CONTOURS OF DARKNESS

She lay across his lap, her head and feet dangling, her dressing gown pulled up over her waist. She squirmed and clenched her buttocks, revelling in the position of exposure to his silent gaze. There was an air of febrile expectation in the room, a kind of sophisticated sniggering which spiced the simple structure of the act with intimations of the wicked. She arched her back and offered her arse for his use.

'I must not succumb', she thought. 'I must remember to stay conscious.'

CONTOURS OF DARKNESS

Marco Vassi

NEXUS

A NEXUS BOOK
published by
the Paperback Division of
W. H. Allen & Co plc

A Nexus Book
Published in 1990
by the Paperback Division of
W. H. Allen & Co plc
Sekforde House, 175/9 St John Street
London EC1V 4LL

Phototypeset by Input Typesetting Ltd, London

Printed and bound in Great Britain by
Cox & Wyman Ltd, Reading, Berkshire

ISBN 0 352 32573 9

This book would not be complete without acknowledging those who helped it reach this form. Foremost are Irene and Evelyn, who lived with me successively through three drafts and bore the brunt of my confusions. Then Maurice, who would not be satisfied until it was as good as I could make it. I owe thanks to Larry, for his technical advice on smuggling; to Beverly, who provided the title for chapter eight; to Bill, my S&M instructor; to Frank, for many, many conversations and the title for chapter four; and to Muriel, for her Aquarian graciousness.

The work is dedicated to Wilhelm Reich.

The relationship of man to woman is the most natural relationship of human being to human being. From the quality of that relationship, the whole level of development of the species can be assessed.

Karl Marx

But he never had this chance to be alone. His body was in the service of others. There was no pause in life. A man was picked up in the tempo of this life, and couldn't get off it. The body had no time to reflect. It spent its energies working for other bodies. It developed co-operative reflexes instead of expressive ones.

Alan Harrington

Perhaps everything terrible is in its deepest being something helpless that wants help from us.

Rainer Marie Rilke

1

Trapeze

They had their words and their deeds; and the relationship between the two functions of their being formed the pattern of their lives. They sought the eternal through the passage of time, and searched for love in the rubric of sex. They huddled beneath their private solutions to the vast problems of their age until they saw that history was a director that used them ruthlessly and without asking permission to include them in its play.

She lay across his lap, her head and feet dangling, her dressing gown pulled up over her waist. She squirmed and clenched her buttocks, revelling in the position of exposure to his silent gaze. There was an air of febrile expectation in the room, a kind of sophisticated sniggering which spiced the simple structure of the act with intimations of the wicked. She arched her back and offered her arse for his use.

'I must not succumb,' she thought. 'I must remember to stay conscious.'

Aaron stroked the damp groove between her cheeks with a limp right hand, watching her tremble as his fingers trailed the entire length of the valley. No expression showed on his face. He operated her body with the bored ease of a locomotive engineer holding the throttle full open across a moonlit prairie. His hand moved insolently back and forth, and with each pass she grew more excited, like a child jumping up and down in anticipation of a treat. It was his greatest

1

pleasure to rouse her to a frenzy of wild thrashing while he maintained his distance and control.

Suddenly he lifted his arm and brought it down sharply, the palm of his hand striking across the centre of her buttocks. She cried out once, a sound of relief, as though a splinter had been pulled out of her skin. The shock was like a slap delivered during an attack of hysteria. It underscored her sexual cycle by punctuating it. Again his hand flew up, and again slammed down, stinging the full firm globes of flesh. He began to hit her in earnest, until her skin grew pink and her legs kicked up and down, and the noises she made were tinged with desperation. He hurt her to the point where she had to scream.

'Do you like that?' he said. He hit her with all his strength. 'Do you like it?' he repeated.

In reply she cocked her pelvis back and shook her head from side to side, acting out the ambivalence of her condition. She hated the pain, especially as each blow fell upon progressively more tender flesh and became excruciating to bear. But being spanked thrilled her; her cunt moistened at the very thought of being upended and handled so rudely. Also, there was a kind of liberation to be found in the intense stimulation of her rear, more so as she yelled loudly each time he hit her. It had been many months before they were confident enough with one another to attempt other forms of quasi-sexual contact; the first time Aaron had slapped her buttocks with any force was when she was straddling his cock, pumping her pelvis into him with sustained fury, and he began to beat a tattoo on her cheeks. The step to spanking as an activity related but not integral to fucking was a short one; and at that it had taken several more months before he could wade into her unabashedly while she wailed in response.

Now, each time they did it, she discovered emotions that she was not ordinarily in touch with, bubbling from her chest as each slap added heat, released energy

2

in her body. It was one of the few times she was able to feel and express her anger.

When she raised her rump towards him, he stopped, and looked down at the form before him. The woman lay in an attitude of utter abandon. Her arse glowed a dull red. The proud deepbark arsehole held only the smallest pucker of tension. Her cunt gave off heavy odours of secretion. She never seemed so desirable to him as at moments like this.

'Beauty is a bawd,' he said. He bent forward and kissed her on the base of the spine. 'Cynthia, how wanton you are.'

She wiggled around and smiled to herself. Aaron spread her cheeks apart with the fingers of his left hand, and with his right began to spank her vertically, slapping the whole length of the crack. A higher-pitched moan escaped her lips, an expression from a different area of her need. Each whack produced a hollow sound until he had opened her buttocks fully and could hit her cunt and arsehole cleanly. She parted her legs to expose herself even further, and again he increased the force of his blows, bruising the tender centre between her thighs.

She began to lose her breath, her self-consciousness, and dived into the waters of ecstatic surrender. She knew he might hurt her but would not damage her, so she could give herself up to the structure of their act, letting him control its content. She struggled against swooning altogether, for in a mindless state she had a tendency to grovel, and afterwards she would have trouble realigning herself with her sense of dignity. She needed to remember that what they did was a mutually agreed upon involvement, and her role as object of punishment was purely arbitrary. She had a vision of his balling his hand into a fist and punching her cunt, and she melted as the image was reinforced by the increased tempo of his slapping. Her mouth fell open and saliva dripped from her tongue onto the floor. She grabbed his ankle and licked his foot. She hovered

3

at the brink of total acceptance, filling up on the energy released by his power.

'This is what I want,' she thought, 'this is what I really want.'

Abruptly, he stopped. A gasp of disappointment escaped her lips. She wanted it to go on forever. She had fallen out of time into the continuum of endless gratification.

'Do you want more?' he said.

The question was not a real one. It was part of their ritual, their tacit agreement to pander to one another's inner agendas. If she wanted him to continue, she would have to beg. He spoke again, his voice low and insistent, suggestive of things that were vile and base, forcing her, through her own greed for sensation, to listen and assent to everything he said. His need to reduce her to a twitching anonymity was only partially motivated by his unconscious fear of women; more cogently, it was the only method he had of transcending the level of ego.

'You don't care, do you?' he said. 'You're just an open hole.'

'Only for you, Aaron,' she told him, which was not at all what he wanted to hear.

He brought the middle finger of his right hand against her outer cunt lips, holding enough pressure just to intimate penetration. He knew that the desire to be entered, to be filled, grew voracious as it was teased, as a hungry animal grows frantic when food is held just beyond its reach. Over the years he had come to understand woman's brute capacity for fulfilment, and he toyed with that propensity as she inched upward, straining to touch the finger with her cunt. Again and again he allowed her to think she was going to have it, and then pulled back a quarter of an inch, listened to her moan in exasperation, and then watched her lift her arse once more to reach for him. She clenched and tightened the muscles in her vagina so that her cunt opened and contracted as it sought to

4

capture its prize, like a goldfish mouthing the surface of the water for food. And when she had raised herself as high as was physically possible, he lifted his hand and with no warning slapped her quivering cunt.

She shouted out in shock and sorrow, and then burst into deep sobbing, the immediate pain of the blow reviving in her all the suppressed pain of a lifetime, breaking through the muscular blocks of resistance, calling up memories whose engrams were covered over with the grey pall of repression. He held himself aloof from her tears, letting her enjoy the fullness of her experience without interference. And when her crying subsided, and she had had enough time to integrate her reactions, he slowly began to arouse her once again, touching lightly, holding out promise of entering her cunt, and then drawing her out, seducing her into baring her shamelessness once more. He hit her again, and repeated the cycle a half dozen times until she lay limp from exhaustion.

She was heavy across his thighs, cutting off circulation to his knees and calves. His cock was crushed against his belly and his back was sore from the strain of holding her. His pleasure was abstract, a blend of visual, tactile and olfactory impressions which merged to shape an entity in his mind, a form he admired for its utter uniqueness. For him, woman was a perennial source of beauty, but in a way that would have astonished any woman he spoke to about it. The female body was a palette from which he derived the colours to create the intensely personal paintings in his soul. He lacked the conceptual means to articulate that to himself.

Cynthia wondered what he would do next. She was having a strangely enjoyable time. With each wave of abuse she discovered deeper layers of truth. She had paid therapists as much as thirty dollars an hour to help her delve into areas of self-perception she was now learning to explore with more directness and thoroughness through sexual encounter. And none of the psychologists had ever fucked her afterwards, as Aaron always did. She was becoming capable of linking her apparent degradation with powers of surrender that subsumed the whole petty world of conquest.

She felt herself sliding off his legs and she twisted her body in order to land on her knees. She stared with twirling eyes at the picture before her: the insides of a man's thighs, black coarse hair, two wrinkled pouches of roughly textured flesh, and the sleek tender tube dominating the entire montage. For an instant the tableau went dark, and a bolt of terror shot through her. At the speed of thought she recalled an incident from when she was two, lying on a rug, her grandfather kneeling over her, dripping his flaccid penis towards her face, and she reaching for it as she would for a toy, and then holding the paradoxically dry succulent skin. The image blended with the reality in front of her. Part of her was still that infant, wanting the intimate touch that bore such enormous connotations of guilt; and part of Aaron was throbbing with the same indiscriminate sexuality that had possessed her grandfather.

When she focused again, Aaron had grabbed his cock and was gently milking it, prodding it to swell. She watched like a person being hypnotised, and when the shaft was three quarters hard, the thick vein bulging from its belly, the head beginning to expand with purple majesty, she found herself swooning into it, her jaw opening in perfect time to be exactly the right size to take his cock inside as she touched it with her lips. He took his fingers away as she swept forward, and looked down in awe as the stiff organ disappeared into her mouth. He felt her tongue and then the clutching of her throat as the pulsating base of the seven-inch cock was covered by her lips and she buried her face in his pubic hair.

'She's swallowed it,' he thought, the idea exciting him more than the reality.

She did not move for a long time, holding her breath,

6

relaxing so she wouldn't gag. He bunched in the middle, slowly folding in half, covering her with his shadow. He looked like a man who had just been punched in the solar plexus, stunned and helpless. She had struck at the centre of his sexual vulnerability: his need to subjugate. By voluntarily assuming the character he would have liked to force her into, she robbed him of his power to enslave her. As any woman in a struggle of wills with a man, her best weapon was agility, for she would almost surely lose in any open contest of strength. The cock lodged in her throat, she made sucking sounds with her lips, as though to pull him in even further and in imitation of someone eating a particularly delicious food.

With great delicacy she brought her teeth together until they at first rested on, and then lightly bit into the rigid cock. She treated herself to a few moments of fantasising what it would be like to bite it off. For that space of time she trembled with the actuality of her ability to destroy Aaron at his core. She tasted the possibility of tearing the immense hunk of meat out by the root, bathing in the shower of blood spurting from the jagged hole, and the severed erection sliding down her gullet and into her stomach.

Aaron felt a tremor of fear course through him. He did not for an instant associate his feelings with the real danger that the woman on her knees in front of him might castrate him with a single bite. It never occurred to him that putting his cock in someone's mouth was an act of the highest trust. Instead he ran through the catalogue of things which usually roused fear in him: old age, illness, and death. He was catapulted into a brief intense meditation on the nature of life, while Cynthia grew giddy at the thoughts which flitted through her brain.

Her chest began to ache and she pulled back, licking the bottom of his cock from base to tip as she disengorged. When he was completely outside her, he drew in a long sustained breath through his mouth, making

7

a sound like escaping steam. And at that point she remembered to suck air into her lungs. They stayed frozen in their attitudes, breathing heavily, sorting out the wildly complex impressions they had just been immersed in. The whole gesture had been so finely tuned, so essentially cerebral, that it barely passed muster as a sexual act at all; or rather, it was as though the sexual gyrations were a pretext for some other, less obvious, form of exchange.

Snapping to like a man roused from a trance, Aaron seized her by the hair and brought her lips to his cock again. This time he used her, rocking her head around to offer different angles from which he could fuck her in the mouth. He pressed in against her temples, covered her ears, rendering her deaf and stoned, reducing her to the single function of cocksucker. He pressed his fingers into her neck so that her jaw relaxed and she opened further to accept his fierce thrusts. And once a momentum had been built, he released her, allowing her to go wild as she went down on him. She sank into a shaking oblivion, emerging as a slobbering animal, lapping and licking and nuzzling into his crotch, her hair wet from sweating, stringy over her shoulders and down her back. She growled as she gnawed at his cock.

He was drawn into the spectacle and began to slide from the edge of the bed. He fell forward like a wounded bear, pushing her back. She moaned and flung her arms around his thighs, gluing her mouth to his cock, begging by sucking to continue to suck. He came to his knees and then toppled over until his chest lay on the floor; she wriggled under him, pinned by the cock which was rammed between her stretched lips. She kicked her heels into the floor as he pressed the full length of his cock deep into her throat, and when he pulled out she fought to keep the erection in her mouth, her tongue flickering vainly to lick it one last time before he removed it altogether.

He rolled the bulk of his body down her stomach like

lava inching downhill until he lay fully on top of her. Her warm thick breasts bulged against his chest, her still writhing lips found his mouth, and her hot cunt pressed against his groin. He reached down to slide one hand under her arse so that he could push his cock between her buttocks as he slid the base of it against her clitoris. Their bodies rocked like buildings in an earthquake as the imperative to fuck, the deep biological spasm of coupling, seized them spontaneously. With a single motion their hips rotated, their genitals swung back until the tip of his cock was at the opening to her cunt, and they joined together in a single movement.

'Fuck ... me ... cock ...' she said as the heavy organ split the furrows of her cunt like the prow of a boat slicing through the water.

'Oh my dear God yes,' she said, and her arms and legs closed about him like the petals of a flesh-eating plant surrounding the insect which had landed to taste its honey. Her limbs grappled him in an embrace which did not allow him any freedom of movement. Blind and driven as a mole in dark earth she forced her way forward until she was completely impaled by the thrusting pole between her legs. The impact of the penetration shocked her entire system, so that she forgot his presence as the bearer of the gift and spun off into grunting grasping convulsions, a unitary reaction to Aaron's cock bursting enormously inside her. As obscene as a twelve-year-old being humped over a garbage can in an alley, she rejoiced in her conditioning. All the years she had been taught sex was filthy formed images which she now brought to life with her body. For a short searing space of time she was being the dirtiest little girl in the world.

He could not match the assault of her unbridled fury of lust. He began to withdraw from the closeness of the contact, and placed himself at a distance, servicing her by holding himself against her, acting merely as the surface she rubbed herself against. He cursed

9

inwardly as his cock began to wilt. But she took no notice of the shrinking penis flopping aimlessly in her cunt, for she had already begun to negotiate the upper reaches of her climb to orgasm. He gave himself up to her use and wished desperately that he could have maintained an erection on order to derive the fullest pleasure from the moment. The energy which was blocked from entering his cock went to his brain, and he became ensnared in his thoughts. And as he drifted off into an interior reality, she pumped into him like a dog in heat, her cunt seeming to want to pull his entire pubic bone into itself.

'You hot-arsed bitch, you murky whore, come on my cock,' went the refrain through his head. But he could not say the words. His momentary impotence made him circumspect, as though only the sustenance of an erection gave him the right to assume attitudes of power, in the way that a bishop will not issue proclamations without holding on to his mitre. He feared appearing ridiculous. It was best when she lay under him, his buttocks crushing her mouth, his hands invading her cunt and pinching her nipples. Then he was able to lavish paragraphs upon her. Now he felt like the male in the embrace of a female black widow spider, paying for his ecstasy with his potency. The sensations in his cock were exquisite, more detailed and erotic than if it had been stiff, but he wondered whether she would climax on his limp penis.

As often happened at such moments, he thought of Cynthia's being with another man. 'If I were someone else,' he said to himself, 'would there by any difference in her reactions? Or is this just a thing she does when she reaches a certain level of excitement, regardless of who is lying on top of her?' Whenever he had asked her about that she had hastened to reassure him that she could be that way with no other man, but there was something about the speed with which she replied that only fired his suspicions further. It was inconceivable that she would lie outright; and yet he found it

10

impossible to believe her. And as his doubt congealed in his mind, the flow of energy between them ceased, like a thread being snapped. Although there was no change in his outward behaviour, the shift in mood changed the precarious balance of their act. She gasped, faltered, made one futile effort to leap to climax, missed, and then slid, tumbled and rolled down in a series of spastic clutchings into a state of tingling frustration. She lay for a few seconds in a fit of listlessness, and then caressed his face and licked his throat in chagrin and gratitude, because she had been so high and come so close. The flavour of ecstasy was still on her tongue.

He waited until she came completely to rest before he stirred. She lay under him like a stricken pigeon. Her mouth was as tender as it had been when she was sixteen and her face had temporarily lost all the lines of experience that had, after twenty-eight years, made her a seasoned woman. To his unfocused mind, to his floating eyes, she was a virgin once more, and he the lover who was the first to enter her. Her attitude seemed one of total trust and innocence mixed with palpitations of expectation, intuiting that she would soon be travelling to frightening peaks of pleasure, sensing that the man would be there to catch her as she swung from one pinnacle to the next. Her cunt was liquid with warmth and his cock mushroomed into hardness once again.

'Oh sweet love,' she said as her legs rose like counterweights on a cantilever bridge, awesome in their scope.

He gazed upon her and sucked in the precious rarity of that open captivity which is the finest favour a woman can bestow upon a man. She unfolded layer after layer of her nature, the beauty of her womanhood overflowing the outlines of her body until each portion of her anatomy glowed blue and yellow. 'This is what I love,' he said, 'when you are this soft, this vulnerable. All your other moods have no real meaning for me.'

'Oh Aaron, fuck me,' she said, 'just fuck me.'

11

For her there was nothing but the waves of heat, particles of cold, currents of air, vibrations of earth. Sensations as fragile as hummingbird wings blended into a single sense of ultimate yearning. She was at the outermost limits of her ability to maintain her awareness of herself as an entity. She evaporated into the consciousness of the enormity of existence and in her careening amorphousness felt the chill breath of death upon her forehead.

'Aaron, hold me,' she said.

Her breathing a ragged sighing, he lifted and lowered himself onto her, his cock bathing in the churning froth of her gaping cunt. He fucked her gently, not letting his feelings flood his awareness of the person who provided him with such unspeakable sensations. They fucked together, each in touch with the other, both in touch with themselves. Where there had been only a him and a her, there was now an us, and in the security of that knowledge they began to fly more freely, like acrobats who have finished their preliminary testing of one another's reliability. He searched instinctively for some deep crevice inside her by following the arc of his own excitation. His cock homed in through its own intelligence. His conscious mind was relegated to the background, to act either as cheering crowd or critical audience. Her legs spread wider, her toes flexed, her heels pushed towards the ceiling. She gave him all the cunt she could.

His pelvis dropped and he brought his cock in from a lower angle. She made a cry like tearing silk and clutched his shoulders, digging her nails into his skin. He pushed his cock harder into her, and held it against the spot where she had been transfixed. A long moment passed in which there was no movement, and then a long low groan began deep in her throat, and erupted as a cry of primeval pain. She felt as though she were giving birth and being born all at the same time. An electric current zipped through her and she bunched herself around him. He slid his hands under her but-

12

tocks and shook her arse until the rocking motion spread from her crotch to her belly, loosening her spine and setting her head to rolling from side to side. She wept without tears and spilled herself out in a hot splashing orgasm which fell upon them like a thundering waterfall.

While inside the vital passage through the centre of his cock, the sperm trigger trembled for the full duration of her climax, threatened to fire, and then subsided into a state of quiescence. He did not come. He could continue to fuck. And he wilted at the thought of repeating the same delirious cycle again.

As he collapsed on top of her, as though on signal, she once again wrapped herself around him and started the low shovelling movement which signalled the beginning of another ride. He became soft in her arms, his mind as throbbingly vacant as a nodding junkie's. In the same way that it had taken spanking and forceful fucking to bring Cynthia to the point where she could contact the feelings which flowed beneath the characterological tensions of daily living, so it required her orgasm to relieve him of all sense of duty and allow him to relax into an unstructured exchange, one in which he did not have to dominate. She rolled him to his side and then on to his back. She sat on top of him, her legs bracketing his hips, her cunt mouthing his protruding cock. She lowered her weight onto his body, and kissed him, her tongue greedy for the inside of his mouth and the responses in his lips that her pressure would give rise to. His lips were slack, and she took advantage of the relatively rare moment when he was no longer doing, but was content simply to be. His passivity translated into defencelessness for her, and all her tenderness was aroused. She slid her legs down outside his, and then on top of his, and moved between his thighs, forcing them to open wider. Her hands cupped his arse and pulled him into her. He traced the outline of her face with his fingers, his eyes closed, gently caressing her

13

nose and cheeks and ears. Like a languorous woman under an energetic man he yielded his body up to her promptings, letting her take him with her rhythms, her methods, her insights.

'Yes,' he whispered.

The simple word was like a lash across her legs. She began to fuck him. Her knees dug into the bed and she rocked her cunt into him with a heavy beat. His knees came up to balance and grip her, and he put his arms loosely around her back. With each thrust he moaned, the sounds bubbling up involuntarily. Her own sounds began as excitement flushed her entire body and she started to flop around, her breasts slapping against each other, her head thrown back, her arse churning in all directions.

'She's going wild,' he thought.

The image, titillating and distracting, had the effect of a grain of sand dropped into the delicate works of a fine watch. At the high velocity at which they were operating, the thought upset the timing of their act. He was ripped away from the immediacy of his involvement like a child being torn from its mother and the extraordinary fucking which had seemed so intensely real, became at once an obscure activity indulged in by people with whom he had only a faint acquaintance. Like a careless participant at a peyote ceremony glancing up at the stars and introducing cosmic insignificance into the drama, he tasted, at the peak of his sexual pleasure, the fear of his own nothingness. Immediately his cock softened and shrivelled into itself. As she felt it leave her she panicked and tried to grab it by contracting her cunt. But the sudden movement startled him and he turned his face to one side as he lost his power once more.

The disgust he felt at himself was mirrored by the expression on her face. Before her humanitarian instinct made her understanding, she gnashed her teeth in frustration. Then she lay down on top of him and held him tightly. They moved into an embrace with the loving knowledge only possible between those who have fought many sexual wars together and have learned compassion through necessity. Without ever having articulated it as such, they shared a deep respect for the difficulties that man and woman share in any attempt at joining together.

'I can't do any more of these tonight,' she said at last. 'You'd better come now.'

She edged off him and lay on her stomach next to him. She was offering her body to be used for his climax, knowing that when he became totally selfish in his fucking he was like a stoker pouring coal into the flames, and she was more than happy at having her cunt be the oven he built his fire in. They looked into each other's face with the knowingness of ghouls. They grew serious. His eyes smiled. Her mouth pursed. He slithered on top of her, adjusting his position until her buttocks slipped perfectly into the hollow of his groin. She continued to hold his gaze, turning to peer at him from over her shoulder. She did not exhibit the least change of expression as he dangled his cock between her cheeks and trailed it over the entire curve. It hardened as he moved, and when it was stiff he slid it between her thighs. Still watching him, she tilted her arse up and altered the cant of her cunt to meet his desire. He pushed forward and the thick organ entered the pink hole. As he penetrated, her lids began to fall. She looked deeply into her, and she let him watch as the overwhelming power of the sensations in her cunt flooded the lighthouse of her associative intelligence. She went under, and until the very end watched him watching her succumb.

Her head dropped forward and he gently bit the tendons along her neck. She raised her haunches until she was on her knees, her thighs pressed along the tops of her calves, her back a long ski slope, her arms along her sides and going inward to her fingers which fondled her cunt lips and rubbed her clitoris. She gave up all thought of everything, including the man who

15

was fucking her, and stepping bravely into the most frightening solitude, the loneliness of bliss.

She was wracked by four orgasms, each a jagged peak of tension which brought her to a pitch of paralysis followed by a long fluttering release. Like a man tipping his hat in the presence of a funeral procession, he toned down the raucousness of his thrusts into her bottom after each of her climaxes, but did not drop his rhythm. When she had spent the fourth time, he knew he would come soon, and pulled out all the stops. Each breath exploded in a harsh bark, his hands formed fists and flew apart into planes again and again, like a man grasping and letting go, grasping and letting go. He fixed his stare on the sight of his cock sloshing in and out with such vigour and her cunt completely relaxed, taking his fiercest plunges crazily.

The trembling began in his thighs and swept up his pelvis and then his spine, until he shivered from his knees to his head, the whole sinuous movement transmitted to her through the single energy focal point of his cock, which fucked her until she was white with screaming. He reared back like a man attacked by the flailing hooves of a maddened horse, and let the sperm shoot from his cock in a series of bursts, spill out, and subside to a dribble, and finally he squeezed out as his pumping reflex continued and she gripped the shaft with her cunt, sucking out the last drops of fluid. He felt the exquisite pleasure that comes to the vampire's victim, the thrilling transfer of energy from one body to the next.

Before he closed his eyes and collapsed beside her, he looked at her round mysterious arse and realised that if there were a dozen men in the room she could kneel like that for the entire night, taking one after the other, letting each fuck her until he came, allowing each of them four and five orgasms, until they were exhausted, and could then just rise, stretch her cramped legs, and feel as though, for once in her life, she had been properly satisfied.

16

2

In The Middle Of A Middle

'I did it again,' he thought. 'Fell asleep after fucking.'

He had fed on fantasies on Cynthia's body for the entire day as he shepherded twenty-nine eleven-year-olds through the prison-like paces of sixth grade. He was in his fifth year of teaching, having started in the Hunts Point ghetto and finding that when he had enough seniority to switch to one of the white middle-class schools, he preferred the black children, discovering in them a capacity for vitality which made the dreary routines of his day tolerable. Cynthia had wondered at his refusal to take a position in one of the 'better' schools. As he sat at his desk, overseeing an inane exercise from the back of one of the reading books, he pictured her at her office, her knit dress clinging to the most delicate curves of her waist, the bulge of her breasts, the cleft of her arse. He had visited her there once, and knew that the other men who worked there watched her whenever she passed their desks, projecting their own desires into the inviting woman. For a moment he pretended he was one of them, and felt the fierce frustration at so badly wanting to touch and lick the sensuous flesh, and having no access to her. And holding on to the feeling of mounting unfulfilled passion, he pictured her naked body under his, as it would be that night, and exulted in the joy of having her. One of the things his relationship with her had taught him was that jealousy was merely the resistance against admitting how much he wanted other men to want her, and have her. In his

17

mind he allowed her to be fucked by everyone, and the more he was free to imagine her with his stable of fantasy-men, the more exciting became her fidelity to him.

He looked at the clock. It was eight-thirty. There were noises coming from the kitchen, and a man's voice. He felt the tension in him building as he woke up further. Some powerful force was working inside him, appearing in his mind as aggressive and violent thoughts, and in his body as a constant restlessness, an amorphous impulse to move, to do. But he had no external goal to fix upon. His energy was flowing, and his psychic gears were meshed, but he lacked a direction. Like so many he was dissatisfied with his job, and had effectively removed himself from all connection with any community beyond his neighbourhood, treating all world and national and state politics as some distant obscene melodrama being worked out among humourless and petty creatures. An older age would have called him disaffected; he thought of himself as alienated.

'I live in an alien nation,' he once wrote on the wall above his bed after an evening of smoking grass and letting his brain explore new patterns of linking the information in his memory banks.

He knew that when fucking between two people was total and honest, the exchange did not end abruptly at ejaculation but subsided into a deep throbbing as the bodies lay with fullest contact between the surfaces, the skin seeming to melt, and their groans and blood floating into one another, their minds homing in on the same vibration and rocking in unison. But the sense of undirected urgency which plagued him had begun to undermine even the sexual act, and fucking was no longer sufficient to dispel accumulated tension.

'Dinner's ready,' Cynthia called from the next room. 'And Conrad's here.'

Aaron was not sure whether he liked the boy, one of the long-haired quasi-students who haunted the

18

Berkeley campus, and their neighbour of five months. He was nineteen, twelve years Aaron's junior, and openly on the make for Cynthia. His rhetoric was radical, and he assumed a knowingness about the state of affairs in society that Aaron found both offensive and compelling. He inevitably felt dull in his presence, a reaction he resented.

As he rolled off the bed and reached for his trousers he caught a glimpse of himself in the mirror. 'I look like a Marine,' he thought, staring at his closely cropped hair. And he felt a surge of hatred for the youth in the kitchen, whose bubbling conversation he could already hear.

'It'll get cold,' Cynthia shouted.

The table was a palette of colour and smell. An unvarnished wooden bowl filled with fresh vegetables sparkled with a dressing of safflower oil and cider vinegar. Next to it a black lacquer bowl of brown rice rich with tamari and sesame salt. Alongside that, a platter of succulent soy beans, simmering in their own juice, cooked with garlic and onions, garnished with half a dozen herbs. A loaf of sourdough bread ranged beside it, while two mugs held chilled apple cider mixed with cold mu tea. Under the cover of a casserole sat a heap of steamed broccoli dripping with melted cheddar cheese. Cynthia wore a thin cotton shirt-dress that came halfway down her thighs. Her nipples were dark and pointed under the fabric; when she moved the faint aroma of recently fucked cunt stung the air.

'Has he got you converted to macrobiotics?' Aaron said. His tone was heavy and quarrelsome.

'Actually, a purist would consider her a revisionist,' said Conrad, his voice lilting in counterpoint to the dense mood. 'The people who run the food shop would shudder if they saw this spread. They all shave their heads and wear steel-rimmed glasses and are as fanatic over food as their ancestors were over revivalist religion. It's just American Gothic in Eastern drag.'

Cynthia smiled at the conceit, the quiet expression

19

she showed only when she was deeply pleased. Aaron veered towards the deep end of his black mood. The bond between Cynthia and Conrad was palpable, and he found it easy to resent their friendliness. A single sharp suspicion exploded in his mind, like a glass shattering on a stone floor. 'Is it possible they are fucking and I don't know about it?' he thought. He entertained the idea for a few seconds; he found it both frightened and titillated him.

Through the window, the sky glowed purple, and the light of the Bay Bridge stretched out towards the towers of downtown San Francisco. For a moment his interior monologue was captured by the external environment, and he experienced a margin of relief. He took shelter in the image of himself as a young man, earning a good salary at a secure job, living in a beautiful urban area, in a deep and complex relationship with a handsome woman, about to enjoy a healthy meal which had been cooked with care and concern, and entertaining a somewhat bizarre schoolboy.

'Americans don't know what good food is anymore,' Conrad was saying. 'We've forgotten. We can't just eat wholesome fresh food without giving it some esoteric or fashionable name, linking it to a movement. Health foods are the new kosher. It's almost subversive not to buy prepacked foods. When they start rounding people up for the concentration camps, not having DDT on your lettuce will be as incriminating as having matzohs in Germany.'

'Smash the state,' said Cynthia, smiling again.

'Coming to Berkeley has turned you into a revolutionary,' Aaron said. 'We should have stayed in San Francisco.'

They gave their attention to the food, not talking, relishing the texture of each of the dishes, getting high on simple taste and nutrition. A silence pervaded the space, a quality that sustained the sounds of wood hitting glass, tooth grinding against tooth, the unceasing hum of the refrigerator, the occasional noise from

20

outside. Conrad, who was feeling the first rushes of the mescaline he had taken earlier, read it as the sense of psychic pressure which always builds up prior to the full onset of the drug's effects. Aaron rationalised the experience by considering himself in a serious mood. Cynthia sat in perfect solitude, feeling herself equidistant from the two men, tasting the flavour of Aaron's cock and Conrad's mind, exciting at the memory of the bulge in the younger man's jeans when he stood up, and wondering whether she would ever penetrate the fog that seemed to surround Aaron's understanding of life. She had changed since their move to the college town, in ways she was still too frightened to look at in all their implications. She knew Aaron to be a good person, sincere in his efforts to lead a blameless life, but he lacked a certain sharpness of insight which Conrad, for all his youthful pretentiousness, possessed in large measure. She had gone to several of the countless meetings that were always being held in Berkeley, once to a group that called themselves Radical Psychiatrists, and then to a poetry reading, and twice to seminars held by a women's liberation organisation. She had come to disdain the large city newspapers, and now regularly perused the underground periodicals. One night, when Aaron had gone to Big Sur for a few days by himself, she read all the sex ads in the back of the *Barb* and with a burst of surprising courage, called one of the numbers. It had run: 'Super hung black stud. Wants white woman under thirty-five. 546–8739. Charles.'

She had reached for the phone three times before going through with it. 'If I panic I can just hang up,' she thought as it rang on the other end. 'Maybe he won't even be at home.'

But the man answered. His voice was like rose thorns dipped in honey. 'Hello,' he said.

She didn't reply, and all at once felt very foolish.

'Is anybody there?' the voice went on.

'Yes,' she said, the word sticking in her throat. She

21

coughed once and said again, 'Yes, I'm here,' and then blushed at the phrase.

'Well, what do you want?' he said.

She blinked at the effrontery of his question. 'I . . . don't know what to say,' she muttered. The deference in her attitude surprised her. In the clear light of electronic impersonality the basic monkey male-female gestures stood out sharply. In a bit, if she got to know him better, she would use her power of redress before law as a fulcrum to wield the lever of dominance in her relationship with him. Her brief exposure to the liberation thinking of the intensely political town had already served to give her a focus on the structure of society as a struggle for supremacy.

'Are you nervous?' he said.

'Yes,' she told him, and relaxed at the saying of it. 'I suppose I am.'

'That's all right,' he continued. 'A lot of women are. They get tight inside when it comes time to come out and ask for it.'

'Ask for what?' she replied, immediately regretting her reflexive feigned obtuseness.

'You want to get fucked, don't you?' he said. There was no leer in his question; it was purely informational. She became aware that she was sitting on her bed, wearing only her panties. The man's presence appeared in the room and he ceased to be a disembodied voice only; she saw him sitting across from her as they talked, and imagined his eyes on her, imagined that he was actually going to reach over and pull her into him. With her free hand she absentmindedly reached up and brushed the nipple of one breast.

'Maybe I do,' she said. 'Do you want to fuck me?' she went on, getting into the swing of the dialogue.

'Are you married?' he said.

'Why do you want to know that?'

'I'd like to know something about you before I answer your question,' he said. 'You know, I get a lot of kook calls.'

'Kook calls!' she exploded, 'I like that!'

'I don't,' he responded gently. 'It's a waste of time, don't you know?' She felt as though she had been walking along the shallow bottom of a swimming pool and suddenly stepped into a deep hole. She could find nothing to say. 'A lot of women are afraid,' he continued. 'They think up all kinds of things. Wonder if I'm a maniac waiting to carve them to pieces, or a fiend who's going to tie them up and beat them. But, really, I don't ever do anything that the woman doesn't want me to do. And that gets far out enough for me most of the time.' He paused. 'Like I said, are you married?'

'No,' she said. 'But I'm living with someone.'

'And he doesn't do it for you any more?'

She bit off an impulse to tell him that she had only called out of curiosity and had no intention of seeing him. And then he cut in, 'Well, but that's none of my business.' He made a sucking sound which could have been a drag on a cigarette. 'So, would you rather come to my place?' he asked.

'No,' she said, 'I mean, I don't know.'

'Listen,' he said, 'I'm six-three, I weigh two hundred and twenty pounds, I have the biggest cock you ever saw, and I can fuck four or five hours without stopping. I like cunt, especially when it's juicy and fresh. I like chicks who aren't afraid to yell and kick their legs. I'll eat your pussy for hours, just chew on it, and lick it, and you don't have to do a thing, just lie back and spread your legs and let it drip.'

His words pressed heavily on her chest and she sank more deeply into the pillows. Her knees began trembling and she let her thighs fall open. She could see the great brute body on top of her, the immense cock jamming her mouth. She had an uncanny sense of its texture and the taste of the first drop of pre-seminal fluid that would form at the very tip. She rubbed her hand down back over her breast and down her stomach

23

to her crotch, letting it lie lightly over her cunt. She was excited by the excitement.

'Of course you like it,' he said, his voice intimate in her ear. 'I can tell by how you're breathing. What woman doesn't want to be fucked?' Her thoughts sped to the two women's meetings she had attended, and remembered the venom in the voice of one of them who had remarked, 'They think we just go around panting all the time, just waiting for them to grace us with their stupid cocks.' She felt that the truth of the matter lay between the stud she was talking to and the lesbian who had flashed such bitter hatred. For her, fucking was the supreme experience, and as far as she knew, dildos included, it was impossible to fuck without a cock. All the sensuality that two women could give one another might surpass in breadth what usually went on between a man and a woman, but there came a point when the vessel yearned to be filled in a simple natural fashion, with the thick pulsating organ that had been fashioned for just that purpose. She wondered how so natural a deed could have come to have such sinister social overtones.

'I'll give you what you only get in fantasies, all the things you think are perverted and dirty. I can teach you how to accept all the parts of yourself that you have cut off. You'll find yourself licking the floor and sucking my feet, begging me to let you eat my arse out. I'll come in you from behind and make you climb the wall. When you leave here you won't be able to pee for a week without remembering what I did to you, and then you'll be ready to come back.'

Her mind half on his words, half on her thoughts, Cynthia began to rub her cunt through the silk of her panties. She felt the hardness of the mound, the softness of the lips under it. The warm flush of pleasure charged her loins and her fingers started to move with more precise purpose, tracing the vertical slit down to the musty spaces between her buttocks. She reached up and brought her hand over the elastic top, and then

24

slid it down the inside of the fabric until she touched the opening of her cunt, the wet pubic hair.

'You will come until you think you can't come any more, and then I'll take you places you didn't even suspect, places where everything is teeth and nails and shrieks. I'll take you to the jungle, baby, and throw you to the tigers. And when you get hooked, I'll get some friends to come over, and we'll smother you with hard-ons. Three or four men, all like me, putting it in you everyplace, in your arse, in your mouth, in your cunt, between your tits, all at once. Hands and tongues and cocks all over you. And you down there rolling and lapping and swallowing everything we give you.' He waited a beat. 'Did you ever have somebody piss in your throat after he came in your mouth?'

She moved her finger in and out of her cunt, penetrating an inch and slipping up to rub her clitoris, giving herself the sensations she wanted and revelling in the geography of the canyon between her legs, its strong supple walls and delicate ridges. The fact that her cunt was awesome and beautiful came to life in her consciousness, and she was enveloped in the joy of loving it. As she finger-fucked she considered for an instant that he might be masturbating at the other end of the wire, and the thought enflamed her. She strained to catch some clue in his voice.

'Can you come over now?' he said. 'I can meet you some place public, and if you don't like me you can leave without trouble. Otherwise I can take you to my place and fuck you clear up to your eyes.'

She tried to speak but didn't want to interrupt the flow towards climax. Her hand flew faster between her thighs, her pelvis rocked up and down, and her belly clutched and released in a series of spasms. Half sitting, half lying, the phone in one hand, her breasts lolling on her chest, the nipples wrinkled, her mouth open and her tongue sliding from side to side, unabashedly fingering herself to bring herself to orgasm, she presented a classic picture of depravity.

25

'Are you still there?' he said, and she let out a small sharp cry, at first guarded, and changing into an open bleat of pleasure. She was coming and she didn't care that he knew what she was doing. He was outside of her, a force without a face, and she sagged into the open enjoyment of the exquisite moment. His voice took on a note of suave complacency and he said, 'Well go ahead then, frig yourself crazy.'

As a dog that has long been pent up and brought to an open meadow will strain at the leash and then bound wildly into the free space when the latch is removed, she sprang from his words and sank into her own orgasm. She moaned and cupped her cunt as the crucial excitement level was reached, and let herself pump spasmodically as the tension was released. Her heart welled like water from a deep spring, and her mind vibrated until it had shaken itself free of all thoughts.

A long time passed, and the only sounds were of her breath and the puffs he seemed to be taking on a cigarette. Then he spoke, calmly, reassuringly.

'You see what can happen just over the telephone. Imagine if we really work together; think how far you can go. Admit it now, haven't you just experienced things you never have before?'

She pulled herself together. 'Yes,' she said.

'You owe it to yourself to see me,' he added. 'I'm very reasonable.'

'You sound like a psychologist,' she said.

'In fact, I used to be. Now I'm a therapist.'

'You call this therapy?' she said, shaking her head to clear it.

'Why not?' he countered. 'The biggest problem in the country is sex. People are either puritans or pigs. When I fuck somebody, they learn something about themselves. And what is therapy if it isn't a means to self-knowledge?'

The thought struck her like a clap across the back

of the neck. 'You don't by any chance charge money for this?'

He laughed. 'I'm too experienced to be giving it away any more,' he said. 'Fucking a woman the way she needs to be fucked, usually against her resistance, is hard work.'

'Christ,' she said. 'What do you do for pleasure?'

He didn't answer. 'It doesn't sound to me like you're going to come and meet me tonight,' he said.

'I'm sorry,' she replied.

'Me too,' he said. 'I'll just have to put you on my long list of kook calls,' and then hung up, leaving her hanging, feeling as though he had stuck a long rusty pin into her as his final gesture, his act of revenge.

'It was delicious,' said Aaron. 'I take back all the unkind things I've said about food fanatics.'

Cynthia regarded the man she had been living with for three years. Her stomach was full and she felt the sweet contentment of sexual satiation coupled with physical well-being. She was intensely aware of Conrad's eyes, and his look which never rested from seizing her body. He was looking at her nipples, while not staring. There was a lack of focus in his face, and she marvelled that he appeared so soft, almost like a girl, his long blond hair a glimmering waterfall, his expression as peaceful as a child's sleep. Aaron, as usual of late, was looking at nothing. The drama in his mind held all his attention, and his face was vacant, also peaceful, but like that of someone massively dosed with a strong tranquilizer, or of someone recently lobotomised. And co-existing with this emptiness was a scintillating vibration of animal energy. Even sitting still he exuded the air of a football player who has just crossed into the goal after a ninety-yard run. When she examined herself honestly, as she was coming more and more to do, especially after her long talks with Conrad, she admitted that it was Aaron's primitive force which kept her glued to him. Her knees

27

still grew weak when she just thought of him on top of her and in her. She would have let him fuck her in the middle of University Avenue on a Saturday afternoon if he wanted to. She knew she could leave him, but while with him had no desire to be able to resist him.

She understood that some basic decency would keep him from ever attaining a position of power or wealth, and after their move to Berkeley had made peace with her fate. Aaron would make a career in the ghetto schools, and she would make a baby or two, and they would age quietly. A distant voice within her cried out against the decision, shouting something about a greater fullness possible for a woman than as the attachment that went with the man. But no viable alternative seemed possible, and she did not even have the vocabulary to think about the question in a vigorous manner. She dismissed all her vague misgivings, and wrote her mother a letter telling her about the move, talking in terms of 'wanting to be a little closer to playgrounds and parks,' and hinting very strongly that she and Aaron would soon be giving their relationship legal status. She judged that they were on their way to becoming a classic couple.

But after a month in their new apartment, she knew that they had, unknowingly although in full view of themselves, stepped in exactly the opposite direction to that which they thought they were choosing. The question of marriage, which was never openly spoken about but which permeated their psychic and emotional atmosphere, and served as a barometer which indicated and forecast cycles in their relationship, lost its flexibility and play; it ceased being an issue which served largely as a frequency upon which to pass communications, and became a weapon which glowed dully in the corner, waiting to be used in one way or the other. Aaron's energetic ennui, which he hoped to sublimate into the ritual of social acquiescence, blossomed into a burning restlessness; and Cyn-

thia's doubts about her condition as a woman materialised into small volatile acts of secret sabotage. She had
never told Aaron about the phone call.

'When I withhold something from him, and he
doesn't know I'm doing it, it makes me feel he's
extremely stupid,' she thought.

'Fanatics are just people who take themselves seriously,' said Conrad, picking up the thread of Aaron's
line which best served as a springboard for beginning
a rap which interested him. 'After all, what's the difference between Lee Harvey Oswald and the Pope? They
share the same ruthless conformity to the rigidity of
an ideal, and all their sentiment to the side, have no
actual concern for the damage their behaviour does to
any life around them. Each serves a private solipsistic
God.'

Aaron, who had been raised a Jew, bridled at the
comparison. His years of religious conditioning still
operated inside him, and while he could show the
entire Roman position to be bankrupt in a rational
conversation, his emotions still reacted with the
reflexes that had been trained into them. 'I suppose
we have to include the Weathermen in that group,
then,' he said, once again argumentative.

But with the grace of a master in aikido, Conrad
used the momentum of Aaron's thrust to throw the
attacker off balance. 'Unless you accept the possibility
that at least some of them are acting not out of principle but out of necessity. That they blow up banks for
the same reason you breathe air. If they didn't, they
would die.'

'It's interesting how you always find winning rationalisations for the actions of your friends, and deny the
same niceness to those you think are your enemies.'

'A paranoid has to be good to his friends,' said
Conrad. 'They're all he has to rely on, in the whole
universe.'

'Oh, Conrad!' said Cynthia, her voice warm with

29

tenderness, her heart touched by the sudden insight she had into the profound loneliness of the boy in front of her, so young, so brilliant, so terribly balanced. She needed to go to him and put his head between her breasts, for just then, and for a long time; what he lacked was the woman who would be his mother, the mother that for all the common complicated reasons he was not able to love when he was a child. 'He just needs to be held, that's all,' she thought.

But she projected into the future, wondered about Aaron's reaction, about what it would feel like to have Conrad's face pressed into her, and she checked her impulse. Conrad looked into the other man's eyes. 'Who are your friends, man?'

The question was like the golden ring one grabs for on the carousel. It was not the acquisition of the hoop that was important, it was the strength and steadiness necessary to reach for it that made the experience worthy. With unaccustomed candour Aaron replied, 'I don't think I have any friends. I was close to some people when I was young, but we grew up in separate directions. They all stayed back East, married the girls next door. I had three or four engagements, but none lasted. I went into therapy, found out a lot about my fears, and decided not to try to fight them any longer by exposing myself to the situations which gave rise to them. I decided to travel, saved money, and took off on a trip around the world. I made it as far as Egypt.'

Aaron raised his head and for the first time seemed to be aware that there were others in the room, that the voices he had been hearing were something other than the embodiment of his inner drama. He felt a peculiar lightheadedness, a combination of his strange reactions to the earlier fucking, and the food, and the odd emanations which were coming from the circle he sat in. Conrad hit the first full rush of energy released from the mescaline, and his body tingled as though he had just plunged into an icy pool after a long steam bath. He was able to continue the conversation, but he

30

felt that he and Aaron were two jet pilots in parallel planes talking to one another as they hurtled forward, faster than the speed of sound. Cynthia, for the first time, saw that she would very much like to have both of them in bed at the same time.

'I went to see the Sphinx,' Aaron continued. As he spoke he went inward again, and Conrad shifted his gaze to Cynthia, who caught the full blow of his glance. They locked in on one another, and stared at the perfect nakedness of one another's being. It was an astral fucking, a revelation on the most exalted plane. The words that Aaron spoke fell into the space they all shared, and provided the framework within which all the other changes took place.

'It transfixed me. I had been doing things like whisking through the Parthenon in forty-five minutes, and the Sistine Chapel in fifteen. But for the first time, when I saw that sculpture, I stopped. I stayed for eight days and nights, not changing my clothes, not shaving, barely remembering to eat. In the day I was baked by the sun, and at night chilled by the stars. And that statue came to life! I could see it dancing and flying. I could see it being built, and was transported back in time to when the Pharaohs ruled. I remember wondering whether I might die and be buried right there at the foot of the Sphinx. It seemed to me then the most beautiful thing that could happen to me. I guess I was mad. I had lost all touch with the twentieth century, or rather, I realised that time was not relevant to what I was.' He frowned, struggling for the proper expression. 'I mean, I saw that all time was the same thing, no matter what shape it took. It was just time. And then there was eternity. And for a while I was exhilarated by what I took to be a great truth. I sat in the hot sand and glowed for it seemed to me that somehow I had solved all the problems that man has ever faced. And a peddler came up to me, and scrutinised me until I was forced to look him in the eyes, and he smiled, the most knowing insinuating smile I

31

had ever seen, and I was forced to drop my gaze before him. And in a wheedling voice which for the first time I understand as sopping with mockery, he said, "Perhaps the good sir would like some fruit while he sits thinking about the nature of the world." And upon his saying it, my mouth began to water. I had to have some fruit. When he charged me an exorbitant price, I didn't care. I pressed money into his unwilling hands. I heard what sounded like a great whistling wind and when I looked up, the Sphinx was laughing, in great sand-sweeping gusts. "There may be a storm," he said. But when I looked past him, everyone else in the area was walking about at their usual pace, and the day was absolutely still. The man next to me stood up abruptly and walked off behind me without a word. And the next day I collapsed. I woke up in a small American hospital, was treated for exhaustion and dehydration, and dismissed. When I told the doctor about my experiences, he explained it quite simply as a period of prolonged psychotic hallucination brought about by my debilitated condition.'

'What a load of shit,' Conrad said.

'Well, how would you explain it?' Aaron asked.

'Fuck explaining it,' Conrad replied. 'The real question is, did you learn anything from it? Did it expand your mind?'

'The only lesson that seems valid is that if you sit bareheaded in the Sahara desert and don't eat or drink for several days, you will have extraordinary experiences.'

'No wonder you don't have any friends,' Cynthia said. 'You don't have any imagination.' She was embarrassed to see Aaron, who was chronologically a man, appear fatuous in front of Conrad, whose younger mind seemed so much deeper. But to her surprise, Conrad defended him. 'He's got more imagination than he can handle,' he said, 'and he's afraid of it, so he holds it down.' He turned to Aaron again. 'I'd like to give you acid,' he said.

Aaron cocked his head. 'When?'

'Now,' said Conrad, and reached into his pocket to remove a capsule filled with white powder. 'Right now.'

Cynthia flashed a thousand scenes in which the machismo being enacted formed the central element, from John Wayne movies to fistfights in her old neighbourhood. It thrilled her to see two males in their essential maleness acting upon one another. In distinction to the competitive aggression that such a scene usually entails, the contest before her was benign, and all the aggression was dialectical. It was as though Conrad had issued a challenge which, instead of stating, 'Let's fight to see which shall win,' had said, 'Let's struggle with one another so we may get to understand our own and each other's strength.'

She was not surprised when Aaron reached over and picked the capsule up. 'What's the point?' he said. 'I'm sure everything I've read and heard about LSD is true. I will have insights and see sights and feel my feelings very profoundly. It's only the intensity of insanity, it doesn't point to a way of life.'

'What happened after you came back from Egypt?' Conrad asked.

'I decided not to go back to advertising. I moved to the coast and took a teaching job. I met Cynthia. Here I am.'

'That trip changed your life, didn't it?' Conrad said. He leaned forward and his energy flowed off him like water down a cataract. He was approaching the first peaking of the mescaline, a capsule given him by an acquaintance he had run into on Telegraph Avenue, which he had taken on a spur-of-the-moment impulse. He had wanted to go to Tilden Park and spend several hours with the trees which he considered to be the sources of his deepest relationships. His highest ecstasy was to take mescaline and lie for hours along the thick branch of his favourite oak friend, feeling the sense of ageless life that coursed through its centre, relishing the roughness of the bark, and wallowing in

33

the dance of sunlight through the leaves, the liberating oxygen they released, and the rich smell of green. But he had decided to stop at his house first, and on the way had seen Cynthia sitting on her front stairs, taking the air while she waited for her rice to cook. She invited him in, and he found himself detoured.

Now his words fell with explosive weightiness. 'It's not what you *think* you understand when you take acid that counts. That part's already programmed. It's the actual chemical change that makes the difference, the re-circuiting of the pathways in your nervous system. Do you dig that? You don't *know* different; you *be* different. You're absolutely right about all the cosmic experiences; that's only a movie. Unless you fight it. And that's like fighting evolution. That's refusing to grow into what you were meant to attain.' He nodded at Aaron's hand. 'Take it. Don't be afraid to be afraid. Get dumb.'

'What about me?' Cynthia said.

The men turned in unison, homing in on her vibration. Conrad, thrown from the back of his bucking monologue, was at a loss for words and sat there blinking. His right hand fell into his lap and began inadvertently rubbing his cock. At the level of concentration they were operating at, his action was not relegated to the incidental. They all copped to the fact that Conrad's gesture was his actual answer to the question. Aaron watched the interaction as though it were a play in a foreign language.

The young man blushed, but he did not turn away from Cynthia's smile of warm amusement. She was regal in her regard, openly holding the power, the choice of saying yes or no at any time to Conrad's desire, and aware that if she admitted him into her, she would be agreeing to an opening of herself which would make her into someone very different than she now was. The glove was now thrown down between Conrad and her, and she understood that she could not take refuge in the fact of being a woman; the challenge

34

to wrestle with herself by encountering him matched the one which had been offered to Aaron.

'He's really a revolutionary,' she thought. 'He is dedicated to change.' The idea of becoming lovers with him struck her as overwhelmingly attractive. Since their first casual contact as neighbours she had grown closer to him in a slow circular pleasant way, and now realised that she trusted him. He was able to bring out the most daring aspects of her without ever threatening or judging. And he was always straightforward about what he wanted.

Aaron saw in a stroke all the possible combinations in which Conrad and Cynthia could make love. He accepted that she could have a relationship with the youth that would rival, if not surpass, what she had with him. It was clear that it was his duty not to interfere with what she was having from Conrad. But his ability to swing free from jealousy when the situation was still in seed form had not stood the test of Cynthia's actual taking up with another man. He did not know whether he could withstand the experience without acting badly. And he could not conceive of humbling himself before the others; he was sure that Conrad would pity him and Cynthia would despise him, a combination his ego would not survive.

He felt a hand on his arm. 'I'm not cutting you out,' said Conrad, 'I'm dealing you into a different game. That's all. And you'll be confused, and you won't know what's happening, but that's only because it's new territory. And I've been to places that are just as fantastic as anything you can get to. We're both the same kind of thing. And I'll just keep reminding you that the panic you feel about to break loose is just the energy of the animal that's been penned up, whipped, caged, ever since you were born, ever since civilisation began. It's just the man in you wanting to come out all the way, and being afraid, because of all the voices whispering inside you, and all the policemen walking around outside you.'

'You're hypnotising me,' said Aaron.

'Just like the Sphinx,' said Conrad. 'Maybe you can explain to yourself what happened after you stayed in front of that thing, but you haven't come to terms with why you stayed in the first place, what its power was.' He squeezed Aaron's arm. 'I'm not out to hurt you, man,' he said. 'I just want to fuck your old lady, and I don't want it to be a bum scene. So I want us to get straight with each other. That's all.'

'Will you two fuck tonight?' Aaron asked, his voice ragged.

'Just with our minds,' Conrad replied. 'We won't do a cock and cunt scene until it's cool with you.'

'And what if it never gets cool with me?' said Aaron, suddenly feeling anger.

'That's your choice, isn't it?' Conrad answered.

'And what about you? Do you want to fuck him?' Aaron turned on Cynthia.

She closed her eyes. After such a long time, the simple honesty of saying and hearing words that were not being used as evasive tactics was ravishing her soul. She had no alternative but to speak the truth. 'We're heading for a dead-end,' she said. Her voice came out as very old and very wise. 'We have to admit it. We've been trying to shovel ourselves into a comfortable grave. And I don't know what it is about Conrad. He excites me and frightens me, sometimes he disgusts me. But he makes me feel alive, so very much alive. And I'm beginning to think I really don't care about anything else except that feeling.'

'And you don't get that from me?' Aaron spoke, his voice heavy with anticipatory dread.

'Only when we fuck,' she said. 'And for the past few months, not even then all the time.'

'See it through,' Conrad whispered to Aaron. 'This is the chance to get into all the closets that you've kept locked all these years. Let everything out, let us see you, and then you can see yourself. And stop being so hung-up on whether that chick wants to fuck somebody else besides your precious self.' He waited for several seconds and then added the appellation with full irony. 'Man,' he said.

As though he had known it all along, as though he had been aware for years that he would be doing what he was about to do, with an air of mordant resignation, he brought his lips down and pulled the capsule off the palm of his hand and into his mouth. He had seen that in his profoundest part what he needed most was to take a single decisive step, to do something irrevocable. With a sense of rueful calm he picked up a glass of tea and cider and washed the drug into his stomach.

3

Little Signs In Lava Flow

They had been like a person in whom an infection was
festering, but who was afraid to let himself be sick, to
let the illness run its course so the body could rid itself
of its poisons. They continued to shape their relationship into normative forms, wordlessly hoping that by
assuming the social shapes of content they could bring
their psychological states to heel. For Aaron, the need
to identify himself with the image of success as defined
by the worldview of his parents, warred with the
impulse to break loose into some as yet unmapped
territory of life. Like an explorer who follows a stream
with desperate faith that it will lead him to an undis-
covered realm, and yet fearful of luring himself into a
savage place which holds nothing but a violent end, he
navigated the cycles of his existence. Cynthia, whose
origins lay in the sprawl of a large proletarian family
whose children saw new clothing only at Easter,
reached for the middle-class respectability her mother
had held out as the greatest salvation she could aspire
to in this lifetime. But she shared with Aaron the
spark of rebellion, the sign that the truths born of
exhaustion and struggle, the dim wisdom that the previous generation had fashioned out of its defeat, were
not to be accepted, even if it meant years of wrestling
with their total conditioning. Their move to Berkeley
was the last effort to surrender to the patterns which
had been programmed into them, a final attempt to
escape the fierce worm of discontent that thrashed
inside them.

They took a place in an old wooden house, a handsome building which had once embraced a single family in gracious style. Over the years, with the growth of the university, it had been bought by a developer and subdivided into four erratically shaped flats, one having access to the attic, one with a bath and closet tacked on like two snails to the outside of the structure, and the two downstairs apartments facing one another through a wall as dramatically incongruous as the one which sections Berlin. With the more recent onslaught of what had come to be called Manhattanisation, the building had been marked for destruction, to be replaced by a six-storey square concrete tomb whose sprawl would involve the destruction of the spacious back yard, and all the trees, bushes, flowers, grass, insects, worms, and microscopic life it supported. A neighbourhood effort had, four years earlier, won a zoning regulation which temporarily delayed the victory of the bulldozer, but the owners still champed at the bit, pouring time and money into a constant corrosive effort against the status quo, knowing that sooner or later the people would drop their vigilance, and the proper city officials be persuaded; then the venerable home could be destroyed.

Their neighbours ranged from the very old to students; oddly, there were no children on the block. Bank tellers and radicals shared facing views of the street. Aaron and Cynthia were soon, like everyone else, nodding and smiling to the people they came to recognise through daily contact. On the third day they were approached by a grey-haired woman who confided that she was delighted to see nice young people moving in, for she was sick of students and blacks and girls with brassieres and men with beards.

But the tension of their own lives kept them from involvement with others, and the diversity of types precluded the establishment of any single dominant scene they could get into. It was Conrad who had come closest to entering their balance of exclusivity, one day helping Aaron to carry boxes of books up the flight of stairs, staying to talk, offering grass to smoke, receiving an invitation to dinner. They had accepted him as a good omen, a harbinger of the changes they were hoping for. But after a few weeks, when his influence started to affect their lives, they saw that he had a different meaning for them than they had at first suspected. For Cynthia he became a key to the freedom she had been only dimly able to conceive of, while Aaron understood that the slight young man with the angelic face posed a serious threat to the tenuous grip on conventional stability he had come to manage since his return from Egypt.

'What do I do now?' Aaron asked after swallowing the capsule. Cynthia looked at him as though he had just slashed his wrists. In her mind, LSD was still a thing of mythic proportions.

'The best thing is to lie and listen to music,' Conrad answered without hesitation. He had offered the drug spontaneously, but only after Aaron took it did he realise that he had been working for this moment for many months. 'These two must be part of my karass,' he thought. 'There's no other way to explain why I'm getting this much involved with them.' He watched Aaron for any signs of regret, and to his satisfaction, saw none. 'The acid won't hit for at least a half hour,' he went on, 'and it's good to be relaxed when it comes on.'

'And you're going to be my guide,' said Aaron, shaking his head, speaking half to himself. 'It's strange. I don't really trust you.'

'I'm just here to see that you don't panic and do something silly, that's all. It's your trip. And any shit you want to lay on me, just go ahead. When I gave you that tab of acid, I took on your karma for the next twelve hours. For me that's a sacred deed.'

Aaron stood up slowly. He looked at the two of them,

40

his eyes questioning first one and then the other. 'I feel very much alone,' he said.

'That's what it's all about,' Conrad told him. 'Go ahead, I'll be there in a while. I want to talk to her about what's going to happen.' He paused. 'She's real, too.'

Aaron began to get angry, and suddenly it didn't matter any more. At that moment he was truly most absorbed in his inner state, and actually didn't care what Cynthia and Conrad did together. It occurred to him that having Cynthia interested in another man was in many ways a blessing; it relieved him of having to be the only source from which she derived all her male energy. In a moment of relief he saw that her taking Conrad as a lover was a liberation for all of them. The jealousy and fear of loss which would assail him later were covered by the initial burst of insight. He smiled. 'I've been thinking about taking acid for a year. I can't believe I've actually done it.'

'Wait, man,' Conrad answered. 'In a couple of hours you won't believe anything of what you now think is so important.'

Aaron turned and went into the next room, ostentatiously swinging the door shut behind him. Cynthia half rose from her seat, following an impulse to go with him, but Conrad reached over and held her shoulder. 'Let him be,' he said, 'let him stand by himself.'

She sat down. 'I'm frightened,' she said.

Conrad fished into his pocket and pulled out a piece of hashish wrapped in tinfoil and a small brass pipe. 'What's the worst that can happen?' he said. 'He may find out he doesn't really want to be with you, or maybe you'll discover you don't want to be living with him. And then you'll break up and go on to something else. So what? That's all life is, coming together and splitting apart. What are you holding on to anyway?'

'I don't know,' she answered. 'I feel attached to him. I love him. We have a heavy sex thing between us.'

41

The young man lifted an eyebrow, the gesture making him appear cynical far beyond his years. 'I know that kind of sex trip,' he said. 'A lot of huffing and moaning, thrashing around, shouting "no", getting fucked up the arse and slapped in the face. It's very low-level, a dead end. Pretty soon you'll be using leather. It's because you aren't straight with each other and can't just fuck right out and dig it. It's just a lot of noise.'

Her lips tightened and her eyes narrowed. His dismissal of three years of intimacy with a few cold phrases infuriated her. 'How do you know that?' she said, her voice icy.

He crumbled a few pieces of hash into the bowl of the pipe. Without looking up at her he said, 'I listen outside your window, how do you think?' And before she could respond he glanced up and into her eyes and added, 'Several nights I've put a ladder against the building and climbed up to look at the two of you. And I know everything you do. I know what your face looks like when you're on your knees and getting rammed from behind, I know what you do with your mouth when he's sucking your cunt lips and can't see the expressions on your face, I know how you roll your hips when you're tired of fucking and are just trying to get him to come, I know that you don't always swallow his sperm.'

The room tilted crazily in front of Cynthia's eyes. His words had the effect of demolishing all the solid points of reference by which she manoeuvred through her perceptions of the world. In a stroke her privacy had been brutally invaded, its contents examined and evaluated, and the intruder had shown no more interest in having seen the most intimate aspects of her sexual and emotional being than he would in watching a passing cloud. She didn't know whether she hated him more for what he saw or for his refusal to be excited by it.

'You fucking faggot,' she said, not even aware that she was going to say those words.

From the next room came the opening strains of Bach's First Suite for Unaccompanied Cello, played by Casals, the resonant sound seeping through the walls. Conrad lit the pipe with elaborate slowness, holding the match over the deep brown chunks until they glowed, and then abruptly blew it out, and sucked the resulting white smoke deep into his lungs, holding it a long time, and exhaling with a soft explosive puff. He toked again, and held the pipe in front of him, offering it to Cynthia.

Resistant, on edge, she nonetheless brought her hand up and took the stem between her fingers, held it to her lips, and sucked a mouthful of the smoke. From the first taste of it she relaxed, and toked three times before sending the pipe back. She had smoked marijuana sporadically after being introduced to it at a party she attended with Aaron, and like most people under thirty accepted it as a staple, although minor, pleasure in life. But after smoking with Conrad, she began to develop a different orientation to the weed, using it as a tool for explorations into her psyche, allowing it to work its potent magic on her mind. It was through Conrad that she first tried hashish, and she rapidly became addicted to the sensation it produced. She entered into a battle with the entire army of inner prohibitions and outer regulations to have more of the drug. Mornings after a heavy smoking bout she would promise herself to use it no more, and like a Puritan after visiting a whorehouse, was filled with recriminations, wondering whether she was sliding down the path to ruin.

One night she had voiced her fears to Conrad, who brought her to a crisis by saying, 'Only you have the right to tell you what to do. Maybe you need to become a drug addict for a while. It might be just the medicine to cure you of having been a zombie all these years. Don't be afraid to kill yourself a little. It's just the

43

bullshit part of you that's dying. Being real doesn't mean being nice.'

He had taken her for a walk and waxed on about the repressive nature of society, the monster which attempted to crush the freedom of the individual. 'Look,' he said, 'the buildings, heavy square concrete cages that keep the people from the earth and sky. The streets destroy all movement except along one of two axes. The streetlights destroy the softness of the night. Look at the tight constricting shoes. You know that old Sufi saying, "Wear shoes and the whole earth is covered with leather." And the clothes, all to insure that we don't get to see one another's genitals. It's a jail. And the whole thing is based on the fear of the body, of the animal that we are. And so we've become unnatural creatures, destroying ourselves and all the rest of life on earth. Did you ever read the line of Leary's? "I hereby declare that world war three is now being waged by short haired robots in an effort to destroy the web of free wild life on the earth by the imposition of mechanical order." '

He had stopped at the entrance to the campus and in a voice loud enough to be heard by the loungers and passers-by he said, 'This civilisation is all stupidity. All the rules, the explanations, the governments, the laws, the jails, the armies, the schools, it's all a power play, it's the game of masters and slaves. Listen to the voice inside yourself. When you smoke hash it's that voice that is set free. And then it's up to you to have the courage to hear what it says.'

The clarity of his vision, impressed upon her when she was sensitised by the hashish, had radically altered *her* vision; she was indelibly stamped with the power of his worldview. Later she was able to dissemble, the super-ego pointing out that his speech was merely the product of a youthful idealism coupled to extremist thinking, and her id providing the energy for enough guilt to allow her to dismiss the contents of what he said. But the effect worked inside her, beneath all her conscious shufflings. She continued to use both marijuana and hashish and she found her feet pointing more and more in the direction of what was nebulously termed The Movement.

'It's a weird thing to listen to,' said Conrad as he filled the pipe again. They had slumped into their chairs and were enjoying the release of tension throughout the muscles of their bodies; their eyes were already bloodshot, and their pulses raced with the accelerated beat of their hearts.

'It's all he plays anymore,' Cynthia said. 'I heard it stoned one night with the earphones on. It was beautiful. It was like Bach and Casals became one person, and the music didn't belong to one or the other, but both of them at the same time. It was as though their souls blended together in the music.' She lapsed into a revery of memory and sound, sinking into the dream that she and Aaron had fashioned from their incompletion and need. Conrad spun off into his thoughts, speeding down the ski slopes of his mind in great powdery rushes that distracted him from all external stimuli. They took on the roles of strangers with each other, as impersonal as people in a waiting room, tied together only by the common purpose of attending the same event. It was a precious moment in which communication ceased, and a blessed communion enveloped them.

'You know,' she said, her words distant, 'there's more to Aaron than you might think. Maybe he does wear a suit and has short hair and isn't hip to all the latest movements, but he's really very deep and can be incredibly sensitive. And more than all that, he's a good man. You should go see him at his work sometime. He's the only teacher in the school who cares about the kids.'

'I know all that,' said Conrad. 'I wouldn't have kept coming around if I didn't see what's inside him. And I wouldn't take a night to guide him through an acid trip

45

if I thought he was a waste of time. He's a beautiful cat, but he's still swimming around in a lot of shit.'

'Don't you?' she asked.

'Sure. And he gives me as much as I give him. The only difference is he doesn't know yet what he's got to give. I'm still a kid in many ways, but in some areas I don't have any confusion left.' He kept talking but his attention went inward again, and his words came out hollow, disconnected. 'I want him with us.'

Cynthia started. 'Us? Who is *us*?'

'The people,' Conrad said. 'The real people.'

Something in his tone called forth a quality of conditioned hysteria that manifested itself as an attitude that might be found in one of the news magazines. His choice of terms gave rise to visions of conspiracy in Cynthia's consciousness and she recoiled slightly from the man who had so suddenly come to assume a demonic form, an agent from a dark underground. She wondered whether association with Conrad was dangerous, whether she and Aaron were being watched because of it, whether they could be arrested. The whole world of wire-tapping and midnight seizures, of narcotics scandals and bombs in cellars, which had been to her a dim tabloid melodrama, came to life in the form of a slender boy, someone who just six months earlier she would have called a hippie.

'Who are you?' she said.

Conrad laughed. It was a rare expression for him. 'I'm just me,' he said. 'I don't represent anybody, I don't belong to any organisation. I'm just one of the people. Us. There are no membership rolls or rules. There's just people. People who are alive. People who know, and don't keep pretending that the world is something other than it is. And we are the revolution, because we aren't dedicated to anything except life. All life. You know that if the oxygen-carbon cycle of the atmosphere is thrown too far off balance everything will die except certain primitive forms of moss. When Jesus said that the meek would inherit the earth he included more than just human beings in his vision.'

She shook her head, she had no experiential tools with which to grasp the concept he was shaping. 'It doesn't make sense,' she said.

He thought a moment and then laughed again. 'Think of the Mafia,' he said. 'They call their operation "*our* thing" and recognise one another by sight. Only we aren't interested in amassing power and wealth. We just want to derail the train the species is taking to its own doom.' He looked across the table and watched the woman with the wrinkled forehead and wondered how much of what he said could possibly penetrate the web of prejudices she had concerning his way of life, in what ways she was translating his words into ideas that did not accurately reflect the reality he was describing. 'We're just friends,' he said at last. 'We live any place, and we do many things. Some are farmers, some blow up banks, some run book stores, some deal dope. There are mothers and children. You know, we are a society. A network of friends. And when we meet one another, even though we've never met before, we know who we are.' He put his elbows on the table. 'The FBI now has special schools to teach their agents how to act like us. As though having love in your heart and intelligence in your eyes was something you could achieve on the basis of attempting to deceive your fellow human beings with the purpose of jailing them. They're incompetents who haven't worked out the principle of cause-and-effect on any higher level than by understanding that pulling a trigger will fire a gun.'

He sat back in his chair, his breath heavy in his chest, his golden hair shimmering like a halo and tumbling to his shoulders, his face glowing with exalted purpose. 'And when we meet people who want to break out of their bags, we help them. Only because we want life to continue.'

'You make it sound very altruistic,' she said. 'I

thought you were doing this because you wanted to ball me.'

'Sure,' he shot back. 'It's part of the same thing.' His eyes burned into hers, and for the first time since he had met her, he let the full blaze of his desire be visible. He had confessed and she had heard, and now they were ready for the act for which all the palaver concerning the state of the species had been a necessary foreplay. In an age when fucking grew boring either through fidelity or unbridled promiscuity, he had learned to infuse his lust with a sense of context and purpose, guarding against the horror of the aimless orgasm. In the same way that certain esoteric eastern sects laced their sex with the spice of mysticism, Conrad had come to surround his erection with the garland of social significance. When Cynthia finally did spread her legs for him to enter, she would be taking in not only a man, but the vanguard of the entire liberation front. The uncomic purity of his motivation and the actual deadly seriousness of the world condition saved him from ludicrousness. She hadn't had another man in over three years, and she yearned to define herself in some other way than was possible within the parameters permitted by Aaron's body. She was not unfulfilled in the areas in which she and Aaron romped together, but she had become aware that was only one small section of the universe of her sexual potential. Without saying it to herself in so many words, she wanted to find out what lay beyond her role as a complement to a single man. She had the smallest intimation that to give in to Conrad's request was only the introduction to a path whose development she could not foresee. But already the walls of her secure self-definition were crumbling.

The sonorous lines of the music swelled throughout the house as she rose from the table and walked deliberately to the window, turning her back on Conrad, and stood looking out into the night. Her head was swimming and her knees were weak. She knew that she had taken the first step, and wondered whether he would understand her silence and stance as an invitation.

She waited a long time, unknowing of what went on behind her, feeling the backs of her bare legs tingling, her arse trembling, her spine poised in a delicate curve beneath the thin fabric. She strained without movement, attempting to sense the presence behind her, and just at the moment when she was sure she had misread the mood, his hands rested on her hips, paused, and then slid surely and softly around front, over her belly, and up to her breasts. She sighed, closed her eyes, and collapsed against him.

All softness and shaking, she melted into the hard flat chest, the muscled thighs, the half-erect cock. And like a skilled danseur he spun her around, catching her about the waist, and gently crushed her to him. She wobbled slightly, at once afraid and committed, and then flew against his body, her arms circling his neck, the length of her clinging like wet cloth around his frame.

All considerations, all questions of age and loyalty, all problems of time and place, disappeared, and they became male and female simply, exulting in the shared beauty of their union. Conrad nuzzled her throat, worked his mouth under her chin, and onto her lips, where they were swept up into the unique rapture of the first kiss, the first meeting of breath and tongues.

For its duration, they were eternal. The long months of preparation for the massive turmoil of energy, built by disciplined denial and released by the mutual permission to ecstasy, found their culmination in the embrace. They dived into the tingling awareness of their deed.

Like a wave that has been called from the deep ocean by the far-ranging attraction of the moon, swelling into fuller and more perfect form until it sweeps majestically in upon a rocky shore and there breaks with a roar of triumphant power into a turbulent splatter of shimmering white foam and disappears as though it had never been, so their kiss rose to its cataclysmic climax as their stretched lips sought to swallow one another's mouth and their lungs like bellows sucked the air from their chests and discharged it through their nostrils, leaving them cemented by the force of the single vacuum they had become.

Externally, there was no movement; their hands were still, their eyes closed. All the force born of their contact was inside the bubble created by the intensity of exchange. And to an outside observer, their separation would have seemed violently abrupt. They just burst apart, stood back a foot and stared wildly at the mystery they had helped to create, already propelled back into context, but still trailing a wake of strangeness. And then they clung to one another tightly, like people who had jumped at the last minute from a car that had gone on to plummet over the edge of a steep precipice. They found no comfort in one another's arms, only the imperative to push on further into the void.

Aaron lay on the couch and pondered the question of self-honesty. He had read almost a dozen books on LSD and felt prepared for the experience that was about to begin. And yet knew that no amount of intellectual prestructuring could contain an episode the very purpose of which was to transcend the limitations of the conscious mind. Given the circumstances under which he took the drug, the paramount issue in his mind was his relationship with Cynthia.

'They could be fucking on the kitchen floor right now,' he thought. 'And I'm not even interested in going in to find out.'

Foremost among his ruminations was the understanding that there was no way to keep Cynthia from having sex with Conrad without continuing to sacrifice a great deal of his autonomy. She would be faithful, but only at a price, the price he had been paying for three years, serving as the reservoir she went to to

50

fulfil all her needs. They were together as often, as much, as a parent and a small child, and more than once he had reasoned that they were playing out childhood patterns upon one another. He blocked out the details of the movie which starred Cynthia, cunt agape, slobbering into Conrad's mouth. There was something about her, more than with any other woman he had been with, that made her nakedness seem precious. When he fucked her and slipped his hand between her buttocks, the crack slimy with her secretions, it was unthinkable that another man should know that, or that she could let herself be touched in that way by anyone but him. And because it was impossible to acknowledge, he could let himself enjoy the fantasies of her in that role. But with his most erotic daydreams about to materialise, perhaps in his own house, he pulled the plug on his interior projector. He wondered whether the acid would force him to face what he now so easily put aside, and whether it would push him into areas of disclosure that were even more volatile, those parts of him that wanted to be rid of Cynthia, to have her gone and not acting as a constant drain and distraction, compounding his basic confusion. It occurred to him that under the influence of the drug he might even be moved to tell her of his excursions.

His thoughts sped back to a night several weeks earlier when Cynthia had gone to spend the night with a friend. He had found himself walking towards the bay, through the black neighbourhood, when the sound of jazz hit his ear, and he stopped to listen to the cool, sweet, wise music dance through the salt air. On impulse he went into the place, a long narrow room with a bar, a stage, and two dozen round tables. He waited until his eyes adjusted to the dim light, nodded to the bartender, and went to sit by the wall, ordering a bourbon and spring water when the waitress came by. Three musicians played, a piano, a bass, and drums. They operated like people who knew one

51

another and their world so well, who had come to such a thorough acceptance of life, that they need pay no heed to where their playing led them. They spun out run after run with no rehearsal, no forethought; with nothing but sheer elegant style. They produced lines and harmonies that they would never reproduce, and which would never be recorded.

Everyone in the place was young or black. Aaron sipped his drink and felt slightly out of place. Since moving to Berkeley he had become sensitive to his appearance as anomalous in many of the sections he walked in. He closed his eyes and disconnected considerations of the external. He let the music wash over him like a cleansing waterfall, and with the gift he had for entering internal space, he was soon immersed in the stream of sound.

When he came to, the set was ending, and he found himself staring into the eyes of the bass player. The man's lined face was a mask of compassionate indifference offering no comment, exhibiting no personality. 'I don't even want to know you,' it said, 'just to watch you from behind my stage.' Aaron had the uncanny feeling that the man could read his mind, and if asked could recall the past and peer into the future.

Then the woman came and sat next to him.

It was clear that she was a whore, and Aaron, switching his gaze from the white-haired man, looked full into her face and with relaxed certainty knew he would go home with her. She was in her late thirties, broad in the waist, with heavy legs and still firm breasts. Her face was flat, the nose broken along the ridge, her lips bulbous. In any sense that he had ever used the term, she was not attractive, and her expression of deep boredom lessened what little appeal she had. He had no desire to fuck her, and yet was powerfully pulled. She looked as though she could teach him something.

'How much?' he said.

'Forty dollars,' she replied.

'For a week?' he said, his voice mocking.

She looked at him blankly for ten or fifteen seconds, as though she had been hit a chop on the back of the neck. Then the response rose inside her; he could see it the way one sees a sunrise. And when she fully understood that he was joking, the laughter tumbled out like a series of puffing breaths of someone who had just run a long distance.

'I'll give you twenty,' he said, estimating that to be five dollars more than the absolute minimum. But he wanted a certain largesse from her, and knew that it would be more easily forthcoming if he paid for it, as it is necessary to pay for anything one receives from another, either in money or in services, or in the toll taken by the simple fact of having been worked on by another.

She nodded. 'Don't plan on spending the night,' she said.

The waitress returned, her manner more formal, and Aaron paid for his drink. He stood up and the woman followed suit. As he turned to leave he glanced towards the stage; the bassist was still watching him. He led the way out and at the door let the woman go first. She took him ten blocks off the main street, past dozens of two-family homes neatly manicured all in a row. 'The black ghetto of Berkeley,' Aaron thought, 'has a higher standard of living than the middle-class white sections of Queens. I wonder if any of these people have ever been to the slum sections of Harlem. It would singe their eyelashes.'

She took him to a brown frame house and ushered him inside. He tingled with an anticipation that was not yet genital. She wasted no time on ceremonies, showing him where the bedroom was, instructing him to take his clothes off, and going into the bathroom. He undressed and she came back in, a white towel draped over her arm, wearing nothing else, like a stunned waiter in an Abner Dean cartoon. He laughed.

'What's so funny?' she said.

53

'It's all very professional,' he said.

She handed him the towel and began to remove the bedspread, peeling it back carefully. 'Well, what do you think?' she said. 'That we're in love?' And laughed harshly again, as she had in the bar, without humour. She stood at the foot of the bed facing him. 'You want me to make it pretty for you?'

A look of pain crossed his face. All at once he wasn't sure whether he would be able to fuck her. He wished desperately he were with Cynthia, with the familiarity of her, and he saw what it was he had sought in the woman, a texture of contrast, something to inject the routine sexual act with unusual excitement, an excitement he could transfer back to his lovemaking at home. The whore watching him saw his struggle, and although she was ignorant of the details, she recognised the pattern. For a second she almost suffocated in ennui.

'The extra touches cost you more,' she said. She turned off the overhead and flicked on a low lamp with a blue bulb, casting the room into a qualitatively different mood, making her skin glow with subtle and mysterious shadows. She bent over to put on the stereo and Aaron noted the absolute blackness that ran down the crack between her cheeks. The electronic ghost of Billie Holiday entered the room, singing as vibrantly as her live body had ever done. The woman fluffed the pillows and smoothed the sheets. She took out a bottle of rye and two glasses from the cabinet next to the bed, went into her handbag and fished out a pack of Pall Mall, dropping it next to the ashtray. 'You get in now,' she said, and he lay down on the soft mattress, pulling the crisp violent sheet up to his belly. She waddled to her dresser and came back with an atomiser, and with a gesture he wasn't sure wasn't ironic, she sprayed a fine mist of scent over his chest. 'You feel better now?' she said.

Without waiting for his response, she went into the kitchen, and he could hear her fiddling with an ice-

54

cube tray. That she could be whimsical without self-consciousness captivated Aaron's attention, and like a million men who have paid for a woman's body, he grew curious about her soul. It was easy to picture her working, as so many black women did, behind the counter of a luncheonette or in a dime store. He wondered how she began this trade of selling the use of her cunt instead of the use of her hands or her back in one of the other forms of wage slavery open to the majority of people in the nation. She returned with a bucket of ice, standing in the doorway a moment, posing. There was nothing lovely about her. Her legs were running to fat, her torso was squat, her entire attitude was one of hardness, her eyes held only calculation.

'This is the deluxe treatment,' she said. 'It's going to cost you ten dollars more.'

'I didn't ask for any of this,' he said. He paused. 'Maybe,' he added. 'I'll have to see how I feel afterwards.'

She walked towards him exuding scorn. She put the ice down and stared him into discomfiture. She turned quickly and was reaching for the light switch, to explode the ambience, to take back the small niceties she had proffered. He reached out and grabbed her wrist, pulling him roughly towards her. He expected her to fight but she just went stiff with distaste. 'Go ahead, *mister*,' she spat at him. 'If you want me this way you go right ahead. You're paying for pussy and pussy is all I got to give you. You can just get on top and bang away until you come. But if you want me to treat you nice, you have got to *pay*.' She took a deep breath and said, more in exasperation than in anger, 'Don't you understand that yet? Anything you get from a woman, you got to pay!'

He looked at her dumbly; the force of her words stunned him and he felt extremely foolish, the smell of the perfume adding a bizarre dimension to the sterile scene. He let go of her arm, and the tension went out of her muscles. She seemed to regard him as though from a great height. 'What's the matter with you,' she said, 'you ain't a kid.'

With a subtlety that surprised him she stretched her back and pushed her arms above her head, exhibiting the sinuous body that still lived beneath the age and weight. Her breasts jutted out and her arse flared. 'I been in this business a long time,' she said, her voice husky and low. 'Don't think there is anything I don't know, a hundred times over.' She leaned forward. 'It's just like with the woman you must have at home. I'll do what you like, but you got to coax me. You got to make me want to do it.' She brought her face right to his. 'You got to make me hot,' she whispered.

'With money?' he said, his voice sticking in his throat.

'It's as good a way as any,' she told him. 'And better than most.'

They hung in the balance, their contract dangling. He wanted to fuck and she wanted as much payment as she could wring from him. Neither was willing to be exploited in any manner by the other. There seemed no way out of their impasse. The slightest indication that either of them might give would automatically be ruled as capitulation by the other. They were like diplomats negotiating at a peace conference, locked into suspicion.

'Then why are you treatin' me so mean?' sang Billie Holiday, her spirit sustained by electric energy. Aaron and the woman heard the line at the same time and in the same way, and with absolute simultaneity acknowledged the absurdity of their situation.

'Twenty-five is tops,' he said. 'I have to work for a living too.'

She straightened her shoulders, tossed her head back, and wrinkled her nose. And to his surprise, she smiled. 'Well, all right,' she said, 'let's do it.' And fell upon him like warm wet concrete, enveloping him, smothering him with flesh.

He got hard instantly, but did not hurry to enter her. Her body was soft and hot against his. For a long time he lay under her, sucking in her presence. He touched her not only at the surface, but seemed to sink into her, the layers of her skin peeling back, allowing him to merge with her. 'I have all of it to feel, to explore,' he thought and grew lightly giddy at the wide expanse which opened to him. He had her entire exterior to lose himself in before he needed to even consider entering her.

He pushed her up and over, rolling her to her back. She let out a grunt of surprise, having thought that he would lie there while she sucked his cock and fucked him. It always amazed her when men paid her for sex and then got on top and did all the work. She tended to have less respect for a man who wasn't easy enough simply to lie back and let himself be made love to, but who had to climb on her and perform. But it meant less energy for her to expend, and she was quite content to close her eyes and let him loose. 'Knock yourself out,' she thought.

Aaron looked down at the strange body like a lion over a freshly killed carcass. Waves of unreality washed through him. It was only the fourth time that he had been unfaithful to Cynthia, and the sensation of having all his familiar sexual attitudes with a woman he had never seen before filled him with a sense of the peculiar. But it was that more than anything else that he had come to experience. He shook his head to clear his mind of thoughts, and addressed himself to the piece of cunt, the piece of arse, the piece of tit, the piece of mouth before him.

He started at her head, licking the coarse hair, gnawing at the crown of her skull lightly, chewing with the side of his mouth. He sniffed and grunted down the back of her neck, getting drunk on the raw smell of her. He had to restrain himself to keep from going in too many directions at once and dispersing the core of excitement now growing inside him.

57

'She's mine,' he thought, 'because I paid for her.'

He licked her forehead like a dog lapping ice, and planted a suction kiss over her right eye, teasing the eyeball with the tip of his tongue, reaching under the eyelid, treating her to a thread of jagged pleasure. He bit her nose and ran his tongue across her cheeks, over her temples, down to her chin, and finally over her lips, teasing her with the unaccustomed sensation. Her mouth opened to say something but he thrust his tongue inside. 'Mmmwhmwmwm,' he said, the rough wetness of her blending with his own saliva, making the cave they created a basin for their secretions.

Aaron nibbled at her lips, kissed them with his own, and sucked them into his mouth. She gasped, trying to catch her breath, and the movement carried over into her entire body, causing her to jerk and tremble. 'You are delicious,' he said. He dived under her chin and fastened himself to her throat, biting the tender tissues, causing her to yelp while she held on to him tightly, as though reassuring herself of his actual presence. The effect of her move was to make him feel he was being drawn in closer, and he clamped on her right ear, tonguing it, sucking it out, and humming so that the vibration tickled her skull. She tossed her hips from side to side, the currents of pleasure buffeting her like winds pushing a small car from lane to lane across a high bridge.

'Why are you doing all this to me?' she said. 'You don't have to make me feel so good.'

He pulled back, and with a sigh of such delight that it surprised both of them, he buried his face between her breasts. What he had had up to that moment was luscious, and he enjoyed it the way Italians relish the ultra-lean meat on the skulls of calves, and their roasted eyeballs and sizzled brains. But now the first substantial dish was being served, and he set to with appetite.

They seemed too big to get into his mouth. He tried to suck one entire breast inside him, beginning with

58

the nipple, letting it slide over his lips, bunching more of it after that, feeling the fibrous matter under the skin soften as he swallowed it, and still more, until his lips stretched and his mouth began to ache, until his jaw would go no further without unhinging, and then with a mindless bravado discarded his human consciousness and became a boa constrictor swallowing a whole pig. Although he was sure it was physiologically impossible, the entire melon breast disappeared and he felt his teeth hit the hard bones of her rib cage. She cried out once, long and loud, tasting fully the impacted visual and symbolic reality of the act.

And then he slid back, feeling each eighth-inch of breast as it came out of his mouth and reshaped itself on her torso. When he had regurgitated half, his tongue could work again and he licked the sombre sodden underpart of the tit until he came to the nipple again, and this time pressed it hard between his lips, mauling it and lashing at it with the tip of his tongue. She squeezed her eyes shut and pounded the mattress with her fists. And he collapsed on her belly.

Aaron waited until both of them had regained their breath, letting the cycle conclude, and then pushed his face into the slack softness of her stomach. He bit the grainy skin until she put her hands on the back of his head, forcing him down, making him burrow deeper. 'You sure are hungry,' she said. Her words released him further, and he gouged into her the way a shark sweeps in to scoop meat from a wounded whale. He could feel the organs against his nose, and the atavistic cannibal instincts all rose up as he lost his sense of balance and leapt into the full ritual, clamping on her hip bones, scratching her thighs, throwing her from side to side to bite the fleshy parts of her, her arse, her calves, her shoulders. For her it was a cacophonous symphony of sensation. Temporarily crippling ripples of indescribable immediacy thrilled through her. Mammoth frissons held her in thrall.

He took her toes and half of one foot into his mouth

59

and set her to writing as he licked the spaces between each toe with his tongue. He lapped the soles of her feet like an abject slave. He made slurping sounds. 'Lordy, lordy,' she thought. 'It's all blocked up inside him.' The men who came to her fell into two categories: those who felt so much shame and guilt that they fucked briefly and left hurriedly, and those who used her as she was meant to be used, as the one place where they didn't have to be afraid to be naked. And over the years she had heard all the stories, seen all the drama, and known all the secrets that the heart of man can hold. She knew more of human nature than any psychiatrist or priest, for unlike the respectable professionals, the tool she used was her total self, and unlike them, she did not forbid the full range of intimacy. Men came and paid her to pee in their mouths, and she watched, dispassionate, as they grovelled under her. And others tied her with leather, and blistered her nipples with lit cigarettes, and she watched, compassionate, as they lorded it over her.

Aaron crept up the length of her legs, his eyes wild, his teeth bared, to her cunt. She saw him coming and closed her eyes again. 'I don't even want to know what's going on inside him' she thought. 'I got enough to do to take care of myself.' And like a woman who watches a man go to his death by drowning so she can get into the lifeboat, she settled back and relaxed to enjoy the voyage.

He sucked at her cunt for almost an hour. Like a violinist who is able to so wrap himself up in the total concentration necessary to produce his work of art, he swept forward, leaving all considerations aside except the fullest, most perfect eating of a cunt possible. He spent aeons on the tastes, the sweet early paraffin secretions, the acrid flow when the sex got dirty in both their minds, the wholesome smell like baking bread right after orgasm, passing almost immediately and reverting to a thin machine-oil flavour. He mar-

velled at the versatility of the organ, its ability to
change its mood the way a chameleon changes colours.

He licked the rare texture of the flesh between the
outer cunt lips and the first bulge of thigh, and then
each of the individual layers, and into the central bud,
looking like the corona formed when a drop falls into
a saucer of milk. She was tight at first, unwilling to
loosen up to the intense assault. He took immense
patience, licking up and down the slit for a long time,
going from the rough bitterness of her arsehole
through the yielding salt softness of her bulging slit,
over the delirious clitoris and into the starched pubic
hair. Finally, he brought his hands up and peeled the
cunt open with his fingers, took a deep breath, pressed
his lips to the hole, and blew inside as though he were
filling a balloon. She gasped and her legs went up
slowly and regularly, like counterweights on an elev-
ator. He sucked all the air out and continued the suction until he had pulled her cunt lips into his mouth
and between his teeth. 'God damn,' she hissed. He let
go, and her cunt belched, the stale fumes from inside
rushing out in a wet gust as she pulsed in deep contrac-
tions. He covered the rippling hole with his mouth and
let its excretion pass into him, taking the full measure
of its vileness with the pungency of its beauty.

Again and again he blew her, until she was weak
with coming, and then he wormed his tongue inside,
feasting on the textures of the lax tunnel, lapping tiny
pearls of dew from the ridges of the cave. And when
he could not ring a single variation more on the theme,
he came up on his knees and peered down on her. His
cock, rousing itself from the hibernation imposed on it
while waiting for the winter of the mouth to pass,
stirred and grew stiff.

She sighed, locked her hands under her knees, and
waited, knowing that in a moment he would enter.
Her cunt felt like a steaming marsh. She had lost all
sense of its firmness. There was only a hot zigzagging
tingling between her thighs, and the hard cock would

bring it all together into a single sharp spasm of completion. She was opened up.

He slid slowly towards her, his cock pressed the fringes of her saturated cunt, and he started to fuck her.

He felt free. He had paid for her time with money, and had paid for her attention with lavish service, and now could reap the harvest of his pleasure unencumbered by any consideration of having to please her. It was in this area that he often came to grief with Cynthia. The inhibitions which kept him from fucking her cleanly, and the lack of expertise which kept her from fucking him fully, forced them into a mutuality, which was most glorious when it was an actual exchange and not a muddled compromise; but it was almost always the latter.

Aaron tingled from the moment he penetrated the woman. He lay fully on top of her, not supporting his weight on his elbows, but letting her have the bulk of his body. He let himself be absorbed, sucking in through his pores all the energy he had lavished upon her. She fed it back unstintingly, holding herself against him, ready to let him gorge himself while he pumped his cock into her.

He humped the small of his back, bringing his cock in at a more vertical angle, rubbing against her clitoris, making her squirm under him, her arse wrinkling the sheet as she moved. He brought his hands under the rolling cheeks and felt with his fingers into the crack, touching the rough kernel of her arsehole and the bottom stretches of her cunt. He kept her wriggling while he planted his hands in the most intimate crevices of her body, letting her feel him feeling her feel her own wanton response. Aaron shuddered and moaned. His mind went black.

She put her hands on his back and dug lightly into his skin with her fingernails. The encouragement cheered him on, and he slid back so that he entered her from the bottom angle, allowing his cock to spring forward to its regular upward tilt. He felt the tender vein along the bottom rub the lower channel of her cunt. Her legs trembled.

'Oh, my poor knees,' she said. 'I sure am going to be stiff in the morning.'

'No pity,' he said, and thrust into her with a more vibrant pitch. He hit a tender spot too hard and she screamed. He pulled back and touched her there again. It was a blunt knife hitting into her core, and he pressed it in once more, increasing the pressure until she realised it wouldn't damage her, and gave into the sensation of being stabbed at her centre. He came at her again and again, causing her to groan, and then cry out in deep throaty moans, spilling her soul out in sound.

Like a tuner listening to the fine vibrations of a piano cord, he tasted her voice until he had homed in on the source he was seeking, slipped his cock up and under to a deeper place inside her, and from the sudden sense of convulsion in her cunt and the column of heat coursing up the shaft, he knew he had found the vulnerable core.

She swooned and was transfigured. All the harshness drained from her features, the weariness, the cynicism, the restraint. She allowed herself the grand luxury of surrender to herself, and was made beautiful by it. He saw her in her archetypal guise, the black skin glistening, the strong body swinging through high jungle grass, the haunches and arms muscled, and her face a broad field of living sagacity, sensitive to the teeming and intoxicating rushes of life within her and without.

'Earth,' he thought, and then, 'Mother.' The two words began as separate conceptual entities and joined in a single meaning. The ancient myths came into vital focus and Aaron lived for a moment in the spirit of the planet.

She began to move beneath him, not so vigorously as to upset his own equilibrium, but with enough gusto to assist, like a horse that enjoys the way its rider feels on its back. Her many years of practice allowed her to maintain a discipline of movement without tampering with the flow of energy which gave rise to that movement. He let his strictures go and let himself move freely. His eyes closed, his mind empty, all immediate concerns dissipated, he gave all his attention to the life between her legs. His cock grew thick and hot and sent sweet tremors into his groin. He fucked her without reserve.

Without warning, he felt his orgasm announce itself. His first impulse was to hold it back for he did not want the intense pleasure to come to an end. But he kept himself from interfering and watched the development take its course. The sensation of coming rose higher and higher, and he relaxed every muscle in his body, especially the sphincter of his anus, and his desire to let go of the bubbling sperm clashed with his desire to let it subside. 'Stop moving,' he whispered to the woman under him. She froze on the spot, and they clung to one another with the silence of submarine officers listening for the fatal hum of ship motors overhead. The ejaculation lost its momentum and slowly evaporated.

With a happy jolt Aaron realised that he had got through a very narrow spot and entered a new level, that he could continue to fuck as he had been doing, staying at the very edge of coming. He shook his head and threw himself back into the fucking, words coming unexamined from his mouth, his limbs fluttering, his torso shifting. He fucked her until he felt her, and at the impact of contacting the reality of the person underneath him, he was grabbed up in an orgasm the way a kitten can be picked up by the scruff of the neck, and was shaken by it, the shudders wracking his body without his having the slightest say in what went on. He came into her with relief and gratitude, and then collapsed on her breast.

She held him a long time and did not move. She was

tremulous with need. Towards the end he had lifted
her utterly out of herself and brought her a way of
being that made all the rest of her life seem drab and
shabby. For a few brief minutes she had soared like
the eagles over the mountains of earth. And just when
she thought she might lift bodily from the bed and
once and for all be free of all the pain and misery that
was her day to day existence, he exploded inside her
and lost all his power, and she tumbled down in the
wake of his ruin.

She felt his cock get soft and begin its slow slide out
of her. She was close to tears. It moved slowly and
slimily, retreating from the niche in her where not all
men went, past the pulsating walls, by the lips, and
then outside. His cock was gone, and a cold breeze like
a wind from the grave flickered over her cunt. It was
finished. And once again she berated herself, again for
allowing herself to forget that the fire of passion stoked
by a man always ends in the cold ashes of loneliness
afterwards.

She stared at the ceiling, tracing the tiny cracks in
the plaster. 'If an earthquake was to hit now and kill
me on the spot,' she thought, 'I wouldn't mind.' And
on the phonograph Billie Holiday sang about life's
being so sad she just wanted to end it all.

Aaron got up and dressed. He felt as though the two
of them had just officiated at some diabolic rite. He
knew her at great depth and yet not at all. He would
almost certainly never see her again, this woman who
had accompanied him through such ferocious changes.
He gave her thirty dollars, indicating that he didn't
want any change. She put on a dressing gown and took
him to the door.

'Why is it like this?' he asked. 'There must be some
way out of it all.'

'You got a plan?' she said.

'I feel so good and I feel so bad,' he told her. 'I don't
know which way to go.'

She held his face between the palms of her hands,

65

like a mother holding her small son. 'I've found it and I've lost it so many times,' she said, 'that I know there ain't nothing but the coming and the going.'

She closed the door behind him and he went back to the empty apartment where he watched a dull movie until he fell asleep. He said nothing to Cynthia the following day, and that night, when they fucked, he wept in her arms. She took it as evidence of love.

4

Blind Vision

With labyrinthine stealth, the acid dissolved the neuron pathways in Aaron's brain, exposing his thoughts to their own reality. He woke up to his own structure, an event which surprised him by coming as no surprise. Nothing changed; he merely realised the fact of his own existence, saw himself as a thing in the universe, in relation to all other things. The world manifested itself to him as though for the first time and the vaunted clear white light turned out to be nothing other than the mysterious glow which imbues the mundane and to which most people, in their usual sleepwalking state, are blind.

He looked about the room. The huge easychair, the fifty-year-old walls with the coats of white paint he had sweated to apply five months earlier, the Woolworth lamps that had seemed such a bargain at the time of purchase, all stood forth, radiating a sense of presence that gave them the aura of being alive. What he did not expect, and what rushed upon him with suffocating speed, was their ominous quality of structure and function. The housing and furniture which had been designed to serve the needs of his body became the parameters beyond which his body could not move. A vision of a monkey bar, of the type that was once popular in the playgrounds he frequented as a child, seemed to symbolise his life, which appeared as an endless scramble from one level to the next, from one section to another. He saw his existence as an exercise in glorified futility.

With astonishing ease he was able to put together all the strands of all the incomplete insights which had plagued him over the years, and at a stroke differentiated between the organic sense of himself and the education that self had received from the moment of conception. The genetic programming which determined everything from his height to his quality of voice, and the social training which infused him with everything from language to food habits, were illuminated, and what was left was an amorphous throb that could not be identified or defined. He conceived of his ego as the full-dress costume of his soul, and saw that his soul was a quality of nothingness, an empty mirror eternally reflecting itself.

'So that's how it goes,' he said out loud.

Unused to the workings of the drug, he stood up quickly and started to walk across the floor to the kitchen. Like most neophytes, his first impulse was to share his grand revelation with others, feeling that he had a message of crucial importance to impart to the race. But the startling physiological changes occasioned by the move, which ordinarily would have gone unnoticed, registered with shrieking impact upon his sensitised system. What had just seemed so stable and rational went tumbling topsy-turvy before the rush of blood and pounding thud of his heart. His body image, to which he was normally unattuned, flared in his consciousness, and the evidence of his senses notwithstanding, he felt himself to be ten or twelve feet tall. All sense of control disappeared, and the calm reality of what he had known while lying on the couch exploded into a nightmarish fancy. The familiar was shown to be intrinsically mysterious. Panic flooded his mind and he stampeded, stepping blindly in front of him, and with an audible crack slammed his shinbone into the sharp hard edge of a glass-topped coffee table.

'What was that?' said Cynthia.

In the sculptured silence following the end of the

music, she and Conrad had listened for sounds from the next room. Their second embrace had led to a spasm of clutching, and Cynthia had reached down and run her palm lightly between Conrad's legs, trembling as she pressed the turgid cock which bulged against his jeans. Part of her aware that Aaron might walk in at any moment, part of her anxious to leap into the unknown, she began to sink, going to her knees, ready to fumble with the zipper, ease the thick shaft out, and take it in her mouth. She had smoked enough, and talked enough, and pondered enough, and now wanted to be filled. That her desire coagulated as a prescience of pungent sperm on her tongue was an accident of more factors than she could tabulate. Like an infant groping for the full breast, she yearned for the loaded cock.

Conrad grabbed her by the wrists and held her up. 'We promised Aaron we wouldn't fuck tonight,' he said.

'You promised,' she amended. She covered his mouth with hers and moaned into his throat. Her hands flew like butterflies over his buttocks. She came close to frenzy and perilously skirted that terrible point at which a woman loses awareness of the man and becomes awash in her inner turmoil. The more she attempted to prompt him, the more distant he became, until at last he stood back from her. He was not prepared at that moment to plunge into chaos with her.

Hurt exploded in Aaron's consciousness with the force of a heavenly visitation, shattering his leg and sending bursts of fire into his hip and side. In his heightened state, he felt the pain both as an experience and as a phenomenon independent of him. The speech he was about to deliver to the others skidded from the field of importance and was replaced by a throbbing meditation on the nature of pain. He remembered reading the Buddha's first precept that existence itself is pain, recalled that he was able to make no connection with the words, and now understood their meaning with crystal clarity. The truth screamed through him like the roaring whistle of a jet screeching low over an Asian village to drop napalm and steel-fragmentation bombs. Scraps of videotape footage were projected from his memory bank and his living room became a tumultuous horrifying battleground filled with half-naked human beings frozen in the avenue of the descending flaming juggernaut.

In a flash which permanently imprinted the knowledge on his mind, all the cruelty of the species throughout its entire history catapulted from the background of inattention into sharp focus at the centre of his consciousness. With extraordinarily wrought tunnel vision he seized upon this single aspect of human nature and invested it with singular importance. At the precise instant when, according to the infantile directions of the so-called LSD gurus, he should have been transported by galleons of bliss, his mouth was filled with the bitter taste of a less disneyesque aspect of life: its implacable brutality. Like the goslings who fixated upon the laboratory assistant who happened to be the first moving thing they saw, Aaron was stamped with negativity as he took his first acid-permeated step into psychic space. Everything else which was to happen during the following twelve hours would not obviate that initial turning.

'We are insensate maddened animals,' he thought, and all the enigmas which caused his frustration seemed solved by that one insight. The conflux of events and ideas which was his life, infused with the energy released by the drug, opened a great silence within him. Everything he was capable of knowing appeared in a vast mosaic before his mind's eye. As though he were a giant who had once been a man, he looked down on the maze he had been stumbling through and could see at a glance the nature and location of all the obstacles which had stymied him. He wished the moment could last forever, that he would always be able to perceive so clearly.

But as he watched, it changed. A palpable awareness

of time overtook him, and he saw himself as but one of its fleeting structures. The span of his life became a single entity, as concrete and finite as the arc of a bridge cable. His individual existence was a strand inextricably woven into the tapestry of history. And as he followed its course, he reached a point where it ended. He stared with amused horror at the spot where his life finished, came to an abrupt halt, was intersected by another line which cut through the very space he would have gone on to occupy. Death, which had heretofore had only a literary reality, came upon him with its actuality, stunning him into sobriety. Mortality, which had been a word, was seen as being as much a part of him as his fingernails. The acceptance of the fact radically reversed all his acquiescence at being subservient to the will of any other human being, and his job, his standing as a citizen, his role as a lover, all emerged as forms of bondage.

Then, like a man sweeping the horizon through a telescope, he turned his gaze to the left and overlooked the past. He was appalled by the chilling simplicity of what appeared. Everything he had been up to that point was nothing but a conditioned reflex which responded to the countless stimuli that had been fed into him from his first moments of being: the chemistry of his mother's bloodstream, the religion and nationality foisted upon him, the thousand little correctives issued daily for years until he was totally programmed to act the way his civilisation deemed he should.

'But there is no freedom in any of that,' he thought. He saw destiny as a blind weaver, a dotty craftsman using the available materials to spin a fabric of unintelligible design. 'I'm a slave,' he said to himself. 'The whole universe, including the very structure of my body, is just one way of defining my complete limitation.'

'He's probably getting his first rushes,' said Conrad. The entire revolution had gone through Aaron's mind in less than a second of chronological time. 'I'd better go see how he's doing.'

He checked her once with his eyes, the glance of a soldier saying goodbye to his lover at the train station, forced to pull the shade down on softness and intimacy in order to join the troops boarding to reach the battle-ground, and walked quickly into the living room. Aaron was bending over, his trouser legs up, checking the damage to his shin. He looked up and saw Conrad coming toward him, stood up quickly to regain his composure, and before he knew what was happening found himself holding on to the young man, his arms around his shoulders, his head on his chest, and the tears spilling unashamedly from his eyes.

There was no need to talk. Conrad understood that deep within Aaron some long-locked spring of feeling had been released, and what memories or forms of ideation or prompting toward action it engendered were of no real concern. It only mattered that the man would weep; from that all freedom followed. Aaron felt the blessed relief of not being embarrassed at what he had always thought was a weakness, and was amazed through his tears that he could accept the embrace of the man who just a half hour earlier had appeared as a threat to his peace of mind. He laughed as he cried, reflecting that the stability he was so frantically hold-ing on to was actually the rigidity born of fear, and for this brave instant, there was nothing to be afraid of. For the first time in his adult life the arms which held him were the powerful arms of a man, seeking nothing but to feed back to him his sense of himself, and not the arms of a woman, which always implied a contract, and could comfort, but could never reassure.

Cynthia, hearing the unaccustomed sound, stepped into the room; and assailed by the unexpected sight of the man she lived with and the man she had been just making love to now locked in a circle of feeling which totally excluded her, was faced with her own crisis. Deeply repressed attitudes of rejection, instilled during the days when six siblings vied for a harried mother's affection and a tired father's attention, marched to the forefront of her perception. She wrestled with a sense of betrayal.

Conrad stepped back, the single most valuable action he had learned during his precocious adolescence. He stood sideways so that the straight line of energy which had gone from Cynthia on one end to him and Aaron on the other became a triangle. Veteran of over a hundred acid and mescaline episodes, his instincts for emotional dynamics were honed to a fine edge. He rarely bothered with content, and addressed himself to structure.

'It's getting a little heavy,' he said. He looked from one to the other. 'Everything that's happening is real, but it's not all there is.' He went to the window and pulled the blind. At once, the ambience altered. 'We're still a couple and their neighbour spending a quiet evening at home. All the shit that's working in our systems gives it a peculiar twist, and that's what we learn from, but we need to stay straight. Otherwise we'll wind up all knotted together in a colossal bummer.'

Aaron listened to the words as though they were in a language he didn't understand. Already he was speeding to another nexus of internal confusion and clarity, the liberated elements of his mind forming and reforming to shape new perspectives. He tried desperately to remember what it was that had just made so much sense, why his tears had felt so good. But his eyes were dry, and the first tinges of nausea were colouring his outlook. Cynthia looked grotesque, a cubist melange of angles covered with melting flesh, a surreal gargoyle. He was certain he was going to vomit.

Conrad led him to the centre of the room and helped him to lie down. 'Whatever you think, whatever you feel, whatever you understand, don't hold on to it,' he said. 'You're just a river, and you're going to assume ten thousand shapes before the night is finished. Don't identify with any of them. Just keep flowing.' His voice, low and lulling, put Aaron in a state of relaxation, and he closed his eyes. Immediately the feeling of illness passed, and he entered a state of consciousness for which there was no conceptual expression. He let go of his environment, of his awareness of Conrad and Cynthia, and sank into himself, to mine the rich lode of his long untapped unconscious mind.

Cynthia sat in the large chair, her lips and hands trembling. She had received the waves of revulsion that had poured from Aaron when he last looked at her, and coupled with her burgeoning feeling of insecurity, they undermined her sense of well-being. She opened and closed her eyes rapidly, and finally looked at Conrad imploringly.

'Why don't you make some tea?' he said, directing her toward an activity, knowing that to be the best therapy for her current state. And as she moved about the kitchen, working slowly and exactly, holding on to the familiar routine of boiling water, washing dishes, clearing the table, sweeping the floor, Conrad sat cross-legged a few feet from where Aaron lay, and took several deep breaths, finding himself keenly aroused by the developments of the evening.

For three hours there was little movement. Aaron lay like a man in a coma; Cynthia shared her time between dozing on the couch and prowling around the back yard; Conrad sat like a stone statue, lost in his mescaline revery. In each of them solitude sang like a loon; there are some places which can only be got to alone, and to these three products of a culture which did not prepare its members for communion with that god who can be found only in the chambers of the heart, the loss of social amenity produced various stages of oppressiveness. Aaron felt as though he had been buried alive, and lived for most of the time with a sharp awareness of the walls of the crypt which contained him. Oscillating between stark terror and currents of omnipotence, he churned silently within the tomb that was his mind. Conrad sailed similar seas, but his experience allowed him to accept the voyage for what it was, a passage through forces which gave man a taste of his utter insignificance in the face of the enormity of creation. Cynthia was cast into paroxysms of paranoia; the stoned withdrawal of the men at a time when she was negotiating her own high reaches threw her mercilessly onto her own resources, and she discovered, with angry amazement, that up to that moment she had defined herself entirely in reference to whatever man she was with, and had no sense of herself as an individual, as a person, except in the sociological role of woman. She saw that her relationship with Aaron comprised only one and a half people, neither of them ever able to attain fullness, except at the expense of the other.

Finally, Aaron stirred. His eyes opened slowly and with the sense of being entombed still dominant, acknowledged his actual physical environment. Like a person who has lived for months on amphetamines and has come to accept that psychic state as permanent, and then stops injecting the drug and descends to the chemically normal equilibrium only to find it massively depressing, Aaron stepped into the world he had created for himself out of the pitiful tools he had been given as a birthright and saw it to be absolutely stifling. Forgetting that the power of the perceptions was due to the increased energy released by the acid, he thought he would have to live for the rest of his life with this frightful aspect. And with an elegant leap of rational intelligence he understood that the awesome immediacy of the insight would be tempered by time, but that its factual reality would continue. In sum, in a few days he would feel better about his condition, reverting to his customary level of consciousness, but his condition would continue to be a denial or a translation of the fierce life energy inside him.

'It's all true,' he said aloud.

Conrad blinked and looked at the inert form. 'How you feeling, man?' he said.

'I've been under a long time,' Aaron responded.

'About three hours,' said Conrad.

'About thirty-one years,' Aaron said.

'Ah.' Conrad added, 'You've seen all that.'

'Yeah,' Aaron said in a low vibrant voice, 'I've seen all that.' He stared at the ceiling. The conversation lifted much of the weight from his chest; they were two solitaries sharing the darkness of the night, the way wolves howl to relieve their plaintive loneliness under stark moons over frozen hills. 'You are my comrade,' he said.

Conrad cocked his head. 'I don't know what that word means,' he said. 'All I know is friends and strangers. And you aren't a stranger any more, and I don't know whether you're my friend.'

'Are you all right?' said Cynthia.

'I feel like the past few hours have been one long breath,' Aaron told her. 'And I've filled my lungs and can be here for quite a while, but soon I'll be letting it all out again and breathing it all in again.'

'The next cycle will be less intense,' Conrad said. 'And the one after that even less so. Until you'll be breathing normally again.'

'Will I go back the way I was?' Aaron asked.

'No point in talking about that,' Conrad answered.

Aaron closed his eyes again, but instead of sliding back into the austere realm of cerebration, he fell into a pool of sensuality, his brain retiring to the task of sorting all the new data and structuring new gestalten to pattern it. He descended into his body.

It was as though a spirit entered the room, changing the very molecules of the air.

There was no change immediately observable to gross perception. Aaron seemed as still as he had been earlier, but to one who could read the language of the body, the difference was marked. Whereas his energy had been flowing up into his brain and inward toward his centre, giving him the appearance of a man in shock, and instilling that feeling of constriction which he had translated into an image of the grave, it now moved downward and outward, charging his pelvis and legs, so that he seemed to swell and radiate; to the degree he had appeared deathly, he now was seen to overflow with life. His thoughts became, instead of the laboratory of crucial considerations, like the delicate riffs of a piece by Mozart heard in the background while fucking. No imitation of sex as such intruded into the atmosphere, for the other two had not yet moved into that realm of expansion which now transformed Aaron and imparted to him a radiant beauty.

Conrad was the first to be affected, noting with almost cynical satisfaction that the contours of the trip were developing along expected paths. The realisation caught him in a bind, for he knew that in a short time the scene would move into the area of orgy, and to succumb to that temptation was too easy for his liking; it also carried the threat of repercussions from Aaron. He did not wish to subject their relationship to more strain than the older man could assimilate, especially under the influence of the drug. In the outlaw life-style that had become his role it was more important to be secure within a narrow ground with people than to indulge in far-reaching romps over untested terrain. Aaron and Cynthia were as much a possible source of help in a crisis as people he wanted to become more intimate with. The two functions were reciprocal, but to pursue one at the possible expense of the other was foolish.

He began to detect the changes in himself which enticed him into the world of sucking and licking and sighing. His legs grew heavy, his groin flushed with heat, his shoulders slumped and his fingers curled and uncurled, as though he were bunching silk into his palms. He looked at Cynthia. She sat sprawled in the large chair, her shirt unbuttoned to her chest, the tie-

dyed fabric a frame for the swell of her breasts. The
bottom of the garment had ridden to the tops of her
thighs and her pubic hair was a black shadow deep
between her legs. His cock stirred. With the knowledge
born of patient observation he could now read the
alterations in her attitude; she was coming undone.

'She's ready for anything,' he thought, and wondered
whether she had the power to be wanton. A woman
come upon with a passion could stand five times the
number of men presently in the room on their ears,
making them perform like so many trained lions, leaping through the hoops of their own desire and over the
poles of their own erections, all the while allowing
them to think it was they who were running the show.
But it would take a woman with absolute confidence
in the sublimity of abandon; one slip and she would
become the wretched object of a shoddy gang-bang.
Conrad made peace with his ambivalence by deciding
to remain passive, taking whatever sensual gifts were
handed him with gratitude, but doing nothing to structure their flow.

But Cynthia did not know how to proceed and was
wishing that one or both of the men would go to where
she was and do something with her. She was intimi-
dated by Aaron's status of tripping and didn't want to
interfere with a process she didn't yet understand. She
could feel the vibrations emanating from him, and
knew from experience that he was rutting heavily.
Conrad's eyes were like hot hands on her body, and
she still tingled at the memory of their encounter in
the kitchen. She closed her eyes and slipped into a
state of imminent waiting.

The three of them sank into a wordless swirl of
sexual yearning. Aaron centred his attention in the
beating of his heart, returning to the awareness of life
as a single throb, a blind pulsation in the dark. The
great complexities he had been dealing with reduced
to the critical moment when the muscle in his chest
contracted and released, contracted and released; once

more he returned to the theme of mortality, but instead of understanding it in imagistic terms, he saw it as the simple physiological question of continuation. From the top of his head to the soles of his feet he thrilled with the simple joy of breathing. For each it was almost impossible to tell which feelings were generated from within, and which were being received from another. They were a circuit the nature of which was determined by the totality of all their impulses, and the communications were too rapid and subtle to be sorted as to origin. Their minds were drenched with erotic images dimly projected, and their mouths were shaped for moans of the ecstasy that can only come from capitulation to a force greater than the intellect is willing to acknowledge.

Aaron brought his hands to his chest, pausing to relish the concrete reality of his own form, and then, something he had never done before, caressed himself gently, sliding his hands to his belly, which rose and fell in a soft rhythm, and to his crotch, where his cock lay in tender readiness. A shiver of sweetness tickled his thighs, and his muscles tasted a sensation akin to the first mouthful of ripe melon crumbling on the tongue. He rubbed the shaft slowly until it swelled, causing a bulge down the right leg of his trousers, to him a centre of almost unbearably precious carnal contemplation, but to Cynthia a focus of temptation.

With great trepidation, she slipped off the chair and moved cautiously to where Aaron lay, walking on her knees. She knew that he had no need of her at that moment, but something about his vulnerability to his own pleasure stirred her to involve herself with him. The sound roused Conrad and he opened his lids to watch as she advanced, the undulating womanflesh going to drench the stiffening male in her pungent juices. To his sight, which at that point beheld the whole world as a fluid mass of shifting sand, she possessed the stateliness of a long-necked dinosaur marching solemnly through tall waving marsh grass. A strong urge to rise to meet her was checked by his reluctance to add to the violence which was about to be perpetrated on Aaron at that moment. He was certain that he did not want to be impinged upon, even by an almost naked, and randy woman who wanted very much to be had by him. Conrad stared at the lolling breasts which preceded her, huge mammalian sensors feeling their way in the dark. His teeth itched with desire, but he held himself with an iron discipline which was becoming his central pride and pleasure, and only watched, the way a jackal will stand at the periphery of the circle where several jungle cats devour a succulent zebra, hoping that some will be left over for him.

Cynthia stopped, reached tentatively forward, and touched Aaron's cock with her fingertips. He flinched as though he had been slapped and brought his knees up like a man protecting himself. Into the domain of subtle vibration he had entered, her touch came as a gross intrusion, and wakened a hundred reflex reactions which frightened him with their clamour. The sense of relaxation had transported him to realms of quiet bliss, and he silently screamed against any request for movement, any demand for him to reach out. She understood his response as a sexual spasm, as in part it was, and was emboldened to bring her head down to rest her cheek against the hard cock that filled out the fabric. He put his hands over her ears, holding her head still, trying to communicate his wish to be left alone. She took his movement as a challenge and began insisting by grabbing his hips and pulling his body into her as she attempted to force her face between his legs. Conrad looked on. The woman's legs, now naked to the ass, were kicking against the rug, and her torso squirmed lasciviously; she presented the classic picture of every man's most rudimentary wet daydream: that of the woman who had divested herself of all defense and pretense and is allowing herself to sail off into an elongated gesture of bestial groveling begging. Aaron pushed her away, and his efforts only served to inflame her; she thought he was interested in another round of their favourite scenario, which always ended with him subjugating her, abusing her, and then sinking bewildered into her arms.

'Why do they fight one another so much?' Conrad said to himself. He had no way of knowing both were, in large measure, still working out the traumas of their childhood and teen-age, when sex was less a shared activity than a series of shivers linked to a sense of shameful wrongdoing. Although they now had adult rationalisations for their behaviour, and more sophisticated forms of presentation, what they did was limited by obsolete dynamics.

'Please,' said Cynthia, 'you have so much energy. Don't keep it all inside. Let me. Let me.'

She tugged at his zipper, staring at the work of her fingers with the look the demented attain during odd moments of concentration. She crooned as she hauled his cock out, the rigid member bending perilously as it was pulled from inside the tight trousers through the narrow opening. It flared in her fist, twitching in anticipation. Aaron rolled his head back and forth on the floor, battling, but with less conviction. Her nose wrinkled, her eyes went unfocused, her mouth opened tremulously, and her head dropped down, her hair spilling on his belly as she kissed his balls and then licked the length of his cock to the violet tip where a single drop of moisture was balanced, like dew on a rose. She sucked up the fluid, enraptured by the taste, and then in a single motion gliding with the grace of a swan, she swallowed his entire cock.

He groaned once, and surrendered to euphoria.

She sucked him lovingly, giving it her total attention, her lips acting as divinators for the explosions of pleasure in his cock, so that she moved unerringly in the way he would have done were he blowing himself. 'Oh you beautiful thick cock,' she said again and again. 'Put it in my mouth.' Her voice lapsed into a patter of gurgles and sputters. 'That's better,' she said after a while, 'so much better.' For a while she experienced the quiet rapture of a baby nodding off on the nipple.

Aaron fluctuated between melting into the flutter of Cynthia's tongue all around the tip of his cock, and the knowledge that Conrad was watching. He imagined what the other man could see, and the result-ant images sparked eruptions of lava through his veins; at once he envisioned the thin curved lips in the expression of imbecilic rapture that emerged when she smiled with a cock in her mouth. Cynthia at first blocked the awareness of the third person, pretending that she was alone with Aaron, but the hot presence behind her could not long be ignored. She swung to the opposite end of the spectrum into exhibitionism, and also projected herself into Conrad's view of her. 'I'm on my belly sucking a cock and showing my arse to another man,' she thought, and tried to match that reality with what she would have thought of such a thing five years earlier, and enjoyed the shock which comes of having one's previous self, dormant within the character structure, wake up to see what a later self has become.

To the degree that she and Aaron kept to their own business, the energy flowed freely between them, reduced somewhat by Aaron's resistance and Cynthia's anxiety. But their increasing referrals to Conrad's presence pulled at their bond, and sought to include him. Fear, inhibition, lack of clarity, all intervened to keep that from happening, and instead they began to perform for him, without knowing they were doing so. Their *act* became an 'act'; yet they were not able to turn themselves into theatre. So her cocksucking was distracted, and his appreciation of what his cock felt like in her mouth was muddled. In a while they became bored, and could not admit that they were bored. Cyn-thia worked her tongue twice as fast, and Aaron started to lose his erection.

At a point where the wisest thing two human beings

can do is simply to leave one another alone, they often, with implacable perversity, proceed to embroil themselves more intricately. Cynthia opened Aaron's belt, grabbed the waist of his trousers, and tugged them down his legs, over his knees and past his feet. She was no longer thinking; it was as though some switch had been thrown in her mind and she was programmed to act out some mordant drama that had its wellsprings in all the unexplored regions of her unconscious. Aaron was still clear enough to know that he ought to stop himself, but he translated that as an imperative to stop her, thus insuring that he would allow the thing to go on. She stooped forward and laid her tongue flat along the sole of one foot, and licked him, without stopping, up the length of the leg, plunging at last deep between his buttocks. She dug her nails into his legs until he arched his back and with a violent twisting motion turned herself over and like a mechanic sliding under a chassis pulled herself beneath his body. And then lay there, panting, waiting for him to succumb to gravity and sink slowly and heavily on top of her. Aaron felt himself come unstoppered. What she offered him was past his ability to resist; he had only to let go and she would offer herself totally in fullest degradation.

'Don't do it.' Conrad tried to project the thought into Aaron's head.

But she began to moan and yearn, and the sound of her aggressive surrender swept him past all considerations of person, and he let the actual and symbolic massiveness of his buttocks swallow her face and crush her wide fragile mouth. With a whimper she licked the crusted shit from his arsehole, and glued her lips to the musty cleft.

She clung to him like a leech to its donor until she needed to breathe, and then let go all at once, her face falling to one side so that the buttocks crushed her cheek. She wormed out from under him and lay still, looking except for her size, like a baby that had just

83

slithered from his loins. Aaron held his breath, for in
the few brief seconds when her sucking lips and pro-
bing tongue had entered his clenched sphincter, he
knew beyond all doubt that she had really wanted him
to release the slow sliding wet fullness into her. A
premonition of the vile filled him with loathing.

Cynthia rose and propped herself on her elbow;
dazed, she swung her head around and found herself
looking into Conrad's eyes. The contact stunned her,
for she could see all that he could see of her, and
knew that nothing was hidden from his view. Her
embarrassment mingled with a wild exaltation as she
recovered a hope that had been lost and even forgotten,
that she would one day meet a man to whom she could
give herself unreservedly, assured that he had the fullest appreciation of what a thing of wonder she was
doing. It came with the delight of a spring breeze, the
realisation that what she wanted was possible if there
were two men: one to enter her through touch, the
other through understanding, thus bringing both
halves of her together. Disheveled, blown, ragged, the
acrid taste still on her tongue, she was blessed with
an awareness of herself as a woman. All her roles,
fragmented aspects of the whole, manifesting themselves serially, bloomed in her consciousness, and she
accepted that she was more than a lover or a wife,
more than a slave or a witch, more than a queen, a
friend, a seductress, a worker. She understood that she
was a human being and heir to the full potential of
the species. Anything that anybody was ever or ever
could be also lived in her. The racial unconscious
opened its doors and freed her of her partial vision.
Through a mechanism she was not even aware of, her
habit of being acted upon was temporarily broken, and
she was able to act.

'What do you want from me?' she said to Conrad
who was assiduously watching all the changes on her
face.

84

'I want to be left alone,' said Aaron, hearing the question and arrogating it to himself.

'All right,' Cynthia said to herself, 'I'll leave you alone.'

She smiled, and, never taking her eyes from Conrad's gaze unbuttoned her shirt and shrugged it off her shoulders. For the first time he saw her naked body as something which related directly to him and his mouth watered. She came up on her hands and knees and walked over to him like a four-footed-animal. Her breasts hung down, her rump shone in the dull light, and her cunt was tucked under, a patch of darkness accessible from behind. He imagined his cock sliding under her arched buttocks and into the sticky centre, and his heart skipped a beat. But he did not move.

They stared at one another like a boy and girl on a see-saw maintaining the contact as they rose and fell, always in opposite directions. A thin fury had begun to build in her, for she was going further and further out to spark some sort of response from the men, and they remained impassive behind the wall of their drug-induced self-sufficiency. The problem which arises the moment two or more individuals share the same space was now magnified by heightened circumstance. But she pushed on, thinking that a critical point would be passed, and one or both of the men would take a hand in directing the sexual proceedings. She sensed Aaron's presence behind her, and using that awareness like a swimmer propelling himself from the side of a pool, she dove in a long arc toward Conrad's crotch. The zipper opened easily, and she eased the limp cock out.

With a sigh, she took it in her mouth. Almost at once she was seized by excitement. She had known no other cock but Aaron's for several years, and the strangeness of feeling Conrad inside her was markedly thrilling. She sucked it in as far as it would go, and held it there, poised between the pressure of her tongue and the roof of her mouth. In the acquisition of a

85

veneer of sophistication and boredom which had accrued to fucking only one man for such a long period of time, she had lost sight of how marvelously dirty the act of cocksucking could be. She remembered her dates during high school, and the boys who were constantly trying to get her to touch them while they struggled to reach her nipples, her arse, her cunt. Having been trained from childhood to regard such contact as powerfully shameful, she almost fainted with the joy of intense sinfulness she felt when she was seventeen and went to the apartment of a twenty-four-year-old man, who was able, through a combination of titillation and coercion, to get her to go down on her knees while he sat at the edge of the bed and put the forbidden cock between her closed lips which with virgin trembling, parted and accepted it inside her. He had stroked her cheeks as she tongued him and whispered, 'Oh yes, baby, suck it, come on you beautiful mouth, gobble it down,' and then very unexpectedly shot his sperm and held her tightly so that she gagged and then had to swallow, feeling the slime sliding down her throat.

Conrad's cock hardened. She licked it while it swelled inside her, and when it reached its full length she pulled back, leaving it exposed. She lay down in front of him, held the base of his cock in her two hands, and began to bounce her head up and down on its crown. She did not stop for niceties; she sucked him like a professional, interested in bringing him in one single rush to a spurting orgasm. She had grown hungry for completion, and wanted the cycle to come to an end in the most direct way it could, with one of the men coming and dispersing the energy which had risen to painful levels of reserve.

She heard a rustle behind her. She twisted her head to the side, continuing to move back and forth on Conrad's prick, and glanced as far left as she could. Aaron was watching her. It was the first time he had seen her with another man, and he was stung by the beauty of her. Even looking into the mirror while she was sucking him hadn't prepared him for the feelings he was now experiencing, the jealousy melting into yearning, the anger exploding into joy. He raked her body with his eyes, soaking up the lusciousness of her charms; he almost wept as he swept his glance from her feet, where her toes curled in pleasure, to her arse, which wiggled like an insect's in the midst of luring a mate, to her mouth, which stretched with such delicate intensity over the enormous cock. To her, his expression was unreadable, the distance, the darkness, and the motion she was involved in conspiring to veil him from her.

All at once she was frightened. She had proceeded along what seemed to be acceptable lines and had assumed that Aaron, by taking the acid, knowing of the electricity that flowed between her and Conrad, had given silent consent to sex between them. She couldn't be sure whether he was glowering at her, whether he was hurt or feeling mean. She knew that he could make her pay dreadfully for weeks afterward if she displeased him. But just then Conrad's cock pulsed in her mouth, and her attention was drawn back to her cocksucking, and she returned to the texture of the silky rim and the tough tender shaft, giving it her loving care. 'I don't have to stay with Aaron after tonight,' she thought, severing her fear. 'I'm a free human being.'

From his relative height, Conrad watched the drama between them. What he could see and Cynthia could not, was that Aaron's right hand was curled around his cock, pulling it in counterpoint to the rhythms of Cynthia's mouth. An odd grasp of cosmic inference massaged his brain while he observed the three of them in their laconic performance. He knew that the event was working itself out according to a plan to which he had only partial insight, and thus was justified in holding back. But he bemoaned the lack of fullness, and wondered why Aaron hadn't got up to fuck Cynthia from the rear while she sucked his own cock. He speculated that the acid had put Aaron on an internal trip, and removed him from the arena of overt passion. Without his being conscious of the process, his attention split into several fragments, a piece on Aaron, a piece on Cynthia, a piece on the nature of the universe, and a dwindling piece on the sensation in his cock. Wrapped in his thoughts, he had lost his erection.

'Shit,' said Cynthia to herself. And with a stroke of boldness which so enlivened her that she almost pissed on the rug, she opened her mouth and let the limp tool fall out, and turned rapidly on Aaron, sliding across his thigh and scooping his cock between her lips. She picked up the same rhythm she had begun with Conrad, like a woman starting her knitting again after putting it aside. She was performing the act of cocksucking for a specific end, to close some crucial gap within herself that could only be bridged by a male organ. The fact that she was switching cocks to accomplish that was a minor consideration. She wanted to feel the pulsation of the thick vein as the sperm gushed out onto her tongue; she no longer cared which of the two men provided the cock to do that.

Aaron lifted his pelvis off the floor to meet her approach, thrusting into her as she closed her jaws over the shaft. Watching her had brought him to a pitch of excitement and his movements were involuntary, following an inner arc of keen frenzy which sliced through the fog of introspection which had enveloped him. He sighed as she went to work on him. 'This time I'll come,' he thought, reverting to the insipid pattern which the brief boost allowed by the LSD had revealed in its poverty.

With thrilling perversity, however, she retreated. Having attained her aim of bringing him out of his shell and into strong contact with her, she was now in a position of strength; she had something he needed and she momentarily blocked out the moral responsi

88

bility for having roused that need in the first place. She teased him, first stuffing his entire cock into her throat, and then pulling back rapidly, right to the rim, and slowly opening her mouth so that the sensation on his cock faded and disappeared. He tried to pull her head down but she resisted, and he was forced to reach up with his cock to find her mouth again. She licked him with her tongue and pulled back once more, repeating this until his muscles ached with the strain of trying to lodge his prick in her mouth again. And when he was at the bursting point, she simply stepped back, turned around, showing him her rump, and sprawled forward, starting in on Conrad, coaxing him into involvement, enticing him to a point where he could feel the ejaculation bubbling in his balls and then stopping.

'It's all a game,' she thought. 'I don't owe them anything, and they don't owe me anything. We can all do what we like.' The drugs she had smoked and the contact high she was receiving from Conrad in his mescaline and Aaron in his acid had raised her consciousness to a state, rare among human beings, where she could perceive the obvious. 'If I could always see this clearly,' she said to herself. 'I would never have any confusion about anything.

Giddy with the power of the individual in a flurry of self-discovery, and chattering with fear that she might be careening down a dangerous blind alley, she went back and forth between them a dozen times until she could no longer tell any difference, having reduced their impact upon her to the single dimension of their maleness, and seeing in that context that there was indeed no way to choose between one and the other.

'They're all the same once you put the lights on,' she thought, giggling to herself at the reversal of the old saw about women.

The men had darker perceptions. Caught in the spiral of their gnashing lust, and put in the position of erection producers, they framed Cynthia as a photograph of a woman gone wild. In their evaluation, stripped of all levels except the apparent, she was a dripping naked cockteasing bitch, her lips red from the friction against their cocks, her arse an open invitation, her cunt redolent with the aroma of heavy secretions. They were being whipped into an unthinking furor of desire as she played Russian roulette with their cocks, rotating them like chambers in a gun until she found one that fired.

Finally Aaron grabbed her. In the second his fingers closed over her skull and twined in her hair, he remembered who she was, and in a single flash the years through which they had passed together materialised and he was overwhelmed with the power of the reality they shared. He recalled how poignantly and terribly he loved her, and how ruthlessly he hated her, and in how many ways they simply rose and fell with one another. She received the impact of his insight as a rush of energy so strong that she could not fight it, and brought her face humbly to his groin, accepting his cock almost reverently. So she gave herself in her own way to something in him which she recognised as superior without knowing what that quality was. And at the precise instant she stopped struggling, he lapsed into nostalgia, and became once more a teenager with a sluggish date.

He flicked his gaze across the room and saw Conrad still sitting there, his limp cock hanging from his fly. He looked down at the woman begging him, with her noises and actions and glances, to do it to her, to make her a receptacle. She didn't care what he deposited in any of her openings, she was urging to be filled. He was struck by the younger man's restraint, and wondered why an acid-head would be practicing delayed gratification. He was annoyed that he had become so active, and judged that he had lost face before Conrad, who hadn't once lost his cool. He hated Cynthia then for having seduced him to this role of ogre, straining his cock into her, gripping her forcibly to him.

'You bitch,' he said. 'Is this what you want? A cock in your mouth while he watches, sees you rolling naked on the floor. You miserable cunt.'

The words were whips across her soul, for they were spoken in honest anger, not the stage voice Aaron fell into when he tried to lash her verbally. Also, it was the first open acknowledgement that there were three people in the room. She grasped that what she had been trying to do was be the bridge between the men, while they, after that initial embrace, had lost all functional interest in one another, in their apathy leaving her stranded, unable to relate to either. The animal in her sprang loose and she let out a long, low growl, arched her back, and snapped her head up, her face a mask with slit eyes and bared teeth; her fingers curled and her nails quivered like knife blades just thrown and sunk in hard wood. Feelings so massively repressed they did not have names bubbled to the surface to show themselves in terrifying expressions and orgiastic contortions. She twitched and jerked and stretched like an epileptic cat.

The effect on the men surpassed all their nicety of intellect. They exchanged a lightning glance which communicated the harsh jungle reality of their condition the primacy of male and female. In an unspoken stroke, Aaron released both himself and Conrad from the social contract in which Cynthia was *his* woman; she became simply *a* woman, and they were two men with precisely the same instinct, now whipped to a thrashing frenzy – to fuck her. They moved simultaneously and fell upon her, the last shreds of Aaron's reserve and Conrad's strategy burning in the heat that erupted from her body. They silenced their perspective with snarls.

As they touched her, she began to fight, her legs thrashing and her mouth and hands seeking targets to bite and scratch. The three of them rolled around the floor like cats doing battle, knocking over furniture, banging and bruising themselves. She was no match

91

for their strength and weight, and they jerked to a halt wedged against the couch, Cynthia's arms pinned by Aaron and her ankles held tightly in Conrad's grasp. She twisted and squirmed, all the parts of her which enflamed the men made more prominent by her exertions. Her breasts rolled and juggled, her cunt flared, her arse tightened.

Aaron brought her wrists together and held them with one hand and with the other rolled her to her stomach; when Conrad saw what he was doing he assisted in the movement, and in a few seconds she was prone before them, more vulnerable now that she could not attack them with her eyes. But as Aaron's free hand swooped down to her buttocks and Conrad inched his way up to a point where he could slide his cock under and into her cunt, she found her voice.

'All right, Aaron,' she said in the kind of voice a mother uses to an unruly child, 'what do you think you're doing?'

In a twinkling the jungle disappeared and they were back in the living room, their social roles grafted instantaneously back to the burgeoning energy, quieting it, making it ashamed. Aaron was once again a schoolteacher who did not know what direction his life should take, and Cynthia was the woman he was thinking of marrying, and Conrad was a strange radical from down the block whom neither of them knew very well. With her tone she injected the air of responsibility into their activities, thus robbing them of their unbridled fullness.

As though on signal, the men looked at one another questioningly and Cynthia stopped struggling, her lax muscles providing a greater dampening of their lust than all her strength could manage. She presented them with indifference, the very quality that they had shown to her when she was attempting, earlier, to prompt them into action. Aaron let her go and turned away, getting to his feet and walking stolidly out of the room, past the kitchen, and into the bedroom.

Conrad, at the very edge of coming, passed his hand once over the head of his cock and the sperm spurted out, providing only relief from the fierce tension, and no pleasure at all; it fell in gooey drops on the carpet. Cynthia, something in her snapping, began to sob.

She stopped after a while, and like a woman coming out of a waking dream, rubbed her eyes. She got to her feet. Conrad sat as he was sitting earlier, cross-legged, his eyes closed. She shook her head and with a gesture so feminine it brought her back to herself, she spread her fingers and ran them through her hair, smoothing it and dropping it behind her shoulders so that it fell down her back.

'Where's Aaron?' she said.

Conrad opened his eyes and looked at her. He almost gasped at the sight. Flushed from the struggle, flowing with the freedom she had found in so fully playing so many roles, she glowed with a strange beauty. Her nakedness made him blink, for it was not only that she wore no clothes, but that she wore no artifice which suffused her with brilliant openness. Despite all his experience, despite the fact that he had seen women in their glory before, he felt, for the first time in his life, that awe-filled and dizzying sense of capture which has, from time immemorial, been called falling in love. And that her first action was to ask for Aaron tore a gash of envy across his soul. For he saw with certainty that she would go to him, and they would claim all the energy which had been liberated, and fuck with such totality and concern as to transport them into a searing paradise of ecstasy.

'It's what I get for getting mixed up with a couple,' he thought, ruefully acknowledging that he had faced this possibility very early in his relationship with the two of them. Simultaneously, he told himself that the wheel turns many times, and one day it would be he who was blessed with the overflow.

'He went into the bedroom,' he said.

She looked down at her body, and back at Conrad,

and the problem was clear to her. 'I think I'd better go to him,' she said.

He nodded. He was already seeking refuge in indifference. She walked to him, knelt down, and tenderly kissed him on the mouth. It was a kiss of regret and promise, but it pointed to a future time, another place. She turned, stood, and strode from the room, her cheeks wobbling as she walked. Conrad felt a pain in his chest.

He rolled another joint, smoked it steadily, and collected his thoughts. In a while the sounds began, the soaring cries of Cynthia's lovemaking, and the groans of Aaron's pleasure. His lips twitched and he smirked at the wall. And as a few others have done on the sad downward glide of a mescaline ride, he consoled himself with the truth that it was not easy to learn the lessons of life; one had to live them and not know till afterward why one did what he did. And more than anything else Conrad felt that all he went through was in the way of preparation for some test or for some decision, the nature of which he was just beginning to suspect.

'Oh sweet Jesus fuck me,' Cynthia cried out.

Conrad gathered his dope and walked crazily out the front door into the cool sweet-smelling air. it was almost four in the morning. He strolled to his house, picked up his bicycle, and pedalled at a contemplative rate to the Marine, where he sat watching the wide expanse of dark blue water, and the harsh yellow lights of the Golden Gate Bridge, until the sky grew pink and the clouds began to show. He was blissfully alone.

5

The Driven

Not a person on the street seemed sane. The mid-morning sunlight froze the pageant of types in their sparkling diversity. Even those who were only there to stroll and absorb were transformed into spear-carriers in the opera of Telegraph Avenue, and Aaron watched the scene unfold as he walked, searching for Conrad, and tried to formulate some conceptual structure which would subsume the disparate and complementary forces of the world he saw with eyes that still glowed with acid rushes.

The most apparently bizarre were the Hare Krishna singers, young men mostly, with shaved skulls and foreheads painted white, wearing orange robes and blue basketball shoes, pounding drums and chanting their single mantram until their minds were dulled through repetition and their eyes came to see the entire complex multiform reality of life through the inverted spyglass of a senescent worldview. They danced in front of a table with pamphlets praising the benefits of their brand of enlightenment, and under a photograph of their founder, a sallow old man with liver-coloured lips and eyes like snub-nosed bullets. The picture showed him adorned in flowing robes and seated on a red velvet throne covered by a yellow silk canopy, and surrounded by forty to fifty of his followers, all earnest American boys and girls.

As though to offset the gaudy diffusion of that exotic sideshow, stolid blacks stood heavily on the edges of the sidewalks and sold the Panther newspaper, in which angry warlords and ideological chieftains thundered their pronouncements and called for the redress of grievances with painfully clumsy articulations. Aaron bought a paper. On the inside front page was a letter from a leader in exile who asserted that 'proof of the pie is in the action,' and warned against all tendencies to get involved in theory to the detriment of practice. Aaron leafed through the pages which detailed prison atrocities, sudden murders by bands of police, and twenty-six rules which had to be followed by all members of the Party.

Leather craftsmen sat up on the concrete, sewing, tapping holes, cutting, piling their inventions in animal skin on blankets, turning the street into a brief imitation of an Eastern market. Occasionally one of them sold something, and completed the exchange of goods and money without the smile which has become almost compulsory in California whenever business is done. These were people who, for the most part, had reduced their physical needs to bare essentials and lived in loose family groupings in old wooden cabins in one of the patches of woods still extant around San Francisco, perhaps in Marin or in the Santa Cruz mountains. They could subsist on a few dollars a day, supplementing their meager incomes with food stamps. They described themselves as righteous dealers and felt they owed no gratitude to their customers.

The walls of the street shrieked with slogans and posters, demanding that political prisoners be released, that the pigs be offed, that the war be ended, that women be liberated. Aaron drank in the jangling panorama of protest and need in a way that he would not have been capable of just two days earlier. Where he had seen what he called undergraduate officiousness he now beheld the immense outpouring of energy and effort these proclamations gave evidence of, and received his first vision of what could be effected if the exuberance of youth were given healthy channels to flow through. But there was no place for it to go, except the deadly route of school, military, and servile employment, and so they frothed with perpetual indignation, and hatched wild schemes to overthrow the existing order. A few small cards, stapled to a wooden partition, proclaimed, with suspicious simplicity, that Jesus saves. Thousands of cardboard sheets of widely varying size and colour offered hundreds of things and services for sale or barter: massages, rides, poetry readings, ecology meetings, opinions, rooms, ideas, food. And thin, drawn young men and women slid up and down the length of the street whispering, 'Acid, grass, speed.'

'Spare change, brother,' a voice said to him.

Aaron looked at him carefully, his reactions measured and gentle as one's tend to be at the tail end of a trip. He noted the disconnectedness of the eyes, the vagueness which comes of living too long without any sense of purpose. He estimated that the man was somewhere between twenty and thirty; he wore his hair and beard that had been growing for several years; he seemed, due to a severe slouch, shorter than his six feet. Over his shoulder the Avenue emptied onto the campus, with its tremulous mixture of eucalyptus groves and squat stone buildings. It galloped over several hundred acres before beginning its stepped climb up the Berkeley Hills, culminating in the great cement Physics building and the guarded Radiation Laboratory which commanded a total view of the majestic valley, the shimmering bay with its elegant bridges, the gaping gateway to the Pacific, and the spiny mountains ranging north and south into distance, mist, and the first grey swatches of polluted air.

'Why do you call me brother?' Aaron asked.

The man answered him automatically. 'We're all brothers in God,' he said.

'And if there is no God?' Aaron went on.

'We're all God, man,' came the reply. 'The universe is one, don't you know? And we're all a part of that.'

97

He smiled, pleased at his own loquaciousness, as though he had made an irrefutable point.

Aaron turned and walked away, forgetting that the man had asked him for money. He was intent on finding Conrad. After he and Cynthia had finished fucking, he was stung by a whiplash of guilt, a sense that he had somehow betrayed a trust that had begun to form between him and the other man. The sex had been the finest since the early days of their living together, when they were still in the phase of discovering one another's bodies, but several times during the welter of feeling he had drifted into the notion that Conrad was still there watching them, and each time that the illusion had burst, he had been filled with a poignant sense of loss. Somewhere a corner had been turned, and, while high energy still flowed through him, he wanted to track down the significance of the night's events.

Both he and Cynthia had called their respective jobs to make excuses for not going in, and Aaron had had a taste of what it felt like to lie on acid. He had difficulty in getting the words out of his mouth. Cynthia lay naked next to him as he called, and when he finished had cooed, 'Let's spend the whole day just making love, we haven't done that in such a long time.' But he could not stay with her and almost panicked when he got up to dress and she grabbed his arm. He couldn't bring himself to say what burned inside him, that after having satisfied himself on her body, he found no further interest in being with her. It was as though he needed the other man to help him confirm some aspect of his identity which close unbroken association with a woman had done much to undermine. He did not have the tools to formulate his problem in historical terms, and did not understand that the unnatural intensity bred in the marriage form had to lead to suffocation. For the second time in their common law marriage he wondered why she had no intimate girlfriends. He had mentioned that to her once and she had put her arms around his neck and said, 'But I don't need anyone but you. Aren't you happy with me?'

Like a puff of smoke that evening appeared in his mind. He saw her again in the bath, suffused with the projected glow he surrounded her with in the early days, the room thick with steam, the water frothy with scented bubbles. He flushed as he recalled the way her long legs cantilevered out when she did a favourite trick of hers, opening her cunt lips with the fingers of both hands and peeking up at him from under her fine golden hair, affecting the leer so popular in sex magazines, but with a gleam of humorous intelligence in her eyes to replace the dull slack stare which mottled the faces of the models.

'I can't get enough,' she had whispered, and cupped one breast with her hand.

He drove into the past, surfacing with memory after memory of that night. They had, as couples often do after skirting an issue, chosen to romp into a bacchanalian mood and each drank a pint of narcotic cough syrup, sinking into a hazy seaworld of blurred perceptions. They fucked once and then slept, and when Aaron awoke she was lying spreadeagled across the bed, breathing regularly in her drugged sleep. Her body had an air of unreality, and the phenomenon kept propelling his mind through a revolving door. He crawled between her legs and spent a long time gazing at her cunt. The lips were flung about in disarray, lettuce leaves of pink and purple, wrinkled and crushed, with his recently discharged sperm oozing out from the bottom and into her hair.

'It's an absurdly ugly thing,' he thought, and saw it as though for the first time, stripped of its connotations. He peeled back the folds of flesh and peered into the small serrated opening, where inside and outside joined. 'This is where the cock goes in and the baby comes out,' he said in a low voice. And then, 'I wonder what my mother's cunt looks like.' It was there, he saw, that the whole problem of sex lay for a man, the need to dissociate the thing he fucked from the thing he issued from. Underneath, her white buttocks spread out like an inviting cushion. And from the centre came a smell like the rotting columns of wood which support wharves in saltwater rivers.

'Cunt,' he said. 'Cynthia's cunt. If Cynthia had no cunt, what would there be of Cynthia?'

The matted hole appeared to look back at him, as though it had its own consciousness independent of any other centres of the body. The importance of that one bit of anatomy to his entire appreciation of her startled him, for he admitted that in any broad view of life the heart and liver and lungs and spleen were all more precious organs, more necessary to her sustenance and well-being. To his drooping mind came the realisation that except for her use in satisfying his sexual needs, she lived as a two-dimensional character in the scenario of his days.

'She is a woman,' he said to himself. 'What does it mean, to be a woman?'

But even as he pursued the train of thought, the brute power of the playground between her thighs captivated him, and he brought his lips forward to kiss the crack, feeling it cold and damp against his mouth. A sheet of energy flapped through him from the point of contact and a deep rumble broke the skin of consciousness, a turmoil of blunt desire which swamped the tentative understanding he was reaching for. His cock got hard.

With none of the common libidinal stirrings he beheld the person beneath him. He had made no special effort to imbue the cunt with any sexual magnetism, and yet it served as a stimulus for lust in and of itself; he needed no fantasy in order to have it arouse him. Since she was unconscious he was able to maintain a rare objectivity while he went about performing the act, and studied his reactions closely. He drew himself over her sleeping form and with great care and patience brought his stiff member up against the soft receptive zone.

Thrills of vegetative ecstasy ran through him and he whimpered as he watched his cock nudge the opening, enter, be swallowed by the hairy mouth, engulfed in its folds, and then slide penetrating all the way into her. She seemed to be at once asleep and responsive to what was happening. Tiny reflexive motions of fucking caught her pelvis up as he drew himself out and thrust himself in, tasting the deliciously small variations in temperature and texture abiding in the different levels of her cunt. For a few seconds it mattered to his enjoyment whether she was awake or not, and then he shifted into a purely behavioural response, satisfied with the simple fact of the action. She lay open and removed, the perfect vehicle for his detached desire. It was a form of fucking that puzzled him, lying in some shadow area between masturbation and actual intercourse. Looking down on her expressionless face, holding his torso up with his arms, his pelvis swung back and forth easily, his knees serving as the fulcrum. She sighed once and he felt her cunt quicken.

For many minutes he rode her as the herald of the coming orgasm. He did not hold back or rush, but remained in the mood of stillness, watching the development of the physiological changes. He saw the act of fucking as a quietly rapturous meditative dance which attained to the perfection of fullness. Then, like a tree running with sap, when the springtime of his seasons sounded its call, he spilled over, lavish in the river of rich white seed which bounded from the pulsating cock into the silent labyrinth between her thighs.

'Berkeley Barb!' a girl shouted. She was nineteen or twenty, barefoot, a complexion already spoiled through bad diet, with stringy hair. She wore a costume of poorly matched pieces, giving an impression of destitution which clashed with the air of insouciance she affected; a thin note of desperation infected her being. The index finger of her right hand was orange from

nicotine. Aaron was snapped from his revery and stared at her. In his abstracted state, he beheld the girl without preconceptions and for a jagged second saw himself as her boyfriend; with that, the hundred differences in their stations in life melted away and he felt a rush of affection for the stranger before him. She looked at him with open distaste. His entire appearance seemed to revolt her, and she ran her eyes from his patent leather shoes to his short hair, taking in the stiffly-creased trousers and white shirt.

'Or would you rather have a *Tribe?*' she said, her voice tinged with sarcasm. The second of the two papers had been born when a large part of the *Barb's* staff revolted against its owner who, they claimed, was a capitalist counterrevolutionary not interested in the true needs of the community of radicals and who, perhaps more pointedly, underpaid his workers. They formed a commune called the Red Mountain Tribe, after the wine of that name, took a strident line on all political issues, and emerged as the foremost example of left-wing yellow journalism on the west coast. The vendor's offering it was a sneering commentary on Aaron's sartorial style and what she imagined was his concomitant value system.

He responded only to her words, too taken by his surprise at the way he had perceived her to react to such an esoteric innuendo. 'I'll take one of each,' he said and handed her thirty cents. Upon taking the money she erased him from her concern.

He continued his walk and the street opened itself at its edges, chic head shops, definitive book stores, restaurants which specialised in one or another type of cuisine, clothing emporiums, shoe palaces. Aaron floated along like a man who had never been there before, for always when passing through on Telegraph he had viewed the street as a jangle of commercialism and unruly people; this was the first time he was able to breathe in the richness of the milieu. Dogs ran loose. Grim old ladies and grimy faced teenagers shared the air that was still sweet enough to provide a contrast to the exhaust fumes of the cars which geared by in chrome contempt.

He entered the Mediterraneum, a coffee house run like a cafeteria in which all the elements of Berkeley's city life could meet over the neutral ground of Italian pastry. It was like Switzerland and no single group was allowed the privilege of claiming it as its own turf. Periodically it would run with disfavour with the street regulars who were put off by the large numbers of straight people who went in, but the management continued its glacial policy, and the place gained in respect for having refused to take its tone from any single faction. He picked up an espresso at the counter and sat down at a round table to leaf through the papers, amazed at the openness of political and sexual rhetoric; one article which explained the servicing of small arms astounded him and the chill wind of revolution whistled into his soul. The print began to swim before his eyes and he covered them with his hands, attempting to stay steady as his reality rocked under him. The last rushes of the acid spun him into an unaccustomed state of consciousness and he lost all context for what he experienced; he felt like a stranger to his time. He wished desperately he could find Conrad, for it seemed there was no one else in the world who would understand his condition as precisely and sympathetically. He took a number of deep breaths, filling his lungs and emptying out, and became aware of his heartbeat once more, of the blood coursing through his veins, of the tingling where thousands of hairs grew out of his scalp. He came to himself and as the external noises fell away he tasted the peculiar flavour of timelessness, that odd experience in which the functioning of the analytic mind is momentarily suspended and the world of mundane perception is suddenly charged with an intangible beckoning presence which seems once and for all to confirm its existence as the true face of the real, against the

103

outraged sensibilities of the scientific paradigm, and the arcane tipsters of the transcendental.

When he looked up again, he saw Conrad, sitting several tables away, deep in conversation with three other men who, except for minor variations, looked exactly like him: the style of clothing, the boots, the long hair, the sinuously cautious movements. He caught himself just as he was about to call out his name and had risen half out of his seat to go over to him, when he judged that such an intrusion would be gauche. In relation to them he felt like a man from a foreign country, speaking a different language. His only connection with them was through Conrad's puzzling interest in him, and he suddenly saw that he and Cynthia must constitute an aberration in Conrad's overall life pattern. He felt foolish and ready to repudiate the past twelve hours as a spell of psychosis. 'I should be home with Cynthia,' he thought, and his eyes were stung with tears as he was gripped in a spasm of sentimentality. Leaving his newspapers on the table, he rose and started to walk toward the street, looking straight ahead; but just as he reached the door Conrad's voice lashed out and caught his attention.

'Hey, Aaron,' he said.

He turned and found the young man grinning at him while the others at the table exchanged glances; Aaron was sure that Conrad had been telling them about the night's events. He felt himself blushing with heat, furious that Cynthia should become the object of smirking small talk.

'Why don't you sit down with us,' Conrad said.

'I've got to be going,' Aaron replied in a curt tone.

'Christ, he's uptight,' he heard one of the men say to the others.

'I'll come with you,' Conrad shot back, leaving his chair and walking from the table without looking back. He put his arm around Aaron's shoulder and went out the door onto the erupting street.

'Is Cynthia all right?' Conrad asked.

'Cynthia's just fine!' Aaron said, his voice sharp with anger.

Conrad read the tone and decided that anything he said would provoke a hostile response. 'Let's go over to my place,' he said. 'I think we need to talk.'

Except for the kitchen, Conrad's flat did not have a piece of furniture in it. The place was a sea of rugs, cushions and hangings, strewn with books and papers, water pipes, clothing. Even the ceilings were covered with fabric, and the overall effect was that of being in a gaudy tent. Aaron was instructed to take off his shoes as he entered, and as he padded down a long hallway with doors lining either wall he glanced into one of the rooms and saw a naked girl who looked fifteen lying sprawled asleep in a purple hammock. They came to a large room in which the three tall windows were stocked with plants that sat on shelves which ran from bottom to top so that the light in the space had the same quality as that one finds in the forest. Just stepping into it was enough to settle most of Aaron's agitation.

Conrad sat on a pillow and rummaged around until he found a small teak box, fished out rolling papers and marijuana, and proceeded to roll several thick joints. He did not say a word, but lit one of the cigarettes and passed it to Aaron, then lit another and began smoking it himself, inserting it between the pinky and ring finger of his right hand which he curled into a fist, and sucking the smoke from the hole formed by his thumb and curled forefinger. By the third toke Aaron was rushing dizzily into the realm of heightened perception; his body grew heavy and he became intensely aware of his physical sensations. Once again, everything but the immediate environment faded into unreality, and only the room, the moment, and Conrad assumed significance. Cynthia and his job and the parameters of his daily life appeared like comets shooting away from him at great speed into space. A cold shiver

105

of fear rippled down his spine as he stepped once more into that awareness of aloneness which he both sought and shunned. The high levels of the previous night were activated by the grass and he took control, for a time, of the choice he had in the mode in which he saw things. He decided what was important, and shucked off all problems whose weight derived from the influence of other people. He finished the first dope stick and Conrad gave him another. They continued to smoke in silence, embraced by the soft oxygen-saturated ambience of the room. And when the proper pitch of attention had been attained, the talk started of its own accord.

'What do you want from me?' Aaron said.

'I don't know,' Conrad told him. 'I want to fuck Cynthia, but that doesn't have anything to do with you. Except the two of you keep pretending it does.' He paused. 'Either she's free, or you should make her a slave, which means that you would have to act like a master, and I don't think you can handle that one. But as it is the two of you don't know what you're doing with each other.'

'She's free to do what she wants,' Aaron said, and as the words came out of his mouth he knew he was lying. 'That's a lie,' he added immediately.

'Bet your arse it's a lie,' Conrad replied.

'I'd like just to fuck her too,' Aaron said after a moment. 'But I have to live with her to make sure she's there when I want her.'

'That's right,' Conrad agreed. 'That's how it works. Now the question is, how do you break it up?'

'You mean, leave?' Aaron asked.

'No, that's not it. I mean, how do you stop playing that game with her?'

'She has to help,' Aaron said.

'No,' Conrad shot back. 'You have to get to be straight with yourself as a man, and then she'll automatically be straight with herself as a woman. Or she'll split, and find some other ninny to play house with.'

Aaron was stung by the epithet, for although it wasn't directed at him, in that context it described him. The exhilaration which grew out of being able to speak so honestly overcame his trepidations about revealing things which could somehow be used against him. Conrad seemed to have such an utter unconcern about anything Aaron said that it was easy to speak freely with him. He estimated that it would be impossible to shock the young man.

'What do you do with women?' he said at last.

'Fuck with them, talk with them, that's about it. If I'm not really getting it on with a woman, either with my head or with my cock, then I'd rather be alone, or with some trees, or with other men.'

In an over-thirty voice with establishment overtones, unaware that he was lapsing into a role shaped for him by *Time* magazine, he said, 'I don't know too much about this revolution you people are always talking about, but it seems to me that what you just said is precisely what woman's liberation is combating. How do you explain that?'

Conrad let out a mirthless chuckle. 'Jesus Christ!' he said, causing Aaron to feel that he had just said something stupid. He picked at the rug in front of him, and after a long while looked up.

'What do you want out of life, man?' he said. The seriousness of the tone and the directness of the delivery made Aaron check his automatic response, which was to dismiss the question as childish. He realised with a start that all the times he had asked himself that question he had been thinking in inane categories, answering it with words like 'better work conditions', and 'marriage', and 'peace'. Now the response flowed out with the power of a waterfall.

'I want to know who I am,' he said.

Conrad nodded. 'And of all the women you have ever known in your life, how many have helped you in that goal, and how many have done nothing but fill your head with hysterics of one kind or another?'

'You're really down on women, aren't you?' Aaron said.

'I love women,' Conrad said loudly. 'But I never forget that they're one kind of animal and I'm another kind. We make babies together, and that's about all the essential business we have to transact. The rest is optional, and you have got to find out how you are going to relate to them. You can't use the patterns society give us, those are all too stupid to even talk about. I have my fix on women, and women and me never argue. A lot of them don't dig my scene, but that still leaves plenty who do. More than enough to get on with.' He leaned forward. 'Don't you see? Once you make a decision about where you stand, you don't have to fight any more. Everyone who has come to the same conclusion finds each other. The rest go live someplace else and do something else. And when you get bored you can always go see what the freaks next door are doing.' He waved his hand. 'Don't believe all this political bullshit. The only question is people, and how we are going to live on this small planet without somebody always trying to make everybody act the same way.'

'I had thought that Cynthia and I had found the same space.'

'No,' Conrad answered. 'You only found each other, like two children in the dark, and you're both hanging on for dear life. Except that the clinging is killing the both of you.'

Aaron put his head in his hands. The talk had exploded into the foyer of the practical, and the juxtaposition of the airy way in which he was dealing with his problems at that moment with the hard fact of Cynthia's powerful presence in their bed clashed like cymbals in his mind. In a quick flash he saw himself returning to the house filled with brave notions based on the grass and Conrad's words, and very quickly spilling it all out into Cynthia's ears and Cynthia's mouth and Cynthia's cunt, and having no energy to deal with the ideas in terms of action. He remembered watching a filmed sequence of a female black widow spider luring a male to her nest, and the undeniable dance of rapture that he indulged in while fucking her, and then his rapid attempt to flee before she pounced on him, pierced his skull with her fangs and sucked his body dry.

'Conrad,' he said, 'I'm afraid of her.'

'Sure,' the younger man nodded. 'A woman can tear you to pieces, and if she likes you, will, if you let her. But you know, you're physically stronger than she is, and she can't do anything to you that you don't allow her to do. You're afraid of what you want her to do to you, what you would really dig.' He narrowed his eyes. 'Have you ever let her tie you up and whip you?'

Aaron bit his lip. 'No, but I do things that are close to that all the time.' He furrowed his brow. 'I almost killed her once,' he said. Recalling the scene in the baroque atmosphere of Conrad's parlour, Aaron spoke with hesitation, the event coming to life as though through an unfocused lens at first, gradually attaining clarity. He had not spoken of it to anyone before that moment.

'I came home one night in a strange mood,' he began. 'A dozen things had gone wrong during the day and my anger started building early in the morning and went right on through the drive home. As I was walking up the stairs, it began to spill over and I remember hoping that Cynthia wouldn't be there so I could just sit and fume for a while.

'But she was, standing in front of the stove. Something in her posture or her vibration made the hair on the back of my neck rise; she had a certain attitude of vulnerability that attracted my feeling the way a rod pulls down lightning. I didn't know what I was doing. I walked up behind her and slipped my arms around her waist, putting my hands on her belly. She was wearing a thin cotton housedress with nothing on

109

underneath and I could feel the fullness of her under the sliding cloth. She closed her eyes and leaned back against me as though she were yielding herself up, I slid my fingers down to her cunt, electricity sizzling where I touched her.

'I began to say something, but the heat from between her legs distracted me, and I plunged into her with all my energy. I forgot where I was and who I was with; some deep and strong feelings were swamping my critical faculties. I bit her neck, it must have been very hard because she cried out, but at the same time she pushed her arse back and rubbed it against my cock. Whatever it was I was into, she was ready to be the other half.

'I pressed into her, excited by the liberty I sensed she was granting me. Her cheeks fit right into the hollow of my groin.' He paused to glance at Conrad who was lighting another joint. 'You know how luscious her arse is,' he added. Conrad nodded. 'Indeed I do,' he sa᾽ i, and the two men smiled at one another, Aaron relieved to be able to talk about Cynthia's body with someone who also appreciated its beauty from first-hand experience. A glow of euphoria puffed through him as Conrad passed the stick to him and smiled again, a signal of camaraderie.

'It's a groove to talk about chicks in the locker room, ain't it?' Conrad said, his whole body relaxing in a deep internal stretch.

Aaron hunched forward. 'She got very soft, and I didn't know where to put my hands first. I held her breasts and rubbed the nipples until they got stiff and wrinkled. I grabbed her shoulders, her waist, her thighs. I pulled her buttocks apart so I could snuggle into her even closer. And she did nothing but be there, and in a way I couldn't figure out, telling me that whatever I did was all right, that she didn't want anything but to feel me doing my thing.'

He stopped and rubbed his chin which had the first bristle of beard on it. This was the first day in over

110

two years that he hadn't shaved. 'I'm starting to talk like you,' he said. Conrad took the joint and dragged on it. 'No, we're just learning how to talk together,' he said, 'and that means picking up on one another's language.' He shot his chin forward. 'But go ahead,' he said. 'What happened?'

'I pulled her dress up to her waist, and her partial nakedness added a shade of obscenity to the tableau. She made a small choking sound and then bent forward, offering me her rear. I unzipped my trousers with one hand, let my cock edge its way out, and then pushed into her again. All I could see was the stove and I felt like a cook balancing the ingredients of a meal. I touched her every place, and it was like the first time I ever put my hands on her, and was pinching and stroking and slapping. Her knees began to tremble. I slid my hand over one cheek and into the crack of her arse, feeling the hair and the heat, and getting high on the smell. Then, it was like stepping into a puddle unexpectedly, one finger slipped into her wet cunt, and I arched my back to bring my cock up and out, to point it. I stepped into her and it slipped right between the lips and into the socket.

'She let out a groan, as though she had just been squashed, and collapsed onto the stove. The wooden spoon she was holding fell on the floor. I reached over and turned the burner off and moved the pot to the back, wondering that part of me could stay so cool while the rest of me was exploding. And then I just settled into fucking her.'

The narrative stopped and Aaron stared off into space, reliving the experience within himself before continuing to dissipate its power over him by spilling it out in words. 'I stood back,' he went on, 'and was like a painter admiring a work I was doing, watching my cock slide in and out of her, checking the colour changes in her cunt and arsehole. She went from tan to dark brown to purple within two minutes, and I was complimenting myself on my good taste in women. You

111

see, it was as though she were only an object that I could use for my pleasure, and had no existence apart from that.'

'That's the problem,' Conrad broke in, 'because that aspect is true, too. We are objects for each other's pleasure, but not only that. Every time you discover something, you get hung up on it and blot out everything else.'

'I felt tremendously guilty,' Aaron responded. 'And that got my anger going again. I braced her by the thighs and pushing her head down until she was bent over like a woman trying to touch her toes. I kept my cock pressed into her, and her cunt felt like it was filled with glue, holding me inside. I was staring down on her and all I could see was the white circle of her arse and the dark slit down the middle, and I kept thinking that somehow the secret to all my problems lay in what I was looking at, if I only knew how to interpret it. Her arse assumed some kind of cosmic significance in my mind.'

'You were really getting it on,' Conrad said.

'I bucked into her, and braced my feet against the refrigerator behind me to ride her hard. Every time I piled into her she bucked and reared, raising her cunt so I could slam into it more powerfully. I was like a steamhammer gone berserk, punishing her cunt.

'She let out a high keening wail, like hearing an ambulance siren screaming through the streets late at night. I went wild, pulled her shoulders back, shook her unmercifully. I put one arm around her throat and with my free hand I . . . opened the oven door. I let her fall forward and her head dropped into the black space. And then, I can't describe with what horrible fiendish exultation, I turned the centre dial and in a few seconds the oven erupted with heat.'

Aaron's hands began to tremble. 'At that moment,' he said, his voice rough with emotion, 'I wanted to kill her. Do you understand? To *kill* her.'

Conrad rocked back on his spine. 'At least you know

it,' he said. 'Most of the rest of us pretend we don't have that inside us, and we try to act nice, and then it comes out in distorted ways. We have wars, we cut each other with words, we rape.'

'But what I'll remember most for the rest of my life was that as the heat engulfed her, her whole body went limp and she said, 'Oh God, yes.' It sounded like a prayer. I pinned her in that position, and went on fucking her. She was sprawled like a dead deer over a pole, and I was some ferocious beast tearing at her with cruel intensity. It was as though I were rooting for something, something incredibly precious, and I was willing to rip her open to get at it. Her cunt has never been so open, before or since, and as I slammed into her the most violent visions passed through my mind, and at one point I saw myself plunging a sharp long knife right into her centre. And all the while wondering whether she might actually suffocate. But I was beyond stopping, even if it meant taking her life. I still can't accept that. Part of me reasoned that she wouldn't die, but I acted in such a way that showed me I didn't care if she did. I was going after what I wanted at any cost. Only I didn't know what I wanted.

'And then it came to me, and I was appalled at the baseness of the desire. I wanted to reach a climax, some kind of explosion. It's clear now that I had taken all the anger I was feeling for all the shit I had to put up with that day, and channeled it into my sex. But right then I just needed to blow apart, and she was willing to be the fuse and the receptacle for my eruption.'

'That's a thing with chicks in this culture,' Conrad said. 'They're trained to sacrifice themselves. I'd like to know what was going on in her head all this while.'

'She told me that the last thing she remembered was realising that she wanted to be murdered, and asking herself whether I would actually kill her. She said it felt like her cunt had begun to peel backwards, covering her arse and her legs and her body until she had become nothing but a huge vagina, and absorbing me in as though she were a pool and I were diving into the water.'

'She's a Scorpio, isn't she?' said Conrad.

'I think so,' Aaron answered. 'Her birthday is November sixth.'

'Right,' said Conrad. 'And you're an Aries. It all comes together on that level, too.'

'So I put all my attention into coming. I blotted out everything else except what happened between my cock and her cunt. My legs started to shake and I had to grip her to keep my balance. She was ravishing, her long legs stretched and bent at the knees, her arse like a table, her breasts hanging like tits on a cow, her head covered with hair inside the black oven. She had stopped making any sounds. I leaped into overdrive and pumped everything I had into her, all the frustration and grief and rage and sorrow, all the repressed feelings that were keeping me from coming alive. And she absorbed it all, and I loved her for doing that. You know? I was loving her for letting me kill her.

'And then I felt it, the great boiling release, the cataclysmic breakthrough, the terribly fleeting solution to all the contradictions. I was coming inside her. My entire body flew apart at once, my legs buckling, my pelvis flapping like a loose sail in the wind, my arms flying, my head jerking back and forth. I felt the sperm shoot out, and I could see it – I mean actually see it, I don't know how to explain this – spilling into her cunt, splashing against the walls, bursting into the deep crevices in the back chambers. And it was as though I were defiling her, committing some heinous sacrilege. Even as I experienced that I knew that was all wrong, but there it was, unavoidably actual. The expression on my face must have been hideously ugly.'

Conrad stared into the images that Aaron's narrative had conjured up. He was translating the story into the scenario he would have played had he been in

Aaron's place. Having seen through the artifacts of sadism and masochism and understood their functions as means to release life energy, he was comfortable in either role, and chose his attitude in relation to the predilections of whatever partner he was with. Although the dominance-subservience game was not one he preferred as a steady diet, when he did indulge in it he approached it with a sense of style. As Aaron spoke he saw Cynthia with her hands tied behind her back and to her ankles forcing her to kneel with her arse raised. He would tickle her cunt with a feather until she begged piteously to be fucked, and then have her list the abominations she would endure for the privilege of receiving his cock. The excitement would come from the degree of desperation she reached and the frenzy with which she kicked about in order to present herself in the most lewd and inviting postures. His cock wallowed in a lazy erection.

'Right afterwards I pulled her back and lifted her to her feet. The thing became a person again, the anonymous woman became Cynthia in my arms. She sagged against me a long time and I could feel a thousand subtle tremors ripping through her. I was poised between joy and regret and didn't know what to say or do. And then she turned slowly, her face mottled and bruised, swam up to me from whatever depths she had descended to, and covered my lips with her mouth. It was like death coming to get me. And I stood there petrified while she silently moved me with kisses.' He passed his hand across his eyes. 'And clanging in me like a fire bell was the single clear desire to hit her.'

'But you didn't,' Conrad suggested.

'I didn't have the courage, not after what I had just put her through.'

'You're an idiot,' Conrad said, his tone sober. 'She was using you just as much as you were using her.'

'But what would be the point in slapping her?' Aaron asked him.

115

'No point. It just would have been the proper thing to do.'

Something about the incongruity of the phrase, calling up as it did echoes of Emily Post, tipped Aaron into a peal of full rich laughter. He saw the seriousness on Conrad's face and laughed all the harder, for the younger man's earnestness reminded Aaron that he was a generation older and could take solace in the fact that no matter how much more Conrad knew, there were still areas in which he was a child. His inability to laugh at himself was one of those. Conrad waited until Aaron's mirth had subsided, welled up again, and fallen away entirely. Then he spoke.

'By "proper" I mean "organic",' he explained. 'Sometimes you have to do things which outrage your reason, but you have to recognise which of those have to do with your survival, and learn to follow those instantaneously, without questioning or looking back. You have to trust that there's a force operating in you which knows more than all your ideas put together. And you begin to test it in small things, like telling somebody to fuck off if they lay shit on you; or slapping a chick when her emotional strength is killing you and you have to defend yourself physically.'

'You sound like you're making a case for murder,' Aaron said, reflecting the sombre tone of Conrad's direction.

'I killed a man once,' Conrad replied. 'And I've been trying to get straight behind it ever since. In fact, everything I know comes from thinking about the night I did it.' He paused. 'I was sixteen,' he added.

'What happened?' asked Aaron, immediately fascinated by the turn the conversation had taken. Like two lovers who lock themselves to one another by revealing the deepest secrets of the heart, the men hung the first strand of the bridge they had begun to build between them. After Aaron's admission of his selfish bestiality, Conrad felt the burden of unburdening himself.

116

'I left home at fourteen,' he said. 'My father was some kind of chairman-of-the-board type for a subsidiary of an aircraft company. My mother was into barbiturates and booze and fucking the latest stud to make the circuit of the Palo Alto rich bitches. I was about nine when I began to dig what was happening, and after I figured it out, it didn't bother me, except the fact that they were pretending that they weren't doing the things they were doing. She used to throw lines about going to the hairdresser every time she left to get laid; it was easy to tell because she always did a big scene with perfume and tight dresses; and my old man had his name on all the church functions and fashionable charity organisations, and I knew he didn't give a shit about anything except money and power.

'So I split. I hitched a ride to New York and lived in the East Village until the winter came, panhandling, crashing. I found out you don't need much just to survive. When it got cold I came back west, stopping in at different scenes and farm communes, going from connection to connection, discovering what was later called the underground. I was so young and lost that most people felt sorry for me, and I was even taken in by straights: once I stayed for days with a Navy captain and his wife, who was a Pepsi addict. And then made it to Berkeley, and learned how to live on the street.'

'Fourteen!' Aaron mused. 'When I was fourteen I was a sophomore in high school and trying to figure out what I wanted to be when I grew up.'

'Yeah, well, I learned all at once. The one thing I wanted to be was alive. That's the most important. Everything else is a tool for survival. I got very tough and lean, and I had the one quality my parents had instilled in me: I was ruthless. I fell in with some people who were calling themselves revolutionaries but were mostly into speed and danger. I felt like a wolf who had found his pack, and we spent a lot of

117

time shooting up, and pilfering grocery stores, and writing slogans on walls.

'Then one of them suggested a hold-up. He said a friend of his had worked at a small gas station in the Sunset District for a few weeks, and knew that the money pick-up was made every Thursday night at ten. He figured we could grab off two thousand dollars – which sounded like a fortune when I used to go days at a time without a penny in my pocket. We decided that two of us should go, and I was one of the ones chosen.'

Conrad straightened his spine. He looked at the other man to see what effect his words were having, for he wanted the perspective of Aaron's instinctive reactions. 'We were very high when we hit the place, and it all went smoothly up to a point. As soon as the man got out of the car, we walked right behind him and into the manager's office. We jostled him in, pulled handkerchiefs up over our noses, and whipped out the two big Bowie knives we were carrying. We planned to tie them up, split in the pick-up man's car, and ditch it a few miles away. The manager had the leather bag ready and my partner picked it up. He opened it to look inside and I flicked my eyes over just to see if I could glimpse the money. But as I did so the messenger, a man in his forties, wearing a black suit, with a pencil-thin moustache, jumped back. I spun around and fixed him with my consciousness. The amphetamine had operated in such a way as to speed up my physiological processes exactly enough to match my mental functions, so there was no lag at all between what I saw and what I did. At that moment, for me, to see was to do.

'It was as though he were moving in slow motion. I watched him as he yanked his jacket open, reached across his belly, flipped up the strap which held the revolver in place, and closed his hand over the butt of the pistol. In that instant the whole scene was frozen. I heard a woman talking in the street, and realised that outside that small building the world was going on as usual. The stupidity of my situation, and the senselessness of what was about to happen, seared themselves into my brain forever at that moment. And at the same time a voice in my head was saying, "He's reaching for a gun, you didn't consider that he might have a gun, he's going to shoot you with the gun, and you are going to be dead."

'At once, the whole tableau sprang into normal speed again, and as he began to swing the weapon around toward me, I was on him, and the knife buried in his belly.'

Conrad sniffed. 'He said, "Ughn", like a bad actor in a third-rate film, and then slid to the ground. The manager staggered back, the front of his coveralls wet with urine. My partner just looked at the dying man, his eyes bulging. "Oh God, why?" the man said and closed his eyes. I watched and could see the soul disintegrating and frothing out of his body like champagne bubbles.'

'Do you want me to believe all this?' Aaron asked.

'It's absolutely accurate,' said Conrad in a flat voice. 'And my first feeling was a strange kind of dry anger, because he had thrown himself away to save some pieces of green paper, money that didn't even belong to him, the company's money. I got all my lessons in history right on the spot.'

Aaron attempted to integrate what he heard. He told himself that he should be shocked, but he felt nothing but a friendly interest in the rest of the story. Its most cogent effect was to make his own tale seem less extraordinary, less fearful.

'The first thing I did with my share of the money was to buy dope. We got away clean, the murder turned out to be nothing more than a footnote to the caper. The cat who was selling me the speed asked me if I wanted acid. I was very unsophisticated about drugs at the time and thought that it would just be a different kind of high than I was used to.

'So two nights later, I dropped over a thousand micrograms on the Point Reyes beach.' He nodded at Aaron. 'What you had last night was about three-fifty.' Aaron blinked, trying to imagine an experience three times more intense than what he had just gone through, and coming right after he had killed someone. Conrad pursed his lips.

'You might say it was pretty heavy,' he said. 'I was by myself, and I went a lot of different kinds of crazy. I saw everything, you dig, *everything*, all at once. And when I had it all together, I saw myself disappearing over the horizon, going someplace where my mind just couldn't follow, like a little kid running after a train that's picking up speed.' He shook his head. 'Our consciousness and our intelligence is less than a grain of sand on the infinite beaches of eternity. Ever since that moment, I have not once forgotten how ignorant I am and always will be when it comes to what creation is all about.

'The next thing I remember is hunger. I had been on the beach for five days, my mind totally blown. I've tried to pull out some memory of what happened, but all I can remember are the waves, and thinking that the waves never stop, never stop.'

He smiled to himself. 'It was only astral travel,' he said. 'I learned about that later, when I started reading again, and worked my way through every title in the Shamballa book shop. But it turned me a hundred and eighty degrees around from the direction I was taking. I started travelling with a different kind of people, people I recognised only by seeing that they were serious in an indefinable way, even though they might laugh a lot. You have that kind of seriousness, and that's what my instinct is following.'

The conversation had gone full circle. They had traversed the past, found the structural similarities in their travels, and surfaced once again in the present, aware at once that they had, through all their talk, never left the moment. There was a change in atmosphere, and they felt it the way certain old men can feel the distant onset of rain in their joints. A cycle had ended and a new one had not yet begun; they sat in a blue interface, waiting, looking like two monkeys on a high plateau smelling the breeze for its messages of life and death.

The girl walked silently into the room. Her eyes were still sticky from sleep. And her skin was imprinted with the outlines and inclines of the hammock. She exuded palpability and her cunt hair was sparse. The subtle vibrations of reverberations of words, and the realities they referred to, stirred around like whispers in church and settled as she smiled, stretched and yawned, like a kitten waked from a nap.

'Hello, kitten,' said Conrad. 'That's Aaron,' he said.

She turned toward him, her hands still curled by her ears, her elbows framing her breast, her wrists tilted, her legs two shapely white columns that led to her cunt. If he had not seen her earlier, he would have believed she was an apparition.

'Want some dope?' Conrad asked.

As a reply she sat down next to him, crosslegged, leaning forward. Without self-consciousness Aaron scooted across the floor until he was part of a tight triangle.

'Me, too,' he said eagerly.

'He's cute,' said the girl.

'He's a tiger, watch out,' said Conrad.

Aaron beamed like a child at a birthday party.

Conrad rolled a thick joint, with finely powdered marijuana as a base, and crumbs of hashish as a topping. Aaron watched his fingers in their deft practiced movements, and realized that Conrad was an expert in hallucinogenic drugs, a man who had learned thoroughly through his own experiences, and was immensely more learned than colleges full of psychologists who derived all their data from reading reports made by other psychologists who used students as subjects to experiment with.

121

'You use drugs a lot,' he said.

'It's my business,' Conrad replied. Aaron looked blank. 'I'm a dealer, didn't you know?' he continued. He grinned. 'I buy wholesale and I sell retail.' He laughed out loud. 'That's the biggest irony of all, you see. I've become a businessman, just like my father.' He furrowed his brow. 'The only difference is that I'm honest in my motivations. I never sell anything I haven't tried myself. And I never keep any surplus wealth. I make enough to keep me alive, at whatever level of affluence or poverty seems right at any given time. I went through a period when I was turning over five thousand dollars a week, and I made my deliveries in a Morgan. But it got to be too much of a hassle to maintain at that volume, so I simplified my externals, and got it to where I only need to sell a couple of dozen lids a week to stay alive.'

'What kind of drugs do you sell?' Aaron asked, his mouth hanging open.

'Grass, hash, acid, mescaline, psilocybin, cocaine, and when I can get it, opium.'

'I'm sitting with a pusher,' Aaron thought, taking the term from his inaccurate understanding of the nuances of the drug world. Visions of police bursting through the door flooded his mind. He saw headlines: SCHOOL TEACHER ARRESTED IN NARCOTICS RAID, and the photograph of the three of them, with black squares to cover the girl's nipples and pubic hair. For a brief fraction of a second he tasted what it means to be in jail; the bars closed behind him and he stood trapped in a small concrete tomb. Sweat blossomed on his forehead.

'But I haven't done anything wrong,' he shouted down the corridors of his prison. 'We weren't harming anyone.'

And the booming voice came tumbling down from the judge's bench, 'Statutory rape, corrupting the morals of a minor, possession of narcotics with intent

to sell. Five years, ten years, fifteen years!' He screamed inside his mind. He shut his eyes tight.

'Are you all right?' said the girl, her hand on his
shoulder.

'Why is it against the law?' he said to Conrad. 'I'm
scared to death all of a sudden that we are going to be
arrested, and I know it can happen, but all we're doing
is sitting here peacefully minding our own business.'

'Ah,' said Conrad. 'You have begun to ask dangerous
questions. You are already a suspicious character.
Soon you will be identified with us, and the stout men
in the blue uniforms will begin to follow you, and listen
to what you say, and tap your telephone.'

'Stop it,' said the girl. 'You're making him paranoid.'

'In America the blatant truth is cause for all the
paranoia anybody can handle,' Conrad said in a loud
voice.

'Fuck him,' she said to Aaron. 'He always starts
doing this when he gets really stoned.'

'Stoned, is it?' said Conrad. 'You go stand on the
fucking street corner and try to sell a little harmless
grass to a friendly face and suddenly get grabbed by
some longhair who turns out to be a narc in disguise
and then spend ten days in jail with real freaking
crazies who might slit your throat in the middle of the
night and pray that your father has more loyalty to
his son than he does to his society so he will come up
with some bail, and then do a shitting and pissing
Step 'n' Fetchit for the judge and get a-year-and-a-day-
suspended-sentence, and then go out three days later
and have to stand in the same spot and run through
the whole scene all over again, and hope that you don't
get caught again this time.'

'It's stupid to deal on the street,' the girl said.

'Well, it's my fucking right,' Conrad said, his voice
agitated. 'That's what I dig doing most, sitting in the
sun on Telegraph Avenue, sitting high, and selling
drugs that will make people beautiful. And if some
stupid motherfucker with a hard-on in his throat

wants to lock me up in a cage for that, then it's come time for me and him to start doing some fighting, because he is a bad man.' He ran his tongue along the glued edge of the paper and sealed the cigarette. He held it in his fingers for a moment. 'Excuse me,' he went on. 'There's no point in my spraying you with my anger, you're not the people who are trying to put me away. And anyway, I don't do much dealing on the street anymore. I have a small discreet clientele, and I make home deliveries. In some circles, I'm considered a celebrity.'

Aaron watched the young man play out his role with interest and affection; this was a side of Conrad he had not known of, and he suddenly felt oddly glamorous; he realised he was doing something which, in another of his life contexts, would be considered extremely daring. And yet, at that moment, it all appeared so natural. With a twinge of amusement he thought of how this whole day would appear as he sat soberly before his students, and the smile had barely begun to form on his lips when he was raked by paralyzing horror. He saw with unmistakable clarity that he didn't want to return to that classroom or any of the life that it implied. Having treated the period of time since he had ingested the LSD as a baroque episode, he was suddenly taken by the understanding that he could easily continue right down the path that had opened to him, and come to view all of his life up to that day as unconscious preliminary to his true existence. It was not beyond the realm of possibilities that he might one day be sitting with a beard and a naked woman, rolling countless joints, taking acid as regularly as most people see movies, and talking open insurrection.

He shook his head violently. 'It's impossible,' he said to himself. 'These notions are the result of drugs and not sleeping. I'll see things differently tomorrow.'

But another voice in his head mocked him. 'These have been the most liberating twenty-four hours of your life,' it told him. 'They've given you a taste of the freedom you've always dimly suspected was waiting for you. All you have to do is continue. Don't go back to the old life. Stay here.'

Like a thirsty man at the edge of a well he fears may be poisoned, Aaron sipped at the implications slowly. Many of the dimly formulated evaluations he had stockpiled in his mind began to find their completion. All the frustrations that stifled him at his work saw their origins clearly. The questions about his relationship with Cynthia that had wracked him in pain leaped at their answers. And yet he could not be sure. For a fearful instant it seemed to him that the only way he had any chance to extricate himself from the numbing maze of his treadmill days lay in an area where he would find himself continually in the role of what he had always considered as outside the law. For at that very moment he was, he saw, a criminal, indulging in actions which carried the penalty of jail.

'What are you thinking?' asked Conrad.

'Whether or not I should turn you in,' Aaron responded, enjoying the drama of his words.

Conrad smiled knowingly, understanding at once the context from which Aaron spoke. But the girl shifted uneasily. 'What kind of game are you two playing?' she said.

'Neither of us knows,' said Aaron.

'Oh, I know,' Conrad said, 'and so does he. But he's just beginning to find out where it's at.'

'I'm glad I'm just passing through,' she said.

Conrad lit the joint and passed it to Aaron. As the older man took a deep drag, pulling it into his lungs, holding it, imitating the way he saw Conrad smoke, Conrad gazed at him with unblinking eyes.

'But you don't have to rush it,' he said. 'All you have to remember is that you never have to make a decision. Only exercise a choice. You don't have to seek anything out. Just say yes or no to what's presented to you.'

And with a fluid motion he turned to the girl and put his arms around her shoulders. He leaned on her until she began to sag, and slowly sank to the floor. He turned her over so that she lay face down, and ran his hand over her arse. He nibbled the back of her neck and she raised her legs from the knees, her plump calves curving toward each other until they crossed at the ankles.

The three of them continued to smoke and talk, watching the afternoon change into evening, the evening give itself up to night. They entered a gentle euphoric communion and gradually, without difficulty, the men took off their clothing and lay down on either side of the girl, whose body had begun to glow in the dim light. Without an abrupt movement or sound to break the spell they were weaving, they began to make love to her, with their hands, their mouths, their cocks, covering her with the overflow of their good feeling. She barely breathed, but vibrated with every touch, every caress, every penetration, lost in a revery of acceptance.

As Conrad covered the girl's thighs with his own and slid his cock into her young wet cunt, Aaron felt her tongue fluttering delicately against his, her rhythms responsive to what happened at either end of her, blending the input so that her subtle movements were in harmony with each man alone, and both men together. As he was further unravelled by the patient fingers of their blissful anonymous sex, Aaron thought once of Cynthia, but as one thinks of a distant dear friend, fondly, poignantly, and with no relevance to the action at hand.

6

Comrade Cunt

'But you make it sound as though all my problems would be solved if I became a lesbian,' Cynthia said.

'Not at all,' said Jackie. 'I just pointed out that what now seems like problems will show up as the product of insufficient knowledge. What we're talking about is expanding the base of your experience. "Lesbian" is just a word, a label, and shouldn't freeze you into a premature understanding of what's involved in the process of entering a relationship with a woman which doesn't exclude the sexual aspect. Ultimately, you are never doing anything but finding out more about yourself. Whether or not you wish to continue to fuck with men is a different question altogether. But if you do, you'll find that you won't be prey to all the confusions that propel you into the sort of difficulties women have with men.'

'Do you ever have sex with men?' Cynthia asked.

'I haven't for several years,' Jackie told her.

'I still have a taste for them,' Maureen broke in. 'But it's not too often that I find a man highly evolved enough to interest me more than physically. Most of them still have a conquest reflex which makes them terribly boring as lovers. And the ones who have a balance of sensitivity and strength seem to have been stricken by a peculiar air of listlessness which robs them of the desire to encounter a woman, and either become asexual or gay.' She smiled. 'Occasionally one meets a man who is simply and truly a man, and then

I give myself to him unconditionally.' She rolled her head around on her neck. 'Until he leaves,' she added.

'Why does he leave?' Cynthia asked.

'Why, that's their nature,' Maureen replied. 'Once they have opened the woman fully and tasted all her secrets, they have no further interest in her. If she wants to rid herself of him quickly, she lets him see all of her in a single night; and if she wishes to keep him tied to her, she feeds him piecemeal, yielding up little tidbits, teasing him with foreshadowings of delights to come. You know the tale of Scheherezade, of course. It is clearly allegory for what I'm talking about. She was able to provide the king with a thousand and one different qualities and aspects of her sexuality and saved her life with that.'

'Doesn't the man have anything to say in all this?' Cynthia said, beguiled by the tenor of the talk.

'It depends on how conscious he is of who he is. If he is a dolt, unable to admit that the only unique thing he has to offer a woman is his erection and therefore incapable of putting his ego on the shelf, he will have no idea that the capsule containing him and the woman has limited air, and will sustain life in inverse proportion to the intensity at which it is lived. You see many couples who have burned themselves out and then go on groping and rooting, looking for any little scraps that might have been overlooked in the initial looting. Their sex usually becomes stale or violent.' Cynthia shifted her weight on the couch; the description fitted her situation with Aaron, and with every other man she had been with, too closely for comfort. 'If he has totally understood his sexual nature, however,' Maureen continued, 'then he can choose to remain passive and let the woman decide the hows and durations of things; or become aggressive, and ransack her at his own pace. I remember a man who unveiled me completely in six hours. His energy was fantastic and I did nothing but open continuously until I had totally absorbed him.'

'Optimally,' Jackie said, 'a man has learned to be passive and aggressive at the same time, and then can make love as good as a woman.'

'How can a man be both passive and aggressive?' Cynthia asked.

'By knowing his own mind,' Jackie said.

Cynthia sipped her tea and the three women fell into silence, letting the melancholy progressions of Satie's piano music supplant their talk. It came from four speakers hung in the corners of the enormous room and suffused the space. Cynthia kicked off her shoes and tucked her legs under her, relaxing in the soft fabric of the couch. She felt comfortable, content.

When Aaron had walked out the door she felt like a whore who had neglected to take her money in advance and had her trick leave without paying. Her first reaction had been anger, and unthinking rage which fanned out from her soul and blistered the air with its vehemence. Aaron sensed it at his neck as he jogged down the stairs and did not hesitate or look back. She clenched her fists and tightened her face, shaking in frustration, emanating black vibrations. But the explosion spent itself quickly, and she was left with only an emptiness the depth of which frightened her. She allowed it to be filled with self-pity. She flung herself down on the bed in an attitude of defeat, and took the peculiar pleasure one finds in that state of recounting how badly one has been treated. She was building an impeccable case for herself as a hapless victim when her reason intervened and pointed out that no one had forced her into anything, that her participation was freely volunteered and often the initiating factor; it noted drily that she had enjoyed a passionate romantic interlude in the kitchen, sucked two cocks in the living room, and fucked majestically in the bedroom, a condition which could hardly be considered as evidence for collecting grievances.

She returned momentarily to a state of calm, and

looked at the clock. 'Well, I'm naked and it's nine-thirty in the morning,' she said out loud, her voice popping out without her conscious projection. It surprised her into a realisation that she never spoke except to someone else, and all of a sudden that seemed a silly prejudice, as though what she said had no meaning unless it was heard by another. She smiled and let herself go on. 'So what if he leaves,' she continued, 'I still have myself.' Then, as though a more caustic voice emerged. 'And if he walked in through that door right now you'd jump right back into his arms.' The thought was unsettling, for she could see the truth of it, and that seemed to negate any autonomy she might lay claim to.

She thrashed her head about as though to shake herself into another frame of mind. It was becoming apparent that she was veering back to the central fact that Aaron after hours of delirious lovemaking, couldn't wait to get out of being in the same room with her. She knew that it was important for him to see Conrad, and did not begrudge him his need. But the way in which he abruptly removed himself after his orgasm, and his total lack of concern about her own needs and wants, stretched the limits of her compassion to breaking point and made him seem almost hateful in her eyes. She could not escape the conclusion that the problems of their relationship had insidiously undermined their very humanity, and that after attempting, with affection and good intentions, to forge themselves into a couple, found that effort produced those very evils they had come together to overcome. It seemed that they should part company if only in the interests of common decency.

This common perception, pinpointing the climax of over a year of growing discontent, gripped her and forced her into the emotion she had not wanted to yield to. Sadness crept over her like a fog, condensed, and was transformed into sorrow. She saw what all lovers see who are at the edge of accepting that there may

130

be nothing essential to be salvaged from continuing in one another's company, that the creature that was them, the thing that was Aaron-and-Cynthia-together, would be gone forever.

'It's like he's dead,' she said aloud, and her heart, like a sky that has been threatening to loose its burden of thunder and rain, burst its prison of fear, and swelled until the sobs and tears spilled out in wild profusion. Deep ragged sounds erupted from her heaving chest and her cheeks glistened with wet. She rolled to her stomach and gave herself up to her unhappiness, crying in cathartic release, the profundity of her feeling sustaining in its fullness the vast turbulence of her spirit. Her shoulders shaking, her finely curved spine rippling, her buttocks quivering, her legs kicking, she clutched the pillow in her fingers and pressed her face into its comforting belly.

She wept because she did not know whether she loved him any longer. And within her, permeating all images and identities, the capacity to love a man gave her life, opening her to life, produced new life. For a long time the rift had been widening, and now he seemed so far distant that he could no longer even hear her voice. The pain was many feelings at once: an anguished clutching at a frayed sleeve, a flat wave of searing heat, a helpless twitching, a melting into grief. The stranger who had left so brusquely was the same man who had most thrilled her with booming joy; she held him and she lost him in precisely the same moment. This terrible duality which tore at her was, however, the only door she knew to the rapture of union, and only in relationship to a man did it seem to attain the devastating tension necessary to give birth to ecstasy.

She cried until there was nothing left, stopping four times, beginning again, winding down slowly, and when it was finished she lay still, floating in the peaceful throb of rejuvenation which follows a storm. All the conditions of her life were just as they had been, but she felt a detachment from them all, a sense that they really did not belong to her. It was something like the effect of marijuana, but more integral, involving her emotions as well as her intellect. Even Aaron appeared to be no more than a character in a book she was reading.

'I don't know how I'll feel tonight,' she thought, 'but right now I don't care if he never comes back.'

She propped herself up on one elbow and looked absently around the room. It made her restless. She lit a cigarette and went to make a pot of coffee. Her movements were rapid, almost spastic. The night's episode and the outburst of the morning, coming after many months of monotonous routine, had jostled her mind and refreshed her body, so that rushes of unaccustomed energy coursed through her. As she performed the kitchen ritual, the day began to present itself as a challenge, a space to be filled. With a start she realised that this was the first day in recent memory which was not either programmed or influenced by Aaron's presence. She recognised that her time was divided between office work, housework, and being with Aaron. The thought disturbed her and she put her focus on the fact that she was now free to do whatever she wanted.

'Now,' she said to herself, 'what do I want to do?'

She sipped her coffee and attempted to plan the day. But lacking practice in letting herself flow with her internal rhythms and discovering her involvements spontaneously, she began to list specific activities. She began to get discouraged when she came to: 'Maybe I'll go to a movie.'

The phone rang.

She was surprised to hear a strange woman's voice on the other end.

'It's Jackie,' said the caller.

Cynthia hesitated. She had no immediate connection with the name.

'We met at the meeting,' she said. 'Do you remem-

132

ber? We were drinking tea together and talking about how unfair it is that secretaries do more actual work than their bosses and get a third of the pay.'

The event lit up in Cynthia's memory. The interaction had been casual and she had been surprised when the other woman asked for her phone number and said she would like to get together informally sometime. She had forgotten the incident almost immediately.

'I called your office,' Jackie said, 'and they told me you were home sick today. I hope you're feeling all right.'

'Yes,' said Cynthia, falling easily into conversation. 'As a matter of fact, I'm not sick at all. My boyfriend and I . . . stayed up all night and both decided not to go to work today.'

'Oh,' said Jackie. Her tone was measurably changed, as though she had stepped back a number of paces. 'You see, Maureen and I – she's my partner – were talking about the meeting, and she was quite taken by you.'

'I don't think I recall meeting her,' Cynthia said, trying to reconstruct the evening.

'No, you didn't. But she saw you when the two of us were talking.' There was a pause. 'And she'd like very much to meet you, and we thought you might enjoy coming over this evening.' There was another silence along the wire. Then the voice went on, with a marked inflection: 'But it seems you're going to be all taken up with your boyfriend.'

The cadences of the sentences produced an odd effect, and Cynthia felt she was being gently prodded, tested for responses. It was not an unpleasant sensation. She cocked her head.

'Well,' she said, 'actually it looks like he's gone for the day.' Suddenly she became aware that she had no clothes on, and tingled with prickles of apprehension that the other woman knew that.

'Oh,' said Jackie, and again her voice revealed a different edge. Like a sculpture that shapes the space

133

around it, the conversation underlined the nuances of the situation. 'Uh, we're at home now and we thought you wouldn't be free until after work but . . . do you have any plans for today?'

Thinking of the list she had been compiling, Cynthia laughed.

'You have a beautiful laugh,' Jackie said, and her words were like a light kiss on the forehead.

Neither of them spoke for a few seconds. Cynthia could hear the breathing through the earpiece. Her chest held a certain heaviness, as though a hand were firmly pressed there. The thoughts flitted through her brain so quickly that she had no time to examine any single one of them, and they created a buzzing in her head.

'I'd enjoy very much coming over,' she heard herself say.

Somehow, although there was no sound to indicate it, she knew that Jackie was smiling. Her voice was clear and warm. 'We're on Grizzly Peak road,' she said. 'You know where that is?'

'Yes,' said Cynthia, impressed by the address.

'It's number twenty-four, the first house on the right after the second long curve. Shall we say in an hour?'

The day shone with almost unnatural brilliance, vibrating with a light that is like nowhere else in the world. As her car climbed, up Hearst Avenue, past the arty North Side with its refined version of Telegraph Avenue's hustle, past the sports stadium, and on into the hills, care fell from her like lint from a rug being shaken. She was caught up in the sensation of flight, and it occurred to her that she need not stop, she could continue driving, moving, letting all her entanglements dissolve behind her. With stunning clarity she saw that the only thing which kept her tied to her responsibility was merely her *sense* of responsibility, a thing she could discard like a burnt-out light bulb. There was no serious intimation of what such a decision would entail, the years of struggle to destroy old habits of lifestyle: rather it was an exhilarating whimsy, a reaction of relief from the almost morbid compression of the past twelve hours.

The house was almost hidden behind a bank of eucalyptus trees, and as she stepped out onto the driveway the perfume of their leaves bathed her in a shower of goodness. The effect that even a touch of nature has on the town dweller, the softness of forest life coming after the regimen of concrete and neon, buoyed her even more. She was feeling quite happy as she knocked on the thick door, and stood with an easy stance, her tank-top shirt and tight shorts showing her figure off in its trim, almost athletic elegance.

The woman who had opened the door took her breath away. As tall as Cynthia but so thin that the first impression one received was that of a skeleton, she wore a deep-brown sheath dress simple enough to have been worn with equal propriety on the beach or at the first night of the opera season. Her hair was black and coarse, pulled back severely to the back of her head, and bunched in an enormous knot. She wore no make-up or jewellery. Her feet were bare, and a bright red dot on her forehead at the point where the third eye is reputed to function attracted immediate attention. She had deep fluid eyes, a full nose, and skin the shade of burnt umber.

'My name is Maureen,' she said.

Cynthia blinked. 'How could I have missed seeing you at the meeting?' she said, the other woman's beauty lifting her out of the reserve she ordinarily responded with.

'Sometimes we are more receptive to what lies around us than at others,' Maureen said, speaking distinctly, almost with an air of patience. 'The world never ceases being full; it is up to us how much of it we wish to drink.'

There was an indeterminate noise behind her and Jackie's voice rang out, bell-like and playful. 'Are you going to let that girl in or begin a discourse on Hindu

135

metaphysics in the front yard?' Maureen's eyes lost their outward-looking cast and turned inward for a moment; then she opened them to Cynthia again and gazed so directly and steadily into her own that she felt a wave of giddiness pass over her. Maureen smiled and her mouth curved with the same delicate lines that grace Indian temple carvings.

'Please come in,' she said, standing to one side.

Cynthia entered the immense room and found Jackie sitting on the floor in front of a dozen balls of twine, a half-finished macrame belt in her hands. Her eyes swept across the space and took in the heavy furniture, the oils on the walls, a massive oak bookcase, a grand piano, the whole of it resting on a thick green rug with gold and red scrollwork design. One entire wall was a single plate-glass window which overlooked a stepped garden surrounded by trees. She was taken by an impression of wealth.

She had sat on the couch, Jackie in front of her and Maureen at her side, and perched in anticipation, waiting for one of the other women to say something. But Jackie went back to her work and Maureen smiled at her silently. Finally, growing a bit uneasy, she had made some pleasantry about the house, and was taken aback when Jackie looked up suddenly and said, 'Do you know why you came here?'

To her own surprise Cynthia bypassed her reflexive response, an impulse to ask, 'What do you mean?' and answered the question directly. 'I was lonely and you sounded very friendly.' She paused. 'And interesting,' she added.

'That's because I was seducing you,' Jackie told her.

'I thought of that,' Cynthia replied.

'And you came anyway?'

'I don't know what any of this is about, but I'm curious, and I don't think that you'll do anything to hurt me.'

Jackie nodded. 'You're an honest woman,' she said. 'I don't want you to have any misconceptions about our

136

intentions. You have a lovely body and a potentially exciting mind, and we no longer care about relationships which involve one and not the other.'

'And my emotions?' Cynthia asked, finding the words flowing easily from her mouth, experiencing an immediate rapport with the tenor of the talk.

'We are women,' Maureen cut in, 'we have the same feelings.'

Cynthia relaxed into a pleasant tingling; no sense of urgency tugged at her. She could not help but contrast the state with parallel situations she had experienced with men who wanted to fuck her, and the way, no matter how sophisticated they were, all their words and actions were covered with thin beads of sweat. It was the first time in her life that someone was making a sexual overture by appealing to her intelligence, and the experience was exhilarating. The conversation had gone very quickly into areas of intimacy and politics, tumbling almost at once into the question of the lesbian adjustment to the sexual problem.

'You've been to only two meetings,' Jackie said when the record ended, 'but that should have given you enough evidence to see that the whole question of women's liberation can't be understood unless you face the issue of sex between women fully. If we attain all the economic equality and political rights we ask for, they mean nothing if at the end of each day we return to a position of serfdom in relation to some man. And I have absolutely no doubts left about the fact that only in learning to love a woman can a woman put her relationship with men into any kind of real perspective.' She inclined her head toward Maureen. 'We saw you at the first meeting, and were struck by some quality about you that made us curious, more than just wanting to have sex with you. And at the next meeting I approached you to learn more. It was clear that you were at a stage of dissatisfaction in your personal life that was leading you to explore new possibilities. Most of the women who go to those meetings are at that level. And we were a bit apprehensive that you might be snared by one of the political crazies and end up running a mimeograph machine or organising marches.' She waved her hand. 'Not that I mean to put down those functions, they are unquestionably necessary. But they should be attended to by people whose nature predisposes them for drone activity. I think you have the capacity to bypass many of those stages and come directly to the heart of things. The true revolution lies in the mutation of consciousness that takes place in individuals, and for a woman – as for a man – that quest must bring her, sooner or later, to the limits she places on her definition of her own sexuality.'

'You know,' said Cynthia, 'it's never even occurred to me, in my wildest dreams, to have sex with a woman. It's not that the idea repulses me or anything, but I have no impulses in that area.'

'Then consider it,' Maureen said, folding one leg over the other, the motion as silky as the closing of a fan.

Cynthia's expression was somewhere between a laugh and a mild protest. 'But do you mean you want to go to bed with me?' she asked. 'Just like that?'

'Only in the interests of the Movement,' Jackie said and laughed, a high pealing sound that felt like fingers tickling Cynthia's brain.

'Even if I wanted to,' Cynthia replied, 'why should you be interested? I'm totally inexperienced. What attraction can I possibly hold for you?'

Maureen leaned over and put one hand on Cynthia's arm. The touch was a static caress, suggesting everything but insinuating nothing. 'Look at how beautiful you are,' she said. 'That's reason enough.' Cynthia turned toward her and Maureen went on. 'And we are sincerely interested in helping you. Each of us has struggled, as you now are doing, to make sense of the confusions that wear you down.'

'Have you known each other long?' Cynthia asked,

the intonation shaping the question to mean, 'Have you been lovers long?' In addition to the effect they were having upon her directly, she was also taken by watching the balance between them. They rarely communicated to one another directly through words, and yet she had the sense of their constant mutual inclusiveness, as though they were wrapped in a constant embrace which was all the more powerful for not being visible to gross perception.

'I was an exchange student at the university seven years ago,' Maureen said. 'Jackie was a doctoral candidate in psychology. We met at a recital by Bismillah Khan, began talking about the parallels between Jung's thought and Eastern religion, began to like one another very much, and within a few months took an apartment together. We were still naive although we had a very high estimation of our intelligence. We had our separate affairs, and consoled one another for our troubles with men. Then a friend of Jackie's, a chemist, gave us some LSD he had synthesised, and we took our first trip. And that blew the cover off everything. We saw that what we took as superficial frustrations were the tip of the iceberg of human stultification in our society, and the problems we had with sex, which we had been sweeping under the rubric of "well, that's just the way things are," were an indication of how crippled we were. Like you, we began going to meetings, and joined in the strident caterwauling that so many of our sisters still, unfortunately, find necessary to maintain their courage.' She stopped, curved her spine and flexed her neck, giving the impression of a cobra unfolding its hood. 'We became deeply involved in activist extroversion, and it was killing us because we are both basically inner-oriented people. Then one night, after a particularly gruesome day, we were lying in our living room, talking, trying to relieve one another of our confusion, when in the middle of a sentence something popped inside me, there was a tear in the veil that had been covering my eyes, and I saw

139

that none of the rest of it mattered, that the woman who was lying before me was the dearest thing to me in the world, and I had been running around looking everywhere for what was in my very home all the while. A strange force filled me and without a word I slid forward, took her in my arms, and kissed her with all the passion of which I am capable.

'We made love all that night, and since then I haven't been unclear about who I am or what things mean.'

'A few months after that,' Jackie added, 'almost like a blessing, my father died. I had been living on an allowance from him for years, and in his will he left me his entire fortune. I bought this place and we have been spared the necessity of working at jobs that would make us tedious.'

Cynthia realised that she had been holding her breath through the whole narrative. She relaxed her chest and looked from one to the other. 'It's very beautiful,' she said, 'and you're both lucky. But why can't you just enjoy what you've found? Why do you drag in all the politics and get involved in a cause, especially when you look down on that sort of activity?' Cynthia voiced questions which she hoped would not give offence. She had come, in a short time, to enjoy their company immensely. There was something about their complete assurance about their roles in life that she envied, and wanted to explore that without, on the one hand being intrusive, or on the other hand seeming to promise that she would acquiesce in their desire for her. She tested her feelings and found that she was without prejudice. She could imagine Maureen's lips on hers, and the notion was faintly exciting, but not in the least compelling.

Jackie pointed to the library. 'There are a dozen books I could recommend offhand to deal with that issue,' she said. 'If you're interested I'll lend a few to you. They all deal with the connections between economic and psychological realities. But that's all in

140

the realm of theory and has no meaning until one has had the experience with which to weigh the ideas. We have been lucky, as you say, but most people aren't, and we couldn't enjoy what we have if we didn't work to teach others what we know.'

'That's the most altruistic rationalisation for a seduction I have ever heard in my life,' Cynthia said.

'We're experts,' Maureen said simply. 'Why pretend to fumble?'

'And if you share our bed, there will be more than enough heavy breathing and salivating. Right now we only want to bring you to a rational choice, so that in the middle of a tangle of limbs you don't sit up suddenly filled with doubts as to what you're doing.'

Maureen removed her hand from Cynthia's arm and the loss of contact underscored how gentle and unobtrusive, but continually present, the touch had been. 'Sex is a choice one makes,' she said. 'Once the conditions are favourable, one says yes or no. Seduction is a game that allows us to pass the time while the voice deep inside you makes up its mind. It doesn't matter what you think up to the moment of action; it's the action you choose that counts. Our liaisons are picked for us by forces of which we have little knowledge, and we need only to recognise them, and then accept or reject them. Your will is free, but what it is given to act upon has been determined.

'I can accept what you're saying, but none of it makes me feel sexy,' Cynthia said.

'That's because you still think of sexiness as that conglomerate of feelings that arise when your desire is roused by a male in heat. The biological potency of that kind of energy is undeniable, and it has a specific purpose to insure that the species is propagated. But it is *only one mode*.' Maureen leaned forward, took a long flat cigarette from the coffee table, and lit it deliberately with a purple-stemmed match. Cynthia watched, the way a cat will observe a fluttering moth, and only broke her gaze when she spoke again. 'With a woman sexuality is continuous with sensuality. We tend to forget that after so many brutalising experiences with men whose passion ends abruptly at the ejaculation of sperm.' Cynthia thought of Aaron's actions that morning and stirred uneasily. 'When you are sensitive to yourself, you are sexual in everything you do, because you are alive to your senses, to the vibrant qualities of your body. As women we have one sexual duty, to produce children. But once that function has either been discharged or declined, our sexuality becomes a different thing entirely. Jackie and I have already made love to you, and have been doing so since you walked in. We have been touching you with our eyes and ears and words and gestures and intentions. If you see that, and acknowledge it, then taking off your clothes and fucking – if I may use that word for lack of a better – is merely a continuation of the process.'

'Why need it come to that?' Cynthia asked.

'It doesn't have to,' Jackie replied. 'It's just what happens next. I might turn the question around and ask, "Why, at the very point when two women are at almost total closeness, do they arbitrarily draw the line at physical contact?" '

Maureen blew out a cloud of smoke. 'Have you ever wondered,' she said, her words widely spaced, 'why men seem to derive such pleasure from licking a woman's cunt?'

Cynthia twitched involuntarily, the question catching her up short with its graphic power. Her first memory was of Aaron, his tongue lapping the walls of her cunt, his lips sucking greedily at the opening, smacking sounds arising from between her thighs. She could feel the bristle on his cheeks scratching her skin, and his teeth nibbling her clitoris. It was always very exciting for her, but never fully satisfying. She found that in the midst of her revery she had come to look full into Maureen's eyes. She was caught in the woman's gaze, her ego momentarily losing control and

142

flying into the vortex of Maureen's power. It was as though she could look into her mind.

'It is the cunt which attracts them,' Maureen went on, 'it's smell and taste and mystery and texture. Have you ever been that close to a cunt?'

Cynthia was snapped out of her trance by the realisation that a question had been asked. 'I've examined myself in a mirror,' she said.

'But that isn't the same,' Maureen said. 'You miss the pulsation, you get to know nothing of how it moves and changes, of how it can be the smallest, most precious bud, and in the next instant swell to a cavernous mouth that threatens to engulf you. Most importantly, you get to know nothing of what it feels like to have a woman surrender her centre to you, to give her most tender opening to your tongue and teeth and lips and fingers. You have known that only vicariously, through the activities of the men who have flung themselves between your legs, but never directly.'

Cynthia felt the dampness between her buttocks and became sharply aware of the fact that her cunt bulged against the seam of her shorts, that only a thin layer of cloth kept it from access. She experienced an odd sense of nakedness, as though the women talking to her knew her anatomy and its responses better than any man she had ever known without ever having seen her nude. She realised she was very close to some kind of crisis.

'And even in the role you have experienced, as recipient, you haven't known your responses in their fullness. Until you have had a woman there, doing with a sensitivity born of self-knowledge what a man can only do through laboured practice . . . well, you have not the beginning of an idea of how glorious that can be. For who can know the nature of a cunt better than a woman?'

'Ask the woman who owns one,' Jackie broke in.

'Precisely,' said Maureen. 'The woman who makes

143

love to you is yourself, and gives you what you know you really want.'

'But she can't give me a cock,' Cynthia said.

Maureen brushed the question aside with a flick of her wrist as though she were chasing a gnat. 'Find a man for that,' she said. 'If you're really still interested. Sex between women doesn't necessarily preclude heterosexual activities. It underscores them so you see them for what they are, and surrounds them, so you understand their limitations and don't get swamped every time a fleshy rod is poked between your thighs.'

'I like men,' Cynthia said, wondering as she spoke why she was trying to derail the train of Maureen's thought.

'Do you?' Jackie cut in. 'Do you really? Think about it a moment.'

In the space which followed, Cynthia felt the eyes of the others on her. They seemed to keep her thoughts off balance and she attempted to wrestle with the question, but there was no handle to grab it by. Two pictures flashed in her mind, the one of herself lying sated under Aaron's body and the other of herself lying next to him while he slept and she churned with some undefinable dissatisfaction.

'Remove the cock, and what do you have?' Jackie added.

Cynthia suddenly saw Aaron standing before her without clothes, all the attitudes and postures of his character manifest in his naked body, but nothing at his crotch but a smooth expanse of skin. He came toward her, the familiar look of lust in his eyes, and the sight of him filled with such intensity and no phallic focus with which to direct it presented a model of such ludicrousness that the laughter spurted out from between her lips and she lapsed into a fit of giggling. She looked up to find the other women smiling warmly at her, and she saw them suddenly as two tight-rope walkers in precarious equilibrium operating at the edge of a finely honed tension, relying on one another's steadiness to keep the wire from shaking. Imagining Aaron's presence in the setting was like thinking of a gorilla in an operating room.

'We're not going to creep up on you,' Maureen said, shifting the mood during the brief interface. 'But what can happen to you if you come to bed with us?'

'I don't know,' Cynthia told her. 'It just seems so alien to me.'

'Look at me,' said Jackie, 'am I strange to you?'

She stood up. Wearing faded paint-stained jeans and a work shirt with the top three buttons open, she looked like any of thousands of Berkeley housewives, like Cynthia herself, who appeared in the supermarkets on Saturday afternoons. She was several inches shorter than Cynthia, somewhat heavier, with thick thighs and a short waist. Her breasts were full, and Cynthia could see the tips of her nipples clearly outlined, emphasising the fact that she wore no bra. Her own brassiere suddenly seemed an artificial halter and her self-consciousness about wearing it grew. She had for some time debated with herself about being free enough to let her breasts hang from her body without obstruction, but was held back by the thought of the stares she would attract on the street. Jackie's expression was one of penetrating calm, and her eyes held an amused taunt that Cynthia found both disquieting and fascinating. She received a brief glimpse of what a thin line separated her from the jaunty attitude Jackie wore so easily.

'I am a woman, just like you,' Jackie said. 'I have known every passion and fear and feeling that you have. I've gone wild in the arms of men, men more exciting than any you have probably known. And I've tasted every hesitation in doing what's being offered to you now. Believe me, you are going to lose nothing. Even if you decided to continue your relationship with your man, knowing us will make it stronger, if it deserves to survive at all; or destroy it, if it isn't worth saving.'

Cynthia became light-headed. The notion that she would actually succumb to their offer and in a few moments would be feeling their hands on her body, their tongues in her mouth, their cunts... She stopped the flow of images there. 'What's holding me?' she thought. 'I've gone to bed with men whom I've trusted and liked less than I do these two.'

'Why don't you take your clothes off?' Maureen said. Cynthia turned to her. 'I – I couldn't,' she replied.

'Oh, you will go on being a child,' Maureen told her. 'How long do you think you can hide? Like a virgin pretending to be shy. But don't stop, it is very becoming. Your cheeks are flushed and your breath is shallow. Open your eyes and look at what's in front of you. We don't want to plunder you or conquer you or make you have our baby or get you to fall in love with us. We are the same as you. And we're inviting you to a communion, a sharing with us. Do you understand the difference? We've all had the same experience, we all have the same organs, the same responses. There's no contest we have to engage in. We can be as free as we want with one another, go as deep as we want, fly as high as we want. Together. Isn't that obvious? We can go to places where you can't go with a man. *Can't.*' She spoke the last word with a gravid finality.

'I feel like a specimen,' Cynthia said. Her palms were moist and she was uncertain of her reactions. If the two of them had closed in on her at once, she did not know how she would respond, whether she would fight them and flee, or give herself up to the moment.

'That's only because the two of us have a much stronger bond between us than exists between you and either of us. And because we've been very much involved with you.'

'How was that?' Cynthia asked.

'You were something special,' Maureen said. 'After Jackie took your number, we talked about you and were looking forward to seeing you at the next meeting. But after a few weeks it became clear that you weren't coming back and had probably fallen back into your old scene. We pondered calling you a long time, because we both wanted your body, and both intuited that you would be more to us than a passing trick. We refined our minutest vibrations to get every bit of analysis we could out of the scanty data we had, and found ourselves very turned on thinking about you. And then we decided to have Jackie call, and concluded we would be absolutely straightforward in our approach and hoped you would respect that enough to really listen to what we were saying, to feel it as it pertains to you, and not treat it as a theoretical discussion.'

Cynthia heard not so much the content of the words as their penetrating clarity and honesty. She was convinced that they were telling the truth about themselves, and for her that was the pertinent quality. She understood that at the moment she didn't care about all the reasons why they wanted her, or even about the things they wanted to do with her. What gripped her was the rare sweet honesty of their communication. Being with them threw into shadow the half-life of dissembling and camouflage she lived at her office, and the world of murky emotions she shared with Aaron. She suspected that freedom for her would mean more than the ability to have sex with women. But it was the freedom that she wanted. She was tentatively prepared to try unusual vehicles to attain it.

She leaned forward. 'I like you very much,' she said to Jackie, 'and I'm a little afraid of you, I think,' she told Maureen.

Maureen stood up and walked around to stand next to Jackie so that the two of them faced her. Cynthia was able to see them as a single gestalt, and the effect was very strong. Long and short, dark and light, hard and soft, mental and physical, they bracketed all the contrasts. She looked into Maureen's eyes and then into Jackie's and then back again, switching her gaze rapidly until she realised that the two women were watching her with a single consciousness, and she was able to perceive the unity which bound them. They were the embodiment of the ideal Cynthia had dreamed about when, as a young girl, she had indulged her fantasies about a Prince Charming coming by to take her away from the squalor and make her his own.

Her legs trembled. The two women seemed to be evaluating her the way a connoisseur would look over a piece of fine china. She recognised the attitude from many years of having watched men do the same thing. But in this situation she felt none for the ordinary reactions, neither flattered nor degraded. She performed a small series of movements which reflected her ambivalence, patting her cheek, turning her head to one side, touching the instep of one foot with the toes of the other. All the while they held her in the embrace of their observation, and she saw that they could see everything which went on inside her. She grew flustered. She wondered what they knew about her that she didn't know herself; she acknowledged their greater experience, and that coupled with the strength of their presence was almost enough to convince her that her wisest course was to put herself in their hands. 'It would only be for the afternoon,' she said to herself, 'and it will always remain an experience to look back on.'

She held their stare and returned it until the three of them were locked in a circle of mutual recognition and responsive to all the levels of exchange that took place among them. 'I might not be doing it for the reasons you might think,' she said at last.

Maureen spoke and her voice came out like an oracular proclamation. 'We all have our reasons,' she said. 'What you are now thinking will become a part of what we are all feeling. We are moving toward an end to separateness, don't you see? We are renouncing the discontinuity of the male and entering the continuous flow of the female.' She said the words with tremendous fervour and then walked forward until she stood

148

a little forward and to the side of Cynthia. 'Take off your clothes,' she said, 'and that will be the sign that you will spend time with us without the false restrictions which forbid us to love one another's bodies. Let us see those full soft breasts which are our breasts, the breasts of woman, and the deep pulsing cunt which is our cunt, the cunt of woman.'

Maureen held her hand out and Cynthia grasped it. Maureen pulled and Cynthia stood up. Jackie walked to stand on the other side of her. Up close the two women she had a sudden memory of a moment on the desert. It had been a little after noon and the temperature was almost a hundred and thirty degrees. The air was so clear that mountains hundreds of miles away showed minute details to her naked eye. She stood in the shadow of a huge barrel cactus, having stepped out of the car to taste the power of the day, and unexpectedly she had become one with the plant in a moment of transgeneric empathy. For a few scintillating moments out of time she knew exactly what it was to be that plant and remain unmoving in the lonely stretches of cracked earth, bearing the brunt of the sun and the bitter cold of the night. Now she looked from Jackie to Maureen and saw herself through their eyes. She looked at the white curved legs, the short pants which outlined more than they hid, the flat belly rising into round bulging breasts. She saw her sensitive mouth and moist eyes. She saw a young woman, lovely, nervous, unknown, but wanting something that she had spent her life hungering for without being able even to define, and wondering whether here, with these two others, she might find another piece of the key.

'I . . .' she began to say.

'Yes, you,' Maureen said, and brought her fingers to Cynthia's lips, holding them there, and then trailing her hand over her chin and throat, onto her breast, over her belly, and across to her hand, bringing palm against palm, fingers between fingers.

149

'The words become absurd,' she said, 'because we all know the same thing.'

'Everything you're feeling now, we've felt,' Jackie whispered, and came a step closer to take Cynthia's other hand into her own. 'This is our greatest pleasure, reliving through you the rapturous moments of our own first lovemaking.'

Cynthia's throat was dry. 'I don't know what to do,' she said.

Maureen brought her lips against Cynthia's ear, and when she spoke it was more the effect of the breath that moved her than the content of the vocal message. 'Do nothing. Be everything. Go into yourself and find who you are and when you emerge through the expressions of your body, we will be there to hold that movement in our arms.'

They walked with her into the bedroom, Maureen's arm around her waist and Jackie leading her by the hand. There was a buzzing in her brain and everything she looked at was darkened by a violet hue. With every few steps an attack of trembling shook her legs. They had her lie down on the great circular bed which dominated the centre of the room with its posts and curtains and the round mirror which was cemented to the ceiling over it. She knelt on the edge of it, crawled to the centre, and rolled over on her back. Before she closed her eyes she saw herself looking as though she were floating idly on the waters of a zebra-striped lake.

Maureen and Jackie lay on either side of her and for a few minutes did nothing but watch her, their eyes drinking in the body which they were soon to uncover and taste. Then, as though on signal, they came toward her and began to kiss her hair, her temples and her eyes. At first tentative as a mother brushing her lips against the forehead of a sleeping child, when they reached her cheeks they pushed their mouths into her with a greater pressure. Cynthia felt them as questions on her skin but was not ready to respond. Then their lips glided to hers and she felt the first jolt from their contact, the electric fusion of their mouths. The reaction began in her stomach and rolled to her head with the jagged velocity of a tyre that has spun loose from a speeding auto and is careening across the width of road into the blackness beyond. She made a sound in her throat and her hands curved up to cup the necks of the two women who were kissing her. Their tongues fell from the rapidly opening mouths as Cynthia flushed with a sexual yearning she had not thought would appear that afternoon. Ready to proceed with the programme as though it were an experiment from which she would learn something, but not really enjoy, she thrilled with surprise at her nascent feelings. Maureen and Jackie moved closer until each of them had hooked one leg over one of Cynthia's thighs, and as they swam into her on one end, they slowly pulled her open at the other. Cynthia sighed as they opened the portals to her cunt and her tongue curled and swept back and forth until it was seized by the others and held for a tingling moment. The structure collapsed and their lips, writhing like snakes, flew into the turbulent centre. They gave themselves to the dance they had created, their energy going into the unity of contact instead of between any particular personalities. They strained to press their mouths against their mouths until it seemed they would bruise the tender flesh. Cynthia rode the crest until she could not absorb the tension and then her lips flew open once more, wide and gaping, wanting penetration. The others seethed inside her, licking her teeth and cheeks, burrowing into the opening as though they wanted to devour her. They bit her lips and let saliva drip into her throat. Cynthia swallowed them whole, accepting all the sensation they showered upon her, and then surged up to reply. Her tongue, that arcane organ of intelligence, spoke without the resonated breath it usually uses to make words; it talked directly through touch, discarding the cumbersome vehicle of projected speech. The others felt, and understood, and replied. And for a very long time the three women, their bodies locked and vibrating, moved their mouths in a wide shifting embrace, their tongues slithering in silent sentences. The messages which were passed could never be conceptualised. Some were humorous and she smiled inside herself; some were sad and her eyes grew moist; some were so beautiful that she took the hands of the others and pressed them to her own breasts.

They did not separate for over half an hour, and when they finally broke apart, having felt the split welling within them, knowing the time had come for the cycle to end, and saying a thousand goodbyes to the moment which would never be that moment again, Jackie and Maureen fell away with their heads touching Cynthia's, their hair all intertwined. 'Oh my God,' Cynthia said, realising that the whole time had been one single kiss, one sexual torque of consciousness.

She opened her eyes and saw a picture of three women. During the entire time she had lost all concern over gender; the experience was so thorough, so complete, so implacably right, that she was totally absorbed by it, and her everyday standards of judgement took a timid seat in the back row of her mind. Maureen lay to her left, her dress wrapped in wrinkled tightness around her body, caught in the cleft between her buttocks; Jackie was lying face up and Cynthia caught her eyes in the mirror. They looked at each other and for an instant it seemed to Cynthia that Jackie's reflection was her own; she could sense no difference between herself and the woman next to her.

Jackie rolled to her side and took Cynthia's head in her hands. Switching from the image to the reality, Cynthia beheld the face that peered into hers. 'I've lost my boundaries,' she said.

Jackie kissed her, pursing her lips and delivering a series of puckered caresses on her mouth. 'There is no end of getting naked,' she said between kisses. As Cynthia gave herself to the tiny explosions of physical

152

affection, Maureen's hand slid down her side, over the hip, and to her cunt. Cynthia gasped at the touch and as the breath escaped her, Jackie sucked it into her lungs.

'I ... am ... going ... to ... taste ... you,' Maureen said as she moved down the length of Cynthia's body. Her fingers undid the top button of her shorts, slowly pulled the zipper down, and peeled the fabric away from her skin. Cynthia tensed as she felt herself exposed, and then relaxed as the garment was rolled to her thighs, past her knees, over her feet, and cast away. Maureen was crouched between her calves staring into the tangle of hair at the juncture of Cynthia's legs, legs which sensed the presence of the other woman and slowly spread apart to offer access to the dark centre. The outer cunt lips parted as the thighs pulled open, and for the first time in her life Cynthia prepared to yield herself to a woman.

Maureen stretched out at full length on the bed and laid her cheek on Cynthia's pubic bone, taking deep breaths to smell the heady aroma that wafted up from the opening to her body. She nuzzled into the hair, licked the furrow alongside the crack, and with a single deft gesture, brought her fingers into the folds and parted the cunt like a fig. She looked at it steadily, her eyes lidded, her chest heaving with emotion, and with a tiny whimper fastened her mouth on the wet sticky furrow.

Cynthia groaned, her voice echoing in the caverns of Jackie's throat. Jackie pressed her tongue into Cynthia's mouth, causing her to bring her knees up, thus opening her cunt even further to Maureen's kiss. Each of the women had one end of her, and they used her body like a wire to hum through. As Maureen's tongue explored the convoluted cathedral of cunt, teasing every fold and sipping every drop that oozed from the serrated centre, Jackie ravished the mouth which grew more and more slack with open wonderment. Her hands curled at her chest, her legs bent at the knees,

153

her head rolling slightly from side to side, little cries puffing from her throat, Cynthia was like an infant in the throes of pleasure, as Maureen and Jackie sucked the ecstasy from her pores.

The two roommates began to talk to one another with Cynthia as a medium. As Maureen set up vibrations in her cunt, Cynthia let the expression bubble out through her mouth; Jackie, receiving the message, responded by tapping a complex code with her tongue, causing Cynthia to tilt her pelvis, squeeze her thighs, and let her cunt flutter and melt. At one point Cynthia saw the pattern and understood that as she transmitted the communications, she also translated them; her body was a highly subtle and complex instrument for the processing of meaning. She was able to revel in the voluptuous sensations of the act at the same time she analysed its component parts. To be able to have her mind function so clearly while her body was pregnant with sensuous tumult released the tender feelings in her heart, and she experienced a rare unification of her being.

She opened her cunt to Maureen's mouth, letting its sensitive folds listen to the story told it by the tongue and lips, and watched the ripples up her spinal cord splash into her brain, and wash toward her mouth which transmuted the signals into lollings of her lips, and tensions of her tongue. She swooned to accept Jackie's response, receiving her forceful delicate extended kiss on the receiver of her mouth.

And when the harmony had been attained, the energy began to build, like a dynamo gathering momentum. The tapestry of interpenetration was illuminated with a fierce white light and smouldered with heat. The tempo increased so that they moved faster and faster, Cynthia's cunt and mouth working in synchrony, until the matter ceased to be merely one of transmitting and translating, and entered the domain of secreting and synthesising. The sexual entity they had become spanned the mechanical, the electrical, and the chemical modes. Cynthia's legs straightened to point toward the ceiling, making her thighs a trough; mounting grunts of excitement burst from her chest. Her hands stretched out to pull the two heads into her, the mouth to her cunt, the mouth to her mouth. And at that point, when she was at the edge of gibbering breakthrough, Maureen and Jackie pulled back abruptly, dripping and dazed, leaving her suspended in a stark moment of animal self-realisation, at the brink of exposure, terrible with want.

'Oh, don't stop,' she cried.

Maureen inserted two fingers into Cynthia's cunt, the index and middle fingers of her right hand, whipping them back and forth as they entered so they churned the secretions to a froth inside her. She probed erratically with them, filling Cynthia's cunt with the thrashing configurations of their dance, separating and coming together, bending and straightening, going in many directions at once. It was as though some many-legged spider were inside her, kicking like a man in a giant plastic bag. Maureen's hand went in up to the knuckles, and while her thumb began to twirl around the tip of Cynthia's clitoris, her pinky slipped into the striated anus, already slippery with juice that had spilled out of the cunt.

Cynthia pushed her cunt down, tightening the muscles, engulfing the fingers and sucking them into her. Maureen retreated, pulling out until she was almost totally withdrawn with Cynthia's cunt gaping after her like the mouth of a fish just pulled from thewater. And when Cynthia had held the position to the breaking point, Maureen slid her hand into the waiting hole once more, this time entering with three fingers, gnarled together in a knot the width of a thick cock. But unlike a cock, when they were inside her, they exploded into a fury of movement, until Cynthia felt that a sparkler had been lit inside her and her cunt was crackling with flame.

Her eyes closed, she did not see Jackie's motion and

knew nothing of what she was doing until her wet hairy musty cunt pressed down on her mouth. Her lids flew up in shock but she could see nothing but flesh. Jackie was sitting on her face, her arse on her forehead, her cunt kissing her lips. She had difficulty in breathing for a moment, and then realised she was holding back because of the smell. But as Maureen opened her from below, her inhibitions faltered and she began taking deep breaths through her nose, accepting the rich aroma of Jackie's womanhood. She opened her mouth tentatively and tasted the acid and alkali which flowed out in a pearly white ooze. It was such a novel experience that she was not immediately able to come to terms with a feeling about it. This was a cunt she was licking, the same thing that lay between her own legs and which Maureen was now feeling and filling with such extraordinary sensations. She wriggled her arse on the sheet to meet some of the thrusts of Maureen's fingers, and slid her tongue experimentally into the crack Jackie pushed at her. It was no taste she could define, not bitter, not sweet, not salty, not bland. It bedeviled her because it was at once so ambiguous and yet so definite. It was the flavour of cunt, utterly unique in the world.

She slid her hands up and peeled back the outer lips so she could lick the pink bud at the centre. She heard Jackie suck her breath in through her teeth. As she glued her mouth to the vaginal opening and Maureen rampaged between her legs. Jackie bent forward to bring her face close to Maureen's. The two women moved their mouths together and sank into a deep throbbing kiss. At that moment of connection, Cynthia again felt the current which went through her, and realised that if she moved her tongue and mouth in response to Maureen's fingering of her, a line would go from Maureen's hands to Cynthia's cunt to Cynthia's mouth to Jackie's cunt to Jackie's mouth, to Maureen's mouth and back to Maureen's hands, thus closing the circuit. There was no foreign element to destroy the smooth functioning of the loop, and they continued the movement, again letting the energy build until they were vibrating keenly, Jackie's pelvis rocking back and forth as she ground her cunt into Cynthia's lapping tongue and smacking lips, Maureen's wrist twisting spasmodically as she dug and thrust into Cynthia's pumping frenzy.

It was at the apex of the arc that Cynthia felt the familiar pulsations which signaled orgasm, and as she started to come Maureen slid her fingers out, tore her mouth from Jackie's and fixed it to the throbbing centre, catching the spasms of climax and the juices of abandon. As she moaned in pleasure, Jackie twitched and came quietly, her cunt rotating heavily on Cynthia's lips.

Maureen dropped her head on the mattress and Cynthia reached down to stroke her hair. Maureen took her hand with both of hers and brought it to her face pressing it against her cheek, re-establishing contact with the person whose cunt had for a short time engulfed her consciousness. Jackie climbed off and lay down next to Cynthia. The two women looked into one another's eyes.

'I didn't know you had taken your clothes off,' she said.

'I wanted to let you undress me later, but it all got so heavy so quickly, and when I saw your mouth so hungry and begging to be filled I had to cover it.'

Cynthia looked down at the naked body and reached over to stroke Jackie's breast with her free hand. 'I'm amazed at myself,' she said. 'If someone had told me a few hours ago that I could be so free with a woman . . .'

'Two women,' Jackie said. 'It's different when you're with one alone. The number changes the quality of the interaction.'

Maureen stretched, stirred, and kissed Cynthia on the cunt. 'It's like a hummingbird sipping honey,' she said. 'There's just the constant sucking and the ecstatic buzzing of wings. No purpose in life except to drink the nectar and hum in mindless rapture.'

'Would you like some tea?' Jackie asked.

Cynthia nodded and Jackie bounced off the bed, her breasts and buttocks jiggling. She spun around and smiling broadly said, 'I'm so happy you're here with us,' and skipped out of the room. Cynthia turned to see Maureen sitting up. 'She gets like a little girl when she's very happy,' Maureen said. 'And what are you like when you're happy?' Cynthia asked her. The dark woman's eyes twinkled. 'I come,' she said. The words hung in the air, and as a skydiver plummeting through space will, when he pulls the cord, become a fluffy white object floating, so the projection of the expression on Maureen's face transformed the blunt reply into a flower of humour, and the two of them began laughing, the joke mounting in broadness and depth as they fed it with their energy, until they were holding their sides and giggling uproariously.

'I feel so good,' Cynthia said when the fit had passed. And a crease of worry drew her face into a pucker as soon as she spoke the words. With the suddenness of a cloud passing over the sun, her interior landscape grew dark, and she plunged from an exuberant sense of well-being into a rib-aching gloom. She felt the first tinges of depression.

'What is it?' Maureen said, touching her shoulder.

'I don't know,' Cynthia told her. 'It was like the bottom fell out.' She bit her knuckles. 'I suddenly remembered everything . . . back there,' she said. 'Aaron and my job and the confusion and the tension.'

'But you can leave all that,' Maureen said.

'And do what?' Cynthia asked. 'I wish it were that simple. But I still need to work, and although I'm angry at Aaron today, I'll probably be longing for him tomorrow.'

'Not if you let us help you,' Maureen said.

'Help me? How?'

'You do know that you can come live here?'

Cynthia raised her eyebrows. 'No,' she said, 'that never entered my mind.'

'You really don't know how much we're taken by you, do you?' Maureen asked.

'I don't understand,' Cynthia replied.

'There's nothing to understand,' said Jackie as she came back into the room carrying a tray and a teapot and three cups on it. 'We have more than enough room, and we are terribly in love with you, and we want to save you from that turgid existence you've been mucking about in far too long.'

Maureen squeezed her arm. 'It is easier than you think. We can move you in this afternoon.'

'Why would you want to . . .' Cynthia began, but Maureen put a finger to her lips. 'Let's have some tea,' she said. 'There's no point in talking about something if you haven't felt its call.' She reached over to a low table by the bed and picked up a teak box. 'And we can have some of this to add to the refreshment.'

'Is that the grass that Conrad brought by?' Jackie asked.

'Conrad?' Cynthia said, the name catching her attention.

'He's our dealer,' Jackie told her.

'Is he a young man, about twenty, blond hair, with a small scar on his right cheek?'

'That's him,' Jackie said as she poured the tea. 'Do you know him?'

'He's a neighbour,' Cynthia replied. She hesitated on the brink of telling them the story, but did not want to inject more of her concern into the mood of the afternoon.

'Berkeley's a small town,' said Maureen as she opened the lid to reveal several ounces of light brown leaves. 'It's flower tops from a delivery of Jamaica tan,' she went on, 'sprayed with psilocybin,' She filled a large pipe with the weed, lit a match and held the flame over the bowl and sucked the smoke in. As Cynthia watched her, Jackie put a teacup in her hand. She

sipped the brew as the pipe went to Jackie, and put
the cup down when it reached her. 'I've never had
psilocybin,' she said. 'Will it get me very high?'

'You won't want to go anywhere for four or five
hours,' Jackie told her.

'What time is it?' Cynthia asked.

'Time is an illusion,' Maureen said. 'You're letting
the pipe go out.'

'I think I'm afraid,' Cynthia told her.

'Fear? It's a thing children feel. But if it seizes you,
then give yourself up to it completely. Let yourself be
afraid. Shake and cry, and we will stay with you until
it passes.' Maureen struck another match and held it
over the bowl. Cynthia took a puff and began to pass
the pipe to Jackie. But Maureen waved it back. 'No,
no,' she said, 'not like that. Here, I will show you how
to smoke, and then the fear will disappear.'

'Perhaps I should be thinking about getting back,'
Cynthia said.

'Perhaps you should,' Jackie cut in. 'But stay here
while you do it. There's no rush, is there?'

Cynthia pictured the apartment in her mind, saw
Aaron sitting in the living room. For a moment she
felt a pang of compassion, imagining him in pain, waiting for her, and in the next instant cursed herself for
falling back into the same pattern which had been
choking both of them, the inability to let the other
have his or her own life.

'I can stay the night,' Cynthia said.

'Then put your attention here,' said Maureen, holding yet another match over the treated marijuana.
'First empty your lungs,' She waited until Cynthia had
complied before continuing, and gave all her instruc-
tions slowly, pausing to insure that Cynthia followed
each one along the way. 'Hold the tip of the pipe at
the edge of your lips so that when you inhale you take
in some air with the smoke; it will make the mixture
less harsh. Then take a deep, deep breath, sucking the
smoke inside you until there is no more you can take

in. When you are filled with the smoke, close your eyes and feel it in your lungs. Sense it entering your bloodstream, making your body ring like a thousand little chimes. Can you feel that? And now let it rush like a geyser to your brain, changing the way the whole world is for you.'

The words and smoke danced in her like twin melodies which gathered instruments and voices until they culminated in a mighty crescendo. She felt the roof of her skull lift off and a waterfall of silver light shimmered against her closed eyelids. When she opened her eyes she was rocking back and forth on her haunches and the whole scene seemed to have been covered with a fine sprinkle of diamond dust.

An arc of elation braced her with buzzing pleasure. The future joined the past in the realm of nonfunctional existence, and then she returned to the colours and sounds and smells of the room. Through the french windows she could see only green, and was struck by the silence of the place, removed as it was from the raw screech of traffic. The mirrors above and around her reflected the three of them from a score of angles and she felt surrounded by beautiful bodies. She brought the pipe to her lips and repeated the procedure, this time avid for the scintillating effect it brought about. A thought like a cloud drifted through her mind, suggesting that where she was at the moment was the most perfect place in the world to live and she would be a fool to go back to the cramped life she had been living which now seemed to have absolutely nothing left to offer her but the prospect of having a child, which would only nail her down in the trap more securely.

Maureen smiled lazily. 'Yes,' she hissed, 'into the present.'

The pipe came and went, floating around the circle of their hands. Cynthia filled herself with its magic fumes six times before it was filled again, and then she counted two more before numbers ceased making any sense to her. All external considerations faded, and she entered a deep communion with the chemicals which were penetrating her system and altering her very perception of reality. She was not sophisticated enough about drugs to be familiar with the quality of emergence and disappearance, as the different objects and entities of her inner and outer environment shifted in relation to what was figure and what was ground at any given time in her consciousness. But she was relaxed enough that nothing disturbed her, and like a child with a kaleidoscope who watched the different elements of existence coming together and falling apart, always in new shapes and with changing connotations of importance. At one point the pipe stopped coming to her and she sank back onto the mattress, aware of nothing but the waxing and waning of awareness in her body, as she shrank to zero point and swelled to a mammoth figure of archetypal thighs and mythic breasts.

A deep glow suffused her and she brimmed with the beauty of energy. She curled her right foot to her left calf and flexed the muscles of her legs. Her hands reached up as though beseeching someone to hold her, and then came down flat at her sides, the fingers curled like claws. She dug her nails into her thighs until the skin held their imprint, and then slid her hands up her body until she had cupped her breasts. She touched each nipple lightly. She simmered with sensuality.

Something touched her and she knew it was not physical. She opened her eyes and through a striated mist she saw Maureen sitting like a figurine, her legs folded under her, her hands on her knees, her torso erect. She seemed to be straining forward, reaching toward her, like a dancer tingling tautly on points. There was a beam that went from her mouth to Cynthia's left breast, and it was there that she felt the sensation. She leaned into the flow and yearned toward Maureen, suddenly wanting her desperately, desiring

162

to mingle with her in the overflow of energy that enveloped the two of them.

But Maureen did not move and Cynthia turned her head to see Jackie sitting crosslegged on the other side of her, exerting the force of resistance that kept Maureen from coming forward. Jackie's eyes burned into Maureen's forehead and held her as surely as if she were keeping her pinned down with a pole. Then, with an inner shift Cynthia did not understand, Jackie was looking at her without changing the focus of her gaze.

'It's not very mysterious,' Jackie said, the words coming out slowly, with effort, as though she were carrying a heavy weight. 'The eyes have more than one channel, and I can emit energy toward Maureen while taking in visual impressions from you.'

'But what are you doing?' Cynthia asked.

'Be it to understand it,' Maureen whispered. 'The body itself is the language. The words it shoots out are only the echoes of things already said in silence.'

Cynthia squirmed as the tension built. Every time she tried to figure out what was happening, a pressure like a band around her head forced her to stop thinking. She felt as though she were in a lift whose cable had snapped and was plummeting to the ground far below with accelerating velocity. They were screwing her up to a pitch of need which, when snapped, would hurl her into a frenzy. But she could see none of the intention behind their actions, and began to thrash about, caught in the strong force field like a fly in a web. She shut her eyes and rolled to her stomach, and found that when she changed her direction, her discomfort decreased. She adjusted herself until she lay like a line between them, her head near Jackie's cunt, her legs spread around Maureen's knees. She snuggled into the sheet like a person worming into a trench to escape the strafing planes overhead. She could feel the waves of energy passing over her; her skin glowed with heat and her anus tingled. Her rational mind melted and she became a palpitating organism writhing without sense. And when she was returned to herself, and her body lay before the two women like a sea before a diver, Jackie snapped the psychic rubber band and Maureen shot forward.

She fell with her mouth between Cynthia's cheeks, her tongue already reaching down into the cunt beneath. Jackie fell to one side of them and, grabbing Cynthia by the hips, turned her to her side so that she came at her cunt from the front. Without prompting, Cynthia buried her face between Jackie's thighs and sucked at the cunt between them. They clung to one another like iron filings to a magnet, the power of their pull erasing all distinctions. Each of them imploded with a quiet lust, and they dropped all manipulations of who did what to whom. It was no longer Cynthia being initiated, but Cynthia as a woman among women following the unfolding of a passion that needed no fuel except its own will to endure, heeded no laws except the elegance of necessity. They were three cunts, and three arses, and six breasts, and six hands, and six feet, and three mouths, and brains and hearts. They were a movement moving, a sigh escaping, a climax gathering itself.

'Oh my God, it gets more,' was the last thought that went through Cynthia's mind before the upward shooting glory of the beginning orgy propelled her past the grey semaphors of conscious thought.

7

Sweet Satori Blues

The dream had the clarity often found in those who fall into a profound sleep after smoking marijuana. Conrad's body rolled on the meat which lay on the floor of the van, shifting with the rhythms of the rubber tires slapping agianst the concrete highway. In the front seat sat Jerry, driving through the night, enjoying the hallucinations which time and again tricked him into a false perception of turns in the road, and pondering that, in the face of death, illusion and reality had absolutely the same weight. They were on their way to Nogaies to buy dynamite.

In Conrad's mind, a room appeared, and he viewed it with the ambivalence of one who knows he is dreaming and yet can do nothing but be a passive observer of the inner drama, watching it as one does a movie, with a blend of identification and detachment. It was a dark Victorian drawing room with eighteen-foot ceilings. All the angles were distorted as in a German Expressionist set. The walls were ochre, the woodwork mahogany. Thick drapes smothered all the windows, and the single massive door was locked and bolted. The furniture was ornate and overstuffed, deep armchairs, a pile rug, upholstered lamp shades. Only one light shone, from a lamp at the edge of the desk which dominated a whole corner. It had the quality of being underwater.

On the long couch lay a woman of about thirty, her slim form enveloped in voluminous skirts and accented above the waist by a starched bodice. Her left arm lay at her side while her right forearm was flung over her eyes. Conrad peered through the gloom and looked at her face. It was Cynthia's but transformed through the alchemy of subconscious distortion so that it kept changing aspects. Just behind her shoulder, one leg folded over the other at the knee, his hands in his lap, his lids lowered, his breathing calm, sat a bearded man of almost fifty. He wore a black suit and showed no signs of movement.

'It's Freud,' Conrad said aloud. The man turned to him and held one finger to his lips so as to silence him.

The woman tossed restlessly, her clothing rustling silkily in the quiet air. There was a compelling suggestion of thigh sliding against thigh, of soft moist underthings, and secret places yearning for a hand to enter.

'I can't,' she said aloud, 'I don't have anything to say. Nothing comes to my mind, nothing.' She lay still for a moment, only her heaving breasts showing her agitation; her cheeks were flushed. 'Why don't you speak?' she cried. 'Why do you torture me like this?'

The man in the chair showed no reaction except for the slight twitch by his left eye. He looked down at the form in front of him and an expression of sadness darkened his face. 'It is all so clear,' he sighed, 'and yet she cannot see any of it.'

'It is all useless, senseless,' she said.

The man rolled his eyes toward heaven. This was the ninth month of analysis. Every day, six days a week, an hour each day, for three quarters of a year, and she was still not bringing forth any material he could work with. He was prepared to wait indefinitely for he knew with deep certainty that if she did not quit, she would have to break through. 'The clouds must gather a long time before they release their rain,' he thought, 'and when they do, we can expect a flood.'

As though taking the suggestion from his mind, the woman began to weep, tears trickling from her eyes and down into her hair. Conrad tried to step forward, to go to her and comfort her, but the man motioned him back. 'You do not help her by interfering,' he said. 'She must taste her sadness until the bitterness of it chokes her, and then she will find her own way to herself. You would only make her situation more complex, and distract her from her own feelings.'

'What is wrong with me?' she asked. 'Why am I so empty inside? I have everything a woman is supposed to want, a husband, children, a home. But it is all dust in my mouth. Am I just an ungrateful wretch as my mother told me? Am I really evil?'

The man lifted his head. The contours of the room shifted, and a sound like crackling leaves sounded outside. 'Evil,' he said. 'What does that word suggest to you?'

She was startled by his voice. It was the first time in seven weeks he had said anything to her except 'Good afternoon', once as she arrived and once as she departed. 'Evil,' she repeated, encouraged to have sparked a response. 'The first thing I think of is an animal, an animal covered with dirt.'

'Dirt?' said the man.

'Filth,' she said. 'Schmutz.'

'Ah,' said he, 'sex.'

At the mention of the word a slow blush tinged her cheeks crimson and her lips trembled. Her hands flew to cover her breasts and her knees locked together. She was as chaste and wanton as a nun in prayer, desiring that which she found most fearful, penetration by the power above her.

'How beautiful she is,' the man thought. 'What a joy it would be to make love to her, to take her through all those fears, to let her blossom and become free.' He frowned. 'That's all in the past now,' he said to himself, and recalled the years of his engagement and early marriage, when fire had snorted from his nostrils as he sniffed cocaine and was stampeded by surges of raw intellectual power that had women swooning at his knees. But when he reached his mid-forties the whole process of sex came to bore him, and he poured himself exclusively into his work. To have met this woman when he was still in the beginning passion of discovering the principles of analysis would have been a challenge to his soul, and he wondered whether he might not have developed even further techniques with her to rouse him. Now he was content to channel his energy into the hope that she would break through the confines of her neurotic paralysis.

'And if she does,' he said to himself, 'where will she find a man?' He recalled meeting her husband and seeing at once that he was obsessive, a classic anal retentive. 'Oh, theses compulsives and hysterics do seem to seek each other out,' he had mused. Now he consoled himself with an idea. 'Well, if she is cured, I will suggest a month's visit to Rome. She will find a man quickly enough there who will extort the moans of ecstasy now locked in her fluttering breasts.'

The woman twisted her head to look back at him and saw him still sitting impassively in the chair. Conrad attempted to catch her eye but she seemed to look right through him. 'I wonder what he's thinking,' she said to herself and bit her lip. 'If he would only speak. But he's told me that I must proceed totally on my own, that he's there only to assist at crucial moments. But what if I never have a crucial moment?' For perhaps the hundredth time, doubt assailed her. 'What if he's a charlatan,' she thought. 'What if he's actually just another man like my husband, more clever but just as unable to understand what's going on inside me?'

'Please,' she said directly to him, 'you must help me.' As she looked at his face, an expression of stern coldness seemed to pass over his features. His face darkened with wrath. His eyes burned with malevolence. She shrank away from him, suddenly convinced that he was very angry at her, would leap from his chair and strike her. She turned from him, half fearing and half hoping that he would fall upon her and cover her with blows. And at that point, for no reason she could think of, she recalled her father, a man she hadn't seen for almost twenty years.

Her memories raced back to her childhood, a world of confused yearnings and rigid schedules. Days were spent in listless lessons with a governess and formal encounters with her mother. Evenings were a progressively more anxious preparation for her father's homecoming, for they never knew when he would be in one of his black moods and make the house tremble with his terrible wrath.

One night returned with absolute clarity, and as the details of the evening came together in her memory, she closed her eyes tightly as though to block it out of consciousness. But it burst into her with the power of a fist, and she curled into a ball on the couch, uncaring about the impression she made on the doctor. Conrad peeked into the mind of the woman of his dream.

She was six years old and sitting at the dinner table. Her mother had discovered her playing with the neighbour's son of the same age; they had been in the attic with their clothes off, examining one another's bodies. When the door opened she was lying on a trunk, her legs apart, with her playmate inserting his fingers into the slit between her legs. Her mother had whacked the boy and sent him home, and then slapped her until she was dizzy, all the while shouting, 'Just wait until I tell your father, wait until I tell your father.' When he came home, her parents went into his study and did not come out for fifteen minutes, and when they did her father stared at her as though she was something terribly ugly.

'I think you had better come with me,' he said at last after the meal had been eaten in stony silence.

'Don't be too hard,' her mother said.

He took her by the arm and led her into his bedroom. He closed the door behind him, and she recalled the rush of blood to her head and the roaring sense of dizzyness as he walked toward her. 'You have done something that is so shameful I can't even speak about

169

it,' he said, 'and what I am about to do is to teach you never never to do anything like that again.' Her eyes went wide as he took off his jacket and slowly unbuckled the wide leather belt around his waist.

'Come here,' he said and grabbed her around the waist. Her breath caught in her throat as he lifted her off the ground and laid her across his thighs in a single motion and sat at the edge of the four-poster bed. 'And this is to insure that you feel this properly,' he said, his voice sounding distant and choked. The woman on the couch squirmed as she relived the intense frightening excitement of the moment.

His hands went up her legs, lifting the dress over her waist. He pushed it until it covered her torso and head, and she lay wrapped in darkness, unable to see what was happening below. She felt his fingers tugging at her panties, pulling them down and off her body. She blushed until she thought she would burst into flames, knowing that the naughtiest part of her, the part she was never to even think about or touch, or let anyone else see, was bare and expose to her father's eyes. The pungent smell of his trouser leg and the exact shade of brown of the rug under his feet, the giddyness of being suspended and the pressure of his legs against her belly, all came back vividly.

He rubbed her buttocks with one hand and said, 'Now, we'll teach you what happens to wicked little girls.' His fingers tickled and for a moment a current of pleasure ran through her, and without thinking she contracted her cheeks, pulling them in toward the centre.

'What?' he said, and grabbed the flesh in his fingers. 'Oh, you are a dirty little girl, an evil little girl.'

There was a brief pause, a whistling sound, and the strap hit hard and flush across her skin. Before she had time to register the effect of the blow, he hit her again, and then again. A slow burning began, barely painful at first, but growing deeper as the strap continued its relentless punishment. Soon she felt that her flesh was being sheared off, and she howled in anguish.

On the couch the woman clenched her fists, curled her toes, and whimpered. The man in the chair watched. 'Hmm,' he said, 'there seems to be something going on inside her. Perhaps after she goes through it the words will come at last.'

The little girl lost all control. She beat her arms against his legs, she kicked violently, she screamed at the top of her lungs. But the more she reacted, the more heavily he beat her. She reached a point where she felt she could no longer bear what was happening to her, and saw in a flash that she had no choice for she was pinned by a strength greater than her own. Unconsciously, she surrendered, and her body went limp. His arm rising and falling, his eyes locked in a hypnotic stare at the rash-red buttocks and the first hint of a crack beneath them, his breath whistling in and out of his mouth, he was blind to his own actions.

He let the strap fly out of his hands and brought his hand down on the firm curved arse, and as his lips working noiselessly brought one finger forward, slipped it between the defeated thighs, and thrust it rudely into the tiny vagina. She groaned once and lost all control of her bladder, letting a stream of urine splash onto his lap, down his legs, and into his shoes.

'Pig,' he shouted.

At that moment the door flew open and her mother came in. 'Max,' she screamed, 'my God, what are you doing to her?'

And he had stood up calmly, dumped the child off his lap, and said in a narrow voice, 'See what an animal she is, she pissed all over everything.' And left the room deliberately, leaving her to stare up into the dawning envy in her mother's eyes.

The woman on the couch felt the heat in her groin, that same sense of peeing freely, forgetting all concern and letting the warm liquid spurt and dribble from the hole between her legs, making the hair sticky and

171

salty, slick and pungent. She linked it to all the times she had begun to feel some excitement between her thighs when her husband imposed himself on her physically, as he did, his body rigid, his jaws clenched, his eyes unseeing, his hands turned into knots. And always she would retreat from the warmth, always hold back.

She was intelligent enough to know that the man she had sex with did not allow her her fullest range of feeling and expression, but she suspected that there was something deeper in her problem, something she could not find by herself. And then had heard of the wonderful doctor that all society was gossiping about, the man who gave woman the freedom to have orgasms.

She rolled to her back one more and wondered whether she had come to the root of her neurosis. Her body went slack and her legs tingled with anticipation. She felt her breasts as quivering mounds on her narrow chest, and her mouth was an open invitation. Warm pulsating life throbbed in her cunt and the room was filled with the oceanic aroma of her secretions. Conrad began to get an erection. The man sat up in his chair.

'Now,' he said to himself, 'if she escapes transference on one side, and the strictures of the super-ego on the other, she will make it through to the articulation. And once she says it, she will be free.'

'No,' said Conrad out loud, 'it's time for action.'

'Right on,' said Jerry, staring through the windscreen.

The characters in Conrad's dream paid no attention to his shout. The woman brought her legs up slowly, deliberately. She moaned and reached her arms up in a silent prayer for someone to hold her, to take her beauty in his arms and bring it to fruition. The man's chair creaked. He leaned forward, his eyes closed to what he did, and waited for the words to come, listened intently for the words.

Conrad sat up.

'Who's Cynthia?' Jerry asked, looking at him through the rear-view mirror.

Conrad shook his head to clear it of sleep. The pressure in his bladder increased sharply each time the van swayed. 'Can we stop?' he asked, 'I have to pee.'

Jerry drove for a few minutes until the shoulder widened and he pulled over onto a grassy space which overlooked a steep drop. They were on Highway 1, deep in the embrace of Big Sur, going south between the awesome powers of the mountains and the ocean. The two men swung out of the wide doors and tramped to the edge of the precipice to stand side by side and relieve themselves on the rocks below. There was no moon, and the stars burned with a blue-white light. Behind them the hills loomed as fearful shadows, guarding the tract of untouched wilderness that stretched eighty miles inland. There was no other evidence of human presence anywhere in sight.

Conrad zipped his fly, stretched, and walked back a few feet where he sank to the ground and sat crosslegged facing the sea. 'She's the old lady of the man who was in my room when you came in,' he said.

Jerry turned to face him. 'That was a strange scene,' he said. 'He looks like a pig. It really blew my mind.'

Conrad smiled. 'You went through a few changes,' he said.

Jerry ran his fingers through his hair. 'You called out her name four or five times when you were asleep. It sounded like you were really suffering. What's your scene with them?'

Conrad reached into a leather pouch hung around his neck and fished out a small piece of hashish and a tiny wooden pipe. Jerry had come to his house to tell him that the money had arrived, and they could proceed with the plan to pick up the explosives. Conrad had been approached several weeks earlier by another member of the violent faction of the underground and asked if his grass contacts in Mexico could also supply

173

dynamite. Conrad arranged a deal with Arturo, his dealer and friend of several years, a man at whose house he had shared peyote and whom he could trust implicitly. And Arturo, after a few days of his own explorations, had returned with the news that it could be done.

'I have a cousin,' he said. 'He drives a milk truck through the border every day for almost the year now. The guards don't even make him slow down anymore. When you have the money you will come down and meet me here. We will put the dynamite in plastic bags in the bottom of the vat. Then my cousin will drive to his station. But first he will stop at a garage in the American section of the city. You will meet us there, and we'll make the transfer. You give me half the money when we load the stuff, and the other half when we put it in your truck.' He had smiled. 'It will be very easy. We can lift it right from the warehouse. It is very good quality, straight from Czechoslovakia.'

When Jerry had burst into the room, Conrad was privileged to watch the incarnations of the two extremes of his social existence meet face to face. He was amused at both their reactions, Jerry jumping back as though he had stepped on a hot coal, and Aaron turning with with fear. When Aaron had stood up and began dressing quickly, Conrad wanted to say something to reassure him, but realised there was nothing he could do at just that moment. He knew why Jerry had come, and the business was too dangerous to allow Aaron to stay around even for a few minutes. He misjudged Aaron's susceptibility to shock, however, and did not know that the incident was to be a prelude to Cynthia's disappearance. He made a note to himself to straighten the situation out when he returned from Mexico.

Conrad pondered Jerry's question as he lit the pipe, and relaxed into the aroma of the resin as it mingled with the damp green smell of the forest and the rich salt air from the ocean. The spirit of the night was vast and far removed from the concerns of the men who travelled through it. He handed the pipe to Jerry, but to his surprise the other man waved it away. Conrad looked at him questioningly. Jerry was dark-skinned with curly black hair that covered his head like a giant pom-pom. Just a little over five feet tall and perfectly erect from the two hours of hatha yoga he practised daily, he struck a sharp contrast to Conrad's tall blond sloping California look. Conrad had known him for several years, seeing him sporadically and never knowing in advance when he would pass through. They had taken LSD together a number of times and shared the intimacy of men who are willing to fight and die for a way of living that neither, if asked, could have articulated to the satisfaction of the other. They were brothers, and that subsumed the rest. Now Conrad attempted to focus on his feelings for Cynthia, analyzing the complex pattern of behaviour he had exhibited since meeting her. He found it more accurate to observe what he did, and from that deduce his motivations, rather than attempting to rely on introspection.

'I don't want to just fuck her,' he said. 'I could have done that months ago.' He held the pipe toward Jerry once more, who again indicated he wanted none of it.

'Are you off smoking?' he asked.

'I don't do dope any more,' Jerry told him.

Conrad blinked. 'What brought that about?'

Jerry ignored the question. 'So, if you don't want to fuck her, what do you want to do with this chick?'

Conrad took another deep toke before answering. 'I'm sick of the city,' he said. 'The more I'm around people the more I'm getting to hate them. The whole scene is just getting so sick I can't cope with it any more.'

'You're telling me,' Jerry said with a trace of sarcasm.

'You want to blow it up,' Conrad went on, 'I want to

175

get away from it. Trees are the only things I can really relate to any more.' He paused. 'I'm thinking of splitting.'

'There's a few communes I can turn on to,' Jerry said.

'Farther than that,' Conrad replied. 'I know where there's a cabin in Idaho. Fifty miles of forest in every direction. Even the rangers don't know about it. I can pack in brown rice and soy beans, and eat off the land. There's enough nuts and berries and greens to feed a million people who know how to eat right. Plus all the game. And a stream nearby with water so delicious you never want to drink anything else.'

Jerry smiled. 'And what are you going to do there?'

'*Do?*' Conrad said. 'I'll just *be*. What is there to do? Run round like crazies trying to score all the time? All you need is food, water, air, and shelter. I'll just get stoned and stay stoned and spend my life digging creation.' He ran his fingers over the grass in front of him. 'Everybody's insane,' he went on. 'You know that. Why hang around any longer?'

Jerry sucked air in through his teeth. 'And this Cynthia, you want to take her with you?'

Conrad frowned. He had never formulated the question so baldly even to himself. But now that it was presented, there was no way to step around the awareness of the intention that had been propelling him for several months. He nodded. 'I think I want to live with her,' he said.

Jerry stood up and walked to the very edge of the cliff and stared straight down. Conrad's stomach lurched, for the ground was soft and it would not take much for it to give way and send his friend sailing into space, his body breaking on the boulders beneath. 'Do you know,' Jerry said suddenly, 'when we blew the bank in Santa Barbara, it was the clerks who put us down the hardest?' He snorted. 'Can you imagine? The clerks. People who spend their lives pushing pieces of paper around so the Giannini family can own more of

176

the world than it already does. It was a real kick in
the arse to be attacked by the people we were trying
to wake up to freedom. It changed our heads a lot.'

Conrad listened to the monologue, wondering where
it was leading. Jerry walked back from from the lip of
the cliff and sat down in front of Conrad. 'This woman
is straight, isn't she? She must be, to have an old man
like that.'

'Well, that's the thing,' Conrad began. 'I said the
same thing to myself. But there's something different
about her. I mean, she really is unhappy with how
she's living, and she's looking for something more.'

'Enter our hero,' Jerry said. His voice became
sharper. 'Everybody wants to change. But how many
are ready to risk their suffocating security to make it
happen? How old is she?'

'Twenty-eight,' Conrad told him.

Jerry sighed. 'A stiff cock hasn't got any ideology
or common sense,' he said. 'She's too old, man,' he
continued. 'At that age very few people have enough
honesty left to radically alter their lives.' He looked
down at the ground and did not speak for a long while,
and then peered into Conrad's eyes. 'You must be
really hung up on her,' he said.

'I think I love her,' Conrad whispered, the word
sounding strange in his ears. He had not ever used it
to describe his feelings for another person.

'You're such a fucking kid,' Jerry said, but his voice
was warm. 'So hip, but still hungry for romance.' He
cocked his head. 'And you've never fucked her?'

'No,' Conrad said. 'I had a scene with her and Aaron
the other night. I gave him acid for the first time. I
had a beautiful thing going with her in the kitchen,
but then I had to take care of him. And by the time
he was cooled out, the two of them started working out
a lot of shit. She gave us both head, and then followed
him into the bedroom.'

Jerry fixed Conrad with a glance. 'Look,' he said,
'you want to poke your cock into that lady's cunt, and

177

that's a healthy American impulse. Nothing to be ashamed of. And you're getting to an age where you're beginning to scratch around for a mate. And that's cool. But for Christ's sake don't get the two things confused. You're a revolutionary, and she's a nice middle-class chick who's opened up your nose. And you want to take her to go do a Tarzan and Jane trip in a broken-down shack. How can you even think of living with somebody until you have it cooled out with them all the way down the line? How many changes does she have to go through before she even understands where you're coming from? And how the fuck do you think you can take on a grown woman? You're a bright boy, but if you get locked into a scene with her, she'll be having you for breakfast within a month. Living with a woman is the hardest thing a man can do. Don't stack the odds against yourself.'

'I really haven't thought it out that far,' Conrad said. 'The idea of making it into the woods isn't something that's going to happen for a while. And I hadn't connected it with her before just now.' He picked up two stones and hit them against each other. 'I don't want to hurt anybody,' he said.

Jerry took a deep breath and looked up at the sky. The black between the stars was pregnant with revelations for whoever was ready to gaze into it long enough and with the proper spirit. But he brought his eyes back to earth, where he was capable of exerting an influence. He had spent most of his early twenties in an ashram in India, practising asceticsm and following the precepts of a teacher. But the string had run out and one day he realised there was nothing in that place for him any longer, and had returned to the United States to become involved in the world of radical politics, his predisposition for the most rigorous wing of any given involvement leading him directly into the company of the Weathermen.

'They're hurting us,' he said, 'all the time. The wars and the stealing were bad enough, but now they're

178

actually poisoning the fucking air, killing the oceans, wiping out species after species. You want to get away from it. How long do you think there'll be any place left? That little paradise of yours will probably have a Holiday Inn on it in ten years. And that precious forest of yours will be cut down and covered with concrete. And what are you going to do about it? Spend your time trying to convince one chick that she'll have better orgasms with you than with her boyfriend?'

Conrad opened his mouth but Jerry swept past. 'I know the scene with straight chicks who are just starting to come out. It's really delicious to give them an education. You get to be the first one to show them what real ecstasy is. You get to be the first one to fuck them on acid. And while they're learning, there's part of them that's still really scared, and so they hold on to you, making you feel like the biggest man in the world. And nine times out of ten, all you get is a slave on your hands. Is that what you want?'

'What else should I do with my time?' Conrad responded. 'Blow up banks? You yourself see how useless that is.'

'You can join us in our next stage of operations,' Jerry told him. He pursed his lips and waited a moment before continuing. 'Most of the people haven't evolved to a new understanding yet, but a few of us see which way the wind is blowing for the seventies. The trip was to make use of symbolic violence. We figured that if we hit a few office buildings or draft boards the old folks would wake up and ask themselves what was wrong with their society that their children had to protest with dynamite. But after each hit, there would be a blurb in the paper and a mention on the six o'clock news, and everybody would go back to watching the ball game. The only results we got from that was to draw the feds down on us and to turn the people we were trying to communicate with against us. They picked up the slogans that the media fed to them and we were branded as madmen and criminals and agents of a foreign power.'

Jerry rubbed his beard and inched forward. Conrad listened to the words with reserve. He understood and respected Jerry and his people for the chances they took and the fervor that moved them. They were part of his family. But he had never been inclined to join their activities past acting as one of their drug connections and occasionally helping to procure explosives for them. The reasons he had been thinking of retiring from all society, for he felt a kinship with only the most radical members caught in the middle of his context was what drew him to Aaron, for he recognised that the older man had the same problem in an entirely different dimension.

'Six of us met a few months ago to rethink our objectives, and decided that it was too late to salvage anything. I don't know if the species has come to a dead end or it's the period of Kali Yuga, but it's bleak everywhere. Even the socialist countries have become just another form of power trip, hierarchies with different criteria for dividing master and slave. With the current drift of things, it seems the only alternatives are war, pollution, or worldwide dictatorship. *And that's what the people want.* I mean, that's the explanation we finally came up with. It isn't a bunch of bad guys keeping everybody else under their thumbs. If the people wanted to be free there wouldn't be the armies that are used for repression. We came to the conclusion that protest can't help because the ones we are protesting to, the people themselves, are asleep in their chains.'

Conrad slumped down and relit his hash pipe. The words were articulation of thoughts he had spun out himself. But to hear them spoken so forcefully by someone whose very life was a dedication to changing the conditions of society was oppressive. 'So, what is there to do?' he said at last.

180

'Destroy the machine,' Jerry said flatly. 'Destroy their technology.'

Conrad looked at his friend and wondered whether, in his intensity, he had lost his sanity. He had come to his own conclusions that the whole world of political society was a simple-minded game of cops and robbers, and the people who played it were, no matter how high their IQs, functional imbeciles. He had stepped free of it one night when the acid he had taken opened his heart to the reality of the infinite universe, and the blazing mystery of existence once and for all reduced the feverish machinations of manwomankind to a dull dangerous charade. Part of him beat in sympathy with Jerry's ideas, and yet another part speculated that he might be deluding himself with his apocalyptic vision.

'I know what you're thinking,' Jerry said quietly. 'And nobody knows better than I do how hopeless the whole thing is. The old civilization is dying and the ones who own the deeds to its empires and dogmas won't let go, and they will kill without compunction anyone who tries to take the reins of history from their hands. But we have no choice but to try. It's our actions that define us, so we must act according to what we understand.'

'What kind of things did you have in mind?' Conrad asked him.

'If we can get it together,' Jerry said, 'we plan to go after bridges, tunnels, dams, reservoirs, power stations, computers, anything that holds the nation together technologically. We figure that once the brothers and sisters get the idea, there will be thousands of us working to destroy the functioning of the cities and towns.' He spat on the ground in front of him. 'The next step is to tear the whole fucking country down to the ground, make centralization of power difficult or impossible, and let the people sort it out for themselves, without governments, and armies, and mammoth industries that amplify their basic stupidity. The only thing wrong with America is the civilization that

181

lives here, so all we have to do is destroy the civilization. And for us, that means the machines.'

Conrad let the words sink in before formulating any response. He was able to see that the notion was utterly unrealistic, and yet knew that empires had crumbled and been toppled before. There was no good reason to believe that America's time hadn't come, and Jerry's vision might very well be the way it would come about. 'A lot of people will die,' he said.

'Think of New York with its supply routes cut off,' Jerry replied. 'Or of San Francisco with the Golden Gate and Bay Bridges blown up.'

Conrad imagined the span from the city to Marin and the tens of thousands of cars which crossed it each day, feeding the complex of businesses which directed the flow of labour in the area. The most chilling thing about the vision was its feasibility. He shook his head. 'It's not my scene,' he said.

Jerry smiled. 'Give it a few years,' he said. 'After you try feeding Cynthia on cock and dreams for a while.' He put his hands behind his neck, arched his back, and yawned. 'You probably need to get it out of your system,' he added.

'You don't even know her,' Conrad said, surprised at the petulance in his voice.

'You see, hanging around with the middle class is fucking your mind. You're bringing it down to the level of personalities. If she's a woman and you're a man, there are certain programmed rituals you will have to play out with each other. And you'll go through hell if either one of you doesn't understand that, and thinks you should spend your time trying to fight what's been destined in your genes and prescribed by your culture. It's just biology, Conrad. Why are you trying to make something special out of this woman?'

'There's something she has . . .' Conrad began.

'She has a pussy,' Jerry cut in, 'a hairy slit between her legs, and two tits hanging off her chest, and a mouth to stick your cock into, and an arsehole to use

182

when you get bored with the other holes. She's just a thing, no different from you and me. And she's useful and pleasant sometimes, and a big drag other times. She's not an angel and she's not a devil, she's just a human being.'

'Is that how you think of Susan?' Conrad asked.

'Susan's dead,' Jerry said.

Conrad's jaw dropped. 'Dead?' he repeated. 'What happened?'

'I think it was a heart attack.'

The words expanded into the night, their meaning reaching as far as the physical vibrations carried. And when the sound was absorbed in the wide spaces beneath the sky, the silence rushed in and the thousand voices of the shore could be heard, the rustling of the leaves, the insects launching their message through the grass, the waves carving caves into the cliffs. The mood of the night deepened, and at a stroke Conrad felt himself as nothing more than an infinitesimal glimmer of consciousness at the edge between a sweeping continent and a mighty ocean, on a globe of rock where untold trillions of entities swam and crawled and flew. He was stung by the awareness of his own insignificance beneath the stars which seemed to mock anything a man might aspire to, and beneath death, which laughed at all the human virtues and vices. He had known Susan, tripping with her on two of the times he had seen Jerry, and had made love to her once, an idylic dance in a redwood grove near Lagunitas. He tried to grasp what it meant for her to be dead, but his mind could not penetrate past the word.

'We were on Steven's farm in Minnesota,' Jerry went on. 'We had been on the move for almost half a year and needed to hang out for a while. We spent a week just sleeping and fucking, and then Bob showed up with more dope than I have ever seen in one place before. He had everything. We dropped acid that night, and the next afternoon, and before I knew it we were shooting speed and smack and everything except peanut butter. I don't know why I got on such a trip, I usually need to keep my head straight. But it just got to be the thing that was happening and I thought, 'What the fuck, I'll just let myself move with it. More and more people kept showing up and by the fourth day it started to look like one of those trips that never end. Some strange collective spirit took hold and we got unbelievably high. At one point there were about seven of us watching Steven fuck a sheep and none of us could talk anymore; all we could do was grunt. It was very freaky, but beautiful. I mean, it was as heavy as anything I ever saw in India. We were blowing all the repression loose, shitting out accumulated karma all over the place.

'I lost track of Susan and didn't see her for a day or two, and then I found her in the cellar chewing on mushrooms that Steven's old lady was growing there. When she saw me she said, 'Look what I found,' and pointed to a gallon jug of homemade amyl nitrate. Just the thought of all that juice made my knees weak, and she pulled me down on top of her, right into the dirt. We began grinding against each other, very slow and hot. We were so fucking close to each other. I could feel her against me, but I was also inside her feeling me. I was loving her so much I thought I would burst open. We had been together for five years and there wasn't anything we hadn't gone through.

'Then she reached over and tipped the bottle and spilled some of the liquid onto an old rag that was lying nearby. Just smelling it from that distance made me dizzy and I could feel rushes beginning inside me that were stronger than anything I have ever had to handle. She put her mouth over mine and pulled the cloth between our noses. Her eyes were swimming inside mine and her lips kept moving as though she were trying to tell me how much she was feeling and how much of it she was giving to me. Her cunt was so hot that I felt like I was pressed against a radiator.'

He looked up from the ground and at Conrad who watched without blinking as the tale unfolded. 'I don't remember the next few minutes. I went into a spin that took me someplace I couldn't even perceive. Susan was moaning, "Put it inside me, please, Jerry, put your cock inside me." I was at a point where I didn't even have a body. But I knew what she was feeling, and I reached down inside myself to the spot my guru had helped me find, and through sheer will I made my cock get hard.' His eyes searched Conrad's to be sure that the other man understood fully. 'I did it for her,' he said. 'I have never used that power at any other time in my life.

'My cock went inside her and she melted all over me. She stopped being a person and became pure protoplasm, pulsing and oozing under me. I sank into her and what we did wasn't like anything I had ever called fucking. We were in an entirely different world.

'And then she pulled out of it and whispered, "I'm almost there, Jerry, I almost made it all the way," and she tipped the bottle onto the rag again, letting the stuff soak in. "Give it to me," she said, "give me all your strength. I want to touch the bottom." And she clamped the cloth over her face, breathing it in through her nose and her mouth. I felt myself going under and I fought against it. My cock was screaming in her cunt and my mind was roaring like a hurricane at full force and my heart was bursting like an exploding star. And through it all Susan was calling me, pulling me into her. She was all the woman I ever hoped to know in this life and she lay in my arms like an open wound yearning for me to become one with her. My will braced itself and held. Like a man being burned at the stake I felt the flames consume me, but I would not give myself up to them.

'And then, something strange happened. I began to come but instead of the sensations of expansion and feelings of ecstacy, a cold horror gripped me. I wrapped my arms around Susan but she had become something beyond my power to know. I looked into her eyes and I could see *her*, I mean, her herself, the woman she was. And then she began receding, slowly at first and then with terrible speed, moving away into distances that seemed infinite. "Jerry, save me," she said. And then she was gone.'

He liked his lips. 'At that instant I came inside her, bubbling over and bucking into her. I lay still on top of her a long time, and when I roused myself I tried to shake her awake. I called her name. Something clicked inside me. And I knew.'

'She was dead?' Conrad whispered.

Jerry did not speak for a few minutes, and when he did his voice had returned to its usual dry quality. 'The next morning we dug a hole on the side of the hill overlooking the fields and buried her there.' He glanced at Conrad's pipe. 'I haven't been able to take any drugs at all since then.' He frowned. 'Or any woman,' he added.

'Jesus,' Conrad said.

Jerry reached over and grabbed his arm, a rare gesture for him. 'Listen,' he said, 'there's one thing I learned in all of that, and I'll tell it to you now, and probably never say it to anyone else again. When you start to love a woman, you have to be ready to die with her. Otherwise it's all lies. Don't use the word love unless you have accepted death.'

Conrad's eyes glowed. 'That's it,' he said, 'that's the thing I feel with Cynthia, but I didn't know how to explain it to myself. She makes me want to die.'

Jerry regarded the young man gravely. A dozen evaluations ticked through his eyes. He took a breath and then broke into a slow rueful smile. 'Well, then,' he drawled. 'I take back everything I said.'

'Don't laugh at me, Jerry,' Conrad said. 'I need to understand it.'

'You'll find out,' Jerry told him. 'Maybe I'll come visit you in Idaho.'

They stood up, brushed off their trousers, and

climbed back into the van. Conrad drove and Jerry sat crosslegged in the front seat, his attention removed from the past and cast into the future, where it curled around the five thousand sticks of dynamite they were on their way to pick up.

8

The Frigid Orgasm

Florid fantasies flushed through Aaron's mind. It was one in the morning and there was no sign that Cynthia had been home at all during the day. He arrived at the house petulant with paranoia and defensive from the guilt he felt at fucking the girl in Conrad's living room. He suffered the letdown which follows a period of concentrated drug use, and was shaken by the startling arrival of the short man with the black hair, and his own subsequent fumbling flight from the scene. As he walked hurriedly back to his own place, he soothed himself by concluding that he had fallen into a world that was too dangerous and fast-moving for him, and formulated another resolution to discipline himself in the virtues of what he had defined as normal living: the work which give him security, the woman who shared his bed, and the apartment where nothing unruly entered. All the insights which had thrilled him now showed their subversive underbellies; all the glimpses into freedom whirred about him like ghosts, mocking him with what they had earlier used to tempt him into renunciations of his life style. The previous five months of relationship with Conrad and their culmination the night before were placed under the heading of irresponsible flirtation with insanity, and in the firmness of his putting it all down, he nimbly neglected to acknowledge the deep frustrations which led him to search out new modes of understanding and action.

It had not occurred to him that Cynthia would not be in the apartment, and it took him several minutes to assimilate the fact. He went through all the rooms, seeking not her so much as her presence. He poured a glass of milk and took it into the bedroom, where he kicked off his shoes and lay back on the mattress. His proclivity was to lie back and play a rerun of recent events through his head, transforming his experience into a kind of filmic narrative and thus gaining some perspective on it. But the very absence of Cynthia, which gave him the time and space to reflect on his situation, deflected his energy into brooding on her whereabouts. It was not long before his mood coagulated into a jealousy of activities which, so far as he knew, had no basis except in his imagination. But the power of that function has been able, throughout history, to seduce men away from the actual and into the swamps of the speculative.

He reached for the glass on the table next to the bed and noticed that his fingers were still trembling. He recalled the scene in Conrad's living room, and the wild man who had burst in, looked once at Aaron, and jumped back as though he had stepped on a snake. Aaron, the impress of the girl's kisses still on his lips, naked and smelling of sweat and saliva and vaginal secretions, had been seized by an atavistic embarrassment, and could think of nothing but getting his clothes on. The man looked like pictures of radicals he had seen in the newspaper accounts of revolutionary violence; he had, to Aaron's eyes, none of Conrad's gentleness, but seemed capable of killing without qualms. He had turned to Conrad, only to find him smiling as the girl slept with her head on his belly. He felt instantaneously excluded and left abruptly, his thoughts stampeded by panic.

'He's never been interested in me,' he said to himself as he walked down the dark street away from Conrad's house. 'He's just been trying to soften me up so he can get to Cynthia.'

Now, as he recalled the scene, the memory of what Cynthia looked like as she lay between Conrad's legs,

189

her lips wrapped around his cock, flashed in his mind and erased all the channels which led toward Aaron's spending his time in ruminations about the past forty-eight hours; he lurched into the theatre where Cynthia starred in a tour de force performance on the explication of the obscene. He saw her in a hundred positions of abandon, each following the other with the rapidity of rippling playing cards. She was surrounded by men who strained toward her, slobbering to reach her body. And in the scenario he wrote, unaware that it was his need for purgation which shaped Cynthia as the whip with which he would flog himself, she opened herself everywhere to let them in. She lay in the classic pose of lasciviousness, her legs spread wide, her knees in the air, her arms out at her side, her mouth pursed, her eyes smoldering and wanton.

'I don't know where she is,' he said to himself, switching back to the Cynthia of space and time, and not the movie star of his mind. He realised that it was the first time in years that he was not either with her or cognizant of her location. That he had not the slightest idea of how to reach her staggered him, and braced him with the awareness of how much he had come to take her for granted. 'Right now she could be on her back with someone working his way inside her,' he thought. The words danced over the tender tissues of his brain. 'On her back ... on her back ... on her back,' went the refrain, the phrase hypnotising him with its suggestion. And then the others came. 'On her knees ... on her knees ... on her knees,' and 'in her mouth ... in her mouth ... in her mouth.'

He recalled the morning and what it had been like to fuck Cynthia on acid. Ecstasy and insight vied for supremacy as the delicious sensations he found in her cunt sparked metaphysical fireworks in his mind and he found it impossible to keep his attention on the two centres at once. The result had been a mounting anger. After following him into the bedroom where he had begun to find a modicum of peace in the darkness and silence, and rousing him to fucking, she had rolled over on her stomach and let him perform over her, while she did nothing but revel in the rapture of the moving cock. The beauty of her utter vulnerability spurred him on to deeper penetrations and more excruciatingly subtle variations, which brought her cunt to life, hot and wet and responsive. He worked at her like a surgeon with a sledgehammer, operating with brutal delicacy. But by the time he came he had become so wrapt by his own virtuosity that she had ceased to exist for him except as a passive audience which did not even acknowledge the cycles of expansion and contraction which ran through the sexual act. He had left her abruptly, partly because he was angry, but also because he was disgusted by the entity which the two of them became when they fucked. Now he wondered whether that might have prompted her to vengeance, to seek another man to use as a weapon against him. There was no time at which he was able to think of her as existing in her own right, and not merely as someone whose definition came through her relation to him.

'This is crazy,' he said to himself several times, 'she'll be home any minute.' But the minutes piled upon minutes, the hands of the clock creeping toward a point where he was forced to admit that she would not be returning that night. The licentious images pulled at him, and he fought against them the way a man will struggle with the waves that roll inexorably in to obviate all his attempts to reach the shore, sap his strength, and finally drown him. Anxiety clouded his reason and kept him from asking himself the few simple questions which would have put the situation in perspective and allowed him to change his mood. Like an actor whose audience has left the theatre but who is compelled to go on with the drama, Aaron wrestled with his erotic demons until they conquered his whirlwind of baroque constructs which lacerated him with the thin whips of fantasmagoric possibilities.

191

Like a man whose nausea has begun to trigger a reflex of vomiting, Aaron attempted to suppress the upheaval. 'I ought to have learned the last time,' he thought, recalling his experience in the desert and his subsequent resolution to let nothing shake him loose from the rigidly defined parameters of his life. He longed to return to dullness and disquietude in order to be rid of the torment of enormity which engulfed a man who even momentarily discards the shields of routine and ambivalence. To take a clear step in any direction brought consequences that, like a genie from a bottle, could not be controlled once the cork had been pulled unless one knew the secret of taming it. At that moment Aaron did not, and did not want to, know how to deal with such forces.

Cynthia appeared large-screen before his eyes, the leitmotif of his lonely opera. She turned a dozen different ways at the verge of taking a man inside her, his cock tentatively nudging the cunt which had become so precious over the years, and which, although he did not note this to himself, he had begun to find tiresome. He saw her lips pucker, her forehead wrinkle, her hands flutter, as the shaft slid slowly between her legs. He heard her moan, and her arms went around his neck, her cunt swimming in the balance of the jewel motion of her hips. He watched her face change as she slid down the chute of surrender, her eyes closing, her mouth stretching wide, her expression melting to one of unutterable pleasure, and then heard the faint gentle sigh of release puff from her throat. 'Oh,' she said, half in wonder, half in affirmation, and he clenched his fists in anguish and beat them against his thighs.

He suffered scores of such scenes. At one point, lying like a catatonic wired to a pornographic computer, the multiple harmonics of all erotic probabilities sounding discordantly in his mind, he observed as she sat in a strange apartment, two men across from her, and allowed them to look as she fondled herself, building the tension until they would have to burst the bonds of restraint and hurl themselves upon her. She jiggled her breasts with her hands and rubbed her fingers over her crotch; she twitched her arse and licked her lips with her tongue. She smiled into their lust and showed them that she knew what they felt, and delighted in it, and wanted it to reach a peak of boiling frenzy before she would split herself apart at the seams of all her openings and swoon at their assault. In a word that has come to lose the voluptuous connotations impossible in an age in which women have lost contact with the glory of their sexuality, she *tempted* them.

Three hours passed in a melange of anguished variations on the single theme of Cynthia's wayward cunt, and by four in the morning he was spent. He had held vigil to Cynthia's fucking and lit candles to her orgasms; he had prayed to her infidelity and sung hymns to her lust; he had watched, down to the tiniest detail, the movements of her fingers over the anonymous buttocks that pumped into her with such glee, and he had burned with hateful envy at the thought of the pleasure the other man was feeling in finding a woman who fucked so amorously, a woman he was certain he had lost. And like a priest after a sacrifice, when he had stabbed her so often that his own agony was relieved, he turned from the altar with a sense of shame disguised as righteousness.

He stirred and looked at the clock. 'I'm supposed to be at work in a few hours,' he thought. He shook his head. The idea of standing in front of a classroom filled with children and attempting to pretend interest in their acquisition of masses of data recorded in texts that were masterpieces of oversimplification to the point of falsehood was shriekingly unreal. If Cynthia was not back by the time he had to leave, he would not be able to mask his agitation well enough to fool the sensitive evaluation of his students whose true education, beneath all the rigamarole of their programme, was to learn to read the feelings of their

193

teachers well enough to manipulate them to their own ends. He decided that he would take the rest of the week off, that more than anything he needed time unencumbered by outside demands.

His thoughts drifting toward the realm of the selfish and the pragmatic, he relaxed enough to begin to feel his great fatigue. It had been almost forty-eight hours since he slept last, and he was ready to succumb to his physical and emotional exhaustion. His eyes burned, his limbs grew numb, and a kind of fuzzy lassitude spread from his brain into his body. He reached over and flicked out the lamp, stretched once and without removing his clothing closed his eyes for sleep. But like a man in the last rushes of an amphetamine high, a core of him remained alert. It burned with a disconcerting intensity, and with a child's gesture of self-reassurance, he put his hand over his cock.

He lay in that dangerous state halfway between wakefulness and sleep, where revery and reality mixed to conjure an intimation of understanding. With his lids lowered, and in the dark, it was as though he could still see the room. Familiar and drenched with associations, it now presented itself to him without the comforting sense of spatiality between objects. He became the ceiling; he was the walls, the chair. He entered the flow of impressions and became one with them. But without the ability to articulate his psychic state, he fell prey to its contours, not understanding that consciousness is merely a reflection of phenomena and has no substance in itself. He was joyfully empty, but did not know it. Were he of a different culture he might have been quietly thankful for being blessed with the only true bliss which is man's lot on this earth: the trembling awareness of being itself. At such a time, when he ought to have been fortified with conceptual models which allow an appreciation of mystery without a flight into either mysticism or rationality, he had nothing to guide him but the rigid infantile paradigms of a low-level civilisation. He possessed

194

only a grab-bag of orthodox Catholic dogmas, pressed
into his mind by rote as a child, and the muddled social
science of entrenched imperialism. There was no way
for him to subsume his experience as it passed through
him, and he seized the most primitive mode of
expression as a means to clutch, as though it were a
lifeline, what he could salvage of the identity he felt
most directly: his male sex. Like a baby in gurgling
exploration of its genitals, he opened his trousers and
let the limp penis fall out.

For a long time there was sensation without an
accumulation of form; he fondled and manipulated his
cock simply to feel himself, to reassure himself. The
major structures of his life shaken to their foundations,
he returned to the source of life to find a base to build
upon. At that moment, the elements he had come to
depend upon, to invest with a quality of permanence,
showed themselves in their actual limitation. Only
the eternal was eternal; all of its manifestations were
provocative shapes of time, doomed to a dance of
emergence and extinction. Having been purged, willy-
nilly and without his full prior consent of his attach-
ments to his social role, his ego entanglements, and
the very woman whose energy he had come to rely
upon as a source of revivification, he was prepared
to enter the realm of raw sexuality, without images,
without cooperation from another, without any illusion
as to its nature.

His cocked stirred, thickened.

But never having been trained to flow only in its
own channels, the sexual energy, once roused, spilled
heedlessly into the other centres of his body. Most
destructively, it roared into the domain of intellect and
gave birth to a legion of images. And at that instant,
when he might have, even for a second, stepped free
of the spectrum of ideas through which he had been
habituated to perceive the universe, he slid back into
the trap of conditioned thought, and once again began
to use that distortion of the life force as his misguided

reference point from which to deal with reality. As his cock got hard the solace of fantasy oozed over the gaping insights into the actual nature of things, insights which caused him to seek refuge in oblivion.

From the recesses of his subconscious where he had feared to go, a creature of exotic qualities emerged to serve as his partner in the ritual of masturbation. It was Cynthia's body, wedded to Aaron's mind, his projection of what it might be like to have the full promiscuity of his nature living within the flesh of a woman, with what he conjectured was a woman's ability to simply walk out into the street and procure all the sexual provender she might want.

Had he been able to detach himself from the process he might, again, have learned something not ordinarily accessible. He could have used the experience to apprehend some of the secrets which male and female, each constituting one half of the secret of man-womankind, keep attempting to shout, whisper, and speak to one another across the chaos of their divisive desires. But he was swept forward by the mounting excitement in his cock, and, like many men who reduced their sexuality to the barometric variations in that organ, had his vision obscured by the shadow of his erection. That sensitivity which disdains concentration and is the quintessence of organic intelligence was crippled by the narrowing need to ejaculate. He sought to discharge the very tension he had fled to as a refuge, thus creating the rack which was to pull him apart.

As he massaged the thick base and fondled the sensitive velvet head, and progressed to a more frantic jerking of his hand up and down the shaft, he felt his body as hers. He imagined the cunt between his legs, and opened to a phantom cock. He tasted the mixture of apprehension and release with which a woman accepts penetration into her centre. He swam into physical chances which, had he seen them from outside, would have astonished him. His left arm floated through the

196

air and caressed his nipples, the fingers drumming a teasing tattoo on his chest. The hand slid between his legs and he felt the soft cleft between the buttocks. His chest swelled with yearning, and the outline of flat curved breasts pressed again his shirt. His legs were open, and shook from side to side as though wanting to rise up and clasp the waist of someone above. A shift of attitude restructured his consciousness and it was Cynthia's arse which accepted the touch, Cynthia's breasts which pointed toward the heavens. As he was she on his own bed, he was she as she might have been at that very moment, lying on another man's bed. For a split jagged second there existed six distinct permutations of the single deed: he was himself masturbating, he was himself as Cynthia masturbating, he was Cynthia being fucked by another man, he was the man fucking Cynthia, he was the man fucking him, and finally he was a point of awareness outside himself observing the entire process. His own hands caressing his own buttocks became, the hands of another man holding the weight of Cynthia's cheeks as her wide yielding cunt mouthed his cock with its wet kisses. The two cocks merged into one pole going in two directions at once through the double-ended cunt. The excitement of the concatenation of forces plunged him recklessly into a further pursual of the evolving image. He was like a consummate mime playing his complex role in stark silence, and the vivid pictures told no story except the struggle of a single confused man trying to find, amidst the proliferating uncertainty of his life, the expression in which he might find truth.

Then hoarse cries charged from his throat, his chest tightened, his thighs trembled, his pelvis thrust up and down in quick rhythmic bursts. He was approaching climax, and as he felt the sperm gathering force, a lever clicked in his mind, and as a man whose car has skidded on a wet road can do nothing but watch as it slides toward a concrete wall, he saw himself come to

197

the brink of orgasm. His cock throbbed as Cynthia's cunt sloshed in fierce metageometric configurations around the other man's cock, and by keeping all the points of the multi-levelled eruption in synchronisation, he had the three of them come at once, the unknown man discharging into the hot hairy vortex between Cynthia's legs, Cynthia shuddering with deep pulsations, and Aaron shooting an arc of sperm high into the air to land delicately for a moment in its exposure to the world outside the body, and then fall to splash in thick drops on his belly.

Congruent with his nature, as the white viscous fluid exploded from the tube designed by the ironic fingers of evolution to function precisely as a cannon to attain sufficient force to launch new life, he suffered the brunt of the recoil, sensing it as a dull sickening swoosh which breathed on his soul and caused it to shrivel. It was merely the biological dues a man pays for pleasure that has been grated onto the sexual act to insure that the species propogates itself. It was the reason why fucking is, for a balanced man, a labour of love which he undertakes only for the most exalted or most practical reasons, either to beget a child or to share his sense of the sublime with a woman who can appreciate the sacred quality of the act.

Yet Aaron knew only disappointment, for he shared his vision with a fantasy, and his seed found no warm deep niche within which to bury itself. He winced, turned his head to one side, and flung himself into sleep, to lie for a few hours of respite from his dreams.

When he awoke, Cynthia had not returned. It was eleven in the morning, and the sun threw an oblong of bright yellow across his chest. There was a brief instant in which his consciousness flourished without context, and then with sudden weight memory fell upon him and crushed him with despair. He sat up quickly to relieve the pressure, but the feeling had already sunk its barb into the emotional centre and

198

began to burn with the sour pain of a cactus thorn. Cynthia's absence was palpable, a force as powerful as her presence had ever been. In the clear light of daytime his fear retreated just past the point where he might confront it, and was replaced by a bitterness which gave him an illusion of strength. He sat at the edge of the bed and stared at the wall, his eyes not focused, and gravely admitted that Cynthia was, at that moment, in all probability looking into the eyes of another man as he made love to her. He reasoned that he might have been able to accept her night of passion and excuse it on the grounds of the turbulent emotions roused the day before, but the notion that she should wake up in a strange bed and with a calm mind give herself to another tore at all the threads of affection inside him. The jealousy which had sprung from the poignancy of loss was now laced with tips of hatred, which formed the first line of defence against pain.

He put his hand to his cheek and was surprised at feeling the bristle which had begun to look like a beard in process. With his hair uncombed, his face unshaved, his clothes rumpled and stained, he bore little resemblance to the man who had returned so confidently from work two days earlier consumed by a desire to take Cynthia in his arms. And while he could ruefully admit that the break between them had been threatening a long time and may have been for the best, he boggled at the ferocious speed and abrupt manner with which it showed itself.

He looked down and saw that his cock still hung from the open zipper, and he roused himself to change his trousers and shirt, throw some water on his face, put his shoes on, and light the first cigarette of the day. As he dressed he realised that he would not be going to work this morning either, and decided he needed the rest of the week off. He reached for the telephone, knowing he would have to lie again, that there was no way he could address the principal as a man, explain in a straightforward fashion what was happening in his life, and simply say he needed time to pull himself together. The tale of drugs, multiple sex, and association with radicals would be cause for instant dismissal; and as he dialled the number he wondered how he he would be able to integrate himself once more into that world of schedules, programmes, and superficiality. He faced the bleakness of having attempted to swing from one context to another, failed, and fallen, like Icarus in the painting by Brueghel, unobserved into the anonymous sea. That he would force himself to continue what he had difficulty in referring to as teaching was a foregone conclusion. He had seen with impressive intensity that, given his propensity for extremes, any further efforts at breaking loose from the system would hurl him quickly into the world to which Conrad had given him an introduction. Yet the thought of submerging once again into the miasma of the classroom made it difficult for him to breathe.

He was put through to the assistant principal, a black man of fifty with whom he had worked for two years, and who now seemed as distant as a telephone operator. He had painstakingly climbed up the hierarchy of the San Francisco Board of Education by steadfastly refusing to do or say anything which was not covered by one or another of the countless regulations which braced the bureaucracy like stays in a corset. Aaron recited a list of symptoms, was told they had a substitute for the week, and they hoped he felt better soon and were looking forward to seeing him again on Monday. When he hung up, the sound of the receiver hitting the cradle crashed in his ear with an unsettling finality. His alternative to going back was to put himself up for sale in the employment marketplace once more, and the mere thought of searching for a job, with its boring and humiliating ritual, made his knees weak.

At that he realised that the same was true of finding

another woman. He went into the kitchen and began to put breakfast together, gathering bacon and eggs and coffee, finding a quick spiteful glee in his freedom from the bland grain mush that Cynthia had taken to fixing in the morning, and which he, out of laziness, glumly spooned down. As the strips of pork started sizzling in the pan, he mused that there was somewhere in the world, right then, a woman that he did not know who would one day be involved with him in the deep complexities he now shared with Cynthia. The idea exhilarated him and made him tired at the same time. It amused him to imagine what she might look like, and he gave himself over to the construction of a body, shaping the parts to create an ideal type for his present mood. She materialised before him, taller than Cynthia and thinner, with smaller breasts and a narrower arse. Her mouth was more full and her eyes were green. Her cunt had an archetypal grandeur that had him smiling to himself in anticipation, and he had progressed to the first caress of her thighs when the water in the coffee pot boiled over and broke the spell.

As he turned down the flame, cracked two eggs into the sizzling bacon grease, and put two slices of bread into the toaster, the rankling voice of the super-ego called an end to the honeymoon, reminding him of the patterns of his past. He had lived with two women before Cynthia and each relationship had, with variations, been studies on the same theme: the inexorable march of personal appreciation into sexuality, and from sexuality into ruin. A new woman was merely fresh information; the structure did not change. And at a time when he was having to accept that he did not have the courage to break out into a more daring lifestyle, he was constrained to admit that there was no evidence that a marriage with another woman would turn out any better than the previous three. The lesson of his acid experience concerning the almost unassailable power of one's conditioning now showed itself in one of its concrete manifestations. The only functional models he possessed with which to think about relationships with women were lifelong monogamy and bachelor promiscuity. He had tried both and found each unsatisfactory and impossible to maintain. He wondered whether there was some way to mix the extremes of behaviour to find a comfortable middle way, but the very changes in attitude he was too timid to undertake were the only viable means to find an alternative method of dealing with the dance between the sexes.

He sat down to eat, confused but calmer. The first few mouthfuls of food entered the ambience of his inner state and radically altered it, infusing the system with a rush of energy. He felt stronger at once, and the shift of focus from his brain to his stomach took the sting from his thoughts; he began to return to an awareness of his body. The floor solid beneath his feet, the chair firm against his back, the table hard under his elbows, he gradually ceased being a creature of entanglements and became a man with presence. He straightened his spine and heard the vertebrae crack.

'I really have nothing to worry about,' he said to himself, and treated himself to a space of forgetfulness in which nothing mattered but the tastes in his mouth and the rapid revival of the trenchant tunnel vision which he habitually identified as good spirits. No sooner did the shift in psychic posture establish itself on the basis of the infusion of fuel through his mouth, than he started to mount another production on its back. Now he was the *Playboy* man, a suave sophisticate with a funky pad and esoteric sports car. Like ivy growing up a wall, a spate of fantasies twined their way up the image. Chronically incapable of accepting the unadorned reality of his condition without dressing it in some costume from the rack of unfulfilled wishes, he toyed with pictures of himself speeding along the shore highway, a well-groomed woman running her fingers through his hair and imploring him with her eyes to make a savage spontaneous love to her. Unconsciously he flexed the muscles in his arms.

The sharp unexpected ring of the telephone caused a startled reflex which spun his head halfway around. With that strange conviction which often makes a person more certain of his hunch than is justified by any law of probability, he knew it was Cynthia. He sat immobile, as though she could detect any movement in the house while her electronic summons probed its rooms. The rings continued, and he counted as they assailed his attention. Eight, nine, ten, eleven, and then silence. All the while he held at bay the entire world of confrontation which awaited him when he would see Cynthia again. He did not want that moment to be just then, and he would not have been able to answer, if he asked himself, whether he would have preferred Cynthia's message to be that she was never returning, or that she had innocently spent the night with a girl friend and was on her way home to his arms. He had temporarily sealed off access to the stormy submarine world of their relationship, and while he might later want to dive into it once more, at that moment he wished to maintain an aloofness from its complications, a distance in which to take an unhampered breath.

He decided to spend the day away from the house, to seek strength through removal from what seemed like the web to which the spider might return at any moment. He did not think of her as evil, having had his more terrible emotions burned away during the night; she was simply a force he did not want to deal with for a while. Leaving the dishes on the table, he put his money and keys in his pocket and left through the back door, cutting through the yard, and coming out on the next street over. It was another cloudless day and the air sang with vitality.

Aaron had a deep love of walking. His happiest days had been during boot camp in the service when his company was taken for twenty and thirty-mile hikes.

There was something about the rhythm of moving forward at a good pace, the easy swing of the shoulders, and the regular deep breathing it brought about, that pacified his spirit and brought his body to life. It was one of the few times he felt free, for the primal simplicity of the exercise washed his mind, and his penchant for introspective rumination was dispersed. Watching the curves of the land change, passing by trees and rivers and hills, sensing the spaciousness of the sky and the gravity of the earth, he attained a joy which no other activity gave him.

He walked with no goal in mind, changing directions at a whim, zigzagging through the streets of the town, absorbing the changes in tempo and texture from section to section. He climbed to Arlington, followed its tree-lined ascent to the edge of Berkeley and into Kensington, and then doubled back to hike as far as the Rose Garden where he breathed in the sweet perfume of its flowers and gazed out onto the panoramic view of the bay. From there he descended once more to the plain, thinking of how beautiful the land must have been when only the Indians lived there, before the imposition of concrete and steel and industrial fumes and great ugly bridges. It had been quite a while since he had enjoyed such a solitary meander, and he wondered whether the nature of his job, with its restrictions on mobility, was not essentially harmful to his well-being.

By the time he had reached the outskirts of the business section, a pleasant physical fatigue had made his legs heavy. It was a healthy contrast to the exhaustion which came from struggling with his thoughts and emotions. As he paused at a street corner to wait for a light, his eye fell upon that advertised massage. It hung over a storefront window which was covered by heavy curtains, giving it the air of a gypsy fortune-telling place. The thought of a shower, a steam bath, and a rubdown exerted a strong appeal. He felt tired and grimy, and in need of an actual and symbolic cleansing. He had never been in a massage parlour before, and the novelty of the idea tipped the balance in its favour. He was somewhat apprehensive, but he crossed the street and went inside.

The first quality he perceived was its dimness. He stepped into a long narrow waiting room painted institution green, with a worn carpet on the floor. Along one wall sat four young women in a row, like hostesses at a dance hall. In unison they turned their heads to stare at him as he entered, and he walked the gauntlet of their eyes to a desk at the far end, the domain of a fifth woman, noticeably older than the rest, who managed to make her automatic smile seem personal.

'Can we help you, sir?' she said.

'I'd like a massage,' he told her, and his words struck an incongruous note in the thick atmosphere. He shifted his weight to one foot. 'How much is it?' he asked.

'We charge twelve-fifty for a one hour massage,' she rattled off, 'and that includes the use of the shower.'

'Do you have a steam room?' he went on, sensing some undercurrent which he could not yet define.

The woman smiled again, and this time her lips held the slightest trace of humour. 'I'm afraid we're not that well-equipped,' she said. She paused a moment. 'Would you like to go in now?' she added.

Aaron nodded, and the woman looked past him to the line of girls. 'Who's next?' she asked.

Aaron turned to see a thin grey girl of about twenty-two stand up. Her attitude had the same stolid air of defeat as the woman in *The Absinthe Drinkers*. She seemed monumentally weary, and he wondered whether she would even have the strength to rub his body for an hour. She came up to him, smiled without looking into his face, and shuffled past through a curtain to the left of the desk. She stopped and looked back. 'This way,' she said.

On the other side was a hallway with four doors on either side of it, spaced several feet apart. She took the first one on the left. 'The shower is down the end of the hall,' she told him, 'and then come back here.' It was only when he turned from her and started for the back that he realised that the place was a whore-house, and the insight shocked him. He was sophisticated enough to assimilate the data instantaneously without tripping over it, but he trembled a little from the impact of finding the activity right off a main street in the middle-class section of Berkeley. Had he gone at six in the evening he would have found businessmen just returned from their offices stopping in before going back to their wives.

In the tiny shower room he took off his clothes, and undressing in that place aroused him in a way that reminded him of his teen-age. There was something smutty and forbidden about it which took him back to damp gropings in the back seats of cars. He relished the element of naughtiness, as proper to sex as seasoning is to food, which had almost been rubbed out by the pornographers on one hand, with their crude hyperboles, and the sex-hygienists on the other, with their claims that sex was as wholesome as brushing one's teeth.

He soaped himself three times, making sure that all his crevices were clean. He did not know exactly what sort of activity would be offered and he felt a certain shyness about presenting his body to a strange woman, lying under her while she explored him with her hands and eyes. He reflected that he rarely took as many pains when fucking Cynthia, and it occurred to him that it was the lack of a certain level of care, such as professionals insist upon, which often took the fine edge off the sex life of the lay amateurs.

He dried himself and padded out into the corridor, his clothes in a bundle under his arm, and went into the room where the girl waited. It was a cubicle about seven by nine feet, as big as a prison cell, with a massage table in the middle and a smaller table in one corner, holding an array of oils, lotions, powders, and electric appliances. He dropped his clothes on the chair by the door and turned to the girl. 'Should I leave the towel on or take it off?' he asked.

'Any way you like,' she told him.

She wore a skirt that fell to her ankles and a white short-sleeved blouse. Her dark brown hair, lacklustre and without body, was pulled behind her head and hung in a ponytail halfway down her back. The sallow face and eyes which always glanced off at an angle from the direction her nose pointed suggested a pernicious illness, a massive vitamin deficiency which had affected her soul. He unhooked the towel and held it out to her, and when she took it her attitude seemed to cry out for violation. She was the kind of woman who infects men with the itch to strangle.

He lay down on the table and looked up at an unfinished plywood ceiling. 'Do you want oil or powder?' she said. 'Whichever is easier for you to work with,' he answered. She reached for a bottle of yellow fluid. 'The powder makes me sneeze,' she said, an apologetic tone in her voice.

Aaron closed his eyes and waited. He was slightly tense from anticipation, wondering how the offer of sex would be made, and whether he should do or say anything to initiate the contact. She poured the oil on his chest, letting it trickle between his nipples and down to his navel, put the bottle down, and with both hands spread it over his entire torso. She stood to the side of the table and leaned over, bringing her hands up from his belly in a straight line to his throat, increasing the pressure as she reached the pectoral muscles, and then moved down again, tracing a line to his hips, stopping, and coming to rest on his belly. She made a dozen passes, and with each one seemed about to touch his nipples or descend into his pubic hair, but she always missed, always came close. Aaron speculated that he was being teased and found himself straining his body so that her hands would go where

207

he wanted them to, producing a tension which defeated any benefit the massage might have had.

She changed rhythm and on the next upward swing dug her fingers into his shoulders, finding and attacking a knot of concentration that was painful to the touch. He shuddered with relief as she worked the tightness out of the muscles and tried to relax under her ministrations. He saw that the greatest benefit and pleasure lay in passivity, but that was a state he had difficulty attaining. The erotic portrait of himself lying naked under a woman who, for a time, was bonded to service him, did not allow his accepting the simple reality of her touch on his skin. In the same way that a person will look at an abstract painting and ask what it *means*, Aaron was unable to accept a caress without leaping to ask where it would lead.

'My name's Charlotte what's yours?' she said all in a single phrase.

Her voice startled him; hearing the mundane ritual of introduction under such extraordinary circumstances made him smile. For, after discounting the fact that the establishment of a business context gave their current tableau a socially acceptable rationalisation, it was somewhat bizarre to reach a point of nudity before exchanging names. He opened his eyes and looked up at her. Under the stimulation of her hands his perception of her changed. In the way that a piece of bread will hold value in direct proportion to the hunger of the person holding it, so a woman will manifest beauty in exact measure to the degree of a man's desire for her. What had been a thin mouth was seen as sensitive lips; and what had been a distraction in her eyes came to appear as a demure look.

'My name is Aaron,' he said.

She nodded, as though he had given her the answer to a question which had troubled her for years. He was taken by a curiosity about her, and like many men before him had the fleeting notion of asking her to go to his place later. But at that, the thought of Cynthia intruded and the situation he had gone there to forget slipped into the room. Charlotte picked up the bottle again and poured oil on his right leg, tracing a thin line from his toes to the top of his thigh, and then rubbed it over the surface with a circular motion, sliding up from his ankle to his knee and stopping short at his crotch. He kept looking at her and wondered what he would feel like if she were Cynthia, giving massages to strangers, looking at a succession of cocks, stroking body after body. It was the only handle he had with which to grasp the woman in any human aspect. Only an analogy with someone he knew could let him see her as anything but a machine geared for anonymous intimacy.

As she moved her hands up his leg she came to within a fraction of an inch of his cock, slid away and then back again, almost touching it but stopping short. He had to exert his will to keep from rolling on his side, pushing his cock toward her. Unschooled in the joys of being teased, and increasingly uncertain as to whether his initial insight into the nature of the place was correct, he began to compound his frustration into greater tension. He sought the release of having his body soar up and into her, to feel his hands on her flesh, grabbing her arms, and forcing the tantalising fingers to hold his cock. It was grandiloquent testimony to the power of the sexual drive that after thousands upon thousands of fucks in his lifetime, after two nights of multiple scenes, and just a few hours after masturbating, going into a place to treat himself to an hour of relaxation and refreshment, he was once again working himself up to a pitch of excitement in his struggle to have his genital organ fondled.

What made the situation, from a standpoint of sanity, somewhat more bizarre, was that the woman had no desire for him; she was merely available. There are certain times when a woman wants a fucking, and she will transmit that request on a board beam to all men in the area through a system of vibrations, clues and overtures. It is only dull male pride that leads a man to think there is something in himself which calls forth the woman's passion. The stud with the correct chemical composition will be drawn to the rutting female and they will couple for a given period. It has nothing to do with the so-called civilised aspects of behaviour, and the talk, contracts, and social rituals are rationalisations to make the animal truth of the matter palatable to weak sensibilities. The deep grooves of acculturation have all but wiped out the indifferent manifesto of the biological summons, and consideration of property and propriety have come to assume more importance than questions of humanity.

But this woman had no interest in being fucked, and Aaron's sudden stirring underscored the basic nature of male sexuality. A man may be walking by a wooden fence and be told that on the other side of a knothole a woman, any woman, has snuggled her cunt or her mouth or her arse against the opening, and will, unless his conditioned inhibitions restrict him, glibly stick his cock into the waiting receptacle. To the degree that he has refined his libidinal urge he will construct a hierarchy of qualities concerning precisely what he prefers to be placed behind the fence, but that reflects a change only in the superstructure of his essential character.

As Charlotte's kneading his muscles released energy in his body the way pumping a handle will raise the level of water in the pipe, he translated the accumulation of feeling into a preparation for the action which seemed called for by the milieu. The more she massaged him to ease him into a state where he would appreciate the sexual favour she would, for a price, offer him, the more tight he became. She was aware of what was happening, but not interested; it seemed odd to her that he was unable to relax, but her purpose in being there was to make money to live on, not to solve the psychological problems of the men she dealt with.

210

She oiled his left leg and repeated the pattern, but with a difference. For his cock had been inclined to the left, and when she moved her hand to the top of his thigh, it brushed against the tip of it. The touch was casual and momentary, but to Aaron it was electrifying, like sliding against a woman's arse in a packed bus when she is wearing only a cotton dress and brief panties underneath. But Charlotte's mood did not change; she worked with the same dispassion, the same lack of personality. She swept her fingers against his cock a number of times and it began to grow hard, like a lizard waking up. It was a peculiar feeling to have his erection flourish for a woman who remained coldly uninvolved with his reactions, but he did not balk at such niceties. He ignored the touch of her hand over his entire leg, and only waited for the brief instant when it would approach his centre. Like a psychologist who has learned the superiority of sporadic reinforcement, she found his arousal increasing if she did not touch his cock at every pass. He tightened his sphincter, forcing the penis to swell with blood. He held his breath, waiting for her hand to seize the shaft and relieve him of the accumulating tension. And just when he was sure he could take no more, she abruptly stepped back and said, 'All right. Roll over on your stomach.'

The instruction was like cold water thrown on two dogs stuck in a genital spasm. He went into instant shock and his erection shrivelled. He was like a fire hose from which the water had suddenly been cut off, and he collapsed in upon himself. He obeyed her heavily, reversing his position on the table as she turned her back to him and busied herself with her equipment. He saw her setting an electric timer.

From his new vantage point, he lost the sense of thrust which had propelled him toward her, and was forced to yield total initiative into her hands. It relieved him of responsibility and for the first time since lying down he was able to let himself go a bit and relate to the purpose for which he had come in the first place: to enjoy a massage. He adjusted his bulk and settled into the thin mattress. He took a deep breath as he felt the oil hit his spine.

'You have a nice back,' she said. 'Do you exercise a lot?'

'I used to,' he told her.

She smoothed the balm over his skin and worked silently for a few moments. Aaron felt a pleasant calm enter his being, and the level at which he related to the woman changed.

'Have you been doing this long?' he asked her.

'A few months,' she said. 'The woman who owns the place taught me how to massage.'

'And you make a living at it?' he went on.

'I guess,' she answered. 'I only get paid for what I do, and if nobody comes in I just sit there, sometimes for four or five hours, and don't get a penny.' She rubbed his neck. 'I'm too lazy to work,' she added. 'I guess this is the next best thing.'

Now that he was temporarily forced to forego the possibility of sexual contact he could appreciate the second half of the rubdown. He felt her warm hands across his skin, following the contours of his bones and muscles, giving him the essence of what love is: the healing massage. He abandoned his thoughts and succumbed to her rhythms as she chased the tiredness from his body, stimulating his circulation, giving him a sense of solidity by acting as the living limitation to his physical boundaries. Her movement was like a dance which he saw with his nerve endings, and he sighed repeatedly as she worked up and down the length of him, across the flat planes between his shoulder blades, into the fleshy buttocks, and down the muscled calves. It occurred to him as he lapsed into sweet ease that he was receiving more concentrated physical attention from this sad stranger than he had received from Cynthia in a year. He wondered idly why it was that people who begin to fuck one another

212

end by not touching each other except to achieve a sexual response. 'What a great treasure we sacrifice for that limited genital stimulation,' he thought, but he did not pursue the idea as the sensations on his back claimed all his attention.

Charlotte rubbed the fatigue from his shoulders, from his feet. Her fingers found the tensions in his neck and sent them scurrying. She pulled his toes and tickled his soles. He drank in the luxury of the treatment and flashed a montage in which he was dressed successively as an oil-rich diamond-heavy pasha of the middle east, an Indian nabob, and a Chinese mandarin, in each instance surrounded by young girls abasing themselves before him, licking his body with their avid tongues.

He heard a click, and Charlotte took her hands away. The massage was over. She stepped back and returned to her supply table. Aaron lay still for a moment, having barely begun to open up to the process, and then stretched once and rolled to his side. She turned around and looked at him. A thin wall hung between them and there was a thick silence in the room.

'Do you want a local?' she said at last.

'A local?' he said.

'Down there,' she said, flickering her eyes at his cock.

'*Down there*,' he thought, and in a phrase it was all summed up for him. The terminology, used to dodge possible police intrusion by referring to a hand-job as a local and to his cock as 'down there', placed the sexual act in a framework of absolute sterility. Aaron shook his head. 'What did I expect?' he said to himself. 'Passion?' He looked up.

'Sure,' he said.

'It's ten dollars extra,' she told him.

'Twelve-fifty for the entire body, and ten dollars just for the cock,' he said. 'That seems disproportionate.'

'That's what it costs,' she continued.

213

He lay on his back, spread his legs, and put his hands under his head. 'It's all yours,' he said.

She walked to the edge of the table and without looking down took the limp cock in her hand, letting it rest on her palm. She brought her other hand over it and began to stroke the top of the shaft, as a little girl will pet a kitten. Her face showed no expression and her body was erect; she looked like a factory worker at an assembly line, making small adjustments in a piece of fine machinery. It was the minimal sexual act possible, the sheer manipulation of the organ until it reached a state of tumescence and an excitatory level triggered the ejaculation response. His cock did not get hard.

'If you don't enjoy it, I don't think anything is going to happen,' he said.

She looked at him as though he were mad. 'I don't have anything to do with it,' she said. 'You're the one who's paying for it. *You're* supposed to like it.'

'Doesn't it give you any pleasure at all?' he asked.

'It's all the same,' she told him. She gently squeezed her right hand and coaxed some energy into the cock. It responded quietly and bulged slightly in her fingers.

'Do you ever do this when you don't get paid for it?' he said. 'Do you have a boyfriend?'

'I had a boyfriend,' she replied. 'He got killed in the Army. And then I went out with a lot of guys and got pregnant, and I got an abortion. And then I worked for a movie theatre, but the place got held up twice and I got scared and quit. And then somebody told me about this. And it's all right. Some guys take me out and buy me things.'

'And do you sleep with them?'

She shrugged. 'They always want me to, and I don't mind. Some of them want me to tell them what I do with other men while they're fucking me.'

Her laconic recital excited Aaron more than the stimulation she conferred on him. He felt his excitement return.

214

'I'll give you five dollars extra if you'll suck it,' he said. 'Do you like to suck cock?'

Incongruously she looked over her shoulder. 'We're not supposed to do that,' she said.

He reached up and slipped his hand up her leg to her arse. The thin hard buttocks contracted but she did not move away. He stretched his arm and pushed his fingers into the crack between her buttocks. 'Suck it,' he whispered.

She bent over at the waist like a performer taking a bow, allowing his hand to plunge between her thighs and lodge at her cunt, which offered no clear delineations through the cloth. She held his cock between the second and third finger, as though it were a cigarette, and took it between her lips with a single swoop, pulling it inside her mouth with her breath. But it was not, somehow, what he wanted. She remained cool and detached, as though cocksucking were no more extraordinary than eating a plate of spaghetti, and he found that the raw sensation, in and of itself, was not enough to rouse his lust. She sucked the limp penis with the *sang-froid* of a child sucking its thumb, and he strained to elicit some special response from her.

'Take off your skirt,' he said.

She turned her head, the cock still between her lips, and looked at him with opaque eyes. 'I want to see your cunt,' he said.

She straightened up slowly, and brought her hands to her waist. 'We can't make any noise,' she said, 'they'll fire me if they find out.'

'Come on,' he urged, 'it will be all right.'

She untied the cord and dropped the skirt to the floor, exposing almost shapeless legs which rose to a pair of white panties imprinted with red and violet floral patterns, of the type sold on market stalls. He watched intently as she peeled them from her pelvis, snaked them down to her knees, and stepped out of the elastic top. A tuft of coarse hair sprung loose from its constriction, a thick deep bush which did not go with the rest of her body. His hand shot out and slid between her thighs, one finger immediately working to worm inside her cunt.

She leaned over again, and with the same clinical air, pulled the skin of his cock back with one hand, exposing the head more fully, and swept the thing into her mouth with a swish of her tongue. He lay back and let her work as he attempted to prod her into a flurry of excitement by rotating his finger inside the lips; her cunt remained dry. They went at each other for a few minutes, her head bobbing up and down and his hand wriggling, like two craftsmen attempting to shape intractable material.

She tried every trick she knew: biting the base of the cock firmly as she licked its head with her tongue, letting it lie in her mouth and coaxing it with her breath, sucking it so hard that it stretched an inch through sheer elasticity, and swinging her head from side to side so the cock hit against the insides of her cheeks. His finger wiggling inside her was faintly unpleasant, like having sand in one's shoe, but she was willing to tolerate more than that to successfully complete the act. She knew that if he did not come he would not pay, and there was no way to extract more than the price of a massage from him without his calling the police.

Aaron approached mild desperation. He had come in for a massage and been led to expect sex; then given a massage until he no longer thought of sex; and then been offered sex in such a way that he could not enjoy it. It was rattling him to have this woman calmly accede to his demands, let him use her cunt, and suck his cock with all the motions, but none of the emotions, of abandon, and withal show no more interest in him than if he were selling her a pint of milk. Finally he felt her remove her mouth; her lips were wet and her cheeks were flushed, but that only served to accentuate her noninvolvement, the way that rouge merely highlights the lifelessness of a corpse.

'What's the matter?' she said.

'I can't come this way,' he said.

'Do you want to fuck me?' she asked.

As an answer he swung his legs to the floor. 'You lie on the table,' he told her.

She glanced at the door behind her. 'We can't make any noise,' she reminded him, and then crawled onto the table. 'How shall I get?' she said.

'Lie on your back,' he said.

She stretched out, her arms at her side, her eyes fixed on his. 'Put your finger in your cunt and start rubbing it,' he said.

She opened her legs slightly and brought her right hand to the patch of hair. She bent her index finger and slid it neatly between the outer lips and into the centre. He jerked his head up as a signal for her to begin, and she dutifully started the motions of masturbation, sliding her finger in and out of the hole. He watched her for a moment and then climbed back on the table, moved over her until his knees were at her armpits.

'Open your mouth,' he said.

Her lips parted until they formed an oval.

'Wider,' he told her.

They kept stretching until her mouth made a perfect O.

'Put out your tongue,' he instructed, 'and start licking.'

Then, as she lay under him, her hand stroking her cunt, her mouth pulled wide and her tongue lapping the air, like a mannikin wound up and enacting the gestures of sex, he took his cock in his hand and began to pull it.

'Keep your eyes closed,' he said, as he stared down at her face. She obeyed him, and with that his cock started to get stiff. He tightened his buttocks, hunched his shoulders, and bent forward. His left arm came down and he leaned on it for support. He jerked the cock frantically, with small rapid motions, keeping his hand close to the tip so that the head would receive constant stimulation.

'I'm going to come in your mouth,' he hissed. 'And you're going to swallow it all.'

Charlotte seemed unconcerned, and continued to act out the part he had written for her. He felt a flash of anger and if they were not behind a partition of a massage parlour, would have slapped her. He had no thoughts in his mind and made no connection between what he was doing and what had happened with Cynthia, nor with his deeper feelings about women in general. Having gone through life operating at the surface of his attitudes, he had never contacted the rage which roars beneath the ingrained reflexes of politeness, and thus had no idea of the tender human feelings that lie beneath the layer of destructive impulses. By pretending affection, he denied hatred, and deprived himself of true caring for others. He had always stopped when his journey into himself brought him to the gates of violence and fear, and so never discovered the realm of love that lay beyond. By adhering blindly to his normality, he became dangerous; and if the setting had permitted he would have responded to the complementary dynamics in Charlotte. Having neither the genetic nor environmental advantages which had been Aaron's portion in life, she did not even have plump respectability to hold on to; her only shield against the dark forces inside her was the vapid existence of an unhealthy uneducated girl from a family of migrant fruit pickers who had come from the midwest in the thirties and been trapped in a poverty made more bitter by its contrast with the lush land whose produce they packaged, and the affluent lives of the people who held pieces of paper with which they claimed ownership of that land. In the place where Aaron found a need to destroy, she nursed an unconscious desire to be killed. And were they on a deserted beach late at night, playing out the drama they now enacted just ten feet away from the sunlit bustling streets of Berkeley where people exactly like themselves walked about in patterns of conformity, he would have ended by smashing her face until it was bloody and then choking the life from her body.

As it was he had to compress all his fury and frustration into the restrained silent thrashing of his fist curled around his cock.

'God, I wish you hated this,' he said, wanting desperately for her to feel defiled so that his act could have meaning for him. He narrowed his eyes so that she was blurred in his vision, and he could blot out the fact that she went on mechanically. He made himself believe what he needed to believe, that she was torn apart between the forces of desire and revulsion. And when he had perfected the image in his mind, the sperm spurted out onto her face, splashing on her cheek, on her lips, onto the curling tongue, and down into her mouth.

Complying with his directions, she licked the spunk from her face, closed her mouth, and swallowed it. Then, as though a switch had been thrown, the finger in her cunt stopped moving and she opened her eyes. She looked up at him and to his intense amazement, she smiled warmly.

'I'm glad you came,' she said. 'It made me feel bad to see how much trouble you were having.'

Aaron slid back, climbing off the table, and stood next to her. Disgust with himself began to well up in his chest. She sat up and put a hand on his arm.

'Are you all right?' she asked.

He shook his head. 'Oh,' he said, 'sure, I'm fine.' Her concern disconcerted him. 'Thanks,' he added. 'That was beautiful. I've never done that before.'

She leaned forward conspiratorially. 'A guy once paid me twenty-five dollars to pee in his mouth,' she said. A flicker of amusement shot across her eyes. 'I felt funny doing it, but it was easy money.'

Like a man fighting nausea, he beat back his feelings of depression. The few hours of relief he had been

219

feeling since eating breakfast had fortified him, and he struggled against slipping back into the sense of emptiness, of being lost.

Charlotte slid off the table and dressed methodically, carefully slipping her panties on and pulling her skirt up to her waist. Aaron went to the chair where his clothes lay, and put them on slowly. He wanted to stay a few more minutes.

'You have to give me the fifteen dollars and pay the twelve-fifty at the desk,' Charlotte said.

He pulled the bills from his pocket and gave them to her. She held them in her hand and looked at him questioningly. Abruptly he stepped forward, put his arms around her waist, drew her to him, and kissed her on the mouth. She did not move away, but did not respond, and after a moment he stepped back once more. His eyes burned into hers.

'If you want to see me after work,' she said, 'I can meet you someplace.'

And with her words a terrible prophetic truth appeared to him: the women would always be different, but the moment would always be the same, and he saw himself going through the years seeking in their arms an end to the pain with which their eternal otherness pierced his heart.

'I don't think I can,' he said, 'I have a girl friend I live with.'

Charlotte tilted her head forward. 'Most of the men who come here do,' she said.

'Well, good bye,' he said, the formality sounding grotesque after the scene they had just shared.

'Come back again,' she said, but her voice had already begun to fade into a monotone of impersonality. He watched as the stranger before his eyes once again donned the mask of a stranger, saw that the few moments were over, paid for.

He turned slowly away and began to go through the door. He looked back and saw her stripping the wrinkled oil-stained sheet from the table, and as he spun around to leave almost bumped into another girl who was leading another man to one of the other tiny rooms down the narrow hallway.

9

Klein Worms

'Each human being has a single folly, a characteristic preoccupation which defines that person's refusal to relinquish the reins of desire,' said Clive, tossing his head so that his mane of hair shimmered around his head. 'Unfortunately for the history of our species, most of us rarely choose a harmless hobby to indulge in, but get caught up in pursuit of one of the classic vices, dedicating ourselves to the attainment of wealth or fame or knowledge or sanctity. In our generation, the fashion is the accumulation of experience, some seeking variety, others tending towards intensity. The problem, from a psycho-economic point of view, is that folly is the primary shield we possess to protect ourselves from truth, which demands effort, and an ability to sustain a fair amount of terror. If the choice is between some socially sanctioned form of foolishness and a silent inner eye fixed on the nature of reality, there are few who would decide for the latter.'

Clive put his palms and fingertips together, before his chest, as though in an attitude of prayer, and closed his eyes for a few seconds. When he looked up again he was staring into Cynthia's gaze. 'When I was younger,' he went on, 'my folly was a passion for women, in all their guises, and in themselves. I worshipped women with such consummate single-mindedness that I equalled any monk in my ability to discipline myself towards reaching some goal. For me, all creation served merely as the backdrop and stage which enhanced and surrounded the beauty of the beloved. I swooned with all the earnest affection of a swain in a Shelley poem. I would often spend an entire day gazing upon a photograph and fondling a lock of her hair in my fingers, counting each second before I would see her again and be able to lavish my attention on her once more.' He picked up the long-stemmed glass on the low table in front of him, swirled the martini around three times, and downed the remainder of the drink in a single gulp. 'Until I had imbued her with such unearthly perfection that she glowed with celestial virtue and became the purest of all things to ever have existed in this universe. I beheld her with such exalted vision that her every breath assumed meaning, for each moment that she remained alive was an occasion for one more prayer of intense thanksgiving. And to the inexperienced, I was irresistible. And it was, of course, only the naive woman who interested me, for only she had not yet learned to guard her vulnerability.'

Cynthia sipped her coffee. She had not yet fully recovered from the shock of walking into Jackie's living room and finding a man standing there, leaning against the window at such an angle that it seemed he was about to fall. He was talking when she entered, and had not stopped once during all the time she was with him. Well over six feet tall, with gold-glinted auburn hair cascading over his shoulders and down his back, wearing tight violet velour trouser and a black leather vest open down the front, his face was like that of Botticelli hermaphrodite, and there was the faintest hue of silver lipstick on his mouth and a delicately applied blue shadow over his eyelids.

She had awakened three quarters of an hour earlier to find only Maureen lying next to her, already awake, stroking her belly. Before she had time to open her eyes completely, the dark woman slid to her and half-covered her body with her arm and leg. Cynthia's first conscious moment was the sight of Maureen's smouldering eyes pressing into hers, so that as her waking ego coalesced to begin another day, it was imprinted with the urgency of Maureen's desire. She had no time to think before she found herself in a deep embrace, the thin curved lips nestling into her own. When she took a breath, the air came from Maureen's lungs.

Without saying a word, Maureen lay on top of her, her legs together, her hands tight in Cynthia's hair, pulling it back so that her face lost the defence of its features and became the raw mask of the person she was. Maureen looked at her a long, long time, seeming to read some tremulous message in her skin. She sighed and kissed Cynthia again and again, stopping after each score of kisses to pull back and gaze at her again in that poignant way which made her appear so sad. Her mouth was never the same twice; it always presented a different texture, a new mode of expression. Cynthia gave way under the prolonged continuous assault upon her lips and tongue. Maureen's body was hot with urgency and calm with patience, and Cynthia could do no more than offer the ever-opening gift of her mouth to the exquisite demands of Maureen's virtuosity.

Then, as naturally as a seed bursting open and pushing its way into the light, Cynthia was called to the moist dark centre between Maureen's thighs. An unmistakable pressure urged her to go down; like a hand inside her chest, heavy and ineluctable, the force seized her will. It did not come from the other woman, but from within herself. It was an impulse that demanded recognition. She slipped her hand down Maureen's back, over the protruding vertebrae of her spine, and onto the thin buttocks. Her breath came in ragged gasps and her sight blurred. She clamped her fingers into Maureen's muscles and began to pull herself down along the length of her body, and as she crumbled in a chaos of feelings, Maureen's mouth closed on hers one more time and sucked the vulnerability from her lips.

'Oh God,' Cynthia whispered as she tore her mouth loose.

'But having effected this transmogrification in my perception of the woman to the point where she transcended all imperfection, I then proceeded to ravish her, methodically and with precision, burning in her the flames of my rage to defile the beauty I had come to adore: I used my cock and hands and teeth to arouse the beast in the breast of the angel I had created.' Clive drew a Gitanes from the pack in the inside pocket of his vest and lit it with a wooden match. He had the assurance of the experienced story-teller who is able to do a bit of stage business knowing that the audience will hold its attention on him, waiting for him to begin again. 'I did not rest until I had brought the two elements of her essential nature to fullest flower at the same time,' he said through a cloud of smoke, 'so that I might know the ecstasy of holding both ideal form and formless energy in my arms at one moment, all in the person of a single enraptured woman, and then watch as her tender heart and delicate mind swooned before the voracious animality of the body which contained them.' He frowned and stared into the space in front of him. 'But each time, and there were dozen of times, that I attained my goal, I found that the woman was of no further interest to me. And like an artist who has finished a work and is anxious to proceed to his next project, I put her behind me.' He nodded at Jackie. 'It was my dear sister who finally forced me to see that the material I was using was the souls of other human beings.'

Cynthia nestled more deeply into the couch. Jackie's arm was over her shoulders, and her hand was idly stroking Cynthia's breast. Cynthia crossed her legs and felt her cunt quicken each time Jackie touched her nipple. She still found it somewhat strange to be sitting naked in front of a man she didn't know while the woman at her side fondled her body. But it was pleasant to have conversation and physical stimulation at the same time, without the currents of one impeding the flow of the other. It was one more entry to be filed in the notebook of events she was keeping in her mind. She thought again of what had happened after waking up. When she had started her rocking ride down the contours of Maureen's body, she had seen with brutal clarity the desire which drove her was indistinguishable from the same feeling which, so often in the past, had sent her slithering to Aaron's cock. The insight surprised her, and opened an understanding into the difference between the wellspring of her own sexual drive and the object it cathected to. The question of promiscuity, ordinarily a fairly theoretical concern, flashed in her mind with an uncanny vividness, and she saw at a glance how it would be possible to sever all connections between what she was feeling sexually and the person who gave rise to those feelings.

Maureen, sensing the purpose in Cynthia's movements, fell back, closed her eyes, and let herself go slack. In a single complex gesture, Cynthia licked and kissed Maureen's mouth, chin, throat, breasts, and belly as she worked her way down the long twitching body. Her mouth was a succession of leeches and wasps-under-glass, leaving sizzling rashes as it leapfrogged and lapped the dark rich flesh. The sound which came from her was a mournful wail that dipped into a whimper and exploded into a shout of primeval yearning. She drew a breath and lowered herself to Maureen's cunt, gaping at its presence. The outer lips of the hole flared like nostrils on a rearing horse, the middle fold gaped in throbbing openness. The cunt was black and dark purple throughout the entire shell, with the opening at the core like a blood-red pearl. It seethed like a dragon facing battle.

'Oh yes,' Cynthia said, and brought her trembling mouth to the glandular orifice, sucked the cunt between her lips, and slid her tongue into its pulsing centre.

'Oh Cynthia,' Maureen moaned as her hands went to the top of Cynthia's head as though in benediction. 'My sweet Cynthia, my darling Cynthia, Cynthia my dearest love,' she crooned.

Later they had lain locked in one another's legs, their cunts kissing, and done nothing but feel the heat flowing from hole to hole, bathing in the emanations from one another's body. They held their eyes steady as their mouths fluttered with flickering smiles. 'This isn't how I planned to start this day,' Cynthia said, her first connected sentence of the morning gliding flatly out on the space between them.

'What is your plan?' Maureen said, imitating a Hungarian accent.

'I've got to get back,' Cynthia told her.

Maureen disengaged and rolled off the bed. 'Why don't we talk about that after breakfast?' she said, and left for the back yard, to do her morning yoga, parting from Cynthia with a shower of kisses and caresses. Cynthia lay back and stretched, relishing the delicious tingling of her muscles as she prepared to get out of bed. And as she sat up, the first thought to come to her mind was Aaron.

He appeared to her the way dead people appear to the living in dreams, with frightening intensity and sharpness, but disconnected from any relationship with immediate external reality. She could see him in her mind, but could not feel him with her body, all sense-memory of him having temporarily vanished. He was a presence she could not avoid, but neither could she relate to him. She wondered what he was doing and whether she should try to reach him. There was nothing special she needed to say at that moment; her reaching out was for reassurance. Without judging her action she picked up the phone and called his school. When they told her he wouldn't be in for the rest of the week, she felt a pang of worry, and called their apartment. The phone rang eleven times, and she had the peculiar intuition that he was in the house but not

227

answering the phone in order to punish her. She knew him well enough to realise that he was almost certainly steeped in a swell of jealousy, and she wondered what she would tell him of the night's activities. She smiled to herself when she saw that to tell him the truth, that she had spent the evening with two girl friends, would halt his flow of suspicion. She doubted that even Aaron's imagination stretched to the point where he appreciated the fact that women could be an even stronger temptation for a woman living with a man than other men might be. His pride would not allow accepting a woman as a sexual rival.

'Maybe he's with Conrad,' she said to herself as she hung up the phone. The thought cheered her. She saw the young man not only as a possible sexual partner, but as a friend, someone she could confide in. She knew with absolute certainty that she would tell all of her adventures to Conrad, and enjoy his responses and listen to his advice. And upon that, she also admitted to herself that she would fuck with him. It was clear that, although it contradicted her image of herself, if she and Aaron split up, she would not spend a long period of time in tearful loneliness, but would call Conrad immediately and have him take care of her. She knew that his liking of her went deeper than wanting a casual affair, and was prepared to lean upon his affection, like a convalescent leaning upon the arm of a nurse. She mused that it would be pleasant to do nothing for several months but have Conrad fuck her, feed her good grass and hashish, introduce her to mescaline, and show her the workings of his life. And failing that, she had Jackie and Maureen to support her for a while.

She ripped herself away from the direction of her thoughts, for a great deal depended on Aaron's state of mind, and her own reactions to seeing him again. She looked around for her clothes, but they were nowhere in sight. Instinctively she went to the closet and found Jackie's wardrobe, hanging like a fashion display, with one article of clothing to fit exactly each of the several dozen social scenes a sophisticated wealthy woman might visit, from an elegant evening gown to a pair of tailored tennis shorts. Cynthia could not suppress a moue of chagrin at the money and taste exhibited in the layout, especially in light of the fact that on the three occasions she had seen Jackie she was dressed in the same jeans and sweatshirt. Cynthia's things weren't there and she decided it would not be irregular in that house if she remained naked. She closed the closet door and spent a long time looking at herself in the mirror, seeking for any change in expression to indicate that the night's and morning's lovemaking had wrought some external differences in her. But she saw nothing extraordinary except for a flush over her cheeks.

'I am now technically bisexual,' she thought. 'I wonder what that means.' She had spun around and swept into the living room, where she stopped short upon seeing Clive.

'That's my brother,' Jackie had said. 'And he's been watching you sleep for a good part of the morning so you don't need to worry about his seeing your body now.' Cynthia had fallen into the classic feminine response, dropping one hand over her cunt and covering her breasts with her other arm. At hearing Jackie's words, she felt foolish and let her limbs fall to her side. 'Come, sit by me,' Jackie had said, 'and have some coffee.'

Now Clive snuffed out his cigarette. It had a trace of lipstick around the base. 'But to see one's folly is merely an intellectual exercise,' he went on. 'One is stuck with that particular form of aberration until one finds another to replace it. Never an easy task, and especially difficult for a man who has spent almost a decade perfecting the skill of debauching women. For at the heart of all folly, including my forays into meta-physical sensuality, is an aching loneliness so profound

229

that I dared not, and still dare not, face it. It wasn't until later that I understood that my very anguish was what gave me power over the women I possessed. They were taken by my surface charm, but it was the deep vibrations in my soul that chained them to me. I think they found in me an echo of the fear that stands at the doorway to all human experience, the horror of this mysterious life, this whirring silent world in which we dance like ghosts to a music which has no recognisable source. They allowed themselves to hope that not only would I understand their pain, but that my strength would help them sustain it. And so they gave themselves to me, the way a cripple throws herself upon a statue that is reputed to have miraculous powers.'

He put two fingers of his right hand to his forehead, his thumb on his chin, and closed his eyes. His brow furrowed and he seemed gripped by a spasm of cerebral intensity. Cynthia watched the man, taken by his almost theatrical air of control, the measured cadence of his speech. Having resolved that she would leave that morning, she was able to relax and enjoy the interaction with a man she would have, just the day before, found grotesque had she seen him on the street.

'But that is why folly exercises such power over our lives,' he continued. 'We make it a shield against the night. My guilt for my years as a sexual scavenger was largely ameliorated when I realised that the women were using me to their ends, fully as much as I used them, and it was merely my puffed-up male ego which allowed me to think that I was the only one writing the scenario. And so they clung to me, woman after woman, letting me infatuate them with promises of paradise, and debase them in baroque sexual rituals, only to be flung out once more into their solitude, wiser perhaps by having one less illusion concerning their nature. To me they became one woman, changing faces and bodies, but manifesting as a single flow of mood and muscle, sentiment and secretion. And I clung to them, a reasoned madman unable to accept responsi-

230

bility for his life, and forging his weakness into a tool for conquest.' He smiled at Cynthia, the expression of a man who has just escaped being hit by a speeding car. 'Given a different set of proclivities, I might have used all that energy to become a successful banker.'

Cynthia found herself smiling in return, although she would not have been able to describe the humour in his words. The air between them seemed to shimmer as Clive's eyes lit up from within and beamed across the space, setting off sparks of pleasure in her brain. She felt an attraction for him that owed a great debt to his sheer physical handsomeness, but went beyond that into a realm of complicity; like Conrad he was able to give her the sense of being included in on a secret that no one else knew about. It was flirtation of the first water.

'You know that I looked at you while you and Maureen were still asleep,' he said. Cynthia felt a blush creeping across her chest and leaned into Jackie's side. 'I pored over your body in minutest detail, listened to your breathing, and watched your face made innocent by dreaming. I took in your movements and smells. And all during that time I imagined how it would have been had I met you earlier, when I was still ravenous for females wanting to be sacrificed. There is a quality about you that inspires extravagant forms of folly. You would probably make a splendid whore.'

Cynthia blinked at the words. She felt that she should feel flustered, but a pleasant excitement buzzed through her. 'Don't you have any relations with women at all any more?' Cynthia asked, a lilt in her voice.

'I've become a homosexual,' he replied.

'Hoorah for our side,' said Maureen as she glided into the room. Clive's face brightened upon seeing her, the way a landscape will thrill with light when the clouds fly away from the sun. He jumped to his feet and held out his arms. Maureen walked towards him and slipped into his embrace. They touched tenderly and totally, the entire fronts of their bodies in delicate contact. They stood holding one another for such a long time that Cynthia began to feel uneasy, until she realised that she was experiencing minute pangs of envy. What astonished her was the fact that she didn't know whether she wanted to be Maureen in Clive's arms, or Clive in Maureen's arms. They presented a stunning picture, both tall, Clive's light skin contrasted against Maureen's dark flesh, his clothing setting off her nudity.

She pulled back from him, put her hands on his chest, disengaged, and came to lie on the couch, at once putting her head in Cynthia's lap. She turned to lie on her stomach and put her lips against Cynthia's pubic hair, kissing the furry patch softly. Clive lit another cigarette and sat down to smoke as the three women spent a few moments restructuring their ambience. It was the first time that all of them had been awake together that morning, and it was necessary to reintegrate their energy fields and merge their auras harmoniously. For Cynthia to have sex with Maureen was one thing; for her to sit nestled against Jackie's side was another; but when both Maureen and Jackie bracketed her between the power poles of their seven-year relationship, her position needed to be redefined. It was part of the ongoing process of living for the two lesbians to remain sensitive to the changes in atmosphere and relationship produced by the introduction of new people, and they maintained certain quasi-ritualistic ceremonies to insure that everyone in any given circle related to the others on levels understood by all. They were practitioners of a species of psychic technology which pervaded all radical activity in the Bay area, a process whereby all the functions of the person, either poorly understood or denied by orthodox psychology, were educated and tuned to perform with the precision of sophisticated machinery. Such faculties as extrasensory perception, telepathy, movements of electrical fields around the body, and astral projection were treated not as topics for speculation but as realities to be dealt with in day-to-day living. Beneath everything else, the real revolution the two women represented was the awakening of the individual to his or her full potential, although, given their sexual inclinations, they rarely involved men in the process of their teaching.

Cynthia closed her eyes as Jackie kissed her temples and Maureen tickled the insides of her thighs with her tongue. She was intensely aware that Clive was watching, but there was nothing salacious in the fact. It was an almost unique pleasure to have caresses and conversations mixed in such an easy blend, to feel the sexual excitation in her body and the intellectual stimulation of her mind as part of a unitary process, and to have the whole movement bathed in the warmth of honest affection. All of her years in the society she was raised in had conspired to teach her that sex was an activity apart from the rest of daily life; it was to be done in a special place or at a special time or during a special mood. To have several people sitting around talking and fucking, viewing both expressions as functions which interpenetrate, seemed the most natural thing in the world.

Lips covered her nipples and a finger slipped subtly into her cunt. She parted her thighs to let the hand slide further in, but it retreated, and she opened her eyes in time to see Clive sitting back down, sniffing the moist tip of his middle finger. 'Dogs greet one another by smelling each other's genitals,' he said as he saw the look of surprise on her face. 'It shows a higher degree of organic intelligence than the stilted rituals we've come down to.' He put the finger in his mouth and sucked it thoroughly. 'Are there any words which could tell me more about you than a single fleeting aroma from your cunt?'

'Chauvinist,' muttered Maureen as she sat up again, leaning against the backrest of the couch.

'No more so than you, my dove,' said Clive.

'I thought you were a homosexual,' Cynthia said, nonplussed at the rapidity of interchange.

'I have switched to cock as a matter of survival and human decency,' he told her, 'but that doesn't mean my taste for cunt has diminished. This division into homosexual and heterosexual and bisexual is really very tedious. Consider, if you were kneeling on the floor in front of a couple sitting before you, a man and a woman, and he presented you with a thick succulent cock and she offered a pulsing oozing cunt, and someone asked you to choose between the two, wouldn't you think it odd that a question of choice should even arise? In moments of passion, it is the shapeshifting dances of our own mouths that we thrill to, and the genital we use as a prop is really incidental.'

'We're not all narcissists,' Maureen said.

Jackie looked at him questioningly. It was as though she had suddenly dipped beneath the banter to listen seriously to what was being said. She was able to accept Clive's lyrical cynicism as part of his style, and appreciate it as such, but she kept a sisterly eye on the little boy who still wept from a scraped knee or the death of his pet, the child with whom she had shared her childhood, and those posturings never obscured what she knew of his loneliness. She cared for him enough to remember that he was more than the act he presented. She made a wry face.

'Being a hooker is destroying your sensibilities,' she said.

Clive looked at her and responded to the note of concern. 'It's simply a matter of trading one system of perceptions for another. I'm finding that to chase my folly requires a more ruthless dedication than I had suspected.'

'You work as a prostitute?' Cynthia asked.

Clive lit another of his Gitanes and passed the pack around. Each of the women took one and he lit each of their cigarettes before getting to his own. He poured another drink from the frosted pitcher which stood on the table into his glass, and after taking a sip looked at Cynthia. 'Most professional homosexuals,' he said, 'the ones who make an ideology of their rectal idiosyncracies, would have it that I was homosexual all along, and using my involvements with women to deny my true proclivities. The fact that I did not 'come out' until I was almost thirty, and then bloomed all at once, would be taken as *prime facie* evidence. They would discount my argument that homosexuality was simply, at one point in my life, a more convenient diversion than the pursuit of women, and was chosen rationally. But after all, we have but one life to live, and it would seem sensible to experience as many variations as it has to offer within the allotted span, wouldn't it?

'To the degree that I am not deluding myself, I can say that I became a homosexual because I found it a less painful and damaging mode of escape from existential terror than heterosexuality. And I have no doubt but that this is merely another phase of my development, and will pass with all the rest. Although,' and he shot a glance at Jackie and Maureen, 'some would hold that the separation of the sexes is a historically necessary phenomenon, and homosexuality is the preferred mode of any truly revolutionary group. I don't argue the point.'

'I've even heard you defend it,' Jackie said.

'Ah yes, that was the night we went to Sylvia's.' He nodded to Cynthia. 'I smoked quite a bit, something I don't ordinarily do; marijuana tends to make me sociological. And I was struck by a vision of the future, a world in which the sexes have been permanently segregated. I imagined that men and women had been given different hemispheres of the globe to develop their own civilisations. And at the borders between the kingdoms would be a series of orgy houses, a great wall of heterosexual eroticism. And all those who wanted to could spend as much time as they desired there, wallowing in transgenital exuberance.

'In the world of men there would be no further cause

235

for hostility; with the women removed all status symbols would be drained of their potency, all *macho* would be reduced to shadow show. They would spend their time wrestling, their gleaming bodies and rippling muscles delighting in their own strength, seeking combat instead of war, and desiring to win no prize, except perhaps penetration into the quivering hams of the man one has just pinned to the ground. Having no one to strut for, man settles quickly into harmless activity.

'And among the women all would be gentleness and honour, for with no man to compete for, their bitchiness to one another would disappear. The stridency would fall from their tongues like scales from the eyes of someone who had been blind, until they found the strength which transcends all artifice. They would become a race with three divisions: the wild witches dancing in the hills, fierce and proud; the soft mothers of the hearth, calm and silent; and the gaunt ethereal goddesses who walk alone beneath the moon.

'Children would be spawned in the orgy palaces, and after a brief period would be separated: the boys to one world, the girls to another, never to see the opposite sex again except when they themselves reached maturity and wended their ways to the border between the two cultures, there to revel in the very halls in which they were conceived. There are some who would never visit the heterosexual centres; and some who would never leave them; while most would go a few times out of curiosity, and generally be content with the peace to be found only among one's own kind.'

Cynthia listened with wide eyes, disturbed by the elegance of the picture Clive painted, needing for some reason to find a flaw in it, to mar its sheen of perfection. 'It sounds like a world without love,' she said at last.

'Ah, what a word that is,' Clive said. 'Whenever we are taken to the outermost limits of our condition and there perceive that no possible utopia can ever hope to compensate for the essential poverty of our souls, we reach for the idea of love like a beggar lunging for a coin. But what is it, after all? We sit on a beach and smell the clean salt air and some ineffable joy fills us, and we call it love; or we swoon in our lover's arms, and we say we are in love; we inject amphetamine into our veins and feel indescribable physiological exhilaration, and identify that with feelings of love; we project all our idealised yearnings onto another human being, and claim that we have fallen in love. But all this is to confuse a tickling of the ego with a rapture of the spirit, to make gratification for bliss. For all the conditions we usually ascribe to love are a result of some action on our part, and the one absolute quality of love is that there is no way for us to call it to us. It enters us at its discretion, not at our volition. Whenever we try to trap it or define it or rouse it in our hearts, we remain sterile and dumb. And then, just as we have forgotten about our quest, like a sudden breeze it's upon us, and we are transformed by beauty and power and understanding. Yet these moments are not of our choosing. All we can do is live our pitiful lives, more or less comfortably, more or less intelligently, and be thankful for the crumbs from God's table. It's a gift we can't do anything to have given to us, and it is taken away as capriciously as it is bestowed. Separation of the sexes can only be discussed in pragmatic terms; it has nothing to do with love.'

'Who you sleep with is a political decision,' Jackie said.

'Or a philosophical one,' Maureen added.

Clive took a drag on his cigarette and leaned back on his sitting bones. He let the smoke out in large puffs and with an audible explosion of breath. He raised his eyebrows and looked at the three women. He ran his fingers through his hair.

'You said you were a prostitute,' Cynthia said to him.

'It was Jackie who mentioned the fact,' he said, 'but it's true. I am the queen of the *Cock*.'

Cynthia stared at him.

'*The Flaming Cock,*' Clive said.

Cynthia's expression widened into confusion.

'It's a gay bar,' Maureen told her.

'If you can call that grim pesthole and the ghouls who haunt it "gay", then I guess you might say it is a gay bar,' Clive said. 'But never has a word been so misapplied to describe a condition. The place is the ultimate conclusion of our commercial civilisation. It's where the niceties of personality are discarded and the interest stays focused on the bodies. It's the meat market, the killing ground of human dignity.'

'I can't imagine it,' Cynthia said. 'I don't know what you are referring to.'

Clive hunched his shoulders and seemed to look inside himself. 'Think of yourself lying on the floor in the middle of a largish room,' he said. 'You rub your clitoris furiously and spread your cunt lips open with your fingers. Your eyes are closed and your mouth is open, gaping wide, your tongue curling over the edges. You bring yourself time and again to the edge of orgasm, and always stop, quivering at the brink. You are building desire in yourself, the way a cyclotron gathers energy. Your breasts jiggle provocatively, your arse is a cleft mushroom waiting to be pierced. From your throat breaks a stream of hoarse cries which match the excruciatingly vivid fantasies that splash across your mind like swirls in a Pollock painting. You are in the midst of a most private masturbatory moment, giving yourself to yourself, submitting to the only master you will ever recognise: your own unquenchable need. But while you are exposed in this ultimately intimate manner, hundreds of men cluster around you, old men, young men, lovers, sadists, coprophiliacs, priests, satyrs, heroes, impotents. They comprise the full spectrum of mankind on earth and they have but one thing in common: they are riveted to you by the implacable lust that your performance gives rise to. And what feeds you more than anything else,

238

more than your thoughts or movements or sensations, what makes the moment one of such unimaginable ecstasy, is the fact that they are watching you, wanting you, closing in on you, to use you as a sponge for their raging desire, to plunge their fingers and tongues and cocks into all your openings and cover you with excretion until you swim in sperm and urine and faeces.'

Cynthia took a deep breath. Like a debator trained by Jesuits, Clive had the knack of opening a conversational movement with an innocent-seeming gambit, and then building logically upon that until the listener had been forced into an acceptance of the conclusion by following the line of reasoning. The one difference was that Clive's logic was imaginistic instead of linear.

'I can't dream of ever doing anything remotely like that,' Cynthia said.

Clive nodded. 'That may have more to say about your unwillingness to accept your potential than about the potential itself.'

'But no one does things like that,' Cynthia responded, slightly piqued.

'In the back of the bar I reign in, there is a room such as I have described,' Clive said, 'a large square space with nothing in it except a half dozen foam rubber mats strewn about the floor. It is kept very dark, and after buying a few drinks in the front, most customers proceed to the rear, where there is almost always some chaotic sexual production being mounted. On a busy night there may be as many as a hundred and fifty men in there, in various stages of dress and undress, engaged in acts that range from the passively voyeuristic to the monstrous and sadistic.'

Maureen stood up and stretched. 'I'm going to make breakfast,' she said, 'I've heard these tales of the middle-aged mariner more than enough.' She kissed Clive on the forehead. 'I love you dearly,' she said, 'but this compulsion to describe the details of your sexual hijinks is really very vulgar.'

'It's merely to elucidate and educate that I'm telling all this,' he said. 'All of my stories have socially redeeming value.'

'I'm not sure what I'm learning,' Cynthia said, 'but I must admit that I'm fascinated to hear it.'

'You see, I'm exonerated,' said Clive. He kissed Maureen's hand. 'And please, don't put any curry in my eggs,' he added, 'it makes me nauseous.' He turned his attention back to Cynthia, leaned forward and wrapped his arms around his knees. He rocked back and forth a few moments, looking up into her eyes. His gaze roamed down her face and came to rest on her breasts, and for an uneasily long time he drank in the lushness of her body with frank admiration. He moved down to her cunt, and then trailed slowly over her thighs, down her calves, and to her feet, only to snap his glance back to her eyes, catching her watching him watch her. The look they exchanged hid nothing, and the compact of admitting their mutual sexual attraction was made. It promised nothing specific, but provided a firm base for negotiations.

'A man approached me at the bar,' he went on, his voice lower and more direct. 'He was an Oriental, about forty-five I'd guess, although he appeared younger. He was slightly over five feet tall, wore a suit and tie and steel-rimmed glasses, and looked frightfully intelligent. We appraised one another for a few moments, and he bought me a drink, having only 7-Up for himself. I waited for him to begin the conversation, expecting the usual small-talk as a preliminary, something about the weather or the time. But he remained silent, observing me. I began to get very interested. I prostitute myself for many reasons, and one of them is the fact that from time to time I meet extraordinary people to have sex with. His first words were, 'Are you as competent as you appear?'

'I took his measure, judged that I could supply the level of excellence he seemed to be requesting, and answered, "Yes." "I wonder," he said. "What do you need?" I asked him. His reply came with a *sang froid* that curdled the edges of my sophistication. "I want you to take me into the back," he said, "and feed me to the others." He looked at me seriously. "You understand what I mean?" he said. "I think I've been waiting for you," I told him.

'We stared at one another like two lovers at the edge of a high cliff, ready to lock ourselves in one another's arms and leap in to the chasm before us. "How much do you receive for your services?" he asked me with an easy formality. His breath was light and rapid; what he was suggesting went beyond the limits of the usual swinish rooting that goes on in the orgy room. He had consciously conceived the act he wished to perform, and was prepared to execute it, enlisting a perfect stranger as a partner. But then, we are all members of the same body, aren't we? It takes a broader vision than most people are capable of to perceive that intimacy is merely a matter of recognition.'

Clive shook his pack of cigarettes and found it to be empty. 'Take one of these,' Jackie said, offering him the wooden box filled with English Ovals. Clive picked one up, sniffed it, lit it, and took a shallow puff. 'These are faggot fags,' he said, 'they have no bite to them.' He looked up at Cynthia who was rearranging her position on the couch.

'He appeared well-heeled, so I said, "Fifty dollars." I was all ready to accompany him without payment, for the simple pleasure of working with a man who understood his nature well enough to ask for precisely what he wanted. But it is the heart of playing prostitute to take money for services. Our dear dull dad's will has left me in a position where I don't ever need to earn money again, but there is something about being handed a ten dollar bill after kneeling behind a clump of bushes and sucking a cock through an open zipper, or bending over double in the back seat of a car to have my arse used and abused, which adds the

241

quality of degradation that alone infuses a whore with nobility.'

Cynthia shook her head. 'You're talking backward,' she said. 'How can being degraded be noble?'

'Because it is a service that one sells. Have you ever been a whore? I mean, an honest whore. Or have you spent your life pretending that you are doing something else with men besides getting one form of payment or another for your sexual favours? Taking emotional dues, or social stability, or morning-after affection for the use of your cunt, instead of putting your hand out and demanding immediate real greenbacks for your labour? It is only when you see sex as a commodity that you can appreciate it as an act of freedom. So long as you pretend that the element of buying and selling, which pervades every last vibration in our entire civilisation, does not invade the contract of the genitals, then you flounder about in a constant confusion. To live honestly in this world, you must learn first to be a whore, come to terms with that reality, and then concern yourself with the more ineffable aspects of your intercourse with your fellow human beings.

'He gave me the money without argument, and we sat for a while, finishing our drinks. After a while we rose together and went off to the back, like a man and his second approaching the duelling ground. On the other side of the curtain, it was business as usual. Half a dozen blowjobs, ten or twelve rectal penetrations, an unspecified amount of vague groping and fondling, twenty or so timid voyeurs tentatively fingering themselves as they watched, and on one of the mats a fairly energetic soul who had pulled three men to himself and involved them all in an angular daisy chain. There was not a glimmer of imagination to the found anywhere.

'The man at my side, I later learned his name was Feng, stepped toward the centre of the room and stopped. He stood erect and calm, surveying the scene

242

with the majesty of an eagle. I walked up next to him and after several deep breaths began to undress him. At first it was ludicrous, removing his glasses, loosening his tie; I felt like a valet. But in short order, we were noticed, and while no one else there, I'm sure, appreciated the nuances or understood the interior dynamic of what he was allowing to be done to him, they didn't miss the major point: a human sacrifice was in their midst, someone itching for immolation. I reflected that the deed was not unlike a monk's setting himself on fire to protest the war, except that Feng would survive this ordeal, and he seemed totally unconcerned with the social symbolism of his act.

'I pulled off his shirt, his trousers, his underwear, his shoes and socks, until he was stark naked, not only in body but in intention. Gradually all the other activity in the room quieted down as this slim yellow man, by his sheer presence and the audacity of his behaviour, commanded their attention. I stepped back, wondering how I would proceed, but he took the lead. He bent his knees, put his arms out loosely in front of him, and launched into a long soft graceful dance that I immediately recognised as the swaying pattern of Tai Chi Chuan. He was a master of the art!

'I don't know whether you have ever seen the full ritual performed; it is perhaps the single most exquisite formal pattern of movements ever choreographed by man. In it are contained the fluidity of nature and the structure of mind, in a single comprehensive gesture that takes almost a half hour to complete. It is as though a rock garden could move. Everyone there, including myself, was stunned at first, and I could gauge by the expression of many of the others that they thought he was mad. And, in a sense, of course, he was. But when insanity finds its proper expression, we can only call it art.

'A certain uneasiness went through the crowd, as always happens when the unexpected is sustained. But slowly, the magic of his movements captured us and we sat in a circle around him to watch and marvel at the exhibition. I knew, and I'm certain that some of the others did, that this entire scene was foreplay, an introduction to his major purpose, which, slowly, came into focus. He was manifesting his absolute control of his mind and body, showing us the totality of himself. I don't know the precise instant it happened, but at one point the austerity of his dance was infused with the erotic flavour of the setting in which it took place, and all of a sudden it was as though he were a dancing girl, performing nude for a smouldering audience. For what all the men had come for, to see and touch other bodies, was being fully given to them. Feng ceased being merely an object of contemplation; he became an object of desire. His delicate legs, his sensitive hands, his heavily lidded eyes, his curved lips, his strong buttocks, his nascent cock, were all on display. Several of the men began to edge towards him.

'He brought his movement to a close with the same posture with which he had begun it, stood silently for a moment, and then with a hideously abrupt wolfish grin sank to the floor, stretched out on his back, cupped one hand over his groin, and spread his legs as far as they would go. There was a space of several seconds in which the entire tableau was frozen, and then pandemonium erupted with the unreal quality of a cut tree beginning to topple. Before he was completely hidden by the bodies which swarmed over him, he caught my eye and sent me a glint of thanks.'

Clive lay down on his side, his elbow supporting his head as Jackie whistled lightly through her lips. 'I guess they were at him for fifteen or twenty minutes,' he went on. 'I don't know how many times he was fucked, or had his mouth ravaged by cocks, or his nipples savagely pinched, or his own cock pummelled and pulled. I sat back and kept watch over his clothing and when the energy centre he had created finally dispersed and he was left alone, lying limply on the ground, I went over to him and helped him up. There

244

was not a trace of the man I had met just an hour earlier; the person who leaned on my shoulder was indistinguishable from the victim of every mass rape and gang bang that has been perpetrated since the world began. I mentally tipped my nonexistent hat to him; he was the most highly evolved connoisseur of pain I had ever met.

'I don't know by what impulse in myself I was led to take him into the small room at the very back of the place instead of just helping him dress right where we were. I told myself he probably needed a bit of privacy, and I'm sure that was true. But subsequent events led me to believe that more than my professional responsibility towards a client was involved. I escorted him into a tiny space that was used as a storage room, running the gauntlet of eyes and hands that plucked at us as we passed, and closed the door behind us. I put his clothes down, and he turned to face me. My heart leapt into my mouth. I had never seen such a look of radiant beauty on anyone except myself. All his circuits were open; he had run the entire spectrum from esoteric practice to sub-bestiality, and through it all retained and enhanced his sense of self. If I were prone to using the word, I would say that at that moment I loved him.

'He fell to his knees and threw his face at my feet. He lifted the shoe and turned to his back, and began licking the sole of the shoe, taking all the crust and muck and pieces of filth imbedded in the leather onto his tongue. He grabbed my ankle and began pulling down, indicating that he wanted me to step on his face, to crush him into the ground. I was aghast with empathy. I knew exactly what he was feeling and why he was doing what he was doing. You must understand the setting. In almost Dantesque circles it went from the whole mechanical mindless business of western civilisation in the street, to the bar where several hundred men were estimating the value of one another's genitals and anal openings, to the room outside where

245

the dark rhythms of fragmented orgy were pulsing, to our small cave where, amidst the mops and pails and instruments of filth, this educated product of the world's most advanced civilisation was begging to have his face ground into the dirt. And at the centre of all this, like a compassionate solipsist, I found nothing bizarre, nothing abnormal, nothing freakish.

'He moaned once and then began thrashing about on the floor. "Now you have seen," he said, "now you must finish it for me." If we were in a different place, if I had not been afraid of the repercussions, I would have killed him then, quite methodically have beaten him to death with a thick stick. And felt that I was doing the man a service. As it was I yanked him up by the hair and slapped him with all my strength, splitting open the skin on his cheek. He began to sob then, and all his structure collapsed. He was lost in his confusion. I pulled out my cock, bent him over a rusty sink, and fucked him for a very long time, until he was limp. I didn't bother to ejaculate.

'Later we had coffee together and discussed the nature of folly. It turned out he was a professor of Oriental Religion at the University, was married with two children, and a highly respected scholar. He said that he indulged his strange needs several times a year, and except for these excursions lived an exemplary existence. A normal member of the community.'

He looked up from his tale and gazed into Cynthia's eyes, catching her unaware. 'What's your folly, Cynthia?' he asked.

The question spun through her mind with the accumulated force of the story that had just built to its conclusion, and the answer came out before she could think about it. 'His name is Aaron,' she said.

'Do you suck his cock?' Clive asked her.

'Why, yes, of course,' Cynthia said. 'What sort of question is that?'

'Purely informational,' Clive told her. 'Do you enjoy it?' he went on.

'Usually,' Cynthia said.

'Have you ever sucked a cock for money?' he said.

'No one's ever offered me money,' Cynthia replied.

'What if someone did?' Clive pressed on.

The drift of the talk revealed its direction to Cynthia's mind. However, with Clive it was difficult to tell how much of what he said was simply hyperbole, a kind of teasing, the way a little boy will threaten a little girl by waving a stick at her, pretending he may hit her with it. She did not know how much of his story to believe; she had the distinct impression she was being put on. But everything he said had an unmistakable ring of truth to it, as though he were communicating some important message and the alphabet he used was incidental.

'I don't know,' she replied. 'I suppose it would depend on the circumstances.'

'And the price,' Clive added.

'I don't know what you want from me,' Cynthia told him. She looked at Jackie for some clue, but Jackie's face was empty of expression.

'How much money do you make in a week?' Clive asked.

'A hundred and five dollars, after taxes,' Cynthia said.

'I'll give you five hundred dollars if you'll suck my cock,' Clive said.

Again Cynthia turned to Jackie. This time Jackie responded with a small smile. 'That's really top money,' she said.

'You don't think I should take him seriously, do you?'

Clive fished out a thick wad of bills. He peeled off a number of fifties and twenties, and put them on the table in front of him.

'This is absurd,' Cynthia said. 'What are you after?'

'Consider it a whim of a jaded millionaire,' Clive said. 'Or the gesture of someone who likes you and wants to teach you something about life. Or the desperate appeal of a man who has been captivated by your mouth. Or part of some insidious ploy by a group of white slavers. Or picking up a hand of cards and finding that you've drawn the joker. What difference does it make why we do the things we do? The only important question is whether we do them or not.'

Jackie took her arm from around Cynthia's shoulders. 'I'm going to see whether Maureen needs help in the kitchen,' she said, and stood up.

Cynthia grabbed her hand. 'Wait,' she said, 'I'm confused.'

'Then don't act until you are clear,' Jackie said. 'I don't know what game Clive is up to either, but I'm not his keeper, nor am I yours. I think you should work it out inside yourself and then come to terms with him. How else can you deal with people except by knowing who you are, deciding whether the other person is acting in good faith or not, and then negotiating the contract between you?' She bent forward and kissed Cynthia on the mouth. 'You'll be all right,' she said. 'It's only a question of yes or no.'

She squeezed Cynthia's hand and walked from the room. 'Please make sure she doesn't put curry in my eggs,' Clive said to her retreating back. He swung around to face Cynthia. 'It really makes me nauseous. Maureen thinks it's an affectation.'

Cynthia slid to the edge of the seat. 'I don't know whether I should stay,' she began. But Clive held up one hand. 'The only danger is in yourself,' he said quickly. 'I'm not going to coerce you.'

'I'm a little afraid of you,' she said. 'All that you've told me about yourself today. I'm not sure I can trust you.'

Clive stood up. With deliberate movements he began to take off his clothes, shrugging off his jacket, and snaking his trousers down his legs. His attitude was one of seeming unconcern, as though he didn't care whether she left or not. He kicked off his sandals, and posed before her, waiting several seconds before he spoke. 'I'm just a man,' he said. 'You have known men intimately all your life, beginning with your father,

248

and uncles and cousins, maybe a brother; and then teachers and boyfriends and priests and lovers; you've dealt with men in offices and bedrooms and law courts. You've had men inside you. What do you know about man?'

Cynthia listened to his words and looked at his body. She saw that she had been receiving dual impressions from him, his language soft and flowing, his actions firm and sharply etched. She had come, through long experience, to expect a man to be all one way; either passive or aggressive, and was not satisfied with exclusion of either aspect. That was why having Conrad and Aaron in the same space was so fulfilling; each of them typified one side of the apparent dichotomy. But here was a man who had delved into and cultivated all planes of his experience, and seemed complete within himself. Yet she had trouble believing him, and wondered what she was suspicious of. What he offered was straightforward enough. Her eyes stopped their movement when they came to his cock. It was the smallest penis she had ever seen on a man, popping out from his pubic hair like an elongated button. She found herself beginning to smile before she repressed the expression.

'Not very formidable, is it?' said Clive, watching her look at his crotch. 'It expands to a mere four-and-three-quarter inches, medium thick, although prettily sculpted. You can put five hundred dollars in your pocket simply by putting it in your mouth and sucking it until the sperm splashes on your tongue. I insist, by the way, that you swallow it. The entire aesthetic is ruined if you spit it out. That's a species of reneging. You've undoubtedly had many cocks in your mouth many times, and will certainly have a good many more, unless those refugees from Chekhov convert you to monomania. And I doubt whether you shall ever have such intense gratification from the act as the knowledge, as you do it, that it will mean five hundred dollars in your wallet. And think of how many pretty things you can do with that substantial piece of change.'

'Piece of change?' she asked. 'I don't have much more than that in my savings account.'

'Well, you can double your capital in a single gulp.'

Cynthia smiled at him. 'You do have a way of being convincing, don't you?'

'I'm a fanatic,' he said simply. 'I always promulgate my enthusiasms.'

'And now you're selling prostitution as a way of life?'

'No,' he replied. 'I'm advocating the recognition of the fact that prostitution is our way of life. And all we need to do is to get more sophisticated about how much we charge for our services.'

'But what about reciprocity, two people having sex on an equal basis, without one being the servitor of the other?'

'When that happens, it's rare and beautiful. And we all paste such episodes in our memory books. But think back, after that lucky encounter, when you return for a second meeting, haven't all kinds of subtle shifts begun to take place, changes in balance? Hasn't there already started a jockeying for position? And then the second fuck is chaotic. And by the third you have either decided not to see the person again or else the two of you have tacitly worked out a deal.'

She shook her head. 'You're right,' she said, 'God damn it, you're right.'

He walked around the table to stand directly in front of where Cynthia sat. He put his hands on her shoulders. 'It's just another form of folly,' he said. 'Perhaps, given our historical epoch, the most honest way for a woman to earn a living. You know, a whore gets to meet *everybody* sooner or later; because they all come down to see us, the presidents and the popes, the policemen and the panderers. We get to see them in their most unhypocritical of circumstances, that is to say, when their hypocrisy is most obvious, as they come sneaking away from the "other lives" to visit the underworld. And after a while, you get to know what people are, and through that, you get to know who you are. Because you never have to fawn or seek favour, you never have to be anything but honest and direct. You very quickly become bored with all rigmarole. You develop a keen and steady eye. In a word, my sweet, you become enlightened.'

He leaned forward and his belly pressed against Cynthia's forehead. She neither accepted nor repulsed the contact. She could smell his skin, a dry crisp aroma like the insides of new books opened at the beginning of a school year. 'And what would you have to give up?' he said. 'You are quite lovely.' He put his hands on the top of her head. 'I have quite a few wealthy connections. You could be financially independent within three years. Think of that. Never to have to make obeisance to anyone again. The men in your office who act as your bosses, giving you a pittance for forty precious hours, one half of your entire waking week, having you sit like an automaton and bang away at a piece of machinery, making meaningless marks on countless sheets of paper. And then to have them condescend to bestow a smile or kind word upon you. Why, when you learn the value of what lies between your legs and the power of what's enclosed in your skull, you no longer have to be a slave. You can be master. You can remove yourself from the entire tedious process. The same men who now treat you as a cipher will be grovelling at your feet, begging you to shit on them. Do you know that? Once you accept your strength and take responsibility for your freedom, you will never take second place to a man again, even when you are taking his cock deep into your cunt.'

'I would lose Aaron, and any other man I hope to make a life with,' she said, her voice flat and distinct.

'Marriage is the most vulgar form of folly. As an escape, it is equal with all other human activity. But why condemn yourself to the subway when you could be gliding over the city on a magic carpet?'

'These are just ideas. There's no chance I'm going to become a high-priced call girl.'

'Perhaps. But here is something more cogent. The chance to be the highest paid cocksucker in the world for a few brief minutes.'

She looked up at him. Her chest was heavy. She felt a sudden wave of fatigue. 'Sure,' she said. 'Why not?'

'For the money, right?'

'You bet your sweet arse,' she said.

'Do it on your knees,' he said.

She slipped off the couch and knelt in front of him. His cock was inches from her mouth. She looked at it dispassionately. Removed from all its associations, detached from any inner excitement on her part, it was a flap of skin, no more or less remarkable than a finger or a toe. She was drained of all sexual feeling, and approached her task the way a woman will take on a pile of clothing that needs ironing; it was a thing to be done, and she did not like or dislike doing it. Its major quality was that it would involve time and work.

She brought her mouth forward but Clive held her head back. 'Wait,' he said. 'Before you start, I want you to say something, so we both have everything perfectly clear.' His fingers touched her temples. 'Say, "My name is Cynthia. I am a whore. I suck cock for money." '

The words richocheted around the walls of her consciousness, knocking over all the images that still stood in her definition of herself. For a moment she tried to tell herself that what he said wasn't true, because she would only be doing it once, and mostly as an experiment, although she could not deny that the large amount of money swayed her significantly. But she could not escape the truth that for the length of time she had his cock in her mouth, his description of her was absolutely accurate. And now he was asking that she say it too, so that it became her description of herself also.

252

'My name is Cynthia,' she said. 'I am a whore. I suck cock for money.'

'Start sucking,' he said.

She brought her hand up and squeezed the base of his cock, making it bulge at the tip. The head flared once and the shaft began to swell. She watched with a kind of wonder she had never before attained during a sexual act, astonished by the sheer physiological miracle of the process whereby a cock becomes hard. The almost insignificant tab of flesh was, before her eyes, transforming itself into a long, solid pole, rigid and thick. At its full length it gave the effect of a man just tall enough not to be considered a midget. Any shorter and it would not have seemed like an actual cock, but some toy fashioned to look like one. When it stuck out at ninety degrees from his body, she took it in her mouth.

To her surprise, once the visual impact was removed, his cock was extremely pleasant. Smoothly textured, evenly curved, manageable size. She sucked it all the way inside her, and when she had taken his entire cock between her lips, the top of it just reached the opening to her throat. He could thrust his full length into her and she wouldn't gag or choke. As though reading her mind, he put his hands on the back of her head and pushed her face into his groin. She opened her lips so that the distance between her teeth and her throat would be shortened and he could push in a slight bit more. She wanted to feel the head of his cock sliding a tiny bit into her gullet. And even at that, she found she could still breathe, the air passage wasn't blocked.

Emboldened by the knowledge that his cock could not hurt her throat, she began to suck the length of it in long wet slurping motions, her tongue protruding and her lips parting as she slid forward, her cheeks quivering as she sucked backward. His cock rode in and out of her mouth with smooth regularity, gleaming with the saliva she covered it with. Cynthia became engrossed in the technical facility with which she performed the task, and forgot all other ramifications. For the first time she lost any sense of what the man's pleasure was and tuned in on her own activity. Without articulating it as such, she was working like a professional.

Clive's voice fell into her ears like gentle rain, influencing what she did but not disrupting it. 'You are almost perfect,' he said. 'The pose is classic, on your knees, naked, cheeks caved in, breasts jiggling, arse protruding. And you aren't bothering with fluting fanciness, dallying around the edges of my cock with your tongue. You aren't there to please me, you are there to make me come. And so you cease to be of any concern to either of us, you are too absorbed in your work to let your ego interfere. My pleasure is my business, it is what I derive from the act. For I have paid you to do what you are doing, and I need give you no more. I won't be like your Aaron or any other man trapped by your wiles. I have no need to moan to let you know what I am feeling, or to twitch gratuitously to indicate that you are transporting me with pleasure. My feelings are my concern; you are not being paid to know what I feel, only to produce feelings inside me. I need only watch you as you cover my cock voraciously, the spit sliding out from the corners of your mouth, the froth bubblng on your lips. And listen to your breathing as you attempt to coordinate each breath with so many strokes in, so many strokes out. And I can wait until you are, perhaps, taken by your own stimulation, and give me more than I bargained for.'

Cynthia let the words flow in and out of her. She had reduced all variables to a single objective, to spark Clive's ejaculation. She wondered whether Jackie or Maureen might come back into the room, and found she didn't care. It struck her at once that they wouldn't think more or less of her for what she was doing. They were interested in her, not in her codes of personal behaviour. She couldn't help contrasting that to what

Aaron would do if he walked in at that moment. She reached a brief flash of the picture she would present to his eyes as she lavished her attention on the cock in her mouth. Without her awareness of it, she began to curl her toes, push her breasts against Clive's thighs, and roll her arse around to give her head further momentum. She put her hands on either side of his cock like a kitten kneading the flesh around its mother's tit.

Clive looked down and smiled. 'It's so easy,' he thought. 'They are such simple creatures. Once one has made the proper adjustments in their minds, their bodies revert spontaneously to unbridled sensuality. And the pity is that so few of them realise that, so few understand that they can make their own adjustments and need not rely on a man to set them loose. How much she enjoys it, kneeling and gobbling, letting the cock rampage in her mouth. God knows what's going on in her mind, what rationalisations she's giving herself. I wonder if she truly knows that wantonness transcends intellect.' The sensations he felt were not extraordinary. He had known them countless times with numberless men and women, both as recipient and donor of the oragenital favour. 'I wonder why I even bother any more?' he said to himself. 'There's nothing more in sex that I hope to discover. It's become just a habit, like smoking. Not unpleasant, and not injurious if kept within moderation. I suppose it's as simple as the fact that I enjoy it, and there are few other things I would rather do with my time than idle it away in those infantile preoccupations.'

He felt the first stirrings of orgasm and he put his attention fully on the juncture of his cock and her mouth. 'I'm going to come soon, Cynthia,' he said. 'In less than a minute the sperm will pop out from the tip of my cock and fill the back of your mouth. You know what it will taste like, musty, pungent, salty, bitter, cloying, sharp, all at once. And then it will slide down your throat and you will make swallowing motions, easing the deposit into your belly. Your nostrils will fill with the smell of it, like raw wheat germ in a freshly opened container. And that will be it. My cock will become limp again, and you will hold it in your mouth until it grows too small to make it worth the bother any longer.'

He bent his knees as the bubbling began in his groin. He dropped his hands to his side, let his head fall back, and allowed his mind to go blank. He gave himself up to her insistence, the constant friction of her tongue and lips on his cock. Like a man dying, his world became one of stark sensation, a sloshing sound, a tingling feeling, the whiteness of the ceiling, the smell of bodies in exertion, the stale taste of tobacco. He groaned once and a shudder rolled the length of his spine. His cock jerked and throbbed, and the thick rich fluid spurted out in a series of powerful jets, six or seven times, until Cynthia's mouth was flooded with sperm. His discharge was incredibly copious and she almost gagged at the volume accumulating at the base of her tongue. When she could wait no longer, she swallowed once, taking the viscous syrup inside her, like a teen-age girl downing the last mouthfuls of a malted milk. Her head spinning, she took a deep breath and swallowed again, pulling in the residue. She clamped her jaws and sucked the cock once more, very hard, draining it of any sperm left in the tube. She swallowed the third time, and then let his cock fall from between her lips. She knelt in front of him a long time, panting slightly, her eyes closed, rocking back and forth. She felt utterly spent, and wondered how she could have become so involved in sucking his cock when she had thought she was at such a distance, and was doing it only for a lark. She had never gone through such an intense experience of cocksucking even with Aaron, at times when she was brimming with love for him. And it came to her with undeniable clarity that there might be more to sexuality than she had always believed, that it might be a power which superceded all other human bonds, and could capture her in its demands despite anything she might think to the contrary.

She opened her eyes. Clive was bending over the table, picking up a cigarette. Maureen was standing at the entrance to the room, looking at her strangely. Cynthia shook her head and sat back down on the couch. Clive handed her a lit cigarette which she gratefully puffed.

'Breakfast is ready,' Maureen said, 'we're eating on the back lawn.' She looked at Cynthia for a few seconds longer and then disappeared into the other room.

'Shall we go,' said Clive.

Cynthia stood up. She began to walk in the direction of the kitchen. But Clive caught her arm. 'Don't forget this,' he said holding out the five hundred dollars. He smiled into her eyes. 'Whore,' he said.

They ate on the grass, bathed in sunlight and the smell of eucalyptus. Maureen produced an exotic omelette and a loaf of freshly baked bread. With it came butter, honey, several kinds of jam, and a pot of breakfast tea. It was after eleven when they sat down, and almost twelve when Maureen began stacking the dishes. Clive rolled several joints and they smoked slowly, enjoying their digestion and the sweetness of the air. The day began to slip gears, to lose the sense of time and purpose and move once more into a mood of drifting and observing. Cynthia felt the first tinges of anxiety. Used as she was to a life of schedules and directed activity, the ambience of the house rendered her like a compulsive without her obsessive behaviour. She had no capacity for idleness.

She looked around the circle, at Maureen whose cool exterior hid such scorching ardour, at Jackie whose clear intellect matched her unfailing warmth, at Clive who went through life as though it were his private berry patch. Their naked bodies gleamed innocent in the sparkling daylight. She wondered whether she would see them again, knowing that in a few days this entire incident might appear as though it had been a hallucination.

'I think I should go soon,' she said. Her words were slow and distant, already affected by the marijuana that passed from mouth to mouth.

'Not really,' Jackie said.

'I'm beginning to feel overwhelmed,' Cynthia told her. 'In less than twenty-four hours I've done things I haven't even imagined doing during the previous twenty-four years. And all of this after a traumatic day with Aaron.'

'Still Aaron?' Clive said.

'I've been with him for three years,' Cynthia replied. 'And by tonight the whole thing may be over, but I owe it to myself, if not to him, to find out where we stand with each other.'

'You only have to consider yourself,' Clive said.

'I can't treat people I'm close to like used toilet paper, to be thrown away when I'm finished with them.'

'Nice try, Cynthia, but you going back has less lofty reasons,' Clive said. 'How many times have there been crises in the past? Quite a few, I imagine. And each time the reconciliation has followed the same pattern, hasn't it? Distance, anger, violence, tears, sex, regret, and recapitulation, ad infinitum. Isn't that so?' He didn't wait for a response. 'That's all so tedious; why repeat it now? Why not make a clean break altogether. Tell no one where you are, not Aaron, not your employers, not your family. Take a new name. Wear totally different clothes. Cut your hair. Change yourself.'

She smiled and shook her head. 'I wish it were that easy.'

'No one is preventing you except yourself,' he said.

'Don't you think I know that?' she snapped. 'The only one oppressing me is me. But I have to find my own way.'

'Excuse me,' said Jackie, 'but I think Clive is right

about one thing. If you see Aaron again, it's almost certain you'll be drawn back into that pattern.'

'And if I stay here I'll be drawn into this pattern. I become a victim of circumstance in any case.' She closed her eyes tightly and then opened them again. 'You must understand. I couldn't relax here until I confronted what's back there.'

'I hope you don't get stuck,' Maureen said. Her voice held an uncharacteristic quaver and when Cynthia looked at her she saw that her eyes were moist.

'What is it?' Cynthia asked her.

'I just felt very sad all of a sudden,' Maureen said. 'I got very afraid that we might not ever see you again.'

Cynthia was about to protest that that wasn't possible, but even as she began to speak she realised that there was not a bad chance that she wouldn't return. Life's liaisons often broke off when it seemed they should be just beginning. Cynthia and Maureen watched the fact that this might be the last time they would be together, and shared the sorrow of that possibility. Cynthia leaned forward and Maureen embraced her. They held on to each other for a long minute.

'Well,' said Jackie, her voice plump and reassuring, 'she's only going into town; it's less than ten minutes away. There's no point in whomping up an imaginary tragedy.' She paused. 'Of course we'll see her again.' She took Cynthia's hand. 'It's foolish to talk of permanence, but you know we like you and find you exciting in bed. At any time you want you can come live here and plan on staying a few months at least. And then you'd be in an entirely different place from which to make life choices. Our intuition is that you are meant to become one of our family. I think your going to see Aaron is a mistake. It's a stale scenario. But I don't want to pressure you in any way at all. Do what you have to, and come back when you want to. You don't even need to phone. Just drive up. If we're not home, let yourself in.'

'You don't know how much I appreciate that,' Cynthia said.

'Yes she does,' Clive said. 'It's all figured in.'

Cynthia turned to him. 'I still don't know what went on in there,' she said.

'You experienced a brief taste of one of several real alternatives open to you at this moment,' Clive told her.

'It was interesting to be a whore for a few minutes,' Cynthia said, 'but it's ridiculous to think I can change my whole style of life overnight.'

'Don't confuse making the decision with living the decision out,' Clive said. 'Of course, life is hard wherever you are, whatever you do. But you have some choice as to where you will conduct your struggle, and how you will play the role. I think you can live a fuller life up here than down there with your man and his dying civilisation. It won't be easier here, only more conscious.'

'I don't know how I will ever be able to integrate your talk of revolution and human dignity with forms of behaviour I have always been taught are degenerate,' said Cynthia.

Clive sipped his tea. 'It's the closet queens who shriek the loudest against homosexuality; it's the priests who persecute the saints; it's the financial robber barons who mount campaigns against prostitution. The people have a right to discover their own life styles, without condemnation and persecution.' Clive sniffed and tossed his head as though to include the whole world outside the garden. 'They are zombies,' he said, 'trying to force us to conform to their deadened patterns of living. They can't stand the idea of individual free choice, of arbitrary decisions, of a refusal to conform to any externally imposed standards. They're termites and ants, not true human beings. Of course they have taught you that it's evil to be a whore or a lesbian or a radical thinker. *But is it really?* You have begun to taste these things for yourself, and you have to now ask yourself what is the truth? Does your experience confirm what they have programmed into you? If so, then return to your marriage and your burgher life and peace be with you. If not, then you have to tear the knots loose with your own hands.'

Cynthia listened to the strong words and understood their accuracy. Her eyes shone. 'I wish Aaron could hear you say those things,' she said. 'He's been struggling with those ideas for so long, and has no one to talk to who will help him get clear.'

'Perhaps I'll come by your place,' Clive said. He smiled. 'Does he have a big cock?'

'It's very large,' Cynthia said.

She turned to Jackie. 'Can I have my clothes?' she asked.

While Cynthia dressed in the bathroom, the others took the breakfast things inside and were sitting in the living room when she stepped out, ready to leave. For a moment she simply stood there, feeling her own breathing. Then she stepped towards the door. The other three all stood and walked with her to the front lawn.

'It's hard to leave,' Cynthia said.

'Call me tomorrow,' Jackie said.

Maureen embraced her again. 'Passion is the only freedom,' she whispered in her ear.

Jackie kissed her. 'The revolution begins inside you,' she said.

Clive shook her hand. He held her gaze and then caught her up in his arms, crushed her to his chest, and set her down again. 'As long as everyone else is giving you little nuggets of wisdom to take with you, I'll leave you with these words: Life is what you do while you're waiting to die. Anyone who tells you anything else is probably trying to sell you something.'

She walked to the car, stepped inside, and watched them wave goodbye as she began the winding drive down the hill.

10

Dejà Vu

Standing in the shower, removed from the stimuli of
the world at large, the steaming water drumming
against the tiles and the plastic curtain, Cynthia ran
a soapy washcloth over her body, feeling the coarse
fabric scrub off the grime of the past three days. She
enjoyed the sense of splendid isolation which contrasted with the preceding period of intense socialis-
ation. It was the first time she'd washed since the night
of Aaron's acid trip, longer than she ordinarily went
without bathing. Aaron had tried a number of times
to convince her that frequent bathing was injurious to
the balance of oils on the skin and was an artifact of
television commercials. 'What's the pleasure in washing if you don't let yourself get dirty?' he had asked.
There was no way for her to make him understand
that the ritual of the bath was unrelated to cleanliness;
she indulged in it for its sensual gratification.

Touching her own body was a delight, close to a
psychological necessity. Her self-definition was, like
that of most others, derived largely from her social
identity. She became the person others perceived her
to be. After eight hours at the office she more or less
unconsciously thought of herself as a dull efficient
machine; after an evening with Aaron she was a house-
wife with an appetite for tumultuous fucking; and on
the street she became a neuter, the lowest common
denominator of all accumulated impressions. On those
occasions when she was alone and asked herself, 'Who
am I really?' she found no answer that would yield to

a verbal formulation. Much of her unrest came from the difficulties she had in knowing which of her several selves was the truest, and she was not sophisticated enough to know that so long as she attempted to put value on different aspects of her ego, she would never approach the problem successfully.

She slid the cloth between her legs, rubbing her cunt until it tingled, scrubbing the deep cleft between her buttocks. She lifted one leg and washed its beveled contours, admiring its curves and smoothness of skin. She smiled as she thought of Clive, and pictured herself as a prostitute preparing for an evening with a client, wondering what it would be like to have a certain price, to be an object that men were willing to pay for, as they did for automobiles and other manifestations of wealth. She held her breasts in her hands, pleased with their firmness and weight, and watched the water run in a single rivulet in the canyon between them. Cynthia enjoyed the sensations in her breasts considerably more than those in her fingers, and she puzzled as to why men found touching a woman's breasts so compelling. She was close to understanding that a major portion of most men's pleasure with a woman is not sexual per se, but a compound of power and male pride which flushes at being able to allow a woman to give herself up to her own excitement.

A wave of depression momentarily swept over her and she thought, 'One day I will be old, and all these charms will be wrinkled and flat. My breasts will shrivel, my cunt will get dry. And who will want me then?'

She was propelled into ruminations on the use of sexual criteria as a means of estimating the value of human beings. She stood under the fine spray of water until all the soap had been rinsed away, and remained to bask in the heat of it on her muscles. She mused that of all the people who had passed through her life over the past few days, not one of them had wanted to relate to her without sex serving as a focus for the interaction. She thought of Clive's discourse on folly,

263

and was forced to conclude that sex served as the single most important distraction from a steady understanding of life for her and the people she attracted. She turned the handles, cutting off the shower at its source, and let the water drip off her skin for a few minutes.

'What if I sewed my cunt shut?' she thought. 'Would all those people who want to live with me still find me interesting and appealing?' She marvelled that her multiple array of functions and expressions had been, over the years, reduced to three main channels: fucking, cooking, and working. She was on the verge of accusing the others of venery when it occurred to her to reverse the question. 'If I were unable to have sex at all, how many of them would I continue to want to see? And under what circumstances?'

She ran down the list. Without sex she would lose interest in Aaron very quickly, she would care to see Conrad only sporadically, and would have little cause to visit Jackie and Maureen again. Clive would become a joke instead of a possible pimp. She was amazed at how all other social functions, intellectual rapport, emotional warmth, political involvement, were all laced with the strands of sex. The coming together of any group of two or more always held the same implicit questions: who gets to fuck whom at the end of the meeting? She received a vision of all civilisation as a stilted sublimation, a substitute for simple straightforward sexuality, of everyone she knew as a pack of polite savages, pretending they were interested in everything else except the central driving issue of human society: how the energy gets distributed. Had she a sociological imagination, she would have extrapolated into other realms, and seen the chaos of mankind as a result of the inability to deal with that question in terms of food and other natural resources.

She stepped out of the tub and looked at herself in the mirror opposite it, rubbing the fog from the glass with a towel. Her skin was pink and glowing, her nipples wrinkled, her face beautiful with seriousness,

264

her cunt staunch between her thighs. She was quintessentially erotic.

'And yet,' she said to herself, 'what is it after all? A pole sliding into a hole. A meshing of gears. A conditioned dance.' She peered into her eyes and into the nature of sex, attempting to confront this problem which had been central to all her difficulties in relationships since she was thirteen years old. 'And it is nothing at all. It changes nothing. It solves nothing. It accomplishes nothing. Why is it so terribly important? Is it that we are so horribly neurotic that we are fixated on fucking all out of proportion to the role it should play in our lives? Do we fuck too much or not enough? Or perhaps it's that we don't do it correctly? Is there anyone who knows? Why the burning jealousy, the clinging and running away, the long cries in the night, the urgent efforts at one more orgasm, one more spasm greater than the last? Haven't I experienced that enough times? Shouldn't there come a point where one is free of sex?'

She would soon have to confront Aaron, and she did not know how she would respond. For she had come to see that their problems were rooted in a complex of characterological difficulties imbedded in the structure of society itself. Everything from official corruption to sexual frustration, from the decay of the nation to the nastiness over breakfast cups, were all part of the same piece. There was a clear relationship between Aaron's unhappiness at work and his sexual insensitivity at home, and the very nature of his job was a function of the general brutality of the economic system within which it operated, and the overall destruction of the culture was hinged on its inability to deal with the sexual instinct. The circle closed in on itself and there seemed nothing any individual could do. 'Jackie's right,' Cynthia thought, 'the whole civilisation needs to be turned on its head. But where to begin?'

'I must make a choice of life style,' she said to herself.

'The battle will be the same everywhere. The question is, where will I be most effective, most at home?' She saw that choosing marriage with Aaron or some other man as her pattern, would entail a harsh and bitter struggle to keep from succumbing to the traps of that particular social structure. On the other hand, it was the scene she knew best, and going to live with Maureen and Jackie might seem easier only because she wasn't familiar with the more unpleasant realities of the path. The labyrinth laughed loudly as she glanced down its false exits.

She covered herself with baby powder, pulled the hair from her face and fixed it in a bun at the back of her head. She put on a tattered pink bathrobe, the first present Aaron had ever given her. 'Am I desirable?' she said to her image in the mirror. 'Will he see me and want me? And what will he be taken by? My breasts, my lips, my cunt? What else is there in a woman for a man to look for? Emotions come and go, and affection is a thing of the moment.' She investigated the functions she served in Aaron's life and found that all of them cast her in one or another role of server, ranging from nurse to conversation post, things she had been willing to accede to so long as there was some sense of investment, a feeling that her time would bring her dividends. But what was the payoff? It seemed she would have nothing to look forward to but more of the same, acting as counterweight for Aaron's erratic forays into himself.

'And what do I want from him?' she asked herself. The answer slammed into her mind with the force of a blow.

'Strength,' she said out loud, 'I need him to be strong, to know who he is and what he wants from life. I want him to be bold, courageous. When he stands as firm and brave as a tree for me to lean on, then everything is right between us.' She grinned, thinking what Jackie would have to say to such ideas, for she recognised that her notions were, in the framework of

266

women's liberation, terribly reactionary. 'But what of it?' she thought. 'I can only follow my feeling, and what satisfies me most deeply has to be what's right for me.' She sprayed a mist of cologne around her throat. The picture of her and Aaron, she saw, was Biblical in its contours, and she relished the image of the man at his labours, securing the home for his family, while the woman tended the chores and in the evenings held his head in her lap, stroking his face, until his fatigue left him and he rose to take her in his arms and make strong tender love to her. She rubbed her eyes. 'I'm mired in old-fashioned concepts of relationship,' she thought. 'In an age when those models seem to have no relevance.'

She took a deep breath. 'I wonder what will become of us?' continued the voice in her mind. 'Will I soon be lying on my back, his cock splitting my cunt apart, his arms holding me tightly on his chest? And after all the moaning and sighing, will he let me fall away, no longer interested in me until his next erection? I wouldn't even mind that, if we could keep it that clean. But we will begin to involve our emotions once more, and to raise our expectations. I will look to him to play a part he is not suited to, and he will begin to make demands on my inner life. We will bind ourselves to one another in that terrible bondage which, once fixed, becomes impossible to burst apart without pain and suffering. And then we shall feel trapped, and thrash about to find some way out. And another Conrad will enter our life, or a Maureen and Jackie, and it will be six months from now and the same cycle will repeat itself.' She picked up her toothbrush, covered it with paste, and began to clean her teeth. 'And would it be any different with Conrad? Once his lengthy seduction is complete and I give him what he yearns for, and his cock at last explodes in the recesses of my cunt, will I become just another woman for him, just another notch, another inconvenience, or will he want to start a new dance, in which the only difference for me is that I substitute one man for another?' She rinsed her mouth. 'And all of this because of sex, because we can't fuck, not anyone, not men or women, without that very fucking becoming the chain that binds us to ancient and deadly patterns of relationship. Maybe I should just give it up. Or maybe listen to Clive, and become a whore. There might be more dignity in outright prostitution than in any of the other forms of relationship people have evolved to deal with one another.'

She rubbed an astringent on her cheeks to tighten the skin and made a face at herself. 'What's the point in all this thinking?' she thought. 'All the while I'm trying to figure it out I'm making myself attractive for when he comes home.' She laughed silently, a brief expulsion of air through her nostrils. 'What's a woman to do?' she asked.

The front door slammed, and her heart jumped in her chest. In a flash she saw that she was afraid of what he might be like, and it was that very fear which thrilled her. It was impossible to know what his mood would be, and she considered that within a half hour she could be in bed with him, or packing her bags to leave. She had no preconceptions or guidelines as to her behaviour. She wanted to face him openly, with all her reactions vibrant, and try to see the man she had lived with for so long. Above all, she did not want to lose her perspective, the sense of opening and liberty that had accompanied her on the ride down from the hill. 'I wonder how much of that is an illusion,' she said to herself. 'Well, we'll soon find out,' she added as she opened the door and stepped out into the living room.

Aaron stood there, swaying, looking like one of the derelicts that haunt Third Street in San Francisco. Unshaved, his clothes rumpled, a look of despair on his face, he seemed ready for suicide or some form of salvation, to end his misery or to give himself to someone who promised peace for his soul and soup for his belly. She was shocked at his appearance, and checked her impulse to go over to him, put her arms around him, and give him her warmth. It was a sorrowful realisation that such a simple human gesture was laid about with a hundred psychic traps. It would have been easier to show compassion for a stranger in the street than to the man she had cared for so deeply.

Aaron looked at her as though through a thick haze. There wasn't a part of him that wasn't exhausted or thwarted. The enormous energy which normally coursed through him lay dormant; he was like a powerful elephant that had been shot with tranquilizer darts and could not rouse itself from its torpor. Cynthia had never appeared so beautiful as at that moment. Invulnerable in the privacy created by her secret disappearance, exuding an animal sensuality, enlivened by her bath, and wearing the robe that had a thousand connotations of their life together, she seemed a creature too strong and lovely for him even to approach. In the constant balance of power that obtains in the relationship between a man and a woman, he had fallen into a pit of helplessness, walled with self-pity, and was incapable of asking her for support. These were his feelings, and in the blink of an eye they could change. When he felt hopelessness, he might, in an instant, show anger. The difference between the two of them just then was that Cynthia was aware of how volatile the situation was, while Aaron was too deadened by disillusionment to perceive the dynamics beneath the surface emotions.

The physical distance between them was no more than six feet. But in terms of their willingness or ability to cross that space toward one another, they might as well have been on the opposite poles of the planet. After three years of intense involvement, having shared what they felt to be the truest aspects of their authentic selves as well as having suffered the mutual abrasions of the daily struggle with one another's most petty manifestations, they stared at each other as though they were aliens from hostile

269

kingdoms, wondering whether they should fight, fuck, or turn their backs on one another and pretend the encounter had never taken place.

They stood facing one another, like actors who have forgotten their lines, stuck in their stage directions, waiting for someone to whisper the next word, the next move. A soft tension gripped them and a double awareness enhanced the space. It seemed to them that all the world held its breath, that the infinite unimaginable universe spinning in untold dimensions a tale for some unspeakable listener was but an insignificant detail in the drama of their confrontation. All that they were capable of feeling, they felt in those few minutes, rippling through the entire catalogue of human sensibility without responding to any of it. Like a madly blinking strobe their perceptions of one another flashed through their minds. They saw one another alternately as lover and stranger, the intimacy of their history clashing with the anonymity of their present condition. It was possible to accept either reality, or neither, or both, or reject the entire matrix within which they were frozen, like flies in a spider web. Each of the four choices launched them on a path that was already structured and planned out from beginning to end. The question was, which to choose? To leap once more into the turbulence of sexual relationship? To cease, all involvement on the spot? To attempt the difficulty and pain of beholding each other as both real and unreal at the same time? To continue to drift in ambiguity?

Freedom is simply an understanding of one's limitation, and crucial to all these considerations was the problem of which should make the first overture, who would bear the onus of setting the mood. The moment surged toward some critical point when a decision had to be made. It was past the time for preamble. They were taken to the brink of articulation and asked by history the single question upon which the future of the species was to be judged: is any healthy relationship possible between a man and woman fucking?

Cynthia's nostrils flared; she was too wary to make any overt gesture. Aaron straightened his spine; there was nothing he could say. They waited, like two aerial artists watching the bar swing back and forth between them, unwilling to move until the timing was perfect, until each could be sure that there would be someone at the other end to catch the one who dared to release the safety grip and fly through the air in a single giddy tumbling arc of trust.

'Aaron, take the responsibility,' Cynthia said to herself.

'Cynthia, help me,' Aaron whispered in his mind.

And externally, nothing happened. The drum roll petered out, the audience lost its patience, and the spotlights swung around to some other act which was beginning its fanfare in the centre ring on the ground below. Whatever chance they had had to seize the instant in a spontaneous movement born of the overflow of their feelings was lost, and they fell back upon their calculations.

The moment softened and bent. They returned from the stark heights of their structural dramaturgy and descended into the material reality of the room. They assumed the colouration of their environment, like two chameleons adjusting to the hue of woodbark. Aaron rocked back and forth on his heels, and Cynthia's fingers trembled. They each let the impetus of their separate convergent escapades catch up to the present, and confronted the fact that after all the ruminations they were now faced with the actuality of one another's presence.

'You look terrible,' she said.

'I haven't slept much,' he replied.

The sentences slid into the space like alligators slipping into a stream, the commonplace quality of their message underscoring all that had been evaded. The simple words cut like razors drawn across soft skin.

271

Aaron lifted his head. The fact that she had spoken first, the sound of her voice, and her calm demeanor, filled him with a rush of energy which, to his debilitated ego, appeared as a surge of power. Like a man in shock who had just been given a shot of whiskey, Aaron stirred from his stance. He felt the first stirrings of a return of self-assurance; Cynthia served as a marker against which he could estimate his position.

'I'll make you some coffee,' she said. 'Why don't you get cleaned up? I think there's enough hot water left.'

Her allusion to the hot water heater, a decrepit piece of machinery that had served as their major point of argument with the landlord, was like a door closing distantly behind them. The fabric of their life together torn apart by the explosive events of the past few days, began to be realigned. Cynthia watched the process without fully understanding it. Some voice in her warned, 'Now's the time. If you want to stay honest with yourself, now's the time to speak. Tell him what you've been doing, what you've been thinking.' While Aaron wondered if he would ever mention the fact that he had already killed her in his heart, and was not sure that there was anything to be gained by bringing her back to life.

But sentimentality, one of the seducers of truth, swept through the atmosphere like an aria from a Neopolitan opera. All the accumulated habit of their patterns of relationship rose up to disarm them. And there were no words. Cynthia could not transmit her experience to Aaron; she could only communicate the details of the adventure, a process which would make him jealous. Then her energy would be spent in dealing with his changes, and little would be left to consider her insights. She needed him to be sensitive to her altered state of consciousness. While through his body ran a single mute physiological hope: the notion that he could fuck her again. All else that he felt suddenly became subservient to the throbbing nerve of lust that had been activated by her physical presence. His cir-

cuits were wired in such a way that the ability to fuck
was the central proof that everything was all right;
once he had an erection and was inside her, he would
have claimed her once more as his own, he would be
in control, and he could make the decisions. As it was,
in this ambience of ambivalent equality, he felt
unmanned.

She blinked once and turned to go into the kitchen,
stepped past him, her shoulder almost touching his,
the scent of her hair stinging him like a whiplash. The
mood was too powerful for him to assimilate and he
whirled around as she walked by him.

'Cynthia,' he said, grabbing her shoulder.

'I don't know, Aaron,' she said. 'You've hurt me too
much in the past.'

His lips twitched. 'You're not the only one who's
been hurt,' he said.

She cast her eyes down. 'I understand that,' she said.
'I'm not blaming you. I just don't want to continue if
it's going to be more of the same.'

'Do you want to split up?' he asked, his voice tinged
with accusation.

'Why do you make it sound as though it's only my
decision?' she shot back. 'What do *you* want to do?'

His fingers dug into her arm. His face jumped with
nervous tics. The question was like a thorn in his back;
he could neither ignore it or reach it. His mouth moved
as though to speak, and he realised that any words
which came out would be meaningless; they would be
nothing but noises to vibrate the air. His speech had
lost all connection with his actions, for nothing he said
would hold true even an hour after he spoke it. He
could make no declarations, no promises; and like
many a man brought to the brink of humility by the
circumstances of his life, he attempted confession.

'All I want now is to fuck you,' he said. 'I can't see
past that.'

Her breath was heavy in her chest. She stared at
him as though trying to find the lie she knew had to

be hidden in his words. But his statement was so simple, so bereft of any hidden motivations, she relaxed her guard momentarily and accepted it. In that instant a second door closed behind them. For both of them ignored the reality which the words pointed to. Fucking was not for them an act like eating, a deed to be indulged in and then passed over. In the sexual encounter, they entered realms of intensity which melted their powers of intellect, the way white flame will cut through steel.

'I've never said no to you,' she said.

He stepped forward and took her in his arms, and in the way all the parameters of existence change when a person leaps from the world of air into the world of water, requiring a radically different orientation to all life systems, Aaron's entire personality changed. Where he was rigid, he became soft; where he was uncertain, he became masterly; where he was lost, he found the map to guide him. With every other aspect of his relationship in tatters, this was one area in which some security was still to be found. He crushed her to his chest.

'You're hurting me,' she said.

Had she spoken the words a few seconds earlier, they would have served only to alienate him further, but in the context of his burgeoning desire, her description inflamed him. He squeezed her to him with the implacable slowness of a boa constrictor killing a leopard, holding her through sheer muscular dominance. It was as though he were draining her of blood, forcing her to depend on him for mercy. Her body against his, the smell of her skin in his nostrils, roused him to a ritual of power. She could feel the immense strength bottled up inside him, and her knees buckled at the thought that it would erupt at any moment and be detonated inside her.

'I was half out of my mind when you didn't come home,' he said. 'Where did you go?'

Her detachment fading, she sagged into him. Her

mind remained lucid and she saw that the others had been right, that once she stepped back into the world of her relationship with Aaron, she would be helpless to fight its raging current. She would have to give in and act as a sacrifice on the altar of Aaron's need, and later listen to more of his promises about how the future would be better. She was amazed at how easy it was to yield to his demands. She knew that the fiercer he became, the more gloriously he would fuck her, and being fucked by Aaron was still the core of her existence. As he bent her back bringing her cunt up against his thighs, she recalled the last time she was in the living room with Aaron, and Conrad's presence there. She yearned for the young man the way she looked forward to a drink of cold water on a hot day. 'This may be the last time,' she thought. 'After this, I may have to leave him for good.'

'Who were you with?' he insisted.

It was difficult to continue thinking, she couldn't keep her eyes open. 'I went to visit friends,' she gasped. 'Girl friends.'

'Do I know them?' he said, continuing his inquisition.

'No,' she told him, 'they're people I met at a meeting, I can give you their number, you can call them if you don't believe me, for God's sake you're breaking my back.'

He bit her throat and sucked the flesh between his teeth. The dialogue, his actions, her responses, were not conscious in any real sense of the word. The two of them were like computers that had been programmed with rigidly defined schemata, and could deliver their results within those limits. All their intelligence, education, and good intentions to the contrary, they were enslaved by the rigours of their conditioning. They knew what they were doing, but as that knowledge had no practical effect on the workings of their behaviour, it had no more value than speculation. As he tortured and questioned her, Aaron's conscience attempted to intervene, telling him he had no right to treat another human being in this fashion, even if the other person were, willy-nilly, cooperating. But all ethical considerations were met and overcome by the fervour engendered by the situation and the unassailable argument of his stiffening cock. He stared into space as his mouth fastened on her skin, considering that all his actions and emotions and thought of the past twenty-four hours had been predicted on a fantasy. He believed Cynthia's statement, and its implication that her evening was innocently spent. He saw that without evidence he had assumed that Cynthia had gone to spend the night with a man. 'Perhaps that's what I really wanted to be true,' he thought. 'Maybe I want to be rid of her.' But now she was back, and he was caught up in a massive regression, twisting in the toils of jealousy and lust. He perceived that he was being dragged once more into the morass of their relationship, and he felt helpless to do anything about it as her firm breasts warmed against his chest. 'Why did you come back?' he said, his tone vibrant with regret.

His question struck her as the final insult, and anger ripped through her psyche. She threw all her strength into a single gesture and wrenched loose from his grasp, leaving him standing with his arms out, like a store-window dummy. She faced him with all the sizzling animosity of a drop of water splashed on a red hot iron. Her face was a flag of aggression.

'You bastard,' she spat. Her eyes narrowed. 'Only because I felt sorry for you.'

She did not see the blow coming, nor feel it directly. Her next recollection had her lying on the floor, her left cheek on fire, her eyes watery, and Aaron leaning over her.

She began to cry, the tears bursting to the surface, but she fought back the impulse. Aaron's eyes were already a sea of concern; he was already blaming himself, seeking forgiveness by her acknowledgment of his brutishness. If she gave in to weeping, he would hold her and console her, and his slap would be forgotten. And it was a thing she did not want to forget, for it served as a launching pad from which to hurl herself out of the gravitational field of their relationship. She made herself hard.

Cynthia put one arm over her face, shielding herself from contact with the man hovering over her. There was a long moment in which nothing happened, and then she felt his hand pulling her bathrobe open, exposing her naked body. His fingers pushed the cloth apart and trailed delicately over her skin. Had she been looking at him, she would have seen the expression on his face change to one of mindless lust. His mouth fell open and a thin line of spittle twisted from one corner of his lips. It was as though he were in a dream, and he drooled over her. Had he been a rapist having knocked a woman to the ground, what he was about to do would have been nobler in its motivation than it was. For he did not only desire to possess her, he wanted to subjugate her; if he had been interested merely in his own sexual gratification, his deed might have been understood as an animal act; but he needed to prod her to respond, to make her want what was happening to her. As his hand covered her cunt, a third and final door closed behind them, stealing them into the very reality they had fought so hard to escape.

His middle finger slipped into the fold and Cynthia bit her lip. Like an epileptic filmed in the middle of a seizure and played back in slow motion, her eyes rolled back in her head, her tongue became a curled lizard in her mouth, her body twisted in a long convulsive movement. He slipped into the moist centre of her and she let herself be carried off in a dance of exposure in which all the expressions she had muted and suppressed for a lifetime came to the surface. She threw herself into her gotterdammerung gyrations, unheedful of all its connotations. He had hit her trying to damage her, and she no longer cared what went down between them. Like a well uncovered by an explosion, she bubbled with the disgust, anger, hatred, fear and anguish that her civilised veneer had walled in. The eruption of all the ugliness inside her was so full that it flowered into a fantastic beauty.

Her lips twisted, her tongue circling her mouth and licking her own skin, her fingers curled into claws, her head rolling from side to side, her legs gnarled and kicking, she was like some ancient beast at last pinned to the ground by a stake through its belly, oozing all the accumulated poison of a lifetime. She projected all her negativity, no longer caring that the man who was the target for it all was guilty only through weakness. Aaron gained the final perspective on his situation. He trembled with need and whimpered with loss. He saw in Cynthia the breaking through of the woman he had always desired, the free unfettered animal, and knew that once she tasted that liberty, he would lose her. The crux of all his confusion came clear. His ambivalence about their marriage came from the fact that he grew bored with her whenever she fell below her fullest potential; but grew fearful when she began to explore the avenues to liberty. Thus it had been necessary to support and goad her efforts at growth, and at the same time sabotage them when they came close to succeeding. He had boxed her in a double bind because he was afraid she would outstrip him.

'Cynthia,' he said, 'how unworthy I am to have you.'

She looked up at him. She no longer knew who he was. He was a man, a person. He was one of the catalysts in her transformation toward some other reality. She realised that all her other images had been illusory; Aaron had no meaning for her except as a tool for her own development. All that was important was herself, her own dance, her inner voice.

'You have never been so beautiful,' he said.

'What does he see?' she wondered. 'Who is he talking to?'

They were tied to one another by bonds stronger than either could break. Once in each other's presence they were both fated to continue the drama, pick up where they had left off, the only difference being in the sophistication of their rationalisation. The only choice was whether to come together at all. And Cynthia had chosen to return because she wanted to perceive Aaron after her experiences with Jackie and Maureen. But now she saw that she was addicted to their relationship, that for all its brutality and evasiveness it brought forth a kind of ecstasy that she found nowhere else. She wondered whether she could leave Aaron and continue to visit him, to have these moments with him. An image of her life opened in which she saw herself walking through a supermarket, and like heads of lettuce were stacked, the heads of Aaron, and Conrad, Maureen and Jackie, Clive, each a different brand, each a different price. And she was free to choose whichever appealed to her at any given time.

Aaron surrendered to his sorrow. He was laced with such longing for what lay at his very fingertips that he almost doubled over in anguish. He wanted her so badly he could barely breathe, and yet he knew that the moment he entered her he would lose himself in her. He saw before him the body of a woman stripped of all its civilised postures. He saw a writhing pulsating creature of movement and moisture and heat. He saw the Cynthia he had glimpsed time and time again, but who had always eluded him. And now she was there, in all her ugliness and glory, in all her salaciousness and purity.

She made thick mewing sounds like a kitten choked with milk.

'Oh my god,' Aaron moaned, 'I have to get inside you.'

He leaned back and stripped off his clothing, his body emerging like a figure from stone under the blows of a cold chisel. He fell forward and his mouth covered hers. She made no change to accommodate his pressure. It was as though she continued to lick the air, and the fact that her tongue fell on his lips seemed incidental. She was in the throes of expression and was not concerned with appreciation. Aaron drank her in, revelling in the fact that she did not recognise him by any outward sign. Her wanton impersonality allowed him to free the beast within himself. He grabbed her breasts in his hands, squeezing them harshly, pushing them back against her chest with his palms, kneading them with his fingers. She let out a series of huffing grunts like a woman in labour.

'Gggnhngh,' she groaned.

'Baby, baby, baby,' he crooned, 'come on, let it out.'

He planted himself between her legs and ravished her body with his eyes, in a glance consuming the full soft fleshy desirability of her, going from her wildly gesticulating lips to her lush breasts and the deep belly which stretched taut to the centre of his charge, her pink, guarded, essential, and trivial cunt, source of so much pain and confusion from the day of his conception. With cosmic significance, he brought the opposite member to bear, flourishing his throbbing, hungry, ignorant cock, the bane of Cynthia's existence. He lumbered over her like a great ape, heavy in his legs, and cried out to the ceiling, his voice echoing in the dark room. And then he fell upon her.

His cock plunged into her cunt with the accuracy of an arrow loosed from the bow of a Zen archer. She let out a moan of mingled pain and pleasure as the ruthless organ tore past the dry outer lips, seared the inner lips with its heat, and burst loudly into the tiny bud at the very centre of her sexual soul. She dug her nails into his shoulders as her legs shot straight up in the air. They hung poised without moving for several seconds, glued to the wonder of penetration and invitation, and then wrapped themselves around each other's body.

A great silence enveloped them as they moved into

a different dimension, leaving the world of evaluation and entering the kingdom of immediate realisation. Like a king and queen who had been exiled in a land where their sovereignty was not recognised and then return to their own borders to have their powers restored, Aaron and Cynthia came home, to the one level of being where they could create their own reality.

Aaron's hips moved in a circular motion, and Cynthia twitched under him, an instantaneously hot wet woman yielding to the parabolic passion of a man possessed. At the juncture where their legs met, the bulging cock kissed the sopping cunt in all the farthest recesses of its mouth. They glided into the realm of touch, the primal sensation, and were buoyed up through the ontology of feeling as they smelled the secretions of their act, tasted the sweat on one another's skin, heard their mutual moans, and looked at each other's rolling forms. Like two heavily charged batteries, their forces built up during their separation, they released tremendous amounts of energy into the air and into one another's systems, creating a momentarily perfect union of male and female. His pelvis rocked in the cradle of her thighs and she yearned upward to receive him. They moved together until their fields merged and came to climax in an orgasm of the emotions that was the sweetest experience either of them had ever known. Cynthia licked Aaron's shoulder as he held her tenderly and tightly. They were at the station where all the trains of their essential currents converged, and from the centre there was no way to proceed but back out into the tangled periphery of their involvement.

Cynthia was both happy and confused, for in the midst of all their difficulty they were still able to reach this point of union, and she found that the sum and substance of their relationship was merely an experience, and as such had no more weight than any of the countless other things which happened in her life. It was only the investment of such moments with value that gave them worth, and it had become impossible to gild the contours of their fucking when all the rest of their intercourse was permeated with pain. 'It's everything I can hope for,' she thought, 'and it's not enough.'

She turned her head to look into his eyes, to see if his mind was still attuned to their fucking, or whether he had drifted off into some interior domain. And just then, spurred on by the demands of his cock, Aaron began to ride once more. Obliterating the ethereal pleasure that had been bestowed upon him, he hungered for the grosser fulfilment. He hunched his spine and began to grind his pelvis into her hairy cunt. Her fingers formed into a mudra of questioning over his head, but when she realised that everything else would have to take second place to his drive toward ejaculation, she sighed and gave herself up to the inevitable. She knew that she would respond and offer herself as a vessel to be entered again and again until heat and friction had worked their magic upon her nervous system and he spilled his fluid tension into her. Her legs spread wide, her cunt slack, she let him fuck her as he wished.

Aaron pumped his cock into her. He growled in his throat and pinned her with his weight. He brought his head down and began to bite her nipples. She raised her knees, allowing him deeper penetration. And they started the kind of fuck that they had performed a hundred times, she swooning with sensation as he urged himself on to completion. But some lever clicked inside him, and he dissociated from the sexuality of the moment in order to set it as some cinematographic production, as though the two of them were suddenly thrust before a camera and it became incumbent upon him to satisfy the voice of the director shouting in his ear.

'Hurt her,' the voice said, 'make her cry, make her squirm. You know she likes it. Hit her, bite her hard.

282

Make her go wild. She's just a cunt, a hot crazy cunt. Forget all that nonsense about human relationship. There's only this under everything else. Just your cock making her faint. Stick it in her, all the way in her. Put it in her mouth, up her arse.'

Large drops of sweat formed on his forehead as he worked inside her, like a man straining to finish a hundred push-ups, forcing himself to the limits of his capacity. He slammed his weight between her thighs, crushing her tender cunt with his strokes. She put her hands under her knees and pulled her legs as far back and as far apart as they would go. His cock smashed the walls of her cunt, causing her to wince with trepidation that he would break through the vaginal wall. But the harder he moved, the more she relaxed, and found that she could accommodate anything he wanted to hurl into her.

He lost awareness of who they were and pressed his teeth into her nipple. She grabbed his hair and pulled it until the pain she inflicted equalled the pain she received, keeping him at bay through a balance of retribution. He snarled and shook his head like a dog tearing at a piece of meat. Her nails dug in at his neck and pulled ten strips of flesh down the entire length of his back to his buttocks. The hurt coursed through him like the shock of ripping tendons and fed the conflagration in his groin. Their battle returned Cynthia to her position of distance from her activity. For the few minutes when they had been joined in the sheer exultation of their coming together in a welter of feeling, all the problems that surrounded them had been shunted to the background. Now those questions returned with greater fury and her mind exploded with a thousand jumbled frantic thoughts. But she had no space within which to sort things out, for Aaron's insistence had become monumental. She tore at his skin with undisguised viciousness.

Aaron plunged into recklessness. He knew that if he continued to fuck her in this manner he would come bucking her will, and that such an orgasm would leave him dissatisfied and surly. It was clear that to go on with his physical assault would probably drive the final nail into the coffin of their affection. But like a man about to get into a fight, he needed the excitement of the combat more than his concern for life and limb. He forgot the future and hurled himself into the frenzy of the present.

Cynthia put her hands at his throat and began to choke him. He grabbed her hair with one hand and slapped her again with the other. The blow stunned her momentarily, and then to their mutual surprise she laughed, an eerie pealing sound. With astonishing speed she shot her mouth forward and fastened her teeth on his right cheek, biting down until she could almost feel the skin breaking. Aaron shouted in pain at the same time he bucked into her with renewed vigour.

As his cock and pubic bone pounded the sensitive tissues of her cunt, like a barrage of war ships on a hostile shore, she ground her teeth together and bit into his face, severing the flesh and causing a shower of blood to burst into her mouth. He screamed once, a high-pitched shriek that resounded over the entire street outside the apartment, and at that Cynthia yelled, a cry of liberation that set her entire body tingling. As the hot thick blood spilled over her lips she thrust upwards and tightened her muscles, swallowing his cock with a single vaginal gulp.

He became a screeching nerve against her body, all the myriad postures and character structures of his many roles lighting up like neon advertisements for the human race, overlaid against the basic formless energy which sustained them. He had gone past all convention and she had soared beyond all inhibition. He saw that every idea he had ever held was as ephemeral as the clouds; there was nothing real but the raw insatiable drive of life itself. He had reached the point where he had nothing more to lose, and could literally

284

destroy the foundations of his slavery by demolishing the physical structure in which it had found expression. Their attacks on one another's body were only the symbols for the deeper desire to abolish the conditioning inherent in their bones and muscles and nerve endings. He sought her centre, to become one with that anatomy and attitude of cunt which was indistinguishable from her most private understanding of herself. And with an ululating cry that contained the eternal pain of birth in its cadences and tones, she surrendered the struggle and flung herself into the boiling cauldron of intense occurrence.

She burst against Aaron's body, taking it in its full impersonal strength and hardness, no longer asking who it was that fucked her, or whether the heart of the man cared for her in any special way. She became a free woman, courageous in her acknowledgment that she must take upon herself half the sadness and fear that men and women bear as the penalty for waking up to being alive in one another's arms. She stopped reaching out for him to sustain her in the terrifying dizziness of ecstasy, nor did she shrink from the heights she had attained. And in her own release, she set him loose. She sang out in full-throated totality of being, in complete acceptance of her essential solitude, no longer requiring the man to console her.

Aaron felt her at last, after all the years of despairing of reaching the core of Cynthia. It had been necessary to lose her and destroy her inside himself before he could find the true woman that slept beneath the form of a woman's body. And although he didn't realise it, it had been equally necessary for her to acquiesce to his desire to kill her before she could let him possess her as he needed to. For a few seconds their hearts and minds and bodies merged in a single vibration, a union which subsumed all the names of God.

And then Aaron exploded into orgasm. Trembling, melting, crying out, he tumbled into Cynthia, who held him as a hammock holds a fragile body, cupping and curving her cunt to absorb the seed which spilled from him. She climaxed quietly, throbbing deeply in her womb.

At the precise instant his sperm left him, all his searing intuition and powerful focus collapsed. He felt like an empty tube, no longer useful to her or to himself. It seemed, somehow, in some undefined way, that he had failed at some crucial test, and he whimpered once as his consciousness clouded over and he began to dissemble into sleep.

And the first thought that entered Cynthia's mind as she unhooked her legs from around his was, 'Perhaps I should stay with him long enough to get pregnant. All I really want from him is a baby.'

'You'll have a scar just like Conrad's,' she said.

Aaron lit the pyramid of paper, sticks and logs in the small fireplace and sat back as the flames began to consume the kindling. He put his hand up to his cheek and felt the bandage. Cynthia had washed the wound with hydrogen peroxide, smeared it with vaseline, and covered it with gauze and tape. The night was warm and the fire was like a sweater on a spring evening, unnecessary but reassuring. A bottle of wine and two glasses between them, they watched the fire and listened to the low music coming over the radio.

'Does it frighten you?' he asked. 'The violence, I mean.'

'Of course it does,' she replied. 'But I find it exciting too.'

They fell into silence, pacing themselves before reaching the question that had been asked earlier but not dealt with. They both were aware that they had to come to some reasoned conclusion concerning whether they would continue to live together. It was obvious that the power of their sexual attraction would bind them in a relationship which might be damaging to both of them, compounded as it was by several years of habit, a genuine concern for one another, and a mutual realisation of the immense difficulties which face a man and a woman who attempt to couple. One of the logs began to crackle.

'It's like the old days,' he said, 'when I was living on the Great Highway, before you moved in. Do you remember those long walks in the fog, and then going back to my place and lighting a fire and drinking hot rum?'

'How could I forget that?' she said. She poured wine into their glasses.

'And that tiger rug? Making love on the thick fur and then falling asleep on the floor and waking up in the middle of the night with only embers glowing. I used to carry you to bed and we'd smother ourselves under the comforter and lie so close together, breathing in one another's mouths.'

'It was very beautiful, Aaron. I loved you very much then.'

'What happened?' he asked.

'I think you got bored with being happy,' she said.

He frowned. 'No,' he replied. 'It was you too. Something in you changed.'

She shrugged and sipped at her wine. 'We began to live together and lost our individual identities. I forgot to ask myself what I wanted and began to worry about what you needed.'

'That simple.'

'And all the rest of it,' she continued. 'I began to see that everything I thought was sustaining me was actually stifling me. My job was inhuman, the city got to seem unliveable, and our relationship was holding me back from tasting all the things I wanted to explore. I felt I was incomplete, living in a kind of genteel drudgery.'

He sniffed. 'Pity the poor middle class,' he said. 'We have too much to be resigned to poverty and not enough to feel rich. We can't be capitalists and we're too frightened to be revolutionaries. And the only place we maintain any real life at all is between our legs.

287

And even there we thrash around, unsatisfied with what we have.'

Cynthia levelled a gaze at him. 'What are you going to do, Aaron?' she said.

'Do?' he said. 'What is there to do? Just continue. Keep on living. Get up every morning, morning after morning, until one morning is the final morning, and that will be the end of it. And all of this life, this thing we're involved in at this very moment, will have been a strange dream.'

'I think I'm going to leave,' she told him. He cocked his head, the only indication that he heard her words. 'I have some money saved,' she went on, and a boulder rolled through her mind as she thought of the five hundred dollars Clive had given her. 'And I'll just take off for a while, be by myself, get in touch with who I am again.'

'I'll be here,' he said glumly, his body tingling at her words, his entire system attempting to assimilate the fact that the threatened split was finally taking shape.

'You know the chances that we'll come together again are small.'

He downed his wine in a single swallow and threw his glass into the fireplace. 'Oh, what difference does it make,' he said, 'if I suffer with you or I suffer alone? I'm finished with believing that having a woman in my life is going to make any difference at all in the nature of my living. This notion of trying new lifestyles is a myth. Life is a choice of pain, and changing partners or refusing any partner at all is nothing more than replacing the instrument used to torture you.' Incongruously, he laughed. 'I'm beginning to get Jewish again. You know, I used to hear this kind of talk from my parents and teachers when I was a kid, and when I left that scene I put it down as so much semitic defeatism. But the more I see of life, the more I understand the wisdom of that viewpoint. God is an ironist, and there is no chance for anything but to continue as we've been doing, trying our best to keep from damaging one another, all the while knowing that we are condemned to inflict pain on those we love, beginning with ourselves.'

Cynthia's face twisted into a mask of resistance. His words, and the conviction with which he spoke them, were terribly convincing, especially at a moment when they were sealing the doom of their relationship. But she did not want to succumb to his bleak vision. 'If I accept that, I'd kill myself,' she said. 'I have to keep looking for a way out. There must be some way for us to become something else than what we were raised to be. Even if it means tearing down the entire civilisation with our bare hands.' She thought of Conrad and Jackie and their sweet rational optimism that sustained all their equally dour analyses of the situation. 'We seem to be the only species of animal that is not at peace with itself,' she went on, 'and we have to find the solution to that problem.'

'Our brains are too big for our bodies,' he said. 'We are evolutionary freaks. The civilisation you talk about destroying isn't some abstract monster out there; it exists inside us, it is us. What's the point of running here and there, travelling, forming organisations, getting involved in political struggles, when you can't climb the walls inside your own soul?' He looked into her eyes and his voice dropped to a low calm tone. 'We live here,' he said, 'and if we can't cope with our problems in our home, what chance do you think there is anywhere else?'

A subtle shift took place in her psyche. Beneath his incantation of hopelessness she thought she detected a plea for help. 'Do you want me to stay with you?' she asked.

He reached over and took her hand. 'I'm a man and you're a woman' he said. 'From the structure of our anatomies and the fact that we can reproduce ourselves by joining together, you would think that nature had designed us to live together. But every other single bit of evidence points in the opposite direction. For all we have in common we might as well come from different solar systems.' He paused. 'No, I don't want you to stay,' he said. 'I want to be left alone. And maybe we can see each other when we want to fuck, the way we did when we first met.'

She shook her head. 'It's impossible to go back to that,' she said. 'You know that. There's no point in pretending.'

'Well, then,' he said, 'one last time.'

He pulled her towards him and she did not hold back. His arms folded around her and she pressed her body into his, her breasts and thighs warm against his skin. Like so many lovers who find the sweetest fruit at the very brink of the precipice, they had come to the edge of dissolution in order to taste the exquisite sensations of fucking at the edge of separation. Through everything they felt ran a single thread of awareness: this is the final moment for this, this is the final moment for this. Each touch, each kiss, each sigh, was to be the last. And, although given the truth that there is no certainty in life, such is the case whenever people make love, it is the consciousness of the reality of evanescence which suffuses all feeling with unbearable poignancy. His erection rose once more, but without the stridency and urgency that marked his previous tumescence. She opened to him easily, lifting one leg to facilitate his penetration between her thighs. Gently, they entered one another, lying side by side, his cock nestled in her cunt, her heart in his hands, their minds interlocked. They barely moved, letting yearning take the place of striving. For her it was a single sustained orgasm, a continual swelling and discharge. She held his face in her fingers and kissed him again and again, each contact of her lips a seal of love lost. He held her buttocks and pulled her to him with unfailing strength. From their mouths came an almost inaudible murmuring that swept through the room like the sounds of an underground stream.

The music from the radio entered the space left by

their cessation of talk. The haunting voice of Mick Jagger filled the air, the sound of a man who had been picked by destiny to play a role that is the envy of millions, but which remains a performance, like any other, that only masks the anguish of the spirit sustaining it. The mournful tones of Keith Richard's guitar insinuated themselves into the rhythm of Aaron and Cynthia's fucking, and the knowing words of the song impressed themselves into their brains.

'Childhood living/ Is easy to do/ The things you wanted/ I bought them for you/ Graceless lady/ You know who I am/ You know I can't let you/ Slide through my hands/ Wild horses/ Couldn't drag me away/ Wild wild horses/ Couldn't drag me away. . . .'

As he melted into Cynthia, the power of the music to cast a spell amplified the meaning of the lyrics. He envied the implied strength and wisdom of the man who wrote it, describing as he did the sorrow that binds men and women together, and the ability to sustain the sadness in order to maintain contact with his mate.

'I watched you suffer/ a dull aching pain/ Now you decided/ to show me the same/ No sweeping exit/ or offstage lines/ Could make me feel bitter/ or treat you unkind/ Wild horses/ couldn't drag me away/ Wild wild horses/ couldn't drag me away. . . .'

The tempo changed and the music broke into a lilting phrase, guitar and drums suffusing the piece with a moment of relief. Aaron thought of the time when he had felt such strong ties to Cynthia that he could have said the words of the refrain with total honesty. He wondered whether the trenchant observations of the song were merely an emotional binge, and how its composers would resolve the tension between the descriptions of pain and the courageous declaration of the final lines.

The voice went on, grainy, crackling, faintly wailing, energetically despondent, launching into the final stanza. 'I know I've dreamed you/ a sin and a lie/ I have my freedom/ but I don't have much time/ Faith has been broken/ tears must be cried/ Let's do some living/ after we die/ Wild horses/ we'll ride them someday.' The verse ended in a brief flurry and the last line sang out once more. 'We'll ride them someday.'

Aaron buried his head in Cynthia's throat. This is what he had always been unable to do, to follow the line of his negativity to its inner conclusion, and then still find the confidence to rescue a vision of triumph from its clutches. He pictured himself holding a team of pawing eager steeds with one hand while his other arm held Cynthia tightly by the shoulders. He realised that he would never live up to his own expectations of what a man should be.

Cynthia moaned and a series of ripples rolled up and down her body. Her pelvis twitched a score of times, each movement distinct and conscious. Her cunt swarmed over Aaron's cock and the breath was forced from her lungs. With tears beginning to form in his eyes, he relaxed the last bit of tension in his loins, and let her take him to orgasm by the power of her own climax. They came together, as softly as falling snow.

Neither of them moved for a long time afterwards. They shared the same thought: they would probably never do that again. The next time either of them fucked, it would be with someone else, and while, in the future, this moment would be lost in the mists of forgetfulness, the very fact that they would not remember added to its heartbreaking sweetness. The dark deepened around the houses in Berkeley as a hundred thousand people slept or made love or played the many games people play while waiting for the dawn. And the disc jockey played *Sister Morphine*, as he continued to sculpt the mood of the night with selections from *Sticky Fingers*, the *Fleurs du Mal* of rock.

'Can we stay up all night?' Cynthia said at last. 'I don't want to go to sleep knowing that I'll be leaving in the morning.'

'You're going tomorrow,' Aaron said.

'There's no point in postponing it. If I'm going to go at all.'

He was about to say something which might have deflected the direction of their flow when an announcer's voice, sententious and crisp, broke into the room. 'This is the three o'clock news,' he said. 'Two alleged members of the notorious Weatherbureau were apprehended this afternoon in a suburb of Tucson, Arizona. The van they were driving contained a large shipment of dynamite which authorities say had been smuggled in across the Mexican border.'

Cynthia flicked her eyes towards the radio. The voice annoyed her, but as it continued, an unaccountable fit of fear seized her. She gripped Aaron's arm, as though bracing herself.

'One of the men drew a gun and fought a brief battle with police and was killed on the spot. The other man, Conrad Wilson of Berkeley, surrendered without a struggle.'

'Conrad,' said Cynthia. A cold chill ran down her spine, causing her fingers to shake. Aaron felt as though the bottom had been ripped from his bowels and he tightened his sphincter instinctively. The voice went on, like an alien intelligence announcing an invasion of the planet.

'Interviewed after the capture of the two supposed revolutionaries, one Federal Agent said, "We've been watching Gerard Mohr for several months now, hoping he would make a move like this. We have no information on his accomplice, but we have tracers out and should know more by tomorrow." '

Aaron felt as though someone had hit him across the back of the neck with a rubber truncheon. Cynthia's face began to twitch. They held onto one another like two children in a pitching boat on a stormy sea. Each sentence struck with the sharpness of a gavel on hard polished wood.

'Conrad Wilson,' the voice said, 'was charged with transporting contraband material across a national border, illegal possession of explosives, possession of illegal drugs, and crossing a state line with intent to incite a riot. The arresting officer said that the charges, plus others that would be added when he was formally arraigned, could carry a penalty of up to thirty years.'

Aaron listened as the words rolled into his ears. The picture of Conrad, smiling, gentle, stoned, sitting in his fairyland living room, was horribly superimposed with images of guns, billyclubs, fists, iron bars.

'On the international scene,' the announcer began to say. Aaron leapt up and snapped the radio off. He stood there for a few seconds, shaking.

'It can't be,' Cynthia said.

'It is, all right,' he replied.

She sobbed once, her hands covering her mouth. 'Thirty years,' she whispered, the awareness of that length of time pressing heavily on her brain. It was longer than she had yet lived during her entire lifetime. She could not grasp it.

'And they'll come here next,' Aaron said.

'Here?' she repeated.

'You heard him,' he said. '*Tracers* they call it. They'll investigate where he lived, who he saw. And they'll come here.'

Cynthia swallowed, trying to keep her mounting nausea down. 'What can we tell them?' she said. She was still at the point where acceptance of the reality required a coating of hysteria to scale it down to manageable dimensions.

Aaron balled his hands into fists. 'What do you think?' he said. 'We'll cringe and we'll lie. They'll ask questions and we'll pretend we don't know what they're talking about. "No sir," we'll say, "we thought he was a student. No, sir, we didn't realise he was a radical. No sir, we had no idea he sold drugs. Me, sir? I'm a school teacher. Yes sir, very respectable. Of course, sir, I'll be very careful who I associate with in the future. You see, sir, he was a neighbour, and we

294

were just being friendly. No crime there. Very good, sir. Thank you, sir." SHIT!' he exploded.

Cynthia stared straight ahead of her, not seeing anything. At the very moment she was losing one man in her life, the other was ripped away, to be thrown in prison for more years than she could imagine. She could hear the steel doors closing behind her, could sense the suffocating closeness of the prison cell. The picture burned in her mind and she wondered whether she would ever be without it again. It seemed at that moment that so long as Conrad was in jail, she could never again feel free. His capture was her own.

'But they'll file dossiers on us anyway,' Aaron went on. 'And we'll be implicated.' He began to pace the floor.

Cynthia stirred from her trance, Aaron's words mingled with her thoughts. The realisation that it might be decades before Conrad would make love to a woman again had begun to sear her mind. In the face of that, Aaron's worry seemed inane. 'Good,' she said, 'I want to be implicated.'

He smiled grimly at her. 'Tell that to the FBI when they come.' He tossed his head back. 'This isn't a matter of the emotions,' he said. 'This is people who are ready to kill. In their eyes Conrad is a madman who must be destroyed. And if we are involved, they will put the same judgment on us.' He ran his fingers over his hair. 'I don't advise playing games with the situation.'

'But how can it be?' she said. 'Conrad is the last person in the world who would get involved in anything violent.'

'We don't know anything about him,' Aaron told her. 'He told me he once killed a man. He was a revolutionary. Those visits he paid us were only one of his masks.'

Cynthia gazed up at Aaron and looked at him a long time. 'You talk about him as though he were dead,' she said. 'He was your friend, and you seem to have written him off all at once. Don't you care about helping him?'

He took almost a full minute to answer, letting all the changes course through him before his response came forth of its own accord. The woman in front of him, the man in jail, himself a willing prisoner of despair, all the myriad confusion of his lifetime, came together in a single moment. The choice of who he was and where he stood hinged entirely on the answer he gave.

'No,' he said.

Cynthia remained expressionless.

'Of course, sentimentally, I want to. But in practical effective terms, there is nothing I can do. He took his chances to live as a free man, and I respect him for that. I used to envy him. But he was caught, and now he pays for his beliefs. I am a coward, and I remain at liberty to walk around. That's my jail sentence: I get to live with myself, knowing what a failure I am. That's the way life is. I don't want to make a romantic political affair out of it. The people who arrested him are no different from me. It's hard for me to admit that, but it's true. I do nothing to fight them, so I am on their side by default. How can I help Conrad? I'm one of the people who put him in prison. I'll feel bad about it for a long time, but I see no point in taking any road that will put me behind bars too.'

Cynthia stood up. An iron composure gripped her features. She wanted to repress her feelings until she could be by herself. She turned towards the kitchen, to go to the back yard.

'Do you hate me for what I just said?' Aaron asked her.

She shook her head. 'No Aaron I don't hate you. I understand you too well for that. We just have to go separate ways, that's all.' She walked to the door. 'Will you help me pack in the morning?' she said.

He nodded. 'Where are you going?' he asked.

'I think it's best if I don't tell you,' she answered.

Aaron watched her walk from the room, hesitated a few moments, and then went to the stereo. He switched it on, lifting the tone arm, and dropped it on the record that had been lying there. The sonorous phrases of Bach filled the room. He sat heavily on the couch, closed his eyes, and began the long job of erasing thousands of entries from the files in his memory bank. All traces of Cynthia and Conrad would have to be destroyed before he could rest.

Cynthia ran down the back stairs and out under the open sky. Overhead, the stars burned in steady indifference to the turmoil so distant from them. The air was damp and sweet, and Cynthia stood naked, a white dimly glowing figure in the pre-dawn chill. She looked around the yard and for an instant Conrad's presence enveloped her. She imagined him on his ladder, peering through her bedroom window. She remembered the feel of his arms and the touch of his lips. She conjured up the taste of his cock when she had shuttled back and forth between him and Aaron.

'Was that just two night ago?' she thought.

She lay on the ground and buried her face in the thick grass. She was choked with a feeling that threatened to engulf her if she released it, and clutched her hands over her breasts. Like the legendary child holding a finger in the dyke to keep the waters from flooding the land, Cynthia held her breath to hold back her emotions.

'Conrad,' she whispered.

And at that moment, a bird sang, its clear chirping melody slipping happily through the night and tripping through her consciousness in a stroke untying all the knots inside her. The uncomplicated innocence of its call opened the gates to her feelings and the fearful tension snapped. A deep sob shuddered through her frame as she took a full painful breath, and then her eyes burned with salt and heat. Her shoulders heaved as she surrendered to the spasms of grief, and gave birth to the tears which allowed her to feel her sorrow.

She wept until she was empty. And when she sat up, the first thing she saw was the oak that dominated the entire space behind the house. Her teeth began to chatter as she thought, 'There are no trees in prisons. How will he live without trees?'